About the author

David's teachers often said he was someone who spent all his time daydreaming and living inside his own head. This apparently never changed and he still lives there. David spent much of his young adult life travelling around England for work and in his mid-twenties broke the borders and journeyed to China where he taught English to fund his travels across the land over the course of three years. Most people who receive writing from David these days tend to be in trouble with the law as he busies himself fighting for peace and justice in his home country. Of course, when you're this busy finding time to write is a challenge, and to this day, David will never understand how he managed to write this entire story using a smart phone.

Photograph by Lee Brazier.

MAGIKAL THINKING
VOLUME 1

To Liz

Thank You for Everything
You Do ...

DQZS ROBINSON

MAGIKAL THINKING
VOLUME 1

Vanguard Press

A CIP catalogue record for this title is
available from the British Library.

ISBN 978 1 80016 247 1

Vanguard Press is an imprint of
Pegasus Elliot MacKenzie Publishers Ltd.
www.pegasuspublishers.com

First Published in 2022

Vanguard Press
Sheraton House Castle Park
Cambridge England

Printed & Bound in Great Britain

Dedication

This is to everyone who wishes the world was a little bit more. To those who would prefer an imagined land to the one they stand on. To those who throw on a bed sheet, grab the fire poker and pretend to be a wizard when they have the house to themselves. I'll never grow up. I hope you don't either.

"In remembrance of Prince Philip, a true god among men."

Acknowledgements

To my grandfather, Amos Robinson, thank you for everything. I wish you could have read this.

To my wife, Carey Robinson, without your love, patience and understanding, this book could not have been written. Thank you for having faith.

To Richard Brown, the best sounding board I could have asked for. I'll always appreciate how tolerant you were and all the encouragement you gave.

To Adam Bell, I will never forget the smile on your face when you met me after reading the book. Thank you for getting me over the finish line and thank you for the excellent mead.

Prologue
Seamen

"Are you sure they're down here!"

"He seemed confident this is where they landed?"

"Yeah, a few aeons ago. What if they've drifted off?"

"Drifted off? Do you have any idea how big these things are?"

"We're underwater in case you hadn't noticed. Things float!"

There was a deep, long-suffering sigh.

"You really are stupid aren't you! How did you even get on this mission?"

"Note my ability to swim!"

"Right! And that's it, is it?"

"What more do you want?"

"A thorough understanding of the subject matter maybe?"

"I think I know what they look like, thank you. I do have some myself!"

There was a snort of derision.

"Not like these you don't. Yours are tiny."

An awkward and protracted pause followed this comment.

"Like we're gonna see them anyway. It's too bloody dark!"

"Are you kidding me?"

"What?"

"Wow! Just wow!"

From inside an inexhaustible expanse of darkness erupted a flash of orange, flickering light emitting from a little cluster of fire about the size of a tennis ball which was bubbling merrily as it boiled the surrounding water to steam. It was sat in the hand of a powerfully built man who, despite being very deep under the sea, was wearing nothing but a pair of shorts and a diving mask, the latter of which didn't seem to be attached to any breathing apparatus. A thick steel chain was wrapped around his waist, the other end of which stretched out below him into the dark depths and was evidently attached to something heavy. As the man held up the ball of fire for his companion, who was equally equipped with very little, deep gashes in his face were thrown into sharp relief. One particularly nasty wound seemed to run so deep you could see his brain through an exposed opening in his skull. Yet the man seemed unconcerned for his injuries and neither did the other man who bore similar vicious looking marks.

"Y'know, I always forget we can do that!" chuckled the man without fire.

"I'm beginning to think you may have bludgeoned your host a little too hard, Vepar," said the man holding the flame and frowning with disappointment.

"Nah!" chuckled Vepar dismissively. "No such thing as too hard. Truth be told I'm just a bit thick sometimes."

"You don't say!"

"Anyway, Amy…" Vepar embellished the name churlishly, "…you stand, need to talk. I can see your frontal lobe."

"Well, I… am… airing the brain," said Amy inventively. "And don't call me Amy!"

"Airing the brain?" sneered Vepar, roaring with laughter. "I know I'm stupid, but I…"

"It's called trepanning and it increases blood flow to the brain!" spat Amy defensively.

"What blood?" guffawed Vepar.

True enough, there was a suspicious lack of any blood from such severe wounds. Indeed, the water around them ought to be scarlet from the collection of deep gashes this pair of divers had and yet not a drop of blood could be seen.

"Fair point!" said Amy reasonably. "I'm pretty sure this one died at the fifty-metre mark."

"Mine too. Although it wasn't a bleed out," replied Vepar indifferently. "Too much CO_2!" he added at the enquiring look Amy was giving him.

"You know what that means though, don't ya?" asked Amy as he pushed the fireball down below him and peered into the dark void.

"Yeah!" sighed Vepar gloomily. "You want to do each other or what?"

"You really need to think about how you phrase things before you speak, man!" sniggered Amy.

Vepar grinned at him. "You wish!"

Suddenly the seabed came rushing up out of the darkness. There was a muffled thud as the weight on the chain hit the bottom and Vepar and Amy gently dropped to the ocean floor.

"Where now?" asked Vepar who had created a fireball of his own and was using it to pointlessly glance in different directions.

Amy pulled out a roll of leather from his back pocket and flattened it out to reveal a map burned into the surface. Their destination was marked clearly on the map with a silver rivet, a spot out to sea some distance off the coast of Kithera, Greece. The crude rendering on the square of leather and their dotted destination was not useful from their vantage point at all. However, Amy withdrew a device from another pocket in his shorts which blinked into life and on a bright full colour display showed their GPS location.

"Gotta love the twenty-first century, eh?" said Vepar appreciatively. "This kind of grunt work took years before these little beauties came along."

"I know right!" agreed Amy sounding pleased. "These humans really nail it sometimes. Here, look!"

From the location being showed on the GPS display, to reach their destination they would need to go about fifty-five miles, south-south-west.

"Let's ditch these chains!" said Vepar who, with an impressive display of strength, prised the links apart with his hands and swam free.

Nodding, Amy did the same and together, keeping low to the seabed, the pair swam off in the direction indicated.

After nearly five hours of swimming through a wide rocky expanse and seeing nothing but the odd anemone or eroded clay jar, the ground suddenly fell away before them as the sea floor plummeted and opened up into a canyon. It would have appeared bottomless and without sides in bright midday sun, but in the dark twilight of this auspicious night, it was like staring into a black hole where nothing, not even light, could escape.

"They're never down there!" groaned Vepar.

"According to this shitty map they are!" grumbled Amy with equal dismay.

"Bollocks!" spat Vepar, kicking a rock off the edge into the murky depths and watching it slowly sink out of sight. "This is gonna take all night!"

"You have something better to do?" scoffed Amy. "Hot date? Your pillow finally say, yes?"

"You're a twat!" chuckled Vepar and grabbing Amy's arm, he launched himself forward and swam fish-like into the abyss, dragging Amy down with him.

For what seemed like a very long time Vepar swam ever deeper into the cold and crushing depths of the Mediterranean Sea. Five thousand metres deep and a hundred miles out to sea, Vepar and Amy were finally able to line up their dot on the GPS with the point marked out on the leather map. They were stood exactly where they apparently needed to be, yet no sign of their quarry appeared to them.

After a few minutes of fruitless searching in their immediate vicinity, Amy had the good sense to suggest they fire off several fireballs in different directions so they could see further afield. Soon the ocean was littered with balls of light that floated in the gloom like aquatic fireflies. These small incendiary marvels did a reasonable job in illuminating the area, and though still quite dim, the lights revealed a wondrous playground abundant with sea life.

"Can you see anything?" yelled Vepar who had wandered quite far from Amy in his zest for casting fireballs.

"Nothing," said Amy grumpily.

"If they're as big as you reckon, they can't be that hard to spot, surely," said Vepar who was teasing an octopus that had been stalking a lobster in a bored sort of way.

Amy was turning on the spot trying to see what bit of ground matched which bit of map and growing angry when his efforts yielded no results. He turned it left, then right and then upside down. Then he threw it over his shoulder in frustration.

Vepar chuckled unkindly. "Give it here you baby!" And he snatched at the map as it floated gracefully in the heft of the sea.

Vepar stared at the map thoughtfully, his lips pursed in concentration. After some intense deliberation he said, "Chuck me the GPS!"

Amy passed the device with an irritable toss, snagging the screen with his finger and changing the scale of the display.

"Watch it, dumbass!" groaned Vepar, noticing the adjustment and gingerly clasping the device at the edges of the screen. "Ah, you messed it up!" he added waspishly as he tried to relocate their place on both maps.

"It's useless anyway," growled Amy defensively. "We should be able to see them by now. He must have drawn it wrong. Hardly surprising considering his mental state…"

"Shut up you fuckin' moron!" commanded Vepar in hushed tones, "You wanna get smited or what? Or is it smote? Smoten?"

"Like anyone's gonna hear me down here!" said Amy dismissively, yet he cast his eyes around cautiously when Vepar turned his attention back to the device.

"It's too small!" moaned Vepar, giving the GPS locator a violent shake. "How do you make it bigger?"

"You're such a hick!" sighed Amy. "Just spread your fingers on the screen."

Vepar smeared his fingers over the display making the map shift to the side.

"Not like that, you dope!" said Amy. "Like you're opening someone's eye."

"Oh, right!" said Vepar and he rammed his finger and thumb tip against the screen and dragged them apart with such force it was as if he intended to interrogate the device rather than use it. He eventually got the hang of it though and soon Vepar had wasted five whole minutes zooming around the planet, looking at famous landmarks and sighing blissfully as he viewed the sights of his favourite murders.

"WHERE THE HELL ARE THEY?" roared Amy in a fit of frustration. "The things are massive, it's not like they can be hiding behind a rock." Amy scooped up the lobster that had escaped the octopus and crushed it, because he needed to crush something. "I'm telling you, if we can't see them, they're not here!"

Vepar shook his head and wore an expression like that of a parent observing their child's tantrum for the twelfth time that day. He turned his attention back to the GPS and swiftly located their position. As he was zooming in on the map, Vepar noticed something that made his eyes bulge and his jaw drop.

"Mate, when you say big…" began Vepar in astonished tones, "…exactly how big?"

"I don't know, huge!" blustered Amy. "The guy's one of them primordial entities, the sky given form. They're probably the size of a car!"

"They might be bigger than that. In fact…" Vepar leaned to the side to look behind Amy, "…that might be them there!"

Amy span around and looked about excitedly, but he saw nothing but a moray eel and empty space. Where the light was dimmest the terrain rose a mile or so toward the surface but there was nothing on it, or sticking out of it.

"Are you taking the piss?" growled Amy through clenched teeth. "There's nothing there!"

But Vepar wasn't listening, he was still marvelling at the screen. He kept glaring at the floor and following it with his eyes into the distance.

"It can't be!" said Vepar in disbelief. He lifted his foot to examine the ground beneath it. "But that means we're standing on his…"

Vepar lifted his other foot off the ground in alarm and swam high to get a better perspective. He began firing off more balls of flame this way and that, all around and far off into the gloom.

"What the hell are you doing?" bellowed Amy irritably as an errant fireball narrowly missed his head.

"It's still not enough!" laughed Vepar with a manic edge. "We just can't see that far!"

Amy swam up to him and slapped the back of his head. "Oi!"

Far from being annoyed that he had just been slapped, Vepar turned to look with bewildered amazement at Amy and held up the GPS so they both could see the screen.

"Look at that!" said Vepar smugly.

Amy peered curiously at the screen. It took a second or two to realise what Vepar was showing him. When he did, his eyes widened.

"Y… you found them… on there?" began Amy, but he broke off, looking confused. "But if you can see them on the map like that… they must be…"

16

Amy touched the screen and measured the distance. When he saw the results, he gasped so hard the mask he wore compressed against his face and peeled open a wound near the rubber seal. "Th... th... they're three miles wide... each!"

"Each?" echoed Vepar, shocked.

He cast his gaze to the mile-high mountains lit by the field of inextinguishable flame and let out a long, low whistle. "That is the biggest pair of testicles I have ever seen!"

"No fucking way!" exclaimed Amy with awe. "The rest of it is six miles long!"

"So here's a question," said Vepar with feigned calm. "Exactly how are they expecting us to retrieve a set of genitals the size of a city? I mean where were they thinking of putting them? Not exactly gonna fit on the mantelpiece are they!"

"Dude, did you even read the mission brief?" asked Amy, exasperated.

"The what?" replied Vepar perplexed.

"The brief!" exclaimed Amy loudly. "We all got one, it was on a bit of skin!"

"That was a brief?" chuckled Vepar. "Fuck me, mate. I ate mine, I thought they were snacks!"

Amy opened his mouth to respond but no comment came to mind. Instead, Amy's battered and slashed face fell into an expression of something like pity. Vepar wasn't kidding, he really was a bit thick.

"If you had read the brief, you would know that we don't actually need to move them. We just need a bit of what's inside them," said Amy delicately.

"A bit what's insi... No! No way! I am not milking a six-mile-long, ossified and severed phallus. I didn't do it for Grannus at that hot tub party and I'm not doing now!"

"Prude!" chuckled Amy. "Thankfully, neither of us has to do that. We can enter via the wound behind his gonads. Get straight to the source."

Vepar curled his lip in half a disgusted smile and began to swim toward the colossal mounds and their contents with a much less enthusiastic stroke.

Twenty minutes later they had reached a large cave-like opening behind the mountainous spheres that led into a network of tunnels that branched out like a maze further inside.

"Which way you reckon?" asked Vepar gloomily.

"Up there!" said Amy pointing. "I reckon we could take either of those two large tunnel entrances to get us to where we need to be!"

"Joy!" groaned Vepar.

Leaving little fireballs to float in place behind them, the pair entered the mouth of a wide tunnel on the left which ran almost nine miles into the rocky depths. The journey down was difficult. The tunnel narrowed at inconvenient places and their bodies had sustained a good deal more cuts and grazes from sharp deep-sea coral by the time they had squeezed their way to the end.

"What's he want it for anyway?" asked Vepar as he examined the rocky membrane that stood between them and their goal.

"Not a clue!" said Amy who was also giving the wall a thorough examination. "Might want to drink it for all I know!" he added dispassionately.

"Ugghhh!" intoned Vepar, screwing up his face in disgust but laughing all the same. "That's messed up, mate."

"Hey!" said Amy holding up his hands. "Not my place to judge!"

Vepar grinned his amusement. "Probably nothing but dust now anyway. Maybe he's gonna snort some of it."

"You always go too far don't you!" smiled Amy.

"I've seen folk put weirder things up their nose," said Vepar fairly.

"Can't argue with that!" said Amy who seemed to be gearing up to do something. "Back up a little," he added, checking to see how much room his elbow had behind him.

Vepar had barely moved half a metre when Amy swung his arm back and punched the wall as hard as he could. As anyone but Amy would expect, his fingers, hand and forearm collapsed as the bones shattered upon impact.

A fleeting grimace of pain flickered over Amy's face for the briefest of moments before he relaxed completely and held up his demolished arm to watch it drifting uselessly in front of him. Vepar broke down into a fit of uncontrollable laughter and it was some time before he calmed down just enough to ask Amy if he needed a hand, only to break down into wild hysterics for another five minutes.

"Have you done?" asked Amy testily. "That normally works, must still have too much… God essence in it!"

Vepar laughed even harder. "God essence?" he repeated derisively. "Sounds like a perfume! Eau de Dieu!"

Amy straightened up and eyeballed Vepar impatiently. "Go on then, let's see you do better!"

Vepar held up a finger, indicating for Amy to wait. He then reached into a pocket on the side of his shorts and pulled out an explosive charge.

"Is that C4?" asked a very forlorn Amy.

"Yup!" said Vepar who was wearing a self-satisfied smile.

"You had that all this time?"

"Well, yeah!"

"And you didn't think to mention it before I smashed my arm?"

"You didn't give me chance, mate. You just went buck wild all of a sudden. It was very impulsive, you might want to see someone about that."

"Where did you even get that anyway?"

"It's mine, I brought it from home."

"But you can't… Y'know what, doesn't matter. Proceed!" said Amy holding out his uninjured arm in gesture for Vepar to take his turn.

"You might want to take cover back there at the bend," said Vepar who had already stuck the charge to the wall and was busy setting the timer.

Thirty seconds later a muffled boom preceded a wave of pressure, like an invisible wall, that rumbled down the tunnel and swept over Amy and Vepar, pushing them several metres in the wrong direction. No sooner had they come to a stop when they felt a surge behind them as the water rushed back toward the explosion site to fill in an exposed space created by the blast. When the current settled, Vepar and Amy realised they had been dragged into a larger space and felt grateful for the room to move properly, at least until they saw that another tunnel lay ahead. Amy suddenly looked at Vepar in alarm and then his eyes narrowed suspiciously.

"Did… did you just pee?" he asked with a disgusted look on his face.

Vepar, who had been examining his very crooked and broken toes, looked up at Amy with an expression of haughty indignation.

"No, I did not!" he exclaimed incredulously.

"Then why is the water suddenly warmer?" demanded Amy.

"I dunno, do I?" barked Vepar defensively. "Maybe there's a volcanic heat source nearby," he added reasonably.

With a face that showed he did not believe him, Amy swam ahead of Vepar to avoid swimming in his wake and Vepar hurried after him with protests of. "It wasn't me!" and. "I bet it was you and you're deflecting."

Although the first tunnel had been a narrow and arduous journey, it was nothing compared to the slight and wriggling tube they were now expected to squeeze themselves down. The only saving grace was that it was smooth, but bones still were broken in the attempt, so sharp were some of the turns.

"Good job we're already dead!" growled Vepar, his femurs buckling as he followed Amy around a very tight U-bend.

"Ain't that the truth!" grunted Amy as he heaved and writhed and edged forward inch by inch. "Most of my ribs have popped. I just don't wanna get stuck in here. That's not an eternity I want to experience. And why is it so fucking hot in here?"

Vepar clearly felt the same and began bucking his way forward while trying his best to push Amy further ahead.

An hour. A torturous, almost unendurable hour of squeezing, crushing, pressing and pushing until at last they reached a wide opening that was covered in holes like porous rock. From out of the holes, bubbles were pouring out in great jets that rose to the ceiling.

"It's a bit livelier down here than I expected, mate," said Vepar cautiously. "What's doing this?"

"If I were to hazard a guess, I would say some sort of fission reaction."

"Come again?" said Vepar.

"This whole chamber and all of these connecting tubes, it's a giant nuclear reactor. That's why it's so hot. There must have been a reaction to seawater or something that got it all fired up again."

"How do you know it's nuclear?" asked Vepar bewildered.

"The brief!" sighed Amy. "The dude's entire body is enriched with uranium, it's like his whole thing. Hardly a surprise that there's a significant concentration in here." Amy paused for thought then added, "No wonder his offspring were mutants."

"Uranium? So, it's a bomb he's making," mused Vepar in a hushed but excited whisper.

"Maybe, but there are better places to get uranium from than this prehistoric nut sack if that was all he wanted," said Amy as he peered into one of the holes to examine the chambers within. "Nah, if you ask me, they're making something and they need God gravy as an ingredient."

"And none of the others were in the mood?" said Vepar mockingly.

"Might be difficult when you're as old as they are," chuckled Amy. "I don't suppose you have an extra bomb in those shorts of yours, do you?"

"Not exactly!" said Vepar sheepishly.

Amy eyed him quizzically. "What do you mean, 'Not exactly'?"

From out of a large pocket on his thigh, Vepar withdrew a glass sphere about the size of his fist which sheltered a pale lump of rock of about the same size.

"What's the stone for?" asked Amy who was curious but unimpressed.

"It's not a stone. Sodium is a metal," corrected Vepar in superior tones.

"Sodium? That's a bit convenient, isn't it?" asked Amy with amused scepticism.

"Thought it'd be a laugh," said Vepar dismissively.

"How did that not break in your pocket?" asked Amy eyeing the glass casing.

"Toughened glass! Obviously, a lot harder than this meat sack!" said Vepar.

"No shit!" said Amy holding up his wrecked arm.

"So how're you gonna set it off?" asked Amy, spotting a flaw. "You don't have anything to detonate the glass!"

Vepar considered this for a moment then said, "Yep! Only way for it! I'm just gonna slam it against the wall!"

Immediately Vepar swung the ball through the water as hard as he could but Amy caught his arm, stopping the impact.

"Whoa!" warned Amy. "You know that will tear you apart right?"

"Yeah, so?" asked Vepar who didn't see the problem.

"So, let me get out of the way before you do it!" said Amy with a touch of incredulity.

"Oh, right!" said Vepar with a smirk. "Told you I'm a bit thick! See you at home!"

Amy stood far enough back to prevent injury and gave Vepar a little wave. "See you later!"

Without preamble and in a show of supreme indifference to the notion of being torn apart by an explosion, Vepar rammed the sphere with all his might against the back of the hole he was next to. For a few seconds nothing happened except that some extra bubbles seemed to be coming from that hole compared to the others.

Vepar was about to try again when, BOOM! A flash of fire engulfed Vepar's head before a pressure wave blew it and a portion of his chest apart.

The force of the wave had weakened too much to do any damage by the time it reached Amy, but he was still showered with parts of Vepar's skull and face as they streamed through the water like little torpedoes.

From the hole Vepar had destroyed, dark grey liquid was pouring into the cavern like thick, heavy ropes. The liquid was extremely hot too and appeared to be flash boiling the water as it gushed out. The cavern temperature had risen substantially since the hole had opened and much of the surrounding water was full of rising bubbles now. He also noticed that the cavern appeared to be shaking, and to his great dismay, more of the dark liquid had burst its banks and was flooding the cavern with alarming speed. He heard a gurgling, bubbling sound above him and as he looked up, he saw the surface of the water rushing toward him. His face broke the surface and he felt hot steam prickle his skin.

"Ah, shit!" he said with a defeated sigh. "This is going to hurt!"

He dived and swam toward the dark liquid pooling over the bottom of the cavern and pulled out an ampoule from his shorts. It wasn't very big and appeared to be made of polished bone that seemed to radiate its own dim, but brilliant, white light. Without pause, Amy thrust his uninjured hand into the liquid, the ampoule gripped tightly in his fist. The flesh immediately began to burn and catch fire but Amy did not seem to care. When the ampoule was full, he clamped the lid shut tight and without hesitation swallowed it whole and swam as hard as he could to the tunnel leading to the only way out.

Amy crammed himself into the tunnel and thrashed as hard he could to gain as much ground before… too late.

The pressure that had built up from the steam in the chamber forced Amy through the twisting, winding tunnel he had so struggled through before, at speed. The several miles that had previously taken so long to cross, was traversed in a handful of minutes. Amy was ejected from the tunnel and into the sea in a rush of bubbles, flesh and dark grey ejaculate.

For a night and a day, Amy's battered and broken body, floated aimlessly in the Mediterranean Sea until it finally washed ashore on the coast of Antikythera.

For an hour, his limp and lifeless frame lay on the beach as the dusk tide played with his disjointed limbs. His skin had been almost completely flayed off during his ride up the tunnel and the salt from the sea set his nerve endings ablaze. His mask was gone too and his face was deformed from the many fractures to his skull he had sustained in the many twists and turns. Despite the sorry state his adventure had left him in, Amy laughed, albeit weakly. When the shadow of a small figure silhouetted against the setting sun shaded his face, Amy closed his eyes and smiled with satisfaction.

"Will you send me home now?" asked Amy in a soft whisper.

"Did you get it?" asked the figure.

"Yes!" said Amy proudly. "I swallowed it!"

"Then yes, you may leave," said the figure quietly before unabashedly stamping hard on Amy's head, obliterating what remained of his skull and smashing his brain.

"For the best!" whispered the dark figure to what used to be Amy's face. "You really don't want to feel what I'm about to do next."

Whoever the figure was, he was quite correct. As he reached his hand and arm down inside Amy's oesophagus and began turning him literally inside out, there was no doubt, Amy would not have enjoyed that at all.

Chapter One
All Hallows' Eve

Dr Alfred Braskin, with whom this story starts, lived in Bersac-sur-Rivalier, a remote and sleepy village in the south of France. Although English born, he had opted to retire abroad as he and his wife had always planned, however, his wife had long since passed away so he spent his evenings shuffling around his cottage alone.

During the day, he wrote memoirs and papers on his life's work. He had been an anthropologist and archaeologist in his formative years and had dedicated a large portion of his life to the preservation of an isolated tribe in the Peruvian rainforest. He and his team had discovered them during a year-long expedition which was intended to discover some concrete evidence that would help explain the disappearance of the Mayan empire. The entire project was abandoned in favour of studying these new and remarkable people that time, it seemed, had completely forgot about. The leader of this tribe had reluctantly given Alfred and Bernard, his friend and colleague, an audience out of sheer curiosity. He was most astonished by the array of gadgetry these foreigners had at their disposal and soon Alfred and Bernard were being treated better than the royal family.

After the year had ended Alfred and Bernard had gone their separate ways. Alfred chose to condense his journals into articles which he published once a year, including the odd column for the *National Geographic*.

Bernard, became a professor at Cambridge University where he taught anthropology and religious studies. He often used Alfred's articles in his lectures and was usually delighted to see his own name appearing in the acknowledgements. This of course usually gave him impetus to call Alfred to, 'catch up', but usually resulted in an hour reminiscing about adventures they had shared together as younger men. Alfred always called Bernard on the last day of every month if they had not already spoken, and tonight was October 31st. Alfred, would not be making a phone call this night, or any other night. For fate it seemed had made other, more sinister plans for Alfred.

The weather had turned sour. Wind buffeted the doors and windows of Alfred's cottage while the rain hammered against the roof so loudly it was difficult for Alfred to hear the television. It was playing a French version of *Who Wants to be a Millionaire*. Alfred always got the questions correct, of course, even though they were in French. He had once considered entering the show, but he had earned a healthy wage from his past endeavours and had more than enough for a very comfortable retirement.

Alfred had just finished preparing a selection of cheeses on a tray and had poured himself a generous measure of red wine. He took a quick sip, swilled it around inside his mouth, then swallowed and gave a satisfied sigh.

"Merlot from the *Château St Michelle*!" Alfred stated quite boldly as though addressing a group of wine tasters. "An excellent wine that suits a wide range of cheeses."

He picked up the tray and doddered over to his armchair next to the TV. "Although," he added, peering over his glasses at the TV, as the game show host formed a poor joke about how watermelons are grown while referencing his wife's blouse, "it can do nothing for the plain cheesy!"

Alfred chuckled at his own attempt at sarcasm and made a mental note to tell the joke to Bernard when he called him later.

Next to Alfred's armchair was an open fireplace, upon which two thick logs crackled and popped as small flames danced around them. A flash of white light from outside the window caught Alfred's attention. He waited, counting under his breath then, BOOM, a deep, prolonged rumble of thunder echoed across the sky above him. Alfred had only counted as far as two.

"My word that's close," he mumbled to himself.

He quickly fumbled with a remote control and the TV fell silent. The room was illuminated now only by the flickering of flames from the fireplace. The sound of the storm raging outside dominated his senses and he felt a chill run up his spine. There was another loud booming sound that startled Alfred and he spilled a small amount of wine on his shirt. Something puzzled Alfred though. There had been no flash of lightning.

Alfred got to his feet and shuffled over to the window. Rain sprayed against the glass so heavily it was hard to see anything. Alfred leaned closer to the window, his eyes straining to see past the sheets of rain. Another boom echoed across the room, only this time, Alfred noticed the sound had come from the direction of his front door.

"Who on earth is out in this weather?" he muttered to himself feeling a little aggravated at being shaken by a simple caller to his home.

Alfred left the window and headed towards the door, rummaging in his pocket for his keys. He had not noticed a pair of eyes, glowing red against the black night through the window, that were now following him across the room.

"Who is it?" Alfred called a little tremulously through the oak door.

A mixture of several childlike voices chorused "Trick or Treat", back at him. Alfred gave a cursory glance through the peephole. Despite the darkness and the heavy rain, Alfred could just make out four or five figures, each wearing hoods and rather dramatic monstrous masks, all being distorted by the fish-eye lens.

"Trick or treating in this weather? Bloody parents need flogging for allowing children out in this!" Alfred grumbled as he fumbled with the lock and opened the door.

"Come in, come in!" Alfred bellowed as the wind swept into his living room and swallowed his words.

Someone barged the door and Alfred was knocked backwards. "Thanks old man," said one of the trick or treaters as the group made their way inside.

The voice was not that of a child's, however. It was deep and gruff. In fact, Alfred could hear the group sniggering to each other and realised that none of them sounded even remotely young. They all seemed so much taller too and very broad. The last figure to enter kicked the door closed behind him.

Alfred scanned the group which were now stood dripping water in his living room. There were five in all. Three very large men, dressed in long black robes, their hoods pulled over their eyes, the bottom of their masks just visible in the firelight. There was someone who might have been a man, but they were hunched over and their features were completely concealed by tattered cloth. Whoever it was, they were shivering and Alfred could just make out the sound of what seemed to be whimpering. Finally, still stood next to the door and also wearing a long black robe and hood, which hid any trace of a face, was a child.

Alfred turned to the largest man, who was also stood closest to him and made to speak. He was about to demand an answer to this intrusion, but to his surprise, the child raised a hand and the words stuck in Alfred's throat.

"You are Alfred Braskin, are you not?" whispered the child. It was unmistakably a young boy's voice, but there was something very sinister in the tone. Something that made him sound old.

Alfred didn't speak, he simply nodded his head. The child moved past his companions to look at a wall covered with old photographs.

"Alfred Braskin, noted anthropologist and archaeologist?" the child added flatly.

Alfred nodded once again.

"You have been a difficult man to find Alfred," the child continued, his eyes still surveying the photographs. He paused in front of an image of Alfred and Bernard with the lost tribe of Peru.

"Do you remember the day you met these people?" the boy asked, now turning his head to face Alfred.

"Of, of course I do," stammered Alfred. "It was the greatest moment of my career!" he added.

"Greatest moment of your career!" the boy repeated sardonically. He turned to the man hunched on the floor and kicked him. "Did you hear that?"

The hunched man let out a cry, but his voice was drowned out by the laughter that had erupted among the masked men.

"When was the last time you saw these tribesmen?" the child asked, the pitch in his voice high in mock curiosity?

"S-s-some twelve years ago," Alfred whispered in reply. He was taken aback by the apparent mistreatment of their travelling companion.

"Why so long?" the boy crooned, revelling in Alfred's obvious discomfort.

"To preserve their society!" said Alfred resolutely. "They had been isolated from the rest of the planet for so long, it was unwise to attempt to integrate them into the modern world. We, that is my colleague and I, decided that it was best to sever contact with them at the end of our expedition and ensure that the outside world could not interfere with their delicate social structure and habitat any further."

The boy plucked the photo frame off the wall and held it loosely by his side. "To preserve their social structure and habitat," the boy muttered in a tone of quiet disbelief. "Is that really why you wanted them hidden away from the rest of the world?" he added striding over to the fireplace.

"What, but I, why else would I want to!" snapped Alfred indignantly.

"Do not play me for a fool," the boy hissed coolly. "I know you think me a child but my intelligence is far from childlike."

A moment of silence fell between them and Alfred shuffled nervously on the spot.

"Look, I've really no idea what you are implying," said Alfred puffing himself up and trying to sound defiant. "I would ask you to leave, it's late and I have things to do before bed." And Alfred held out his arm in the direction of the door, gesturing for them to go.

With speed a human eye would miss, the boy had moved across the room and was now standing in front of Alfred, his hand clamped over Alfred's wrist. Alfred, startled at this unexpected action, flinched and tried to wrench his arm free. However, despite the very obvious difference in size, Alfred couldn't pull away.

The boy took half a step back and made a slight motion with the hand still holding Alfred then, CRACK. A sickening crunch filled everyone's ears and Alfred howled in pain. His wrist was broken. He collapsed to his knees and cradled his arm against his chest.

The boy paced behind Alfred, breathing heavily. He leaned his head close to Alfred's and through gritted teeth whispered in Alfred's ear, "You are either a moron or a liar!"

"Please," Alfred moaned. "I don't understand."

The boy hurried past Alfred who cowered as he moved. He grabbed the tattered cloth that was covering the hunched man and threw him to the ground right in front of Alfred.

"You really don't know what you did, you pathetic old man!" spat the boy who was now drumming the photo frame against his leg.

Alfred shot a glance at the photo. He found Bernard's face in the crowd. He was smiling broadly, his right arm draped over Alfred's shoulder, his left around a young, pretty girl's waist. Behind the girl was Pacal Chan, the chief for the Chol mountain tribe. Pacal Chan looked quite disconcerted at being so close to Bernard and Alfred.

"Can you not see it?" said the boy, noticing Alfred's gaze. "That look on the tribe leader's face." He continued leaning closer to Alfred and held up the photo in front of them so as to block Alfred's view of the hunched man.

Alfred shook his head and tried to pull away, but the boy seized him by the scruff of his neck and thrust his face closer to the picture. "Fear!" the boy exclaimed in a very menacing tone.

"He was scared to be in your presence, terrified to be touched by your skin and that look is unmistakably the same today as it was back then, look!"

At these words the boy gave a nod to one of the large men, pointed at the hunched man and waited as the tattered rags were hauled off him. The boy lowered the photo and Alfred's face dropped in horror. Six inches away from his face and some 6,000 miles from where he ought to be, was Pacal Chan. His face was covered in cuts and bruises and he looked horrified.

Pacal Chan gave several furtive looks around the room. He seemed bewildered by his surroundings, but nothing wrought confusion upon his face more, than seeing Alfred, kneeling on the ground and crying.

"Ahau?" whispered Pacal Chan.

"He remembers you!" bellowed the boy with false jubilation.

Alfred rounded on the boy. Despite the pain and the fear clouding his mind, an overwhelming sense of injustice was swelling inside him.

"How dare you!" roared Alfred as he placed the hand of his uninjured arm on Pacal Chan's shoulder and gave it a reassuring pat. "You have no right to remove this man from his home," he continued as he got his feet. "I do not know, nor do I care what ludicrous notion has led you to…" SMASH!

Alfred was cut off mid-sentence by the photo frame being broken across his face. Glass scattered across the floor and Alfred stumbled backwards and tripped over his armchair. He landed with a meaty thud on the floor. Pacal Chan tried to stand but was forced back to the floor by one of the masked men.

"Ahau, AHAU?" cried Pacal Chan.

Alfred was concealed behind the chair. Only his legs were visible, poking out the side and sprawled in front of the fireplace.

"Oh dear," said the boy coolly. "I think he's dead and I didn't even get to the good bit."

The men laughed in unison but the mirth quickly died out, interrupted by a metallic clicking sound from Alfred's direction. Alfred rose from behind the armchair brandishing a shotgun, the barrel resting on his injured arm.

"I've got a good bit for you boy," said Alfred, his eyes wide with triumph.

Pacal Chan's face lit up. He seemed to be reassured by the presence of the weapon. Evidently, he had seen one in action during Alfred's expedition. He looked directly at his captors and began muttering hurriedly in a quasi-Mayan/Peruvian language, gesticulating furiously, as though admonishing a subordinate.

Ignoring Pacal Chan as though he hadn't been speaking at all, the boy took a step forward and in a very flat voice said, "Are you going to shoot me?"

"I bloody well ought to!" Alfred replied.

"Ahau, Ahau!" said Pacal Chan desperate for Alfred's attention. Everyone turned to look at him. He was making shooting gestures at the boy. "Seeba'an, kinsik, KINSIK!"

The boy let out a wry laugh. "It seems he thinks you should gun me down too."

He paused a moment looking thoughtful, then turned away from Alfred and began walking to the far end of the room. He still held part of the broken photo frame in his hand which made crunching noises as it bounced against his leg.

"Tell me," he began again still not looking at anyone, "do you know why he calls you Ahau?"

"Yes!" replied Alfred firmly. "It means high king. He mistook our equipment and gadgets for treasure. Believed us royalty and nothing we did could dissuade him to think otherwise."

As he spoke them, the words stirred a memory in Alfred and he gave an affectionate look at Pacal Chan.

"There is another meaning for Ahau!" said the boy, his voice quiet and solemn this time. "Do you know what it is?"

Alfred said nothing but continued to stare defiantly at the boy.

"No? Then allow me to illuminate you," sneered the boy.

"Ahau also translates to God," the boy began again in a matter-of-fact tone.

"While you may have thought, albeit foolishly, that you were being perceived as royalty from a far-off land, you were actually being revered as Gods from another world."

"Don't be ridiculous," snorted Alfred, unable to suppress a little laugh.

"Is it so hard to imagine?" the boy interjected. "From their perspective you were able to conjure fire from a small metal container, harness the power of the earth to point you north, you rode on giant metal beasts and could trap people in a little wooden box and make them sing for your amusement."

The boy turned on his heel to face Alfred and sneered. "Of course all of that, I expect, paled in comparison to the magical weapons you toted around the village."

The boy dropped his gaze back onto Pacal Chan who was still silently miming a shooting action and added, "It obviously made a lasting impression."

The boy's companions all guffawed at this comment.

Alfred's eyes were wide with incredulity, he honestly didn't know what to say. The boy's claim was so outlandish it was almost comical and yet, could it be possible?

"I am surprised you have not felt it," the boy said suddenly breaking the silence. "When they die, I mean," he added noticing Alfred's eyebrows screw together.

"How would I…" Alfred began but the boy interrupted him again.

"Have you not felt wearier lately? Felt the weighing burden of unrequited faith draining your energy?"

"I am an old man," snarled Alfred. "The only weight I feel is one too many years and the barrel of a shotgun," he added with increasing bass in his voice.

"If you say so," muttered the boy. "Pretend all you like, but the last two weeks have been tiring for you. I know because I am the cause."

Despite being unable to see his face, Alfred had the sneaking suspicion the boy was smiling.

"You," said Alfred with a modicum of mirth in his own voice, "are raving. I have never met someone so young with a mind so addled and…"

"I killed them!" said the boy, instantly cutting Alfred off mid-sentence.

"Wh-what?" stammered Alfred.

"His entire tribe," the boy continued gesturing half-heartedly at Pacal Chan. "I slaughtered each and every one of them in turn. I murdered the children last."

Alfred's jaw gaped open and tears rapidly welled in his eyes, blurring his vision.

"Their cries and screams were filled with pleas for you to come and help them. Even when the last child fell silent, this deluded fool," he pointed at Pacal Chan, "continued to pray to you. It felt pretty good beating him into silence," he added with cold relish in his voice.

The barrel of the shotgun dipped as grief washed over Alfred. He felt his knees weaken, he was sweating profusely and he wanted to be sick.

"I have brought this last tribesman with me out of curiosity," the boy continued ignoring Alfred, whose face was now pale and blotchy. "I want to see it, in your eyes. His death, his faith, his soul."

Alfred suddenly comprehended the full extent of the boy's words and stiffened his resolve. He raised the shotgun barrel once more, took aim and squeezed the trigger halfway. His voice trembled as he spoke breathlessly through clenched teeth, "This tribe will not vanish at the hands of a child and three men in ridiculous masks."

His unwelcome guests gave sinister giggles. "I am not a child!" said the boy coldly.

To which the large man to his right added, "And these ain't no masks."

To Alfred's horror the men dropped their hoods revealing hideous faces, their flesh scarred with ancient symbols, their skin mottled and coloured in varying degrees from blood red to onyx black. A tar-like drool dripped from their mouths as they grinned and their eyes flashed scarlet in the firelight.

The shock of this visage alarmed Alfred so much he pulled the trigger fully on reflex. At that split second, time seemed to slow and Alfred witnessed a series of events unfold that he was powerless to prevent. The boy darted with an unnatural speed across the room, right at Alfred. There was a flash of orange-white light and a shower of red liquid left in his wake. The boy reached Alfred before the shell had fired and clamped his palm over the end of the barrel. The force of the combustion built up against his hand, and having nowhere to go, blasted the shotgun backwards taking Alfred with it. Alfred was sent flying off his feet, his shoulder in agony as the bone shattered from the impact and, as Alfred crashed against the wall, the boy, leaping upon the overturned chair, caught him by the throat and held him several inches off the floor at arms' length. Out of the bottom of his vision, Alfred saw Pacal Chan collapse face first onto the floor, a pool of blood flooding from his neck. The boy brought Alfred's face so close to his own that Alfred could at last see some evidence of a face below his hood. Two pure white eyes stared back at him. They had no pupils nor an iris — they looked dead.

"Can you feel it now?" the boy hissed.

Almost imperceptibly, a silvery blue light flashed over Alfred's eyes for the briefest of moments and the boy sighed with pleasure. "You are the first mortal God to fall, but certainly not the last. Your actions in the past have led you to this moment and caused you to be an inconvenience. However, before you die you will serve my purpose." The boy squeezed his fingers tighter around Alfred's windpipe. "Now tell me, where is Bernard Godfrey?"

Chapter Two
Watching the Watchers

"Coffee, Frank?"

Frank, who had been half asleep, lurched upright in his seat and banged his knee against his desk.

He yelled in pain rubbing his leg. "Bugger me Barry, you scared me half to death!"

Barry, Frank's colleague and best friend since starting at the institute, chortled and repeated his question.

"Yeah!" said Frank. "I could do with a brew. No milk mind and er, three, no, four sugars. Cheers lad."

"Four sugars!" said Barry in amazement. "You fed up with havin' teeth? Mind my mirrors while I'm gone," said Barry as he stood up, grabbed two heavily stained mugs and left the room through a heavy wooden door that closed behind him with a soft thud.

Frank, who was still absentmindedly rubbing his knee, swung round in his chair and peered up at a large map of the world which filled an entire wall. It looked as though it had been etched into dark oily glass, upon which dark rainbows swirled and rippled across the surface. The outline of the map and lines marking the borders of the continents stood out in vivid detail as they glowed silver and gold in the dark light of the room. Every now and then a bright burst of colour would erupt out of the murky background, linger for a moment and then dissipate. In some areas the blobs of light remained, pulsing with varying intensity. Next to these spots in glowing characters, were geographical coordinates and a glyph which related to a key chart upon the desk console.

Around the map and spread across the room were lots of mirrors with the same dark oily surface. Each were different in size and shape, but had identical ornate frames, an odd blend of wood, metal, what appeared to be ancient scripture and very sophisticated looking technology. They reflected the room, but were so dirty it was hard to see anything clearly. There were no normal lights in the room either, the only source of illumination came from the glowing spots on the map.

The door behind Frank hissed and Barry reappeared carrying two steaming mugs and placed one on the desk next to Frank. He then sat in his own chair, blew gently into his mug and took a very loud slurp of coffee.

"Anything?" he asked Frank as he pulled his chair closer to his desk and examined the map as well.

"Nah," replied Frank. "Echo Charlie team are returning to base." He rechecked the map. "Alpha Zulu are on still on route to Macau… ETA eight minutes." Frank paused to take a sip of his coffee, then noticing the enquiring look on Barry's face added. "Unknown entity, but low energy output. Probably a dead relative. There was also a burst near Greece, but it turned out to be geological. I've notified the coastguard. It's their problem, not ours."

"Slow night considering it's Halloween." sighed Barry into his coffee. He paused a moment, then with shifty look behind him asked. "What time is it in America?"

Frank tapped on a keyboard and a holographic orrery popped up out of a lens on the desk and began slowly rotating. The tiny sun floating in the middle marked an accurate representation of where daylight was falling across the orbiting worlds. Frank gave the holographic representation of Earth a little flick with his fingers and it spun slowly on the spot. When America came into view, he poked at it with his index finger and it stopped.

"Two in the afternoon," he said at last.

Giving yet another furtive glance over his shoulder, Barry leaned over to Frank and through a shifty smile whispered. "You, er, you fancy seeing what Jessie Pines is up to?"

Jessie Pines and her husband, Chris, were the UK's latest and longest running celebrity couple. Each famous in their own right, their stardom had exploded following their overly extravagant wedding which had a guest list like the Oscars. As Jessie was a singer, they currently lived in their Californian home as she attempted to win over America and cement her legacy as an international star.

Frank looked round at him and at first seemed outraged. But a mischievous smile spread over his face and he nodded vigorously. He swung round on his chair and began tapping furiously into the controls. A computer display appeared out of the same lens the orrery had before. Upon it a busy search process was taking place. What looked like a massive, hairy ball floating underwater, was spinning rapidly, in short sharp movements. As the search thinned and the ball's surface moved closer, tiny pairs of blurry images popped into view as the hair-like extrusions zoomed past the display. Soon it was clearly showing the state of California, then the city Los Angeles and finally Baldwin Hills where the blurry images suddenly became sharper and animated. It honed in on a house where the hair-like protrusions thinned to just two. Next to one hair two almost identical movies were being played inside fuzzy edged orbs, that rotated around the tendrils core, occasionally overlapping and becoming stuck before peeling apart and continuing on their lazy paths. Next to the other strand, two dark orbs carried out similar movements.

"Ay up, one's asleep!" said Barry. "Leave audio until we know who it is."

Both Frank and Barry crowded the display next to the two video spheres, which were showing the TV show, *Friends*. Except the spheres were not playing the show. They were instead watching a TV which was tuned into the programme. Every now and again the display darted from the TV to a clock on a wall or a nearby window all of which were part of a person's living room. They, it seemed, were watching all of this using someone else's eyes.

The spheres continued to watch the TV for a further five minutes before the person whose vision they had hijacked stood up and headed into the kitchen. Both Frank and Barry bobbed rhythmically from side to side as what they were watching wobbled around. Both Frank and Barry knew that mimicking the motion of walking whilst watching from someone else's head, was the only way to prevent motion sickness, and as a consequence, vomiting all over the keyboard, something that Frank's predecessor had allowed him to learn the hard way.

The disembodied eyes found the fridge and to Barry and Frank's delight, a feminine hand reached forward and opened the door.

"We're in Jessie's head mate, crank the volume and switch to mirror two," Barry exclaimed jubilantly.

Frank adjusted a slider on the console and immediately the sound of Jessie Pines' surroundings filled the room. As Jessie grabbed a can of iced coffee from the fridge, Frank swiped at a block labelled 'two' on the computer display and the view from Jessie's eyes flickered off, reappearing inside one of the dirty ornate mirrors to the right of the map.

The mirror was no longer dirty, but bright and clear and gave the perception of depth. They watched Jessie raise the can of coffee to her lips and heard the thick gulping of her swallowing as she drained the can in one swift motion. Jessie then discarded the can into the bin and headed out of the kitchen and up a flight of stairs. As she reached the landing, she entered a door to her left, and to Barry and Frank's delight, they saw the view of a large, clean bathroom. To complete their feeling of rapture, they saw Jessie's hand turn on the shower. Jessie then left the bathroom via a different door to the one she had entered, emerging into a bedroom. A low rumble of snoring coming from her husband, made the speakers Frank and Barry were using to hear with, vibrate and crackle. Frank gave them a quick smack and the sound became clearer. Jessie busied herself a moment, putting away a few items of clothing that were strewn across the bed and then in a soft voice whispered. "Chris! Chris!"

The man lying under the covers stirred a little then rolled onto his front and continued snoring.

"CHRIS!" bellowed Jessie, which made her husband, Frank and Barry all jump up with fright.

"Ahh jeez babe!" breathed Chris who was panting heavily as he tried to make sense of his surroundings. "Ten more minutes, yeah?" he added as he collapsed back on the bed and buried his head under a pillow.

"NOW!" demanded Jessie and with one arm heaved the quilt off the bed exposing Chris' bare bum which she cordially slapped with her free hand. Both Barry and Frank turned away in disgust. This was not what they had been expecting.

"Shower, quickly!" ordered Jessie from the speakers behind them.

"Are you gonna join me?" they heard Chris ask in a playful voice. They didn't want to look at the mirror again, fearing what they might see.

"Mmm, I guess I could spare three minutes," chuckled Jessie and both Barry and Frank suddenly appeared interested again. But their little bubble of joy was popped abruptly by a sound Frank had not heard in years. Indeed, it was a sound that Barry, who had not worked at the institute as long as Frank, had never heard before. A gentle chiming of trickling chords echoed out of the speakers, repeating in a loop.

"That's nice," said Barry interestedly. "What is it?"

Barry turned to Frank, and to his surprise, saw that his face was wrought with horror.

"Wh-what is it, mate?" Barry began, but Frank held up his hand.

He was counting.

The chord progression played for a third and final time, then all became quiet. They sat in silence for a moment, neither person moving, barely breathing. They turned to the map and watched a string of blue lights erupt in a chain across Africa, then Asia and finally in South America. The blue lights pulsed for a moment and then exploded on the screen and turned red leaving massive blood-coloured blobs on the map.

Frank shot to his feet and yelled "BREACH!" at the top of his lungs. At his words the room transformed. All the mirrors around the room came to life and began switching between different scenes. Some of what was being shown was quite horrific, such as visages of rotting faces, giant insects, snarling beasts and children's toys brandishing weapons. Barry, who had been observing this unexpected turn of events, felt quite sick.

A large holographic eyeball popped into life out of the desktop projector. It spun quickly between looking at Barry then at Frank and pulsed impatiently, as just below, the word 'Login' began an orbit like a moon. Rotating around the centre of the eye like the discs of Saturn were the words, 'Global Ordinance and Divination System V2063971.15' in translucent white lettering.

"Frank Smith," said Frank promptly. "Conclave Senior Co-ordinator."

The word login which had been lazily drifting over the top of the eye vanished as the system cycled at speed through a list of names before settling on Frank which bore his title below in smaller letters.

A female voice with obvious computerised overtones replied. "Please provide call sign and security key."

"November, charlie, nine, nine, five, five," replied Frank who held still just long enough to allow a laser that fired out of the workstation to scan his retina.

"User confirmed, please define threat level."

"Level three, multiple continents."

"Alerting all divisions, seven squads are standing by. Do you wish to deploy auxiliary units to all level two events?" enquired the calm disembodied voice.

"Yes, yes!" blurted Frank who was anything but calm. "Barry, sign in, and monitor the auxiliaries' progress. I need to co-ordinate an offensive with the elemortals. G.O.D., are there any professors on duty?"

"Stand by..." replied the computerised voice. "Yes, Professors Gathercole and Gwozdek are in hall three and awaiting instructions."

"Good. Patch me through to the elemortal living room."

"Stand by..."

Deep beneath the Earth's surface, many floors below the control station in a dimly lit circular room, a little light began to flash rhythmically in time with a beeping noise that filled the room. For nearly five minutes the light and the beeps went unanswered, then with a hissing noise a door slid open and in walked a young girl, her long black hair, which was tied up in a wild messy ball atop her head, bobbed side to side and she rubbed her eyes and yawned widely.

She plodded over to the middle of the room, lazily mashed a button upon a circular table with her fist and through another massive yawn uttered, "G'head!"

"Shui? It's Frank, we have a problem."

"Wha'?" muttered Shui as she tapped a finger on the table which instantly projected a digitised map of the world in front of her. It showed the same as the map in the control station.

"Son of a..." began Shui as she ran across the room hammering on the other doors shouting, "Battle gear people, it's on!" before disappearing back into the door she had previously entered.

Chapter Three
A Force to be Reckoned

Ten minutes later Shui was standing in the centre of the circular room, which was now brightly lit, and accompanied by five additional people which comprised of two more children and three adults of varying age. Shui looked like a delicate little Chinese girl but in reality, was a voracious tomboy and exceedingly forthright. She wore loose, blue silk robes over gauze wrapping and small black plimsolls. Her previously messy hair was now neatly tied in a bun, held in place with chopsticks and she was punching her hand while pacing back and forth in front of a woman around fifty years of age named Wun Chuan.

She too was Chinese, but did not look delicate. Despite her age she had the appearance of an angry old lady with her red ruddy cheeks and severe eyebrows. In contrast to Shui's attire she wore a formal tailored grey suit, trimmed with black lace. She kept impatiently checking her watch every thirty seconds, then sighing deeply and rolling her eyes.

Sat to Shui's left, cross legged, eyes shut and wearing a serene expression on his face was a young boy called Aarde. He was African born, handsome, had a smooth shaved head and was surprisingly muscular for one so young. He was clothed in brown and tan canvas robes which were bound so tightly to his body the material creaked as he breathed. Behind him and playing Sudoku on his phone, was Gyasi.

Gyasi was a jolly looking man in his late forties. His rotund belly caused his long multicoloured boubou to bulge to the point of tearing. Like Aarde he was of African heritage and his skin was exceptionally dark. He too had a shaved head which complemented a very long beard which he stroked habitually as he pondered his game.

To Aarde's left and directly opposite Shui, was Hoowo3oow, a young boy of Native American descent. He was stood bolt upright, his feet shoulder width apart, his arms folded. His head was bowed forward a little and his eyes were closed. He wore a very stern expression, which judging by the deep crease in between his eyebrows was a regular look for him. He was dressed in brown leather and suede and had very long raven black hair which was partially tied back with a small strip of thong.

Huffing on a long-necked ornate pipe whilst sat on a swivel chair just in front of Hoowo3oow and reading a *National Geographic* magazine was Elsu, a member of the Miwok tribe. He too was dressed in leather but he had the appearance of someone who would be attending a rock festival. His long hair was braided and adorned with beads and feathers and a big brown leather trench coat swamped the chair he was sat on in folds. His attire was completed by a pair of large black metal soled boots and a battered leather ranchers' hat.

Plumes of billowing smoke erupted periodically from beneath the brim which floated towards Hoowo3oow and seemed to be absorbed. Despite the obvious differences between the children, they each had two stark similarities, their eyes were pure white. No pupils nor an iris and they all appeared to be the exact same age, although alarmingly when they spoke it was in a mature adult voice as though they were actually in their forties.

"Where the hell is Ignis?" muttered Shui angrily under her breath.

"I imagine he's still asleep," replied Aarde without opening his eyes to look at her. "Maybe you should try knocking again!"

"That will not be necessary," spoke an elderly man who joined the room through a door Shui had just started towards.

The man was called Amos and he spoke with an English accent that would have shamed the Queen. He was dressed in an impeccably smart tweed suit and tie. His grey hair was parted neatly on the left and held in place by a small measure of styling cream. He had a very neat, grey moustache which sat between two very closely shaved cheeks and was bespectacled in a pair of black horn-rimmed glasses, which sat unmoving on the bridge of his nose. He walked with the air of a man who had been in the military, his shoulders back, his hands held together behind him. Yet despite this very formal and meticulous presentation, his face was warm and welcoming. When he smiled, his wrinkles fell happily into place showing that it was a natural and genuine expression.

"Ignis is already on mission," he said to the group at large. "We had a bit of an emergency when two of our students, Sarah and Fiona of all people, got separated on a field trip and caused a riot amongst a convent of visiting nuns and the residents of a care home. Unfortunately, the police were busy with the region's largest criminal organisation who had spontaneously decided to surrender themselves and confess to a multitude of offences. Nothing he can't handle," he continued in a hurry, spying the looks of concern facing him. "But he will be busy for a while, so I suggest we crack on with what I take to be an emergency."

"Er, yeah, quite!" said Shui who sounded a little flummoxed. "Frank, what's the sitch?" she added, as Frank's face blinked into being from a projector in the table.

"There are several auxiliary units being deployed around the world as we speak to all level one and two events," said Frank distractedly. "Professors Gathercole and Gwozdek are providing support and supervision to all level two incursions. We do, however, have a breach which has resulted in multiple level three phenomena."

The table in the centre of the room that showed the world map, now displayed additional windows in which various creatures being viewed by some unfortunate individual, were attempting to attack those nearby. Unfortunately, those nearby were children.

"I think we all appreciate how unique this is, but we can worry about the hows and whys later," said Frank. "OK, Hoowo3oow?"

Hoowo3oow didn't move, he just grunted loudly.

"Yeah… you er, you have two figments and, oh lucky you, a zombie! All South of the border pal."

Hoowo3oow grunted again to show understanding and Elsu stood up and hit him playfully on the back of the head with his magazine. "Be nice!"

Hoowo3oow simply sighed.

"Aarde, you have a tribe possessed by animals in Kenya and an actual mummy running amok in Cairo. Both seem to be artefact based so eyes peeled for talismans, urns, pretty much anything a child shouldn't have."

"Understood," replied Aarde in a polite tone. "Gyasi, did you make a note of that?"

"One sec-ond, near-ly-there!" Gyasi replied in broken speech as he frantically tried to finish his game of sudoku.

Aarde turned around and spotting what Gyasi was doing exclaimed, "Oh, for the love of—" and snatched the phone from Gyasi's hands.

He looked at the phone for a few seconds then quickly tapped on the screen several times and tossed the phone back.

"Finished!" added Aarde in mock imitation.

Gyasi, looking disgruntled, pocketed his phone and began scribbling in a small notebook.

"What about me?" asked Shui eagerly.

"You, m'dear, have got a phantom Kabuki costume in Japan and your favourite — Chinese vampires!"

Shui squealed with delight and began bouncing on the spot.

"The Northern quarter is unaffected," continued Frank who sounded most amused at Shui's reaction. "As such if and when Ignis breaks communications silence and becomes free, he can assist with any incursions still outstanding. Happy hunting, debriefing at zero hundred hours," finished Frank.

Amos stepped forward and cleared his throat and everyone turned to face him.

"As I presently have neither mission nor charge, I will serve as summoner if nobody minds." He cracked his interlocked fingers in front of him and gave his hands a little shake. "I do like to keep busy."

Amos then reached inside his tweed jacket and extracted a black, battered looking leather pouch from an inside pocket. He loosened the drawstring and began to rummage inside. A few seconds later he withdrew a sprig of mistletoe and a shaft of metal. He placed them on the desk, and from a shelf below, produced a purple candle which he lit and placed beside the other objects which he then began to arrange. Then while chanting under his breath, he used melted wax to draw a sigil on the desktop. When the image was complete, he placed the candle in the centre of the sigil and blew out the flame. For a few moments nothing happened, everyone stood in silence just watching the smoke writhing up through the air. Suddenly from beneath the sigil and the reflective surface of the glass, erupted a massive electric blue steed. Upon the mount's saddle sat a large muscular man, his

44

eyes glowed ruby red, a thick black mane of hair swished against his broad back and his body below the waist was that of a serpent's tail which lashed the air menacingly.

"BEHOLD! I AM BATHIN!" boomed the demon in a deep, hoarse voice. "DUKE OF HELL, COMMANDER OF THIRTY LEGIONS. WHO DARES SUM…"

Bathin broke off mid-sentence as he turned around and noticed the group gathered behind Amos looking very unimpressed. "Oh, it's you lot."

"Nice of you to join us," said Amos jovially. "And perhaps we can drop the pretence, you are making an awful mess," he added gesturing to the floor where several items that had been on the desk, including a stack of paperwork, had been scattered.

Bathin sighed with exasperation, dropped his massive arms and shoulders forward and hung his head. "Y'know, normally when I am summoned, I am at least greeted with due respect and all-consuming fear!" said Bathin defiantly. "Oh, very well!" he snapped, as Amos continued to stare expectantly.

Bathin reached to the back of his head and grabbed a handful of hair. Then with a grunt pulled off what appeared to be an outer skin. It peeled away from his whole body, enveloping the steed and vanished in a little puff of purple smoke on the desk. What had been uncovered, as the Bathin form was removed, was a beautiful woman with long curly blonde hair and an Amazonian physique. She was clothed in white silk that seemed to flow over her body like water, accentuating her sensuous form.

"Eyes up here!" she snapped at Elsu whose gaze had been wandering over her frame. Elsu choked on a bit of smoke, went bright red and disappeared under the brim of his hat.

"Nephthys, I apologise but we must dispense with the pleasantries. Time is short and of great consequence," said Amos.

"What's wrong with those weird arty gates you normally use, broken, are they? Someone had at it with an eraser?" replied Nephthys, a trace of bitterness in her voice.

"Not broken. In use and in any case not close enough to our destinations," said Amos politely.

"There once was a time when you summoned me for a pleasant chat, now it's only when you need something and I don't…"

"Nephthys please!" interrupted Amos. "We do not have time for you to sulk. If you would be so kind as to whisk my colleagues to their destinations, then, as I am remaining behind, we can have a spot of tea and, er, a chat."

"Really?" asked Nephthys, brightening. "You promise?"

"Of course," Amos finished with a note of exasperation in his voice. Behind him came muffled giggles as Shui, Elsu and Gyasi tried hard to suppress their amusement.

"Positions please," said Amos and everybody moved together to form a circle around Nephthys.

"Hold your breath kiddies, it's going to be a rough ride," said Nephthys, grinning mischievously.

She turned back to face Amos and snapped her fingers. Purple flames erupted at once beneath each person. The flames became a hand which grabbed them forcefully by the waist and they were dragged into the ground and out of sight. Still looking at Amos, Nephthys allowed her silk robes to trickle off her shoulder and presented her hand for Amos to help her down from the table. As she drew level with him, she moved close to Amos' face. For a brief moment she bit her lip and seemed to take in his scent, then as she exhaled whispered. "Milk, one sugar."

A school bell rang out and lots of young Chinese children poured out of classrooms, dragging their bags behind them and chattering loudly about their lessons. They gathered outside the school gates and slowly their parents found them amongst the throng and after a friendly farewell, headed home. Soon they had all left, as had the teachers and the lights in the building went off.

Darkness spread down the silent corridors, blotting out the shafts of dust that glowed in the waning sunlight. In an upstairs storage room, a small boy and girl still remained. They were crouching in the shadows trying to hide. Both had tear tracks down their cheeks. They held each other tightly, shaking with fear, waiting. The silence was broken by a thump, thump, thump noise that echoed outside in the corridor. They each let out a whimper and immediately clamped their hands over their mouths. The thumping noise stopped. It was replaced briefly by a shuffling noise then, thump, thump, thump once again. The sound grew louder, and to the children's horror, drew closer to the door.

The girl whispered in a cracked voice, "*Wǒ xiǎng wǒ de māmā.*"

The boy put his finger to his lips and shushed quietly. He then grabbed a nearby dusty blanket and pulled it over them both. The blanket was frayed and patchy and allowed the boy to keep a watchful eye on the door through a threadbare gap in the cloth. Thump, thump, thump. The boy gasped with fright. It was here.

The door handle twisted and rattled as someone or something tried to open the door from the other side. It was accompanied by frustrated banging and slamming on the door which rattled in its frame, then as abruptly as it began, it stopped. Seconds slipped by in silence as the children began to wonder if it had left to search other rooms. Breathing deeply the boy adjusted his legs which were beginning to ache from crouching for so long. As he did so he inhaled a lungful of dust shaken from the blanket and coughed. In that instant the door exploded. Shards of wood scattered across the floor, the door handle sailed across the room and broke the opposing window and a cold wind swept the room. The figure of a man was standing where the door had previously been — tall, thin and ghastly. His grey skin was pulled tight against his bones and in places was peeling away to reveal bloodless, decayed flesh. He was dressed in very old-fashioned Chinese garments which were tattered and stained with mud. Thump, thump, thump. The sound filled the air as he began to hop into the room. Under any other circumstance, this method of movement may have seemed comical, but the hungry, bloodthirsty look in the man's wide eyes was anything but funny.

The man reached the centre of the room and paused to survey his surroundings. As if he knew they had been there all along, he turned to face the children. His eyes widened and he began hopping towards them. In a panic the children discarded the blanket and made to dash past him but the man reached out and grabbed the girl with ease. Holding onto her shirt he lifted her off the ground and held her level with his head. The boy frantically kicked and punched the man's legs, but it was to no avail. He grabbed a shard of wood that had once been the door and thrust it into the man's knee

47

but still he ignored him. He seemed unable to feel it. The man opened his mouth wide, unnaturally wide, baring rows of sharp, yellowing, bloodstained teeth.

He moved to bite the girl who let out a strained petrified scream when suddenly, WHAM! The door handle had been fired back in through the window and had collided with the man's head toppling him off his feet and causing him to drop the girl. The boy quickly grabbed her hand and together they fled into the corridor.

They ran the length of the passage trying door after door, but they were all locked. Taking a left at the corner they drew level with the janitor's closet. To their dismay, the closet sprang open and they were dragged inside. Struggling in the dark against a hand held over their mouths they squirmed and writhed but this was no use either, the hands binding them were too strong. But as the girl gave up fighting and relaxed, it occurred to her that the hand against her mouth was soft. Not only soft but small, no bigger than her own. She turned her head to look behind her. As she did so a foot nudged the closet door open allowing a sliver of light to pierce the darkness. The young smiling face of Lin Shui came into view and gestured for her to be quiet. The boy who had also noticed this, calmed down too.

"Stay here and be quiet," Shui whispered.

The children looked back confused.

"Oh right!" she added rolling her eyes. "I mean, liú zài zhè'er, bǎochí ānjìng."

The children nodded their understanding vigorously and Shui crept out of the closet. Shui could hear the distant sound of thump, thump, thump, deeper inside the school. With a last look back at the children she held up a finger, pointed it at them and then pointed it at the floor conveying an 'under no circumstance do you leave' message and then left.

In the gymnasium the mysterious man hopped feebly between the sports equipment. He didn't try to move anything to extend his search. However, he appeared to have given up. He stopped moving, his shoulders slumped forward and he closed his eyes. Minutes passed and the man didn't even flinch.

Suddenly as if being awoken from a dream, he perked up and began sniffing the air. His prey was nearby. He hopped to a pile of soft mats and smelled them. Nothing. He then moved to a collection of vaulting horses and springboards piled in a corner. He reached in between the crevices, searching wildly with his hands, but grasped only air. Frustrated and growing increasingly hungry he began smashing aside the equipment in a vain attempt to locate the children. Unbeknownst to him, the quarry he so earnestly searched for was no longer the children, it was Shui. And Shui knew, unlike the children, that this was not a man per se, but a *Jiang Shi* or Chinese vampire. Another minute passed as the vampire continued destroying everything in his path. When nothing was left to break and no hiding places seemed to remain, the vampire once again, sagged into listlessness. Shui approached him from behind holding her breath, her arms held out in front of her and hopping silently in mock imitation. She knew that Chinese vampires hunted by sensing the mix of gasses expelled from the lungs, indicating delicious, edible, life. Struggling hard to stop herself from laughing, Shui moved her face right next to the vampire's. His eyes were closed and his head was lolled forward. A grin stretched over her face and she convulsed with silent mirth.

Eyes wide with anticipation, she put her lips as close to the vampire's ear as she could reach and muttered "Boo!"

At once the vampire sprang to life and took a swing at Shui, which she dodged. Undeterred the vampire unleashed a flurry of punches and kicks which Shui effortlessly blocked. They sparred around the gymnasium, the vampire unleashing frenzied attacks, anger and confusion wrought upon its rotting face. Shui, smiled and laughed, she seemed to be having the time of her life and continued to dodge and counter the vampire's attacks as she bounced around the massive room, occasionally flipping off a springboard or swinging on a climbing rope.

The vampire showed no sign of exhaustion, and Shui, feeling that she really ought to finish this soon as she still had a rogue Kabuki costume to tend to, decided to end the fight. She moved in close and rapidly deflected a string of attacks before tying the vampire up in an arm bar that held him in place. She wrapped her legs over the shoulder and lower arm of the creature and squeezed. The vampire lurched forward a few inches before writhing in a futile attempt to wrench himself free.

In a very casual manner, as though there hadn't been a reanimated corpse trapped between her legs, Shui rummaged inside her robe and pulled out a piece of parchment. Written upon it were Chinese characters in flourished calligraphy. It was a spell that caused immobility. She licked the back of the parchment and slapped it against the vampire's forehead, where it stuck as if glued. The vampire stopped moving and collapsed to the floor as Shui released her grip.

Clapping her hands together to get rid of the dust that had come off the tattered Qing dynasty clothes, Shui gave a satisfied sigh and made to leave. At that moment and to her surprise, the door to the gymnasium opened. The two children had come to investigate and as they entered the room a gust of wind brushed passed them. The parchment that was stuck to the vampire's head flapped in the breeze for a moment and Shui looked concerned. But then the air fell still and the parchment stopped. All stared at the vampire with bated breath.

To their dismay the parchment fell off and plopped to the floor. Shui gave the children a stern look of admonishment as the vampire jumped to its feet and leapt at the children. Shui, with lethal speed, darted across the floor towards the children too. She scooped up a stake of broken wood and appeared between the vampire and the children before it had even landed. Shui crammed the stake unceremoniously into the vampire's chest and backed into the children ushering them out of the door. The vampire looked startled as it creaked its head down to examine the wound. Then, it reached up and grabbed the remaining wood protruding from its chest, yanked it back out and threw it to one side before looking up at Shui and growling.

"Not made of willow then!" she exclaimed, more to herself. Acquiescing to the fact that no pieces of wood in this place would be suitable to kill the vampire, she shrugged and said. "Ah well, we do it my way."

Shui and the vampire both moved in unison but the vampire was no match for her. With incredible speed and accuracy, Shui unleashed a torrent of punches. Hundreds of blows battered into the vampire as he gradually collapsed further towards the floor. Shui, tirelessly maintained pace and the rigored skin, flesh and bone of the vampire began to disintegrate into a cloud of dead particles. When she had finished, only a pair of legs and arms stuck out of empty clothes. The rest of the vampire floated cloud-like around the gymnasium, settling upon the debris like ash from a volcano.

Shui rounded on the children. "What did I say? What did I bloody well say?" she began as she started pacing back and forth in front of them, waving her arms around in frustration. *"Tā běnlái kěyǐ táozǒu. Tā kěnéng chī diào nǐ?"*

The children lowered their heads. Their eyes gazed upon the floor and they shuffled their feet nervously. Seeing that the children were verging on the point of tears, she softened her tone, placed a kind hand on their shoulders and steered them out of the building into the warm afterglow of the day's sunlight.

After making sure the children were OK and uninjured, Shui walked a few metres away from the children so they couldn't see what she was doing, placed one hand on top of the other and held them out in front of her face, her palms facing outward. She slowly slid them apart, keeping her fingers and thumbs overlapped, which began to form a little window framed by the webbing of each hand. She continued to pull out the window until the tips of her index fingers and thumbs met. She took a quick look over her shoulder at the children, to be sure they were still where she had left them, then whistled a strange song with her throat which came out in a multitude of pitches and harmonics.

In between her fingers, the forest and mountain scenery upon which she stood became dark and murky. Oily smoke swirled in the finger frame, and as it did so, distant voices became audible. They were muffled but distinct and sounded somewhat harassed. A few moments later the murky view focused and became vibrant and Shui was presented with a view of the inside of the control room back at base. She could see the tops of Frank's and Barry's heads passing back and forth at the bottom of the picture and was now able to hear quite clearly what they were saying.

"Auxiliary unit, whiskey, golf, three, seven, what is your situation?" asked Frank who was busy marking off sections on the map and inputting data as Barry passed it over.

The sound of screaming filled the room, but a calm voice cut through the noise. "Whiskey, golf, three, seven to Frank, we have encountered multiple level two entities, the building is riddled with them and they seem to be getting stronger as their numbers decrease. Professor Gathercole is on the sixth floor with a wiccan who may inadvertently be the cause of the disruption."

"Keep me informed," bellowed Frank over the din of yelling and crying in the background. "Auxiliary unit, delta, uniform, three, call in."

"Delta, uniform, three, final sweep in progress," replied a youthful voice that sounded midway between puberty as it sporadically cracked into unintentional high pitches. "Some kids had been muckin' about with a ouija board and it seems like things got outta hand."

"Carry on," replied Frank. "Have Johnson send a report to Barry when you are en route back to base."

"Busy Frank?" enquired Shui who sounded most amused.

Startled, Frank dropped his clipboard and as he hurriedly bent down to pick it up bumped his head against Barry's bum.

"Oh, cheeky!" chortled Barry. "See what I did there... eh... cheeky, coz he touched my bum," he added giggling.

Shui snorted with laughter, but Frank did not seem to find this funny and straightened up looking disgruntled. He drew himself level to the mirror that, while normally would have shown Shui's sight, now displayed her face as a result of the reflection song.

"Have you disposed of the vampire?" he asked brusquely.

"Now, don't be like that," chuckled Shui. "We've had a lovely day, don't ruin it."

Frank said nothing but continued to stare irritably into the mirror.

"Yes," sighed Shui in a bored voice. "Vampire go poof."

"Poof?" repeated Frank sounding confused. "What happened to the incapacitation spell?"

"Fell off," said Shui with the same blasé tone.

"What do you mean it fell off?" demanded Frank.

"Weren't you watching?" asked Shui with a mote of disappointment in her voice. "I racked up a massive hit combo on that last job. You better not be keeping score for the guys, that's not fair."

Frank was massaging his temples with his fingers, he looked on the verge of a nervous breakdown.

"Shui," he began with a sigh. "I'm not keeping score. On this occasion it is not a contest. I am too busy to be monitoring the activities of you lot as the Auxiliaries require my full attention. Please just brace yourself for the next jump."

He had emphasised the start of each sentence with an increase in volume as Shui kept opening her mouth as if to interrupt him.

"AMOS!" bellowed Frank a little more sharply than he had intended.

Amos came into view on a mirror that showed the inside of the circular room. He looked very dishevelled. His tweed jacket was open and his shirt was untucked and unfastened three buttons from the top. His glasses too were a little lopsided and his hair looked as though someone had ruffled it with their hand. It also appeared as though someone was trying to drag him out of view.

"Madam please!" implored Amos as he gingerly wrenched his clothing free from the grip of Nephthys and attempted to straighten his appearance.

"Not disturbing you am I Amos?" smirked Frank.

"No, eh, perfect timing," said Amos in a disguised cough as he batted away Nephthys' hand that had been finger walking across his shoulder.

"If it's not too much trouble, could I request that Nephthys transport Shui to Iwakura in Japan please?"

"Nephthys, if you wouldn't mind," said Amos weakly.

"I never mind," giggled Nephthys who promptly dragged Amos out of view, and the mirror fell dark.

"Was that a yes?" mused Barry. But as Frank turned back to speak with Shui, he was just able to glance a view of her erupting with purple flames before her mirror also fell dark.

"I guess so," replied Frank.

"EMERGENCY! EMERGENCY! FRANK COME IN!" came a voice from the console.

It was partly obscured with static and panicked raised voices but it was clear to Frank that it was the voice of whiskey golf three seven.

Frank and Barry both lurched at the console keyboard and frantically tried to pummel the receive button at the same time. Frank knocked Barry's hands out the way and tapped the button hard.

"Frank here, what's your situation?"

"It's Marco!" replied the voice. "He became separated during the sweep of the upper floors." There was a pause during which the sounds of fighting and banging became more audible.

"Where is Gathercole?" asked Barry.

"He is trapped on the floor above Marco. He is still with the wiccan and they are both working on a banishing ceremony."

"What are they trying to banish?" interjected Frank.

"We're not entirely sure. We thought it was a poltergeist at first but it seems more powerful than any we have come across before."

"I'll see if I can deploy another unit to your location," replied Frank, his voice thick with worry.

"Frank?" the young man on the transmission began again. "There's something else."

Frank looked up at the speaker from which the man's voice was coming from but didn't speak.

"Marco has been having difficulty spotting entities all evening... I, I think he may be losing the sight."

Frank swore under his breath. "Do what you can to help him for now, I'll dispatch one of the elemortals to your location as soon as I can."

Frank tried to bring up the view from Marco's eyes but the oil wouldn't form into the image. Something was interfering with the psychic reception.

He slid across the floor on his chair and attempted to contact Aarde and Hoowo3oow. Two mirrors sat side by side on the wall closest to the big map which swirled and glowed as he waited for a response. The first to answer was Aarde. From the view in the mirror, he was running down a back alley in Cairo. He didn't look very happy.

"Aarde, can I have a progress report please," asked Frank.

Aarde was huffing and puffing as he ducked, dived and jumped around various market stalls, baskets and washing lines as he continued to give chase.

"By the time I had finished in Kenya this mummy had already located the children who had taken the cursed artefact from his tomb and has since swallowed it."

Aarde suddenly bent over backwards on the screen as he slid under a camel that had suddenly walked into his path and he took a deep breath before he continued speaking.

"Phew, that was close. So anyway, his magic power has increased exponentially and he is now trying to return to his tomb to resurrect his wife, or sister, might be his mum... I'm afraid my understanding of the language of the birds is a bit rusty. Either way I doubt it will end well if that happens."

Aarde paused a moment looking thoughtful then added. "Probably ought to tell you he has kidnapped one of the children who had been playing with his treasure. I think he wants to use their soul in the restoration of his... er... buddy!"

A vein had begun to throb noticeably on Frank's temple now and he began to massage his head again.

"I think I'm having an aneurysm," he sighed.

Barry clapped him sympathetically on the back as he sidled past him.

"Do you expect to stop him?" asked Frank, his voice now sounding a little strained.

"Oh yeah!" replied Aarde with an encouraging nod at Frank. "Just before he legged it some of his bandaging got snagged on a broken fence. I'm just running him down till he unravels and the artefact falls out of the stomach he no longer has."

"Oh, er, good... .um, carry on!" stammered Frank who could hardly believe what he had heard.

He then turned to look at Hoowo3oow's mirror and was surprised to see Hoowo3oow staring back. He had obviously been waiting for him to finish speaking with Aarde.

Frank made to speak but Hoowo3oow cut him off.

"IS THIS SUPPOSED TO BE SOME KIND OF JOKE?" he bellowed angrily at Frank.

"Wha... well I... What?" replied Frank who looked most alarmed. When Hoowo3oow continued to speak it was through gritted teeth.

"I turned up to this figment problem you sent me to and what do you think I found?"

"I could not say," replied Frank quickly. "Figments are person specific and it is usually hard to see them as once they manifest the child usually refuses to open their eyes, let alone look at it."

"That was a rhetorical question," spat Hoowo3oow. "This child is being chased by an Indian. An Indian of my own heritage and the boy believes it is trying to scalp him."

Frank's head lolled back, and closing his eyes, swore quite loudly this time. Hoowo3oow was very sensitive towards any bad feeling for his people. He was forbidden, like his colleagues when they became the elemortals, to get involved in the plights of normal human affairs and as such had been forced to sit back and do nothing while his tribe and others like them were persecuted by European immigrants. He did not take it kindly when Native Americans were portrayed as mindless barbarian killing machines.

"What am I supposed to do about this, eh?" continued Hoowo3oow who sounded further incensed by Frank's lack of response.

"Might I suggest education?" said Frank cautiously. "Explain to the boy the kindness and wisdom of the Miwok tribe and see if it changes the aspect of his figment."

"Miwok is Elsu's tribe" replied Hoowo3oow.

"Yeah! Miwoks rule!" whooped Elsu in the background.

"Whatever!" snapped Frank who was now growing impatient himself. A man's life dangled in the balance and he did not have time for angst. "Teach the boy to worship eagles or kill the hunter. Either way I don't have time for complaints. Do your job and report back when you're done. I may need you for another deployment."

Hoowo3oow snorted at Frank and parted his hands which terminated the visualisation.

Frank collapsed back into his chair then swung himself forward and started smashing his head against the console. "That's it!" he said with another bang against the console. "Marco is screwed," bang, "and there is nothing," bang "I can do about it!" Bang.

"Oh, I wouldn't say that," said Barry grinning. "Look who just broke communication silence."

Chapter Four
Ignis Faukesius

On the seventh floor in a block of flats somewhere in Seattle, a young man dressed in a black keikogi lay slumped face down on the floor, half buried in smashed furniture and glass. He was bleeding from several cuts to his face and chest and his forehead sported a massive bruised lump. He stirred and debris clattered to the floor as it fell off his back. The young man surveyed his surroundings, then shook his head and pushed himself to his feet. He scooped up his mask as he rose and replaced it, wincing as it slid over his wounds. An eerie cackle filled his ears and an unnatural wind blew over him. The young man braced himself for another fight.

As if the walls were speaking, he heard a voice all around him. "Are you scared, Marco?" The voice was menacing and cold.

Marco said nothing. He retained his fighting stance and closed his eyes concentrating on sounds instead of sights. A set of drawers flew at speed across the room. Marco heard it coming and smashed it aside with his elbow then moved his back to the wall.

Another maniacal cackle bounced around the room then cut to a whisper as the voice said, "You are so much more fun to play with than children. They cry too easily and die too quickly."

The voice chuckled in a rasping ghoulish tone, then said. "Do you really think you can beat me?"

A lamp sailed through the air this time. Marco just managed to avoid being hit as it smashed against the wall.

"What are you really scared of, hmmmm?" hissed the disembodied voice. "What keeps you awake at night?"

Marco opened his eyes a little and a flash of something ethereal passed by causing him to start a little. The formless, misty object popped in and out of being in various locations around the room then, as if someone had turned off the world, all went black. Marco shuffled nervously on the spot straining to see through the darkness. He kept feeling something brush past his legs and waist and could hear breathing very close to his face. Marco gave a shiver. Gradually, a dim shaft of light appeared in the centre of the room. It illuminated the delicate frame of a small girl sat facing away from him in a huddle on the floor.

"I can see your nightmares, Marco," whispered the eerie voice.

Unable to stop himself Marco began walking towards her.

"You have betrayed your heart, Marco, I know your fear," chuckled the voice again.

The little girl's limbs relaxed and Marco halted.

"You only care for one thing in this world, Marco," said the voice and the little girl's head began to turn around.

As the girl's face came into view Marco gasped with shock.

"Yes, yeeessss."

The voice was sounding excited now.

"There she sits all alone with no one to watch over her, awww what a shame," sang the voice.

"Shut up!" said Marco quietly. He was transfixedly staring at the girl's face, there were tears streaked down her cheeks.

"Maybe I should pay her a little visit, after I'm done with you of course."

"I SAID SHUT UP!" bellowed Marco.

His eyes scanned the room frantically. He felt hot with anger and was becoming increasingly frustrated by his inability to sense and locate the spirit that was tormenting him.

"Whatcha gonna do, Marco?" crooned the voice. "You cannot see me, you cannot touch me and you cannot leave. Like your parents you will soon be dead and no one will be left to care for your…" the voice paused then in a drawn-out rattling breath added. "…sister!"

Marco screamed with anger but as he did so, the girl's head snapped fully around on her neck. There was a sickening crack of bone breaking and the girl with her eyes wide and her mouth open rushed towards him. Marco's scream cut off at the sight of this abhorrent apparition and he covered his head with his arms as the little girl came within inches of him. Marco peeked out from in between his forearms and saw the distorted visage of his sister's face staring back. Her eyeballs were gone leaving two black holes that oozed blood instead of tears. A terrible menacing frown creased her forehead and eyebrows and her downcast mouth was full of razor-sharp teeth that swam in a tar like slime.

"You are not my sister," muttered Marco, defiantly.

The girl growled at his words and grasped his arms. She tried to pull them down but Marco resisted.

"You are not my sister!" he said again more loudly this time.

"Maybe not now," said the voice. "But she will be by the time I've finished with her."

"NOOOO!" roared Marco and he pushed the girl back but his valiant effort at resistance was in vain.

The little girl threw Marco against the wall and began punching, kicking and clawing at every inch of Marco she could reach. Marco, overwhelmed and outmatched, could do nothing but try to protect himself from a handful of the blows. He felt cuts being etched into his body and the top of his head. He felt his ribs break from the power of the punches and kicks, and as blood sprayed from his mouth, he lost sight of his attacker entirely.

The assault continued and Marco collapsed to the ground. Deep gashes appeared on his face and, as though someone invisible had picked him up, Marco rose into the air, his arms and legs dangling limp and lifeless below him. He was slammed repeatedly against the floor, then into the walls, then against the ceiling and back into the floor again. His body was forced over backwards and he felt as though his spine would break. The wooden floor beneath his head cracked and splintered as an unseen power crushed his skull against the ground. Finally, Marco felt himself being lifted up off the floor by his throat, felt an invisible hand contract and he struggled to breathe. This was the end he thought. He knew in his heart he was going to die and he thought once again of his sister, his real sister. That she was alone and that no one would be there to care for her. He had failed her, failed the order and failed himself. Everything began to fade away, not just sight and sound, but touch. It all felt separate and distant. Then something happened that brought him back to his senses and made the crushing hand on his neck loosen its grip.

Two knocks on the door accompanied by a high-pitched squeaky voice as someone said, "Housekeeping!"

A few seconds passed as Marco continued to dangle in mid-air, helpless, but alive. The knocks came again followed by the same weird voice that said. "Housekeeping, you want towels?" The person sounded like an old Asian lady.

Amazingly, despite his injuries, Marco was able to reason that this was a block of flats and not a hotel, and therefore, did not require 'housekeeping'. The spirit that held him, had not reached this same conclusion.

"LEAVE ME!" roared the voice.

"You no worry," replied the high-pitched voice from the other side of the door. "I come change bed, you no mind me." And the door handle rattled as the person speaking tried to enter.

"I SAID GO!" demanded the spirit. "I DON'T WANT ANY BLOODY TOWELS OR BED CHANGES."

The squeaky voice grunted. "You best be no makin' mess in there. Boss man take out of my pay." And the door handle rattled again.

Marco felt his body sway through the air as if someone was winding up a throw, then as the spirit yelled, "GET LOST!" he was hurled through the room, straight at the door. He waited for the impact of slamming into the door, braced himself for the crunching of wood and the pain that would follow, but it never came. Instead, he felt himself pass through something soft and powdery, which collapsed around him with a soft flump sound and was further surprised to feel himself being caught by a pair of small arms and then gently lowered to the ground.

"Are you OK?" asked a friendly familiar voice.

Marco looked up and through blurry eyes saw a young boy's face with wild, flame-red hair and white pupil-less eyes, smiling back at him.

"Ignis?" enquired Marco in a weak voice.

"The one and only," replied Ignis softly. "Rest now dude, I'll take it from here." And he rose to his feet and stepped through soot and charcoal which evidently was the charred remains of the door.

In the middle of the room, and clearly viewable by Ignis, was the ethereal entity that had been torturing Marco.

"Oooh you make big mess, boss man get mad, you pay fix," said Ignis in the old woman's voice he had impersonated before.

"A child?" hissed the spirit. "Are you not afraid?"

"I'm afraid I'm gonna have to whoop your ass!" chuckled Ignis.

Still stood in the doorway, the boy stretched as if limbering up. His clothes were much more casual than the other elemortals. He wore a pair of baggy, khaki green cargo pants, large black trainers and a red vest which was pulled tight over his surprisingly muscular physique. On his hands were bandage wraps, that covered a large portion of his forearms and were bound in place by lengths of leather. The white of the bandages were stained with what appeared to be blood.

"You…" said the spirit looking amused. "…you are going to whoop MY ass?" He emphasised the word 'my' with a laugh.

"Yep," replied Ignis simply as he began striding into the room towards the entity.

"I hardly think so," began the spirit and he began puffing himself up, growing a little in height and mass.

"I am unstoppable, I am untouchable," his voice was becoming manic. "I am what children fear, I am your nightmare, I…"

WHAM! The spirit's sentence was cut short by Ignis smashing his fist into the spirit's face which sent it careening backwards, twirling rapidly as it went.

"You, don't shut up," said Ignis in a bored tone.

The spirit recovered slightly and rubbed its face, an expression of shock was wrought upon its ghastly features.

"Y, you…" stammered the spirit. "You hit me!"

It was obvious that it had been a long time since the spirit had felt pain and from the look of astonishment it wore, it had perhaps never felt pain since leaving the mortal world.

"Well yeah," replied Ignis who sounded very uninterested. "That's what happens when you have a fight… you get punched."

"But this is imposs…" the spirit was interrupted mid-sentence again by Ignis who had sped forward and buried his knee deep into its gut.

The entity wheezed and to Ignis' surprise and mild amusement appeared to vomit black slime before collapsing in a ball clutching its midriff. Ignis circled it, waiting for it to recover before he struck again.

"Y'know you are obviously too weak for this kind of thing, would you like a cuppa instead? We can talk out your problems and come to a peaceful resolution," asked Ignis benignly.

"R, really?" asked the spirit tremulously as it rose into the air once more.

"NO!" chuckled Ignis.

He spun through the air and kicked the spirit in the head so hard the ethereal body lost cohesion and popped, leaving the spirit looking as though someone had decapitated it.

A terrible scream filled Ignis' ears as the head reformed and the spirit wailed in pain.

"OH MY GOD, THAT HURT SO FRICKIN' MUCH!" it bawled.

"God?" smirked Ignis, his eyes flashing dangerously. "And tell me, which God would that be?"

But as the spirit made to speak Ignis clamped his hand firmly over the spirit's mouth and squeezed hard, muffling all sound.

"That was rhetorical," whispered Ignis. "I do not care what religion you once embraced. The idea of a deity is one based on power. That being the case, I am the closest thing to God you will ever experience."

Abruptly and without warning, Ignis was flung backward away from the spirit and toward Marco who had passed out. Ignis hit the floor and slid to a stop at Marcos' side.

"What the…" began Ignis quizzically, as he sat up and glared into the room to see what had forced him away.

Strange, glowing blue glyphs had appeared on the floor around the entity and from where they lay, shafts of light streamed upwards creating a cage preventing the spirit moving. Ignis couldn't hear it speaking but saw it bounce around the bars of light desperately trying to find a way out.

Ignis touched his fingers together and held them at eye level. Then he sang the same throaty, whistle-like song Shui had used earlier.

At once Frank's face appeared in the window made by his hands and Frank looked supremely happy.

"You wanna fill me in?" said Ignis with a raise of his eyebrows.

"Yeah, sorry Ignis. A heads up might have been appropriate." Frank quickly leaned out of view as if checking something then continued. "It would appear that Gathercole and his wiccan companion have got the banishing spell working."

"Peachy," replied Ignis disappointedly.

"Sorry mate," consoled Frank. "I was watching you go at it. I know you had things under control." Frank looked a little anxious, then in an attempt to change the tone of the conversation, added. "How's Marco?"

Ignis looked down at Marco who was still laying unconscious at his feet and sighed. "He's pretty battered," said Ignis mournfully. "He wasn't able to put up much of a fight."

Frank and Ignis both looked at each other and with pained expressions conveyed without words what they both knew. Marco had passed puberty and as he had ascended into adulthood, he had lost the sight, the ability to see, hear and interact with the supernatural. A gift that often came so readily to children but rarely continued into maturity.

Frank sighed deeply. "Bring him home, Ignis and we can…"

Frank broke off mid-sentence, he looked both curious and concerned as he stared intently at something behind Ignis. Ignis, noticing Frank's distracted gaze turned to look over his shoulder and upon seeing what had caught Frank's attention he wheeled round completely. The spirit confined to the cage of light had started to look decidedly different. It was much larger than before and for some reason appeared more solid. The glyphs too had altered. They were now blood red and the characters were backwards.

"Er, Frank?" enquired Ignis. "What's happening?"

"I don't know!" said Frank in a panicked voice. "Let me contact Professor Gathercole and see if he can shed any light on the matter."

"You do that!" said Ignis uncertainly and after a moment's pause added. "Quick as you can, yeah?" as the spirit grew another foot and its increasingly solidifying muscles swelled.

As Ignis watched on, the spirit became monstrous. Horns sprouted from its back and shoulders. Huge talons protruded from its fingers and toes and its lips peeled back as fangs sprang out of its mouth in every direction. The transformation looked painful and the new form thrashed around inside the cage aggressively. What was more, the floorboards beneath it had started to bow and crack under the weight of its now completely physical form.

"IGNIS!" hollered Frank desperately.

Ignis looked back into his hands and saw Frank and Barry who were both looking pale and sweaty.

"It's bad, isn't it?" asked Ignis sounding nettled.

"Terrible," interjected Barry from over Frank's shoulder.

Frank nudged Barry, who was almost hugging him, out of the way and grasped the edge of the mirror to stable himself. He looked faint.

"The banishing spell has gone very wrong." puffed Frank breathlessly. "I have not been able to speak with Gathercole directly as he, from what I could observe, is busy trying to stop himself being sucked into a vortex."

Frank's eyes raced back and forth in their sockets as if looking for answers in thin air. "From the data we have collected since this woeful night began, I can only conclude that the breach which caused this influx of increased supernatural phenomena has allowed something… or someone to contaminate the portal Gathercole was trying to create."

Ignis looked at him perplexedly for a second and then over his hands at the monster. "So, what are you getting at?" he added a little impatiently.

"In short," said Frank shrilly, "banishment isn't an option and the spirit has either absorbed or, more likely, merged with a demon."

"Epic!" said Ignis flatly.

At that precise moment there was a terrible roar as the quazi spirit demon broke free of its confinement. Ignis was just able to hurriedly mutter, "Gotta go!" before the monster snatched him up in a hand that was bigger than Ignis' entire body.

The monster closed its fist around Ignis completely, and squeezed hard. It looked down at its own tense fist and gave a deep guttural laugh. "I believe you were saying something about power and God."

It squeezed harder. "I guess that makes me the closest thing to a deity in this room you arrogant little shit!"

The monster gave one final surge of pressure and to its delight heard a series of cracks.

It opened its hand slowly and inspected the contents. Disappointment followed by incredulity spread across its face. Ignis stretched out over the monster's palm and gave a deep sigh like a person waking up in the morning.

"Oh yeah!" yawned Ignis. "That hit the spot."

He got to his feet and began twisting at his waist and rotating his hips.

"I've had a kink in my back all week," Ignis bent over backwards and touched the monster's palm with his hands. "But I think that sorted it!" he added before springing forwards and headbutting the monster squarely in what he assumed was a nose.

Blood exploded in every direction and the monster toppled over backwards and landed on its enormous rear. The building trembled and shook from the impact of the monster's heavy frame. A sizeable crater had formed beneath its buttocks and the monster appeared to be stuck as it writhed and squirmed in a futile effort to get up.

"Not so much bite in your attacks now lad," growled the monster as it glowered at Ignis, wiping its bloody nose with the back of its wrist.

Despite being sat on a floor that had sunk several inches, the monster was still taller than Ignis and it leaned forward and loomed over the boy as he stepped closer. Ignis looked up into the monster's massive face with a half-bored expression. He sighed deeply, ruffled his hair then stretched out his arm and casually leaned against the monster's boulder-sized bicep.

"Y'know," said Ignis as he began examining his finger nails, "it isn't arrogance."

The monster's face became stony and he rolled his eyes.

"People who are arrogant believe they are better than everyone else, I, on the other hand, know I am better," he added flatly. "I don't presume to understand how you came to be this mixed abomination and I honestly have no idea how much power and strength you really possess, but…" Ignis paused and looked directly into the monster's eyes "…I know it won't be enough," he finished with a wry smile.

The monster who had been quite still and attentive while Ignis had been speaking suddenly began struggling to wrench itself free of the floor. It had become incensed by Ignis' words and was eager to prove him wrong. Acquiescing to the fact he was stuck proper, the monster performed a strange series of movements with its hands and hummed in a throaty and solemn manner. It sounded as though many were humming at once and to Ignis' surprise black pools appeared on the walls, floor and ceiling and from within them crawled out black, hooded creatures. They scuttled across every surface like a swarm of ants and surrounded Ignis. A couple of them approached the monster and set to work pulling it to its feet.

Ignis, wasting no time waiting for everyone to be ready for a fight, launched himself high into the air and landed on top of the monster's head, forcing him a bit deeper into the hole. The creatures that were close to the monster took swipes at Ignis, trying to catch his legs and feet but Ignis had already moved. He ran around the edge of the room on the wall's surface and threw himself into the throng of creatures that had tried to surround him before. For several long minutes, the sound of wailing, of bone crunching and of blood splatting dominated the overcrowded room as Ignis whittled down the creatures ever-increasing numbers with lethal force.

Despite having dispatched a large portion of the attackers already, Ignis couldn't help but notice that there seemed to be more now than there was when the fight had started. He grabbed a creature by the wrist, broke its arm and then swung it wildly in a circle around him. The creatures cleared away from him by either being struck by the flailing limbs of Ignis' victim or moving convulsively to avoid being hit. In the space made by the creatures vacating, he was able to see that the black puddles from which the creatures had originated were still spawning more. He understood in an instant, and to the stunned shock of everyone present, including the monster who had finally managed to get to his feet, Ignis fired off a ball of energy from his hand, which incinerated the puddle at once.

"STOP HIM!" roared the monster.

Everyone surged forward at the same time, but Ignis continued to beat them off and fireballs of energy at the puddles, often blasting it through an attacker who was in the way. It seemed as though the crowd was finally getting smaller, when to Ignis' dismay, every creature that remained jumped high into the air and piled on top of him, pinning Ignis to the floor. Ignis wriggled and squirmed but couldn't get free.

"ENOUGH OF THIS!" snarled the monster as it bore down upon him.

It raised a massive hand and slammed it down upon the pile of bodies, crushing both creatures and Ignis alike. The monster moved all of its weight onto the arm holding everyone down and the creatures squealed in agony.

"It ends here, boy!" it said breathing hard.

The monster glowed red and the creatures beneath its hand seemed to melt and trickle up the thick forearm before sinking into the skin. Veins bulged upon the monster's body and it looked like someone had thrown very sticky spaghetti at it.

With all the creatures gone and with Ignis still pinned under the table-sized hand, the monster raised the other in a fist and brought it down hard into Ignis' face. For the first time that night, Ignis began to bleed. The fist raised a second time, and with tremendous force collided again with Ignis' head.

Ignis managed to jutt out his hands from in between the monster's fingers and opened them both wide as a bright, hot ball of energy formed in each palm. The balls shot forward and struck the monster in the cheek and forehead. A sizzling sound followed trails of acrid smoke that poured from the points of impact. When the smoke cleared, angry red burns were visible on the monster's face. Sadly the monster looked quite unconcerned. Perhaps out of sheer irritation the monster clouted Ignis sharply with its elbow on the side of the head. For a fleeting moment Ignis saw a flash of white light and felt a little dizzy just before another blow came crashing down upon him.

Ignis gave a pathetic whistle as the fist lifted, freeing his mouth and he sang the reflect song again.

"IGNIS!" sobbed Frank loudly. His face was wet with tears. The monster hit Ignis again and Frank flinched, looking nauseated.

"Clear the building!" whispered Ignis before the fist came down again.

"What are y…" began Frank.

"CLEAR THE…" WHAM! The fist struck yet again. "…building." Ignis gasped weakly.

Back in the control room Frank began issuing orders to evacuate the block of flats, not just of Auxiliaries and the professor, but civilians too. He had an idea what Ignis was about to do and the last thing he needed was massive casualties.

Barry stood bouncing from one foot to the other as he stared at the mirror showing Ignis' vision with a pained and anxious expression. Frank could hear the repeated sound of the giant fist pummelling Ignis behind him and he fumbled with the console frantically as he tried to quicken the process.

"C'mon, c'mon, c'mon!" he muttered impatiently as the mirrors cycled through the flats' residents showing them being ushered out of their homes by what they must have assumed were ninjas.

"Barry!" said Frank curtly. "Stop dithering and make yourself useful. Get on the blower to the applied sciences department. I need the coven they've got down there to whip up a massive glamour."

"How massive is massive?" asked Barry tentatively.

"It needs to cover that whole building. Ignis is about to put on a show and we cannot risk such widespread exposure."

"Er, whole building, right!" Barry repeated to himself as he waddled over to the console, brought up a holographic display detailing an immense structure and tapped a section labelled 'R & D'.

He then sifted through a seating plan until he found a desk with the name Richard Brown emblazoned across the middle located in the applied sciences partition. Barry tapped this too and a twelve-inch semi-transparent representation of a man sat at a desk pouring over various blueprint schematics and diagrams popped out of a series of lenses in front of Barry. Over in the applied sciences department a full-sized representation of Barry had appeared in front of Richard's desk. This too was semi-transparent and as such had gone, so far, completely unnoticed by everyone in the office.

"Rich mate?" said Barry.

Richard looked up from the blueprint and smiled warmly. "Barry," he exclaimed exuberantly. "How're ya diddlin'?"

"Bad mate, big job on and time is…" Barry's mind flitted to thoughts of Ignis being beaten and added. "…very critical!"

Holographic Barry and Richard walked hurriedly across the office space, weaving in and out of desks as Barry explained the current state of affairs. By the time they had reached the office marked 'Coven', Richard looked aghast. He rapped hard on the door and a stern female voice answered from the other side.

"Come!" it said coldly.

Richard cracked open the door and peered inside, only to be immediately startled by the appearance of a grey eye staring back him. An old woman's gnarled fingers gripped the door and creaked it open fully.

Inside the room was dark, the only light coming from a handful of candles scattered throughout. The amber light flickered and danced around the room and bounced off white silk drapes and cushions that were positioned in a circle around a girl who wore a white silk robe akin to the drapes. She seemed to be in a deep trance. Several other girls were sat on the cushions around her, they too wore white silk that clung flimsily to their bodies and were concentrating so hard that Barry didn't think they had noticed them enter. All of the girls appeared to be in their late teens or early twenties and radiated beauty and serenity. The old woman gave a small cough to regain Richard and Barry's attention. Both men suddenly snapped out of their stupor and looked up at the old woman so fast their necks cricked. They both massaged their shoulders as their faces flushed with embarrassment. The old woman seemed ancient, she could have been more than a hundred years old, and in stark contrast to the young girls sat beside her, she was dressed in black, thick robes that were fastened tightly around her neck, wrists and ankles.

"Gentlemen, you are interrupting a very important ceremony, I hope that you have a most fantastic reason for such intrusion!" snapped the old woman in a rather vicious tone.

"Oh, it's fantastic all right," mumbled Barry who now seemed unable to look the old woman in the eye.

"Mother Westa, I apologise for this unannounced visit, but it is with good reason, we require the services of your daughters," said Richard, cutting across Mother Westa before she could admonish Barry for his little outburst.

"How many of my girls do you require?" asked Mother Westa with increasing impatience.

"Well..." began Richard rather hesitantly, "...all of them." And he winced as he waited for her to shriek at him.

Mother Westa looked as though she had been slapped with something wet. Her lips withdrew inside her mouth but her eyes gaped wide.

"What possible problem could you have that requires the full might of the coven?" she demanded aggressively.

Richard explained what Barry had told him and when he had finished speaking, he became acutely aware that the young girls had all turned to look at him. Richard shuddered a little, it was so creepy to have this many eyes staring intently at him.

Mother Westa fidgeted with her hands for a few seconds, rolling one over the other then turned to Barry and Richard and nodded.

"Very well, I shall set the girls to purpose right away," she said in a much more subdued tone.

However, Mother Westa had barely finished her sentence when the girls turned their heads in unison to look at her, then spoke together as one voice, "The power required to form a concealment of such magnitude may be beyond our abilities."

Barry deflated on the spot. Ignis was being beaten to death, there was no time for a casual discussion, he needed action and he needed it now.

He made to speak to Mother Westa but the girls cut him off with their unified, emotionless voice. "Barry is correct, time is short. Ignis will strike soon with or without the glamour. We should use the NoMinds. They should be able to increase the area of effect sufficiently."

Barry looked both shocked and amazed. Had they just read his thoughts? But he wasn't even there. Were they still reading his thoughts now?

Richard, noticing Barry disappearing inside his own head, turned to Mother Westa. "How do we arrange this?"

But the girls answered again instead of Mother Westa. "It has already been done," the girls turned their gaze away from the men back to the girl in the centre. She had begun to writhe on the ground as if in pain, yet she made no noise.

Mother Westa grabbed Richard by the arm. "They have started to create the charm, you and Mr Barry here, should return to your posts and give Ignis the all clear."

"Thank you," said Richard and made to usher Barry back out of the room. As they left and the door began to close, Barry took one last look at the girl on the floor. As he did so several deep cuts appeared on her skin, staining her silk covering with blood, then the door closed.

"I hope this works mate," said Richard.

"Me too," said Barry softly. The sight of the girl being sliced open by an invisible force had made him feel queasy. "I'd better go, give my best to Sarah and I will see you Friday for the monthly department meeting."

Richard gave a smile and half a wave, then Barry vanished from sight.

Back in the control room Frank was running through a checklist of residents as the last family ran out onto the street and were kettled behind a security barrier a good fifty feet away from the block of flats by several Auxiliary units all wearing keikogi. They were followed out by Professor Gathercole who had Marco slumped over his shoulder.

"All clear!" shouted Gathercole as he ran to the barrier and a medic.

Frank wiped a large amount of sweat from his forehead and breathed deep, long and hard.

"Ignis?" said Frank with forced calm in his voice as he turned to his mirror. "The building is clear, use whatever measures you feel necessary to stop that thing from getting loose."

Ignis, who had managed to wrench his arms completely free, had hold of the massive fist and was wrestling with it, preventing it from coming down on him again or breaking free. The monster, however, was still exerting a vast amount of pressure and Ignis was slowly sinking through the floorboards as they splintered and cracked beneath his back. Upon hearing Frank's update, he smiled mischievously and dug his fingers into the fist piercing the monster's flesh. The monster let out a howl of pain and tried to retract its hand but Ignis held tight and burrowed his fingers deeper.

"I am impressed!" admitted Ignis. "It has been many years since my blood was drawn... you should take comfort in that knowledge," he added softly.

"Comfort?" barked the monster. "I am going to kill you, that thought should be enough to keep me warm at night."

"No, it won't..." replied Ignis as he dragged the fist close to his chest, "...but this will!"

The monster felt the flesh in contact with Ignis' body begin to burn as if he was holding something red hot. He tried to pull away but Ignis held him tightly in place.

"Release me!" demanded the monster but Ignis ignored him. Smoke rose from where Ignis lay and it became apparent to the monster that the wooden floorboards were beginning to smoulder.

"Wh-what are you doing?" the monster asked, fear returning to his voice.

Ignis continued to ignore him and instead stared serenely into his eyes. The monster could do nothing more than stare back as he felt his whole body being scorched from the intense heat that seemed to be emanating from this little boy.

"What is it like to die?" asked Ignis calmly.

The monster wailed in pain as its skin blistered and charred. When it managed to reply it was through gritted teeth. "I do not know. I am not the worthless spirit you first fought. I am a demon and we do not die."

"Then this should be quite educational," said Ignis politely.

"Don't be obsur..." began the monster but his words trailed off as Ignis' eyes appeared to burst into flames. Within seconds Ignis' body had superheated, glowing like a hot ember in a strong wind. The room around them burst into flames as the ambient temperature soared. The remaining windows smashed and thick black smoke billowed out of the seventh floor into the cool night air.

"NOOOOOOOOO!" screamed the monster as fire arched away from Ignis' body and swirled around them like a solar flare, cauterising the monster's flesh, melting wide deep lashes as if a hot knife passing though butter. Like fiery rope, the flames wrapped around Ignis and the monster binding the pair together. In desperation the monster thrashed around in a vain attempt to free itself but its movements just caused the bonds to burn deeper, searing through bone and muscle with equal ease.

"KILL ME!" begged the monster. "PLEASE, KILL MEEEEE!"

The skin on its face had all but liquefied revealing a blackened, cracked skull as burning waxy spots of meat dripped onto Ignis' face.

Ignis closed his eyes and nodded solemnly, then a second later let out a terrifying roar as his body burned white hot and bright and the room filled with a dazzling light, obscuring everything from view.

The power of Ignis' attack, was felt by more than just the monster. The mirror Frank was using to watch Ignis' fight shattered, showering himself and Barry in shards of oily glass. The coven in the R&D department screamed in one voice as blood poured from their eyes and the flames on the surrounding candles grew so large, they ignited the drapes. Mother Westa, who had been expecting something like this doused the fire with a fire extinguisher and then began to place cold wet cloths over each girl's face, which instantly gave off steam. In the street outside the block of flats, civilians and agents alike recoiled and averted their gaze as the blinding light engulfed the top of the building, illuminating the city as though the sun had suddenly risen. The tarmac beneath their feet felt slippery as it too had started to melt from the heat, forcing everyone to retreat further behind the barrier and behind anything that cast a cooling shadow. For eight seconds a huge plasmatic ball as hot and as bright as a star, dominated the sky turning night into day and vaporising everything unfortunate enough to be within reach of the corona. Then as suddenly as it had appeared, it vanished plunging the world back into darkness.

Professor Gathercole was the first to recover. He stood up and grasped the barrier railing. He couldn't see anything except for a green blob that drifted lazily in front of his vision, brightening a little every time he blinked. His face felt dry and hot, but the cool breeze that had followed in the wake of the giant plasma ball was refreshing. Thunder broke above him, and to his delight, drops of rain began to splatter his face, carving small clean spots onto his sooty skin.

"Is anyone injured?" he yelled.

Many people began to mutter around him, but they all conveyed a response of well-being, aside from being partially blind and rather confused. Gathercole smiled and rubbed his head. So much damage yet no civilian casualties, he had to hand it to Ignis.

"Ignis!" declared Gathercole suddenly aware that he had not resurfaced from the wreckage.

Still struggling to see, Gathercole began to feel his way across the road as quickly as he could, dishing out the occasional. "Sorry!" and "Oops, excuse me," as he bumped into and trod on several people along the way.

The rain started pouring heavily as he reached what used to be the main door to the building. It was still intact and the doors were closed but it did nothing to hide the massive pile of rubble that was once home to forty-five families. Gathercole immediately began pulling bricks and lumps of cement from the heap and casting them into the road. A couple of people yelled "Oi! Watch it!" but Gathercole ignored them and dug more frantically.

"IGNIS!" he yelled again as he moved aside a table and climbed into the mess. A chesty coughing noise broke Gathercole's concentration, and as he looked up he saw the outline of a young boy stood on the peak of this brickwork mountain.

"Lost something?" cooed Ignis playfully before coughing a couple more times.

Gathercole gave a hearty laugh then held out his hand to help Ignis down.

"I wouldn't touch me if I were you lad," chuckled Ignis as he slid down a streak of wet mud to stand next to Gathercole.

Up close Gathercole could now see that the rain was instantly being evaporated upon contact with Ignis' skin and what little clothing remained was singed and smouldering.

"I'm still a tad warm mate!" warned Ignis. "Don't suppose you have any bacon and eggs? I'm starving and my bum is just right for…"

"Ignis? Are you there Ignis?" came Frank's voice. Both Ignis and Gathercole looked around for the source before seeing Frank's worn-out visage distorted by ripples in a puddle at their feet.

"Clever!" exclaimed Ignis jubilantly. "How's the team?"

"All Auxiliary units except those at your location have returned, as have Shui, Aarde and Hoowo3oow," replied Frank, collapsing into his chair. "An exit artist should be with you soon along with a clean-up crew."

"What about containment?" enquired Ignis who suddenly sounded business like.

"Well, there have been news reports from several surrounding states who are confused by an early dawn that vanished. We cast a glamour over the building, so no one who wasn't on that street knows a massive fireball just demolished a building. I have put out a story of a destroyed power substation that was struck by lightning."

Frank sighed and shook his head. "That should hopefully also explain the electro-magnetic pulse that disabled every electronic device in Seattle. At least it will stop people tweeting too much, before they see our version of events on the news."

"All's well that ends well then, eh?" cooed Ignis playfully.

"Hmm, more or less," replied Frank who seemed distracted. "I'll have Nephthys bring you back, I need to speak to you all and I know Amos wants to debrief you on your previous mission first."

"Probably a good thing, my clothes are all but melted. A few more minutes and I'll be stood here in the nude," sniggered Ignis.

Frank couldn't help but laugh at this and felt some of the evening's tension lift, then with a wave, Frank's image rippled and vanished from the puddle, leaving Ignis and Gathercole alone again.

"Can you manage all this mate?" enquired Ignis sympathetically as he looked around at the devastation.

Gathercole grinned. "This isn't the first time I've been at ground zero for one of your missions bud... I'll be fine... AHHH!"

He had finished by patting Ignis jovially on the shoulder and at once wished he hadn't. It was like touching a hot iron. He withdrew his hand quickly, blowing on it and waving it in the air to cool it down.

"Told you dude, I'm hot property," chuckled Ignis.

"Oh, very funny," replied Gathercole as he watched purple flames engulf Ignis and drag him into the ground.

Gathercole surveyed the street. There was debris, soot and dust everywhere. "Does anyone have a shovel?" he sighed quietly under his breath.

Chapter Five
Incognito

"Ignis!" exclaimed Amos eagerly, wrenching himself out of Nephthys' grip for what could have been the hundredth time as Ignis' still smoking form reappeared in the circular lounge area.

"Good to see you back, safe and well," he continued as he marched across the room and out of Nephthys' reach. Amos cast her a shifty look and then added to Ignis. "Er, we must discuss the events of the day at once..." and he began ushering him from the circular room into an adjoining office space that looked almost identical to the one there were already in.

"Shui, Aarde, Hoowo3oow, you and your stewards should join us as well." and Amos held the door open for the three children and accompanying adults as they made their way in looking tired and grumpy.

Amos then turned to look at Nephthys.

"Well Nephthys my dear, I am terribly sorry but we must part company for now."

"Oh, don't send me away!" pouted Nephthys as she attempted to put her arms around his shoulders again.

"Now, Nephthys please," began Amos peeling her arms off him. "I really have a lot of work to do and I must speak with my companions before they turn in for the night."

"I suppose I'll see you again the next time you need a lift," sulked Nephthys who now had her arms folded and was determinedly not looking at him.

"Well, that is your job," replied Amos simply.

Nephthys looked murderous as she spun around to face him.

"That's all you want me for isn't it... my mind," she screamed as she stormed up to him stopping an inch from Amos' face. Her anger seemed to falter, and she quivered. "Why can't you want me for my body instead."

Amos remained stoic and motionless.

"Fine!" Nephthys snapped. "I will head back to my void and await my next summons, but don't expect such a courteous greeting next time Amos, my heart can only handle so much rejection…"

Amos watched her slink back to the centre of the room, swaying her hips seductively as she did so. As she stood on the table once more, she turned to face him and added "…and I know I don't actually have a heart but you know what I mean!" before exploding in a rush of purple fire.

Amos made a sound between amusement and exasperation then straightened his tie and entered the office.

Everybody sat down quickly as Amos came in. It couldn't have been more obvious that they had been eavesdropping. Ignis had been the exception as he was busy changing into a pair of fresh clothes which were identical to the ones that had been scorched off his body earlier. Amos, choosing to ignore the others' attempts to appear innocent, walked over to where Ignis stood, scooped up the tattered and burned rags and pushed them into a bin. "Thanks Amos," said Ignis over his shoulder.

"You're most welcome," replied Amos softly. Then turning to the group asked. "So how did we all get on, hmmm?"

There was much loud chattering and laughing as Shui, Hoowo3oow and Aarde recounted their battles of the evening. Boasts and brags were made about who punched the hardest and who got the fastest kill. Even Hoowo3oow joined in on the merriment. Shui had just got into full flow about her hit combo streak on the vampire she dusted when Barry flickered into view in the centre of the table, displayed once again as a hologram.

"Ooh, sorry to burst your bubble Shui, but Ignis out did you, by two hundred and thirteen hits, when he was swarmed by shadow demons," he said cheerily.

Shui's face dropped instantly and she sat back in her chair with her arms folded and fumed silently as Ignis waved his hands above his head in triumph.

A holographic display of Frank joined Barry's and order seemed to restore itself. Frank seemed a little surprised to be given everyone's full attention so quickly. "Oh, er, I, um, good job everyone," he said lamely.

"Here, here!" added Amos noticing Frank's face turning a warm shade of pink. There was a general muttering of agreement and a few well-meant pats on the shoulder from Gyasi, Wun Chuan and Elsu.

"You all performed admirably," said Amos. "Especially you," he added looking at Ignis. "You endured a savage beating to afford the Conclave time to clear the building of civilians." Amos smiled softly at Ignis in an almost fatherly fashion.

"Yeah, good going mate," said Elsu sincerely. "we all saw you battling with that, that... thing!"

"Indeed," concurred Gyasi. "A demon possessing a spirit? Such things are rare, especially these days, any idea where it came from?" he asked Frank.

"I'm afraid I have some bad news..." said Frank who shifted uneasily on the spot and he sighed deeply before he spoke again.

"The events that transpired this evening are the result of a serious breakdown in the barriers between the realms."

The faces on those assembled at the meeting became grim. This was indeed bad news. Wun Chuan was the first to respond.

"What caused the breach?" she asked in a business-like tone.

"We have no idea, it was too sudden and without warning. I can only speculate at this time that the cause was either the result of a build-up of negative energy in a regressive portion of a realm or..." he paused looking strained as though he was trying to find a nice way of saying something offensive. "...or it was because of a direct attack."

Frank blurted out these last words in a rush like someone pulling off a plaster from a particularly nasty cut.

"An attack?" gasped Elsu. "You can't be serious."

"As serious as a prostate exam!" replied Frank gravely. "The breakdown was deep, it allowed a demon to come into our world without summons, invitation or evocation. Whatever made the hole obviously had some serious power behind it. I have gone over the intelligence gathered by Gathercole over the ouija board fiasco, aside from communicating with the astral plane the ouija board is benign."

Frank turned on the spot to look at Ignis.

"The demon you fought must have come across the breach and seized the opportunity to enter the mortal world. It chose to bind itself to the spirit as it was the most powerful energy source in the area at the time."

"Has the barrier closed again?" enquired Gyasi.

"No, no it hasn't. And it's safe to assume it's barriers, plural. If a demon escaped then who knows how many are damaged and allowing realms to flux together and…"

"And that is why all those other creatures, the mummy, zombie, jiang shi and the like materialised in the presence of one or two ordinary children," said Wun Chuan finishing Frank's sentence for him.

"Precisely!" said Frank.

"Can the barriers be fixed?" asked Elsu who sounded very concerned.

"Yep," said Shui cheerfully. "This has happened loads of times in the past, the barriers eventually heal themselves, they just need time."

"The problem is, however," interjected Frank who was not sharing Shui's light-hearted view, "while the barriers are down, more and more creatures and figments are going to manifest themselves across the globe. Energy that is not natural to the mortal plane will continue to seep through, distorting reality and turning innocent thoughts into very real threats. Basically, our realm is contaminated until those breaches are sealed."

"I see no reason for alarm," grunted Hoowo3oow. "We were made for this very purpose and we will destroy anything that crosses the border."

"Damn right!" said Aarde echoing Hoowo3oow's determination.

"I think they have a point Frank," said Amos. "They faced unspeakable evil today and fought them off without incident, not even any casualties."

Frank's face turned sour and he had winced at the word 'casualties'. Everybody stared at him for a few minutes in total silence before Wun Chuan asked. "What is it, Frank?"

"I wish I could tell you that was right, Amos!" whispered Frank who seemed to be fighting the urge to be sick.

"What do you mean?" asked Amos, suspiciously.

"There were two deaths tonight," began Frank steeling himself. "Two deaths that were supernatural in nature."

"WHAT?" bellowed Shui who stood up sharply, her hands upon the desk, her head leaning close to Frank's projection.

She looked mortified and was making no attempt to hide her accusatory stare at both Frank and Barry.

"Who was it? Why were we not deployed? Why didn't you tell us?"

Shui was getting louder with each question and Frank and Barry's holograms were cowering further into the desk.

"Shui," said Ignis calmly, "let him speak."

Ignis, who hadn't said a word since the meeting began had moved around the table and had placed a hand on Shui's shoulder. The gesture wasn't commanding, nor was it aggressive, but it caused Shui to fall silent and drop back into her chair as though she had been drugged.

"Frank, what happened?" asked Ignis in a voice so gentle he might have been speaking to a baby.

Frank took a deep breath and when he spoke, he did so without looking at anyone.

"Around the time Ignis was being deployed to the Seattle flats in America, an event was taking place in France in a village called Bersac-sur-Rivalier. We do not know what force was at work, but we are sure that it was there because of the breach."

Frank put his palm to his forehead then brushed back his hair and rubbed the nape of his neck in one long drawn-out movement.

"Was it a child, Frank?" asked Gyasi tremulously.

"No, no, oddly enough it was two adults that were attacked," replied Frank who was still rubbing his neck distractedly.

"What attacked them?" demanded Hoowo3oow.

Frank gave a defeated half laugh. "Not a clue."

Amos looked puzzled. "Then how do you know it was supernatural?"

"Because one of our mirrors fired up and captured the last few minutes of life and, well…"

"Show me!" said Ignis. Frank knew this was not a request, it was an order.

Frank tapped a few buttons and he and Barry vanished to be replaced with a pair of oily orbs floating in mid-air. A second or two later they merged and formed a large sphere, everyone leaned closer to get a better look.

The sudden sound of screaming and banging filled everyone's ears. It sent chills running down eight very disturbed spines, then with equal abruptness the orbs changed from oily black to a view of an inferno. Within the display, a pair of hands could be seen thrashing around raking at walls and doors as the skin blistered and charred. Through the flames the onlookers could just make out a figure lying dead on the floor. The poor soul whose body was burning continued to wail in agony as the fire raged on. For several long minutes they watched as this unfortunate victim endured burns that should have killed him long before. The fire was torturing him, intentionally roasting him as slowly as it could. In the last seconds of the footage the burning man collapsed to his knees and looked up for the first time. To the surprise and terror of everyone present, three very large figures could be seen standing amongst the flames, unaffected and unconcerned. Their eyes flashed scarlet and the footage stopped. Their victim was finally dead.

"Wh-who the hell was that?" stammered Elsu.

"Who the hell indeed!" replied Frank whose visage had reappeared. "They masked their appearance with a glamour similar to the one we used on Ignis earlier this evening. Only after they left did they break the charm, allowing their energy to be picked up by our systems. They also chose to leave the same time Ignis turned the seventh floor into a supernova."

Frank and Amos exchanged significant looks.

"That would suggest that they knew what Ignis was up to and were waiting to use his attack as a means of concealing their escape," said Amos darkly. "Do you think the monster Ignis fought was a decoy, an intentional suicide run?" continued Amos.

"Impossible to say for sure, but it's certainly a possibility. It's also possible that whoever those figures were, they were responsible for the aforementioned breach."

"Have you sent an investigation team to the site?" asked Wun Chuan who was now taking notes in a journal.

"Not yet," replied Frank. "The place is crawling with fire and police services. I think it's best to wait till the morning and have two of our lot join Wade from paranormal research and investigation."

Amos looked a little uncomfortable at this.

"Don't worry," said Frank smirking. "We don't need to summon any demons on payroll for this one, our own gates will get us close enough."

There was a smattering of muffled giggling around the table at this as everyone thought of Nephthys' crush on Amos.

"Jolly good," said Amos as his cheeks flushed.

"Although it may be worth bringing Nephthys back along with a few other of her friends after the initial investigation for a chat," said Frank. "See if any of them have heard of what may have caused this barrier problem."

"In the meantime I suggest we all get some sleep," said Amos a little too loudly. Then noticing his over compensation said in a much quieter voice, "We have a new potential to see tomorrow."

"Ooh where?" asked Shui excitedly.

"Here in England over in Leamington Spa," said Amos brightly. "Shui, I'm glad to see you looking so enthusiastic, I would like you and Ignis to make contact."

"About time we had some new talent," said Shui approvingly. "The think tank upstairs has been almost empty for a while."

"That lot a think tank?" chuckled Ignis incredulously. "Are you talking about Demi and Stuart or that pair of nightmares from this morning?"

"You underestimate your young colleagues, Ignis," said Amos in a kind but cautionary tone. "As a group they are capable of incredible feats of intellect."

"And Hoowo3oow is capable of smiling but do we ever see it?" sniggered Ignis with a sideways glance at Hoowo3oow who simply growled in response. "Do we have a name for this new oddity we intend to collect?" continued Ignis, ignoring the indignant look on Hoowo3oow's face.

"Afraid not, we only have a school and a classroom. I have registered you both as students who are visiting the school to view their methods. The class is one for accelerated learning, one of the best in Europe, so I am certain you will fit in well."

On this lighter note and with the prospect of a busy day ahead of them, everyone said their goodbyes and goodnights, and left the room heading for their own quarters. Everyone that is except for Amos and Ignis. Ignis was sat slumped forward on his chair gazing somewhat blankly at the floor.

Amos was on his feet but he seemed to have something on his mind and was keen to share it with Ignis.

"Are you OK, Ignis?" enquired Amos quietly across the room.

Ignis looked up at Amos, his eyes were glazed over as though he had been lost in thought.

"Hmmm? Yeah, I'm fine," replied Ignis unconvincingly. He noticed Amos giving him a penetrating stare and added, "I don't know, just feels a bit…" he thought for a moment then said, "…familiar!"

Amos walked over to him and pulled up a chair. "Familiar how?" he asked sitting down.

Ignis rubbed his eyes and stretched his face with his hand. "Can't place it but something about that demon I burned just… well just… you know it's probably nothing. I'm fried from the fight… literally and it's scrambling my noggin."

Amos smiled paternally at Ignis once more and patted his knee. "You need a good night's kip dear boy. That'll sort you out."

Ignis nodded and stood up giving a stretch as he did so. He made to leave but Amos called after him. "Ignis…"

Ignis turned to face him, and even though Amos was sat and Ignis was stood, they were at each other's eye level. "…Before you go you ought to know something about tomorrow."

Amos looked at him darkly for a moment and peered past him to check no one was at the door.

"This potential you are looking for, do me a favour and tread carefully until you know more about them. Every method we have of observing the world around us, both scientific and mystical, have flagged this person up. Scrying, ghost writing, runes, the coven, energy displacement scans, the whole kit and caboodle, all have made reference to this individual and all show great power resonating from them."

Ignis grinned and patted Amos' shoulder. "Amos my old friend, you worry too much."

"No," exclaimed Amos with increasing fervour. "Perhaps, I don't worry enough. I have also discovered that thirteen men and women have been committed to secure psychiatric wings in the local hospital in the last two months. Each had lived or worked within one mile of the school and they were exhibiting some pretty extreme delusions. One man was convinced he was made of strawberry jelly and kept trying to spoon lumps of himself into a dish. Call me paranoid and perhaps with good reason, but I can't help feeling there is a connection."

"Amos, you are paranoid," said Ignis with amusement. "But that is why you are good at your job."

Amos did not seem appeased by this so Ignis took him by the arm, heaved him from his seat and began walking him out of the room.

"Try to remember that I'm pretty good at my job too," he said with a laugh.

Amos looked at Ignis with a wan smile and nodded.

"I forget sometimes you know," he said softly and Ignis looked puzzled. "That you are not a little boy, indeed that you are senior to me in every respect."

Ignis moved the arm that had been guiding Amos around his waist and gave it a little squeeze.

"Get some sleep," Ignis whispered. "Tomorrow is going to be a long day."

They were in the main circular room now, and Amos, heading towards his quarters, looked back and said, "Are you not sleeping?"

"Not yet," replied Ignis. "Still a bit fired up, going to work off some energy before I turn in."

Amos gave another nod, a little wave and left the room leaving Ignis alone.

Shui was the first to enter the room the next morning, stretching widely as she bumbled in. She spotted Ignis sat on the sofa and playing on the Playstation.

"Didn't you sleep?" she enquired through a yawn.

Ignis peered over the top of the couch at her, smirked at her bedraggled appearance and said. "A little."

A quick glance around the room, told Shui this was a lie as all of their training equipment had been beaten to ruin and lay strewn about the floor in little piles of broken wood and twisted metal.

"Blinking doesn't count as sleep," she muttered as she helped herself to a very large bowl of frosted cornflakes.

Aarde entered next, already dressed and looking fresh.

"Morning," he exclaimed brightly. "Would anyone like some toast?"

"Just throw me some bread chap," replied Ignis.

Aarde fished out two slices from the bread packet and hurled them across the room at Ignis. Ignis snapped his fingers and the white bread, as if passing through a wall of heat, turned crispy and brown, at which point Ignis swiftly snatched one out the air with one hand and caught the other in his mouth.

"Show off," sniggered Aarde.

Gyasie and Elsu, evidently roused by the smell of food, came bustling in and seemed amused by their simultaneous entrance. Both were dressed but not neatly, they had obviously hurried to get into the room and secure breakfast before the bread ran out.

"Don't panic," said Aarde coolly. "There is enough for you both, jam is in the fridge." Gyasi and Elsu both helped themselves to a couple of slices of the toast Aarde had already prepared in a pile and began messily slopping on large dollops of butter and strawberry jam.

"I hope you are going to clean that mess," snapped Wun Chuan who had entered the room at that moment looking revolted.

She was impeccably dressed and sipping from a cup of coffee while doing her level best to ignore everyone.

"Sorry, Wun Chuan," cooed Gyasi and Elsu togther.

"We'll sort it once we've eaten," added Elsu who had a streak of red jam across his cheek.

Elsu was just about to tuck into his third piece of toast, when to his shock, it appeared to float out of his hand and across to a chair opposite. His confusion was quickly allayed, when Hoowo3oow's form materialised in a seating position, toast in hand and a rare smile on his usually stern face.

"Gratitude," he said raising the toast a little in a cheers gesture before taking a bite that consumed half the slice in one go.

Elsu, grumbling and looking like he'd lost a pound and found a penny, returned to the dining counter to get another slice only to find Amos, also dressed complete with tie and waistcoat, and munching on the last slice.

Elsu threw his arms in the air like a child having a tantrum and collapsed onto a beanbag with his arms folded and turned his attention to the Playstation game Ignis was playing. Aarde, having finished his breakfast, was now playing too. They were fighting each other on a game called *Soul Calibur V* and there was much grunting and giggling as their characters belted seven bells out of each other. The first round of the fight went to Aarde.

"Only way you'd beat me in a fight!" chuckled Ignis as he impatiently tapped the buttons on his controller as Aarde made slow motion punching noises during the replay.

"You keep telling yourself that sunshine," quipped Aarde as he readied for round two.

By this point the match had gained the attention of everyone else in the room. Shui was bouncing gleefully on an armchair, her empty bowl threatening to slide off her legs and Hoowo3oow was concentrating hard on what buttons were being pressed. Hoowo3oow always lost and was sure that Ignis and Aarde knew some secret button combination that guaranteed victory. A cheer erupted as round two was won by Ignis with a knockout which turned into a ring out. It was now Aarde who was left tapping his buttons with increasing frustration as Ignis narrated the replay.

"Going up and out he goes," said Ignis as he swung his pad through the air in an imitation of his character's winning blow.

"Bite me," said Aarde, though he was obviously amused.

As round three began everyone leaned forward and closer to the massive television, so much so that it looked like a half-time huddle at a sporting event. The final bout began with much dancing around each other, each being too tentative to step too close and give the opponent the opportunity to start clobbering them. Ignis broke the distance first and unleashed a fury of attacks which drained Aarde of half his health. Aarde parried Ignis' last attack, which left Ignis wide open. Not wasting the opportunity Aarde forced Ignis into a corner against a wall and began thrashing Ignis' character who seemed unable to block. Ignis saw his health dropping lower and lower and began to panic. With a quarter of his health remaining, however, Ignis had an idea.

Holding onto the block button with one hand he let go of the pad with the other and jabbed his index and middle fingers into Aarde's torso in three places, finishing an inch left of his navel. Aarde's eyes widened with fear, he knew what Ignis had done and was powerless to prevent the consequences.

"You, absolute child," yelled Aarde as he forced his forearm over his stomach as if in pain. Ignis, laughing fit to burst and still blocking, had begun counting down from five.

"Four…"

Aarde hammered the buttons harder but Ignis' health was not dropping fast enough.

"…Three…"

Aarde was now shifting uncomfortably in his seat but still hitting every button available.

"…Two…"

"Damn it Ignis!" screamed Aarde as he cast his controller aside and ran towards the bathroom door, slamming it shut behind him.

"…One…" finished Ignis as a loud flatulent noise resonated from within the bathroom accompanied by a huge sigh of relief from Aarde.

Ignis did a complicated movement on the controller and his character unleashed a special move which not only knocked out Aarde's character but knocked the clothes off as well.

"Winner!" chuckled Ignis as he dropped the pad on the chair, stood up and turned to look at Amos. "Had we better be off then? We don't want to be late for school."

Shui, recognising that Ignis had hit key meridian points in a particular order on Aarde's body which had in turn made him involuntarily evacuate his bowls was rolling about with laughter, her bowl laying on the floor with a deep crack in the side.

"Not very sporting," said Gyasi grinning. "But definitely effective."

Amos checked his tie was straight and said. "Perhaps it is best we leave now before Aarde comes back out!" And after wishing the rest good luck with their investigation, Amos, Wun Chuan and Ignis headed toward the elevator with Shui hopping after them trying to drag on the rest of her clothes.

The elevator opened into a gigantic hall which was adorned with scattered pictures and sculptures that stretched from floor to ceiling. All four of them stepped out onto the reflective polished wood floor and heard their footsteps echo along the length of the space before them. Amos led the way up the centre of the room with the others trailing after him.

As they walked, Shui and Ignis both observed the artwork around them. Upon closer inspection they appeared to be intricate paintings of streets in different parts of the world. They were painted as if seen from below the floor, as if looking up out of a manhole which felt odd as they themselves were looking at the floor. Surrounding the paintings were grotesque sculptures of monsters who appeared to be trying to climb out of the hall and into the street picture. Directly above the sculptures painted on the ceiling opposite the street scene were more paintings of hellish vistas, or water drenched caves and the like. This trio of art recurred throughout the entire hall creating a gallery of fact and fiction and each had a small sign standing next to it, with the place name written upon it. Amos came to an abrupt stop next to a sign for 'Stratford-upon-Avon' and Shui bumped into the back of him, she had been engrossed in a view of Tokyo that had a cyborg Godzilla wearing white Y-front underpants on its head like a mask and for some reason was texting on a smart phone.

"Oh, sorry Amos," she said absently.

"Not to worry, here we are anyway," he replied with a smile. "Oh, I do like Stratford, spent a good deal of my Academic years here," he added, drifting off into a reverie.

"Have you two got our kits?" enquired Ignis, snapping Amos out of his dreamy state.

Amos began patting down his pockets. "Let me see, where did I put them?"

Wun Chuan, however, in one smooth motion, produced from her inside jacket pocket a vacuum-sealed plastic package and a glass vial. Shui took the items and tore open the vacuum-sealed packet with her teeth. At once a grey woollen jumper appeared to inflate from inside it. It reminded Shui of a time she had microwaved a lump of marshmallow.

"Is this what we have to wear?" she asked looking at Wun Chuan.

"Yes," Wun Chuan said simply. "This is a standard school uniform colour for English students and while you will not have their braiding or tie colours you will still look like you belong to some sort of educational institution."

Shui held it up and looked at it in disgust. "It's, well, very bland."

"So is England," replied Wun Chuan coolly. "Don't forget your contact lenses. That white eyed look can be a bit unnerving if you are not accustomed to it."

"Did you get me the blue ones like I asked, I always thought I'd look pretty with blue eyes," asked Shui holding up the glass vial to examine the contents more closely.

"No, I got you brown ones. That is the colour your eyes should be," she replied dispassionately.

Shui looked mournful as she dragged on the jumper and fished out the lenses. "You're all smiles and cheer this morning. Did someone pee in your coffee?"

Wun Chuan didn't reply but instead settled for giving Shui a disapproving stare, which made Shui chuckle.

Meantime Amos had located the same for Ignis who was also pulling on a grey jumper.

"I got you green lenses," Amos said excitedly. "A colour natural to those with flame red hair like yours."

"Nice." Grinned Ignis as he plopped one into each eye and blinked rapidly to get them seated. "How do we look?" he asked as he slid next to Shui and pulled her into a bone crushing hug.

"Splendid. Although you may want to turn off your voice modulators, your voice is deeper than mine," said Amos, smiling broadly. "Now we must get going or we will miss our train and be late."

"Train?" asked a puzzled Shui who had just pressed a finger into her neck causing her voice to go up a few octaves.

"Well Stratford is very near to our destination but we will still have to travel by train for about forty minutes to get to Leamington Spa."

"Best get a move on then," said Ignis whose voice had become equally high-pitched and childlike and he walked up to the edge of the street scene picture and raised a leg.

Amos quickly spoke, "*Eo Ire Itum!*" in a very commanding voice that boomed around the room and the picture appeared to come alive.

People were walking past, some even seemed to be looking at the four of them with admiration. There were sounds of cars and bird song emanating from the moving image and a faint noise of people chatting. Ignis waited poised with his foot over the scene then, when the conversation trailed away, he fell forward as if taking a huge stride. But his foot didn't land on the picture. He continued to fall forward, through the floor and into the picture and in a second, he had swung past the lip of the frame and out of sight.

Shui, Amos and Wun Chuan stared into the picture for a few moments with bated breath. Soon enough, Ignis had popped his head back into view and was beckoning to the rest. Wun Chuan and Amos quickly did as Ignis had, falling forward onto the picture, passing through and emerging within the scene. Shui, chose to somersault into the picture. She felt gravity change direction as she passed through the painting and just as she had gone down, she was now falling up. She stretched out at the last second and landed gracefully on her feet just as an elderly couple came into view. The couple saw the four of them gathered around a picture on the slab work floor and wandered over to have a look.

"What is it?" enquired the elderly man as he approached. "Has someone smudged it?"

"I think you'll find it becomes clear as to what it is if you stand over there," replied Amos gesturing to a set of benches outside a music shop.

The old couple walked over to the wooden seats and sat down. At once they both exclaimed how good and clever the picture was.

The image they were now all looking at was a chalk drawing that looked three dimensional if viewed from the right perspective. This particular image displayed a fiery, hellish world as if seen through a giant crack into the floor, out of which demons were attempting to crawl into our world.

"Oh, that's very good dear, did you do it?" the old lady asked Shui.

"Yes!" lied Shui aggressively. "And it hasn't dried yet so don't touch it." Shui then gave a meaningful nod towards the image.

Amos understood at once what she meant and whispered. "*Claudere.*"

He did it just in time too as a group of young men who were laughing and jostling each other about and hadn't noticed the picture walked right over it. Ignis, who had been preparing to flying kick the men clear of the drawing, stood down and relaxed. Meanwhile the old couple, angered by the lack of concern the men had shown for trampling over the image, had broken into a furious tirade of admonishment. Words like 'hoodlum' and 'whipper snapper' were yelled at full volume to the entertainment of other shoppers, while the men, who obviously found the situation funny responded with words like 'grandad' and 'heart attack'.

"I can see it's going to be one if those days," sighed Amos.

Wun Chuan, who had been watching everything unfold with quiet disgust uttered. "It's England! What did you expect?"

The four of them began making their way toward the train station, Shui and Ignis walking in almost complete silence while Amos argued with Wun Chuan as he valiantly tried to defend his homeland and associated eccentricities. This continued all the way into the station and onto the platform, only pausing briefly to purchase tickets and a newspaper from a nearby vendor.

"We are all entitled to our opinion," snapped Wun Chuan. "We don't all have to think England is wonderful."

"That's awfully rich coming from you m'dear," said Amos rounding on her again. "You complain incessantly about anything that isn't Chinese and yet the instant someone utters a home truth about," he drew inverted commas in the air with his fingers. "…'the kingdom under heaven', you get in right huff and rant for hours."

Wun Chuan opened her mouth to speak but Shui bellowed. "Enough!" startling a few other people on the platform and she closed it again. No one spoke again until they were on the train and even then, it was Ignis asking to borrow Amos' paper.

"Thanks," whispered Ignis as he dragged the paper across the table at which they were all sat. Ignis thumbed idly through the pages for a while as Amos, Shui and Wun Chuan gazed out of the train window at buildings, fields and the occasional bird zipping past.

Nine pages in, Ignis turned to Amos and muttered. "Price of energy's gone up again."

A man sat across the aisle in an adjacent seat looked up from the book he had been reading and glanced at Ignis, evidently surprised that a seven-year-old boy would take an interest in energy prices.

The man turned back to his book and had just re-read the first line when he heard Ignis say. "And look, Amos, a local bar is having a Mariano Mores appreciation night. Can you remember when we saw him play? Buenos Aires at the Presidente Alvear Theater, back in what... 1948? That was a great evening. And that woman who thought..."

Ignis broke off his sentence at a meaningful look from Amos, whose eyes pointed to the man with the book.

Ignis turned to look at him and saw his confused and slightly gormless face staring back. Ignis flushed scarlet as Shui clapped a hand to her mouth to prevent herself giggling again.

"He's got brain damage," snapped Wun Chuan tearing her gaze from the window and rounding on the man who instantly stopped gawping and turned scarlet too. "And didn't anyone ever tell you it's rude to stare!" she added and the man quickly faced forward and hid his face behind his book.

"*Si suppone che sia un bambino di sette anni,*" sung Amos with a wry smile.

"*Hai, kore dake soko ni suwatte bogī ka nanika de asobu!*" chuckled Shui, impishly.

Ignis mimed picking a bogey and flicking it at her which earned him a sigh and an eye roll from Wun Chuan.

Thankfully the train arrived at Leamington Spa station just minutes later and the bickering gave way to order as they departed the train and headed for the exit.

The clock in the ticket office said 08.45.

"Excellent!" said Amos. "We have arrived with plenty of time to spare. You are not due in your class until nine thirty so that affords us chance to locate the school and meet the headteacher."

Amos looked left and right as he stepped out of the ticket office and into the street, then turning on his heels and pointing up a long road surrounded by tall white buildings, said. "Um, this way I believe."

They soon arrived alongside some shops, and to Wun Chuan's delight, there was a Starbucks coffee shop.

"Two minutes," Wun Chuan chirped, holding up two fingers before slipping inside.

Amos, who had at first seemed annoyed by having to stop and satisfy Wun Chuan's caffeine addiction, decided to follow her in, saying as he went. "Well, as we are here, I could really go for a nice slice of carrot cake." Thus leaving Shui and Ignis outside on their own.

Feeling bored and in need of distraction, Shui and Ignis began looking around for something to amuse themselves with when they spotted a young teenage boy busking outside the entrance to a shopping centre.

He was dressed in a black T-shirt bearing the brand 'Black Sabbath', a pair of tattered and torn black jeans and humongous leather boots adorned with bits of metal and buckles. His other garment, a black leather trench coat, lay sprawled out on the floor in front of him and sported a few pieces of loose change. The boy had a heavy looking twin-necked guitar strapped around his shoulders and as he played for the shoppers he playfully switched from the top neck to the bottom and back again as part of his performance. His long black hair hung loosely in front of his face and swung back and forth as the boy swayed in time with whatever song he was playing.

Shui and Ignis, both having a great appreciation for a wide variety of music and frankly missing the days when minstrels were the only source of tuneful entertainment, wandered over to listen and pay tribute.

The boy was halfway through 'The Hook' by Blues Traveller when he spotted Ignis and Shui, dancing quite unabashed and with very little grace and co-ordination. The boy finished the song and both Shui and Ignis each threw a five-pound note onto his coat.

The boy nodded his thanks and then gestured silently to his guitar.

"Yes," said Ignis a little perplexed. "It's a very cool instrument." He spoke the last part loudly as though addressing someone who had poor hearing.

The boy rolled his eyes, but still smiling mimed speech then pointed at Ignis and then at his guitar again.

"Do you want him to pick a song?" asked Shui.

The boy nodded gleefully and dragged back his long hair over his right ear waiting for Ignis' response.

"Can't you speak?" enquired Ignis, his curiosity peaked.

The boy shook his head, then pulled back the rest of his hair and raised his head. Upon doing so, he displayed a series of thick, jagged scars that ran across his throat and along the underside of his chin. Ignis made a pained face. The boy then leaned very close to Ignis, and with a quick look around, opened his mouth wide to reveal a stump of flesh that used to be a tongue. Someone at some point in this boy's life had cut it out. Ignis' face showed no sign of either shock or disgust at what he saw as he peered into the maw like a doctor performing an examination and the boy seemed gratified at the lack of repulsion.

"Who did this to you?" asked Shui in a hushed voice.

The boy gripped the top neck of his guitar and began to play in earnest. It was a gentle, solemn song that grabbed the attention of several people entering or leaving the shopping centre and he played with such sincerity and sadness that an eerie silence fell upon the crowd of onlookers.

Shui stared at him dreamily for a minute before exclaiming so loudly that a lady stood behind her jumped. "I know that song! It's *Concrete Angel* by Martina McBride," she thought for a moment as the boy continued to play and as understanding flooded her brain a look of deep disgust wrought itself upon her face. "Y-your parents did this to you?" she murmured, so quietly the words were almost drowned out by the notes.

The boy, who didn't falter in his playing, caught Shui's eye and gave a slow singular nod of his head. Shui fell back into the crowd and seethed at the thought it, clenching her fists and grinding her teeth.

The boy finished the song and a resounding applause filled the small foyer of the shopping centre entrance. People chucked handfuls of silver change and pound coins onto the now large pile of money in front of the boy and resumed their business, albeit in a more subdued and thoughtful manner.

"That was marvellous!" exclaimed Amos to the surprise of Ignis and Shui, who hadn't noticed him return.

Amos was clutching a piece of cake wrapped in a serviette and attempting to wipe his free hand on a hankie.

"Amos Cromwell," he said in a cordial manner, whilst holding out the wiped hand to the boy, who grabbed hold and shook it enthusiastically.

Mid-shake, Amos turned his hand to reveal more of the boy's fingers and said. "That must certainly make playing easier?" he chuckled in an almost admiring way.

Ignis and Shui glanced at the hand too and for the first time noticed that the boy had six fingers on each hand.

"Do the extra fingers work?" asked Shui without any hint of embarrassment and she actually reached forward, held it between her index finger and thumb and began moving it back and forth as if testing a hinge on a door.

The boy gave a soundless laugh, withdrew his hand and in a swift fluid motion dropped to the lower neck of his guitar and ripped out a rapid and complicated solo which, impressively used all of his fingers, including the extra one.

"My word," cooed Amos. "I dare say you may be able to play what a person with a standard number of digits could not even dream of!"

Amos withdrew a pocket watch from his waistcoat and checked the time. His eyes bulged a little as he did so then he hurriedly stuffed the watch away and turning back to the boy said, "It was a pleasure to meet you dear boy, but we must be making tracks, on a bit of a tight schedule I'm afraid. But I do hope to see you play again."

The boy bowed to the group and positioned himself ready to play. As Ignis began to leave, the boy gave a cough and tapped on the guitar.

"Oh yeah!" said Ignis. "I never chose a song." He thought for a moment then said. "Play me out to *Problem Child* by AC/DC."

The boy did as he was bidden and Ignis strutted off up the street bouncing along in time with the music and having a pretend mosh pit with Shui.

As the sun shone, and the music echoed through the tall buildings, Ignis was filled with a great sense of well-being. But like all good things, it would not be long before it ended.

Chapter Six
School Daze

Ignis, Shui, Amos and Wun Chuan arrived at the school at twenty past nine. They strode up the stone steps and entered the main doors which were situated in between two vast stone pillars that were delicately engraved with a multitude of languages, each repeating the school motto over and over again, 'The roots of education are bitter, but the fruit is sweet'.

Ignis recognised this as a quote by Aristotle and smiled. "Wonder how much of the fruit has turned rotten?" he thought to himself.

As they entered the reception area, Ignis noticed how much shabbier it was inside. The grand entrance, which was the school's face to the public was clearly not reflected within. It was instead reduced to the usual chintzy counter and cork noticeboards with various advertisements for school events and important information pinned haphazardly upon it.

The receptionist, a blonde woman with mousey features, had at first seemed busy as she took notes whilst talking on the phone. It wasn't long, however, before the group tuned to her conversation only to realise she was chatting with a friend and was listing various items she needed to buy for a party later.

After several long minutes had passed and no acknowledgement that anyone had even entered the building had been given, Amos leaned over the counter to peer down at the woman and gave a stiff cough. The receptionist ignored him and continued to giggle about someone called Ralph and the size of his head.

After having it stretched rather thinly this morning, Wun Chuan's patience finally snapped. She marched toward the counter, stood shoulder to shoulder with Amos, wrapped the desk hard with her knuckles and waited for a response. The receptionist did at least look up this time, but unfortunately made the mistake of giving Wun Chuan a look of deep disgust before turning her back to them and continuing her conversation. Further enraged by Shui's silent amusement, Wun Chuan reached over the counter, grabbed the phone base and yanked it.

The handset sprang away from the receptionist's hand and flew over the counter only to be caught by Amos who said in the politest manner he could muster. "She will call you back!" before hanging up on the base still clutched by Wun Chuan, whose nails were clawing at the plastic so hard she was etching grooves along the side.

"What the hell are you doing?" screeched the receptionist as she got to her feet and began waving her arms about.

Wun Chuan clenched her teeth and began grinding them loudly. She leaned forward as though about to speak, but Amos, thinking diplomacy might be a better option than murder, cut across her.

"I believe my colleague is attempting to convey her disappointment at being kept waiting while you so rudely ignored us in favour of discussing party plans with your friend." Amos said, almost in a whisper.

The receptionist screwed up her face as her eyes kept darting to Wun Chuan. She was obviously trying hard to prevent herself yelling a stream of colourful abuse at her, but Amos, recognising the danger, spoke again.

"We are here to see the headteacher and time is catching up to us."

The receptionist held out her hand to Wun Chuan, and looking directly into her eyes, said. "Well, you had better give me the phone back so I can call her then, hadn't you!"

Begrudgingly Wun Chuan thrust the phone back at her which the receptionist took, pulling a childish, sarcastic grin as she did so.

Amos and Wun Chuan then retreated to sit with Ignis and Shui and waited for the headmistress to arrive.

In less than one minute, a thin woman in her forties, with her hair tied back in a bun and wearing a black suit similar in style to Wun Chuan's attire, entered the room. She held the door open and beckoned them through, saying, "Good morning, I'm Hilary Penton, so sorry to keep you waiting Mr, er?"

"Cromwell!" Amos finished for her. "And not at all."

"Indeed," said Wun Chuan as she made her way past the principal. "It's not your fault we're running behind!" she added with a glance at the receptionist who was peering secretively over the counter.

"Oh, hmmm, yes well," the headmistress began as she too stared disapprovingly at the receptionist. "Not my first choice, but family favours and all that," the headmistress mumbled, more to herself than anyone.

Together, they all strode along what appeared to be the main school corridor which connected a plethora of classrooms and the main hall.

"I think it best to show you to the classroom first so you can observe our methods for accelerated learning. Then we can all head to my office to discuss enrolment," said the headmistress, proudly.

Amos and Ignis looked at each other puzzled.

"Er, I'm afraid you may have misunderstood the intention of our visit headmistress," said Amos kindly.

The head came to halt mid-stride and turned to look at Amos with an expression of great confusion.

"Not, enrolling? Well then, that is to say, what are you doing here Mr Cromwell?"

Amos smiled placatively. "We are here, headmistress, to observe one of your pupils, to see if they are suitable for a place in our institution."

Amos emphasised the 'your' and 'our' as he spoke which had the effect of drawing a sour expression on the headmistress's face.

"Can I ask which student in particular you are hoping to coerce into leaving?" she said in a suddenly sterner voice.

Amos tittered jovially. "Not a clue!"

The headmistress stared defiantly at Amos, as though she thought he was being intentionally evasive, was perhaps even mocking her.

"So what? You expect to sit in one of my classrooms and see if one them just takes your fancy, do you?" she snapped.

"Not at all headmistress." Amos drew Shui and Ignis forward so that they were between them. "These children will sit in the classroom and er, see if one of them takes their fancy," he added warmly as though this solved the argument. "Meanwhile my colleague and I will join you in the office to discuss the prospect of transfers."

"They are children!" barked the headmistress. "They are hardly qualified to make any…"

"They are both exceptionally gifted and highly intelligent individuals and you would be wise to address them directly and respectfully," interrupted Amos and his voice too had become stern and carried a coolness to it that was quite out of character.

"If I may," began Ignis looking up at the exasperated face of the headmistress. "My friend and I come from a place of higher learning which caters exclusively to the advancement of gifted minds and children," he began, gesturing at Shui who gave a knowing nod as the headmistress looked at her.

"I understand that as an adult, you like many, struggle with the concept of someone like me outweighing you in both intellect and experience, but your pride is not my concern."

The headmistress blinked and pursed her lips as if she had just been slapped but remained silent as Ignis pressed on.

"I am going to observe your classes and should I see anyone of note, I will indeed offer them a place in our institution, a generosity I do not often bestow. I have more influence than either of the," Ignis drew inverted commas in the air with his fingers, "'adults', and you will do well to remember that if you are ever fortunate enough to have us visit your," Ignis looked around the corridor, giving it a cursory examination, "school, again!" he finished flatly.

The headmistress looked as though she had been struck dumb. Her lips were still pursed, but her eyes were wide as her temper fought with her rising embarrassment.

"Now if you will excuse us, we must be attending class," Ignis said to the headmistress with a slight bow. "See you guys in an hour," he added to Amos and Wun Chuan.

"Nice to meet you!" bellowed Shui with a smile and a little wave, as she and Ignis headed down the corridor leaving the adults behind.

They came to a stop in front of a door that was labelled, 'Physics', but had an additional sign taped to the window that said 'A Level, Accelerated Placement Students Only.'

"This must be the place," said Shui to Ignis cheerfully, standing on tiptoes so she could peek into the classroom through the window. "Ooh, they look so serious!" she added with mock wonder.

Just then Ignis opened the door, catching Shui off guard and causing her to stumble inside. Everybody turned to look at her, some of them were chuckling, the rest scowled at her as if trying to communicate silently that such raucous behaviour was entirely unwelcome.

Shui, who had flushed with embarrassment, straightened herself and attempted to look casual as she muttered crossly to Ignis out of the corner of her mouth. "Moron!" before elbowing him hard in the chest.

"Welcome!" said a soft, warm voice from the front of the classroom.

Ignis looked up to see who had spoken and found himself suddenly speechless and breathless. A young woman was smiling gently back at him from the opposite side of the room. She was stunningly pretty, with long golden hair, milk white skin and piercing blue eyes. She was bathed in a warm glow of sunlight shining in through the window and for a moment Ignis appeared entranced, unable to think or move as he drank in her visage.

"All right, pop your eyes back in," chuckled Shui as she barged past Ignis, snapping him out of his stupor.

"Please take a seat," said the teacher, gesturing to two empty seats at the back of the class. "My name is Miss Sterling, but please call me Alex."

Ignis, looking rather sheepish, smiled morosely then sidled through the desks to his seat. Shui was already sitting and staring at him with half annoyance and half amusement.

"Shut it!" said Ignis firmly as he sat down.

"Would you like to introduce yourselves?" asked Alex softly.

Shui was first to stand. "Nice to meet you all," she said with wave. Then as if participating in a self-help group, added in a solemn voice, "I'm Lin Shui and I'm a genius."

"We are all geniuses here." Sneered a boy near the front of the class.

He looked like he was in his mid-teens and his desk was right next to the teacher's. He was wearing a school blazer and his hair was parted to one side and gelled so flat against his head it might have been painted onto his scalp.

"Nooo," replied Shui, the condescension in her voice unmistakable. "I am a genius, you are a nerd. Just being keen on your subjects and paying attention in class does not make you gifted."

The boy's face reddened with anger and he made to speak but Shui interrupted. "You are what... fifteen? And you are in a class populated by children under the age of ten and you are all studying the same subject at the same level. You may be clever but your peers are the geniuses."

There was a general muttering of approval at these words by the rest of the class and Ignis who had been quietly observing the other students got the impression that this pompous boy and his attitude was disliked by most. The boy, though still angered, was obviously lost for a retort and simply seethed as he stared at Shui as if he would like nothing more than to punch her.

"Well thank you Lin," said Miss Sterling.

"It's Shui Miss, I mean Alex," replied Shui happily. "I'm Chinese and we say our surnames first."

"Oh," chuckled Alex. "Well nice to meet you Shui," she added still smiling softly. "And what about you?" she asked looking at Ignis.

Shui sat as Ignis rose and as they passed Ignis muttered. "Good to see you're making friends."

Shui said nothing but grinned broadly.

"My name is Ignis Faukesius," said Ignis flatly as he surveyed the class whose eyes were all upon him.

"What sort of name is Ignis?"

It was the boy at the front who had spoken again as though determined to assert some level of dominance over at least one of the new arrivals.

"And what may I ask is your name?" said Ignis coolly.

"Quentin Farrowfield the third," the boy replied defiantly, though there was a quiver in his voice as he spoke.

"The third?" began Ignis, his eyes burning deep into Quentin's. "*Parlarmi così ancora una volta e sarete Quentin Farrowfield l'ultimo.*"

To Ignis and Shui's surprise, one student in the class giggled at this threat.

They looked over and saw for the first time, a little girl sat in the far corner of the room by herself. She had up until now gone unnoticed and was wearing a look of guilty amusement on her face.

"Oh, Chloe!" exclaimed Miss Sterling with delight. "I didn't know you spoke Italian."

Chloe looked up and, curiously, she looked entirely bewildered. "N-n-neither did I!" she stammered.

Ignis eyed her pensively as he sat back down. The little girl had peaked Shui's interest too as she also stared at her over Ignis' shoulder.

"You reckon that's our horse?" asked Shui in a hushed tone.

"Horse?" repeated Ignis incredulously. "Are you sure you're Chinese, you sound more English than Amos sometimes..." He glanced again at Chloe who, despite not yet being instructed to, had been scribbling calculations on several pieces of paper on her desk. "...You may be right though," he finished thoughtfully.

"Shall we begin then?" said Miss Sterling at last when everyone had settled down again. "Quentin, you will see me at the end of class, I've warned you about your attitude toward students before."

"I wouldn't mind seeing her at the end of class!" muttered Ignis absently.

Shui's jaw dropped. "What is with you?" she asked under her breath.

"Nothing!" snapped Ignis who hadn't realised he had spoken out loud.

"Can everyone turn to page thirty-two," commanded Alex as she drifted back and forth in front of the whiteboard. "We will be starting the chapter on forces today."

The sound of pages rustling as the students rifled through their books filled the room, until everyone was poised and ready for the lesson to begin. Everyone that is except for Chloe. She was attentive but she hadn't opened her book. Alex, the teacher, didn't seem surprised or perturbed by this at all and instead turned her focus back to Shui and Ignis.

"As I understand it you are with us just for today, is that correct?" she asked politely.

Ignis and Shui both gave a curt nod of their heads.

"In that case I do not expect you to take any notes for course work, but please feel free to join in and answer any questions if you can."

Ignis knew Shui was showing great restraint by remaining silent and not laughing or throwing out some sarcastic comment, and as he handed her a piece of ruled paper, he whispered. "If you're struggling to understand the theory just copy mine."

Shui's restraint broke and she snorted so loudly she caused the whole class to look at her once again.

"Sorry... sneezed," she muttered apologetically.

The next hour passed by quickly. Every student joined in the discussions and answered each question correctly. They even took it in turns to write on the whiteboard, a formula for calculating the force behind hypothetical scenarios they had chosen themselves.

Shui, to Quentin's increased fury, had explained, how much force would be required to pull his underpants over his head. She had taken into account his height, weight, expected tolerance for pain, the tensile strength of the fabric and the overall strength of the person doing the pulling, which in this scenario, was Shui. When she had finished writing, everyone had begun to laugh, including Alex. Quentin, had taken a full ten minutes to work out and understand what she had written. When it dawned on him at last, he flushed with embarrassment and scowled at Shui.

When Chloe took her turn, she explained how much potential energy is inside the average human and if it were released all at once, what the resulting explosive force would be. As it happens it would be enough to eradicate a large portion of the UK. This was greeted with much approval from everyone. Everyone except of course for Quentin, who on his go had tried to explain what forces were at work when two cars collided at forty-five mph and what the expected damage to each vehicle would be. He was, unfortunately, wrong and promptly stormed out of the classroom in an almighty hissy fit when Chloe had corrected his equation whilst busying herself by taping ten pens together so she could write several identical lines of text at the same time.

After the class was finished, the students filed out leaving Shui and Ignis alone in the room with Miss Sterling.

"Well, I am most impressed with the pair of you," said Alex beaming at them with delight. "I would say I hope you are going to be joining our group, but I think we would be holding you back."

"Unfortunately, as we explained to the headmistress," began Ignis with a touch of apprehension, "we are not here to see if we should join you, instead we are here to see if any of your number should join us."

Alex looked rather taken aback by this. "You two… are head hunting students?" she asked amazed. "I know you are brilliant but you are, what, seven years old? Such responsibility for ones so young."

Shui smiled indulgently. "You'd be surprised at our responsibilities, Alex," she said and once again Alex seemed startled.

Shui's usual exuberant manner had given way to an older, mature tone and for a split-second Alex could have sworn a woman of years that greatly exceeded her own had replied.

She shook it off, and asked with mild amusement. "I don't suppose you are going to take Quentin."

Both Shui and Ignis chortled. "Actually," said Ignis. "We were interested in Chloe."

The soft expression and sweet voice that Miss Sterling had maintained for the last hour evaporated at once.

"No!" she said, perhaps more forcefully than she had intended.

Noticing the quizzical look on Shui and Ignis' face, she added. "Sorry, but Chloe is a very special girl, I suspect you realise this already but I doubt you understand just how unique she is."

Shui and Ignis said nothing, they simply continued to glare at Alex, silently interrogating her.

"Well look who I am talking to, you two are quite rare yourselves. But I would worry for her if she left. I have developed a good relationship with Chloe and I have been able to give her the support that is not being provided at home... Her parents love her of course but... sorry I say too much."

Ignis took Alex's hand in his and drew her close. For a split second he caught the intoxicating smell of her hair and faltered.

He quickly recovered, and pressed on.

"Ahem, Alex... I am impressed by your devotion to your student... s," he quickly added the 's' for fear of offending. "But I am obliged to discuss a placement with any child whom I feel could benefit from joining our institution."

Alex did not look placated so he ploughed on. "You should know that should we accept Chloe into our fold, she will be guaranteed a lucrative career for life, a career that will allow her to fully develop her skills and intellect in a way no school or organisation can."

Alex's expression softened but she still seemed saddened by the idea.

"Look," interrupted Shui. "When we induct a new student, they are required to be accompanied by a parent or guardian, if as you say support at home is lacking, then perhaps you could come in her parents' place!"

As if she had climbed into a warm bath, the tension and worry drained from Alex's face and she smiled once again.

"I would appreciate that," said Alex gratefully. "I know she is not my daughter, but I feel very protective of her. I can't explain it. There is just something about her that makes me so very possessive. Please talk it over with Chloe, and should she agree, I would be thrilled to offer my support."

"Excellent! Well, I think there is perhaps no time like the present," said Shui giving Ignis a nudge with her elbow. "Ignis...? Ignis... ? Oi!" she bellowed directly into Ignis ear, who gave a start.

He had been entranced, gazing at Alex and still holding her hand. "Wha...? Oh yeah... Good idea, let's go," he tipped an imaginary hat at Alex adding. "Miss Sterling, if you will excuse us," before they both left the room.

"You luurve her!" chuckled Shui as the door closed behind them.

"Don't be ridiculous!" snapped Ignis.

"You friggin' do!" said Shui laughing more loudly now.

"No, I don't!" he retorted more aggressively than usual. "I'm just... well she's..."

"Hot?" supplied Shui as Ignis clicked his fingers, searching for an appropriate word.

"Yes... I mean... well of course she is pretty but... but... shut up!"

They rounded a corner and Shui was just about to continue winding Ignis up even more, when they both saw something that drove Miss Sterling out of their thoughts entirely. Chloe was stood a little way up the corridor. She was backed against a wall and Quentin was yelling at her and pointing in her face angrily.

"You think it's funny, do you?" barked Quentin.

"What?" asked Chloe in a meek voice.

"You tell me!" demanded Quentin. "What did that ginger kid say?"

"Ginger?" muttered Ignis as he and Shui marched closer.

"I don't know what he said," Whimpered Chloe. "I didn't understand it."

"You understood enough to laugh!" replied Quentin, still yelling, but now doing it inches from Chloe's face. "Where are you going? I haven't finished with you yet!" added Quentin as he dragged Chloe back up against the wall as she attempted to slip away.

"Oh, I think a practical demonstration of my force theory is in order!" growled Shui as she rolled up her sleeves and started to head towards Quentin. Ignis, however, held her back.

"Not yet!" said Ignis patiently. "Let's see what she does first."

Shui didn't look happy about this, but she acquiesced and waited all the same.

"…and fixing my formulae for me," raged Quentin. "You think I need help from a snot-nosed little child? Well? WELL?"

Anyone watching, may have expected Chloe to cry at this point. Would have thought Chloe to have apologised profusely and begged for forgiveness. She was after all only five years old herself and was being harassed relentlessly by a boy ten years older and some four feet taller.

What no one did expect, was for Chloe to say. "Yes!"

She said it so quietly that it was almost inaudible. At least it was until Quentin, through gritted teeth snarled. "What did you say?"

Chloe had reached the end of her tether. She looked him square in the face and as loudly as her little lungs would permit bellowed. "YEEEEEESSSSS! You are a big stupid moron and you don't belong in our class!"

Chloe breathed heavily for a moment and then it dawned on her what she had said and who she had said it to. Quentin didn't say a word. Instead, he screwed up his face and swung his hand through the air, aiming a heavy slap at Chloe's frightened face. Shui lurched forward but Ignis held her back! Somehow, he knew she wasn't going to need their help. With speed that would rival Shui herself, Chloe caught Quentin's wrist and bent it so viciously, he yelped like an injured dog. In the same motion she wrought his arm out to its fullest extent and forced him to the floor so fast, Quentin did not have time to react. His face smashed against the floor and a tooth popped out of his mouth and bobbed across the ground leaving small droplets of blood in its wake.

"Why don't you leave us alone!" Chloe sobbed, though very much in control as she increased the pressure on Quentin's wrist, forcing him to remain still. "Why don't you... don't you... go far away and never come back!"

The conviction in Chloe's voice was absolute. It was a childish demand, but it was heavy with authority. For two whole minutes nobody moved or spoke, until at last, Chloe, having regained a modicum of composure released her grip on Quentin who slumped to the floor. Chloe backed away from him, expecting an outburst of rage and reprisal for her actions, but when Quentin finally got to his feet there was an unusual lack of emotion on his face. Expressionless and glassy eyed he simply turned about and walked away as if nothing had happened.

"Impressive," said Ignis into the ringing silence that followed in Quentin's wake. Chloe jumped and turned to look at him.

"A genius and a dab hand at the fighting arts, you are indeed full of surprises," he added with a warm smile.

Shui stepped forward. "Hi I'm Sh..." she began, but Chloe cut her off mid-sentence.

"Shui and you are Ignis, I remember from class. It's funny..." she added with a giggle.

"What is?" asked Ignis.

"Your names. Fire and water," she replied pointing at Ignis and Shui in turn.

"You continue to amaze!" said Ignis who really did appear impressed now. "How many other languages can you speak... or at least understand?"

"I don't know," replied Chloe honestly. "Sometimes I know things, just because someone asked me. Things I haven't studied, stuff I can't even remember hearing or seeing and yet I know as if I always have." Chloe stared into space for a moment, then with a sigh continued. "Sorry, I'm not explaining it well. For all the things I do know, it's ironic that I haven't got the faintest clue as to why I am the way I am."

"Well, it's a pleasure to meet you!" said Shui holding out her hand for Chloe to shake.

Ignis in turn held out his hand to greet her properly but as Chloe took it, something strange and terrible happened, something that chilled them to their very core.

A light, vast and bright erupted beside them in the corridor. It swelled in size and power with tremendous haste and within moments the classrooms, students, the world itself had been obscured by its presence. Ignis and Chloe felt a raw surge of energy bursting from the depths of the phenomena and then, as all that had been radiated from its centre seemed to reach its limit, like a tide returning to the ocean, light, air and time was sucked back into its centre as the explosion became a void. For a few seconds, Ignis stared into its maw, braced against the vortex and was amazed to see stars and planets, nebulas and galaxies all swirling around like a giant cosmic soup. Still dazzled by the corona at the edge of this bite-sized universe, Ignis became aware of a figure stood close to the event horizon. It was a woman and she had pain and fear etched on her face. Before Ignis was able to comprehend this apparition or even identify who she was, Chloe let out a chilling cry of despair.

With agonising accusation wrought on her face and heartbreak hanging heavily in her voice she bellowed over the swirling din of interstellar noise. "IGNIS, NO! YOU DAMN FOOL, WHAT HAVE YOU DONE?"

The voice that came out of her mouth, did not belong to Chloe. It was a man's voice, deep, hoarse and familiar. Ignis, who had fire running through his veins, felt his insides freeze. Bewildered, confused and scared for the first time in his life, he turned back to face the woman on the brink of calamity and saw with a thrill of horror, her form spaghettified as she was dragged screaming into unknown space and time. Their senses overwhelmed, Ignis and Chloe's minds teetered on the precipice of infinity and insanity until, with a rushing akin to being pulled through water at speed, the void vanished, the school returned to their sight and they fell to the floor as their hands parted with Shui stood between them looking mortified.

Ignis, panting and sweating as though he had just run a great distance, got to his feet. He leaned over to help Chloe up but she recoiled, scared to touch him a second time.

"Can't say I blame you!" he panted shakily.

Shui, who was still silent and glancing from Chloe to Ignis with ill-concealed shock, grabbed Chloe by the arm and dragged her upwards. Chloe wobbled unsteadily for a moment as she clutched Shui's jumper for balance.

"Are you OK?" enquired Shui firmly after finally regaining control of her mental faculties.

"I think so," whimpered Chloe as she examined a bruise forming on her elbow which she had bumped as she and Ignis broke apart.

Shui rounded on Ignis. "What the hell was that?" It was evident that Shui had intended to whisper this but, full of excitement, she blurted it out quite loudly which made Ignis jump. "You guys went into some kind of trance just now."

Before Ignis could reply, Amos and Wun Chuan came hurrying down the corridor with Ms Penton, the headmistress, hot on their heels.

"What is the meaning of this?" barked the headmistress as she barged passed Amos and Wun Chuan.

Her question was greeted with nothing but defiant and admonitory stares from Ignis, Shui, Amos and Wun Chuan. Realising that she was not about to get anywhere with these outsiders, Ms Penton turned her attention to Chloe instead. "Chloe, I am surprised to see you mixed up in, in, well whatever this is."

Ignis began to explain that it was no fault of Chloe's, but the headmistress cut him off.

"You had your chance to explain, now be quiet or get out."

"Calm yourself, Hilary!" said Amos. His voice was low but boomed over her shoulder.

"It's Ms Penton or Headmistress to you sir, and I am talking to 'my' student."

"She won't be yours for much longer!" growled Shui, who had moved to stand between Hilary and Chloe.

"Ignis, kindly elaborate on what has happened before Ms Penton has an aneurysm," said Wun Chuan, casting the headmistress a cold glare.

"*Ora non è sicuramente il tempo*," replied Ignis, widening his eyes to convey the need for secrecy.

"Speak bloody English!" roared Hilary. "This is my school and I will not be made to look like a fool."

"A little late for that," snarled Wun Chuan.

The headmistress exploded with rage and drenched Wun Chuan with a torrent of abusive words that did not belong in a school. Wun Chuan listened to her without expression, occasionally adding another sarcastic comment which served nothing more than to aggravate Ms Penton further.

Avoiding the argument, Amos bowed low to quickly chat with Shui and Ignis. "The details can wait," he said hurriedly. "All I need to know right now is if you have found our star pupil?"

Shui dragged Chloe forward so Amos could see her fully. "This is the one!" she whispered and she gave Chloe a gentle pat on the back.

"And you're sure?" enquired Amos, aware that the argument Hilary and Wun Chuan were engaged in was increasing in intensity and volume.

"Oh, yeah!" replied Shui with a weak half laugh. "She is definitely the one."

"Excellent!" said Amos clapping his hands together. "If you and Ignis can head back to the office, I'll, er…" he looked over his shoulder at Wun Chuan and Hilary almost nose to nose as they tried to shout each other down and sighed heavily. "Try and smooth things over here."

"Sure thing," said Shui. "Let's go du-dude?"

Shui scanned the corridor and spotted Ignis walking away. Shui and Amos left Chloe with Wun Chuan and the headmistress and hastened after him, but Ignis, as though he had been waiting for them to follow, turned and held up his hand to stop them.

"Amos, get an agent on Chloe," said Ignis with forced calm. "Until she's inducted and we can help her control her abilities, she does indeed pose a risk to those around her." He rubbed his eyes and then his temples. "Shui can fill you in on most of what happened today, I'll fill in the blanks when I get back."

"Where are you going?" asked Shui suspiciously.

"When I shook her hand," he began almost dreamily, "I experienced a hallucination weirder and more intense than I ever would have thought possible." Ignis screwed up his eyes and gave his head a shake. "Don't worry, I'm fine," he assured them both, though he spoke more to Amos than

Shui, as Amos was wearing his concerned parent look again. "I just need to clear my head, walk it off I guess."

"I understand," said Amos softly. "Just keep me updated, OK?"

"Of course!" said Ignis rubbing his head again, then with a furtive smile, he turned and left, leaving Amos and Shui to deal with Wun Chuan and Hilary.

"Let's get this over with!" sighed Amos wearily.

Shui didn't move. She was still staring after Ignis, who was now nowhere in sight.

"What is it?" asked Amos who had not failed to notice how subdued Shui had become.

"Do you…" Shui began hesitantly.

"What?" urged Amos, his concern rising.

"Do you trust Ignis?" she said at last. "His judgement, I mean!" she added quickly.

"Unconditionally and with my life," said Amos proudly, though it was hard to miss the defensive edge to his tone.

"Yeah," said Shui quietly. "Me too."

Amos, although perplexed, seemed content with her final remark and turned to deal with the bitter argument that was about to escalate into a murder. His ears already tuned to the quarrel, he didn't hear Shui's last words.

"Maybe that's the problem."

Chapter Seven
The Chaos Theory of a Murder Mystery

It was late afternoon in a usually quiet village in the south of France. The sun was set high in a clear blue sky and was brilliantly hot, especially for the month of October. From over the distant fields a chorus of birdsong echoed through the gently swaying trees and was accompanied by the soft trickle of a nearby stream. It would have been a vista to inspire even the most depressed individual into painting with watercolour, had it not of course been for the still smouldering and smoking wreckage of a house that had been razed to the ground the night before.

It had been a great talking point for the villagers, that poor Professor Braskin had burned alive in his own house.

"*Eh bien, il allait un peu mou dans la tête si vous me demandez,*" said Françoise Gagnier, a local farmer's wife who had popped in to the bakery for some flour and a large dollop of gossip. "*Avec pas de femme pour s'occuper de lui, il a probablement laissé la cuisinière sur le.*"

"*Vrai, c'est vrai,*" replied Thérèse Mynatt through a mouthful of scone. "*Honte si, pas de famille pour lui manquer.*"

"*Ah, n'at-il pas avoir d'enfants?*" asked Françoise.

"*Non, je crois que sa femme était stérile,*" replied Thérèse without thought of sounding inappropriate.

The conversation between Françoise and Thérèse would have probably gone on for an hour. False sympathy drenched with callous remarks, all for the sake of having something new to talk about. However, their attention was redirected to something much more troublesome, the sudden and unexpected appearance of four males, two of them adults, the other two children. Each one of them was dressed in quite outlandish clothing and were obviously foreigners as none of them spoke French. As they had entered the bakery, they had been deep in conversation. A heated debate of which the children seemed to have as much an opinion about as the men.

Noticing Thérèse and Françoise staring at them in an entirely unwelcome way, the discussion ended at once and talk turned to the topic of refreshments.

"I don't know about you guys but I'm starving!" said Gyasi, licking his lips as he peered through the plastic sneeze guard at the snacks and pastries beneath. "Don't suppose they sell kelewele?" he muttered earnestly to Aarde who rolled his eyes disappointedly.

"It's France, Gyasi!" sighed Aarde. "I would doubt very much that you are likely to find any form of African cuisine in French bake…"

"Ooh, puff puffs!" interrupted Gyasi rushing over to another display.

"Really?" enquired Aarde, who seemed a little more enthusiastic now.

Upon closer inspection, Aarde realised Gyasi had been looking at profiteroles. Aarde was about to correct him, but Elsu who had also seen the mistake cut him off.

"Yeah, mate. You are gonna love French puff puffs. They're a little sweeter than perhaps you're used to but I'm sure once you get them drenched in hot sauce they'll taste just fine."

Aarde gave Elsu a look of admonishment but Elsu thought he saw Aarde supress a giggle as he turned away.

"What about you bud?" Elsu enquired to Hoowo3oow who was standing near the doorway trying his best not to look awkward.

"Bottle of water!" ordered Hoowo3oow tonelessly.

"Aren't you having any food?" asked Gyasi, who had just ordered twenty profiteroles.

"You forget I caught a rabbit earlier. These grounds are fertile, I should be able to find some vegetation to cook it with later," replied Hoowo3oow proudly. His brow suddenly furrowed however, as he eyed Gyasi quizzically. "What's his problem?" muttered Hoowo3oow.

All heads turned to see Gyasi looking confused and Thérèse on the other side of the counter looking impatient.

"CHOCOLAT?" said Thérèse loudly and slowly. She clearly thought Gyasi was a bit dim.

"Aarde, help me out," grumbled Gyasi imploringly. "This lady keeps asking me a question, but French is not one of my languages I'm afraid."

"Good thing I picked you to accompany me on an investigation in France then, eh?" said Aarde sardonically.

"*Puis-je aider?*" asked Aarde politely to Thérèse who seemed thrilled to hear a sentence in her own tongue.

"*J'ai essayé de demander à ce baffoon s'il aimerait sauce au chocolat avec ses profiteroles,*" snapped Thérèse coldly.

"*Oh, un instant,*" said Aarde holding up a finger to turn to Gyasi. "She wants to know if you would like chocolate with your…" he glanced at Elsu who gave him a sly wink, then with a sigh added "…puff puff?"

"Chocolate?" repeated Gyasi incredulously.

"I said they would be sweeter," chuckled Elsu.

"I'll sort it," said Aarde who wanted nothing more than to leave now and get back to work.

He turned to Thérèse who looked just as fed up as he did and placed his order.

"*Il ne veut pas le chocolat, mais avez-vous une sauce piquante? Et puis-je également obtenir un sandwich au fromage jambon et fumé et quatre bouteilles d'eau, s'il vous plaît?*"

"What about me?" asked Elsu who spoke French perfectly well.

"You can eat the rabbit with Hoowo3oow and serves you right!" replied Aarde as he gathered up the items Thérèse had placed on the counter. She also handed him a little bottle of 'Fire Brand' tomato sauce, which Gyasi snatched up, and after pulling off the cap with his teeth, began to liberally soak the bag of profiteroles with it until it looked like a sack of bloodied vomit.

"*Dégoûtant,*" sneered Françoise who had been watching from a distance and was heaving as though ready to vomit herself.

"*Folie!*" added Thérèse who was turning her nose up at the food so much, her nostrils had begun whistling as she breathed.

"Have we done?" snarled Hoowo3oow impatiently.

Nodding, Aarde gave a handful of euros to Thérèse telling her to keep the change and as he shared out the bottles of water, they all filed out of the shop.

They walked for a good twenty minutes without speaking, Aarde munching on his sandwich, Hoowo3oow taking an occasional sip of water and Elsu watching the rabbit tied to Hoowo3oow's waist, bounce lifelessly against his leg and thinking how little he was looking forward to dinner later.

The silence was finally broken when Gyasi, finally deciding the sauce had soaked into the 'puff puff's' sufficiently, fished one out and popped it into his mouth. For a few seconds Gyasi seemed to savour the taste and looked terribly pleased with himself. But then as he bit into one of the profiteroles, the cream that had been concealed within, mixed with the generous helping of hot sauce inside his mouth and instantly congealed, making Gyasi gag and spit it out.

"What the...? They put cream inside the puff puff's!" he exclaimed, outraged as he squashed another ball in between his fingers and saw cream squeeze out. "I can't eat these, ah, this sucks," he whined as he tossed the bag of dessert snacks into a nearby bin and began to sulk.

"You can have some rabbit as well, if you like!" said Hoowo3oow who obviously thought this would cheer him up.

It didn't cheer him up, and instead Gyasi joined Elsu in watching the limp creature flop about as they continued to walk, silently hoping they would find a McDonald's each time they turned a corner.

There was sadly no McDonald's, just the charred remains of Alfred Braskin's home. To make matters worse, the police forensic investigation team were still sifting through the wreckage.

"Damn it!" scowled Aarde, peering through a cluster of bushes some one hundred metres away. "The police are still here." Aarde watched them bagging up various objects for a few moments, then with a sudden realisation asked. "Er... where's Wade? He should have been here keeping an eye on the site."

Wade was the Conclave's leading detective. As a child he had experienced severe head trauma which had caused extensive brain damage and forced him into a coma. His doctors had given him little chance of regaining consciousness and even less chance of being much more than a vegetable if he did. Against the odds, Wade had not only woken, but he had found a new sense of understanding which no one was able to explain. Able to connect the most abstract of information and formulate an outcome that would have been seemingly unreachable, even impossible, Wade had become a kind of savant detective. With the ability to predict events before they happened with unnerving accuracy and likewise see the past by working time back in his head, Wade was one of the Conclave's most valuable assets. Sadly though his skill, incredible as it was, made him whimsical and he often wandered off, distracted by the irrelevant but fascinating world around him.

"You know Wade, he's probably chasing a butterfly to see if it really will cause a hurricane," muttered Gyasi as he rubbed his growling stomach.

"Guess we wait a little longer!" sighed Elsu bored. "You gonna make a start on dinner mate?" he added turning to Hoowo3oow.

Elsu and Aarde set up a small camp in a small patch of woodland a short distance from the police line. It comprised of a couple of lean tos that Aarde had constructed from loose branches that were scattered across the wood's floor and was covered with several shrubs and brushes to provide camouflage. They were concealed well enough and Gyasi, despite his bulky frame, had managed to drag himself up into a tree to keep lookout. Hoowo3oow had in the meantime, skinned and prepared the rabbit for lunch and had even successfully rounded up a couple of carrots and a cabbage from the surrounding plots. Upon a small fire made from a split log, sat a small pot within which a sumptuous aroma was now rising and filling Elsu and Gyasi's lungs. To their surprise it made them salivate with hunger.

"That actually smells good!" Gyasi whispered down from his perch.

"You sound surprised?" growled Hoowo3oow.

"Ooh, y'know I swear if I didn't already know you had no feelings," chuckled Elsu, smiling broadly. "I'd say they had just been hurt mate."

The stew was indeed good. Elsu, Gyasi and Hoowo3oow huddled round the fire and ate ravenously. Aarde kept watch as he paced across the treetops, leaping from branch to branch with increasing agitation.

"Will you calm down, brother!" said Gyasi after a deep guttural belch. "You're gonna give away our position."

"And how many creatures do you know of that burp to communicate?" aked Elsu, lighting up his pipe and taking a long drag.

Gyasi looked sheepish, but defiant. "If any thing's gonna bring the police our way, it will be the smell of herb from your pipe."

Hearing what Gyasi said, Aarde looked down at Elsu and in an angered whisper said. "Will you put that away!"

Elsu, grumpy but embarrassed, knocked the rest of the herbs from the bowl of his pipe onto the ground and extinguished it with his foot. "Tattle tale," he muttered to Gyasi, who was wearing a satisfied grin.

"I assume, from your erratic prowling," said Hoowo3oow, addressing the trees above him, "that you are concerned for Wade's safety."

"You're damn right I'm concerned!" snapped Aarde. "He should have been here hours ago and nightfall is upon us. He's as thick as he is clever and I wouldn't be surprised if he's lost."

"Wade will never be lost," replied Hoowo3oow calmly. "A man who treats the world as his playground can call any place home."

"Oh, stop being all mystical!" barked Aarde, clearly irritated by Hoowo3oow's spurious reasoning. "We should search the area!"

"And how are we supposed to see in this light?" asked Elsu. "We can't all turn into human candles like Ignis."

"I swear you must just be lazy, because no one is that stupid," snarled Aarde, his patience thinning rapidly.

Elsu said nothing, he just stared blankly back at Aarde.

"Really?" said Aarde catching Elsu's look. "TORCHES! We have frickin' torches!" he yelled angrily.

Elsu looked a little embarrassed but chuckled all the same. "Oh, right! I forgot about those."

Aarde let out a deep sigh and composed himself. "Let's just fan out. Work a spiral until we... Shhh! Someone's coming."

Everyone clambered to the front of the bush covering and peered through towards the site. The police had started to pack away their equipment, they had finished their investigation.

"Who is it?" whispered Gyasi. "Who's coming?"

"It's one of the forensic team. He's coming right at us!"

The person walking towards them was wearing a paper-thin white suit and face mask. Whoever it was seemed to be carrying a large plastic box, that was labelled evidence which clinked on every footstep.

Hoowo3oow signalled for Elsu and Gyasi to lie low and hide. He then crept in a circle around the trees, reappearing behind the officer.

The officer reached the edge of the camp and made to grab one of the lean tos but before they could touch it, Hoowo3oow had swooped upon him and was forcibly restraining the officer with one hand behind his back and Hoowo3oow's hand pressed hard against his throat.

"Guys… GUYS… IT'S ME!" wheezed the man, struggling to breathe against Hoowo3oow's crushing grip.

"Wade?" asked Hoowo3oow relaxing his grip.

"Ah, thanks dude," mumbled Wade rubbing his wrist and throat. "Yeah, it's me."

"Where the… what have you been… what the hell man?" stammered Aarde as he dropped from a high branch and landed in front of Wade.

Wade smiled broadly, held up the plastic box and gave it a little shake. "Been busy!"

"I can see that," said Aarde who was beginning to relax again. "Why didn't you wait for us?"

"Well…" began Wade, tearing off the flimsy clean suit as he spoke. "I arrived here really early and like you was disappointed to see the place crawling with coppers. Well, I pitched up on the other side of that field over there and waited for you guys to arrive," he sat down and smelled the stew that was still simmering on the fire. "Ohh, that smells good! Is there any left? I am staaaaarving!"

"Wade!" said Aarde, Gyasi and Elsu together, eager for Wade to continue his story. Hoowo3oow as usual was stood bolt upright and silent.

"OK, OK, just let me get a bit," replied Wade hungrily. He poured some into a bowl, and taking a mouthful, sighed happily. "Played dude," he said looking at Hoowo3oow. "This is well tasty."

"Well?" said Aarde, trying to sound encouraging.

"Hmmm, oh yeah!" spluttered Wade through a mouthful of vegetables. "Well, the forensic team arrived and began sifting through the debris and I thought 'great', all the good evidence will be gone by the time we get a go," he took another gulp of stew, gave a little burp and continued. "Well after about twenty minutes one of them came over to where I was hiding to take a leak."

Like a good audience member should, Elsu gasped and asked. "What did you do?"

Wade smiled and in a very nonchalant tone said. "I punched him really hard in the neck and he passed out. I think he peed on himself too, because that suit smelled funny."

"So you took his clothes?" asked Aarde, who looked genuinely impressed.

"Yup!" replied Wade. "Then I joined the forensic team and gathered up anything I thought might be relevant, and relevant stuff there was in spades."

"Such as what?" asked Hoowo3oow who finally appeared interested in what Wade had to say.

"Well, I found two charred skeletons in what was the living room, both with broken bones. One had many injuries consistent with blunt force trauma, I expect the poor man had been beaten repeatedly, as some of the breaks had begun to heal. The other had a broken wrist and fresh cracks to his skull and vertebrae. I think that guy was the man who owned the house. I found a few pieces of ID that were still intact in the bedroom. Professor Alfred Braskin."

Wade paused a moment to see if the name meant anything to anyone, when everyone shrugged and shook their heads he ploughed on.

"The other skeleton, I believe, is a male in his late seventies, and South American in origin. I'm speculating here of course but, well, I can't help thinking that this bloke was a native of Peru, possibly even Mayan. I'm quite sure he was kidnapped too, brought here for some reason as yet unknown, but I reckon he knew our Professor and I also think it was this guy…"

Wade pulled from the plastic evidence box a clear plastic bag, within which was a smashed photo frame which had a partially scorched photo melted to the inside and was splattered with dried blood.

"How could you possibly know that?" asked Gyasi sceptically.

"Glad you asked," replied Wade perkily as he pulled out a digital camera and quickly cycled through the images. "The male's skull bares several markers common with the mongoloid race. This is obviously a brachycephalic skull. See the projecting zygomas, the small brow ridge and small nasal apertures?" he said showing a photo of the skull as he spoke.

"Also, despite the fire much of what he was wearing was preserved by a tatty sack that his captors had dressed him in. Here look!"

Wade then pulled out more clear bags full of bits of fabric and what looked like stones.

"This," continued Wade holding up a strip of woven cotton that was embroidered with beautiful shapes and patterns, "is the style of weaving the Mayans used to use to make most of their clothes. While that method is common the design is not. See this?" he asked the group pointing to an embroidered serpent on the fabric. "This symbolises lighting. A sort of praise to the god of lightning who created maize. This is worn to appease the maize deity for a better harvest."

"Yeah, but that's a bit of a leap, mate," said Elsu.

"On its own maybe, but look at these." Wade then raised the bag filled with blackish green stones tied together with some kind of thread. "This is actually jade. It just looks black because of the smoke damage. In Mayan culture the higher society types wore jade skirts atop their clothing to reflect their status. This too…"

Wade produced a scrap of what appeared to be animal skin this time.

"Jaguar skin. This is most important because this would have been worn by a king or at the very least a village leader. It signifies their connection to the heavens and the earth."

The group looked incredulous but Wade pressed on. "There are some quills in here too, I reckon they are probably eagle, maybe even quezal but it's impossible to be sure without analysis, in any case, now you've seen these look at the picture again."

Everyone leant in close and gawped at the image. One by one their faces lit up with confirmation of what Wade had supposed.

"There you see. This is the same guy. I think he was kidnapped because, well for a start he was beaten pretty badly but secondly, this day and age, this guy would be massively xenophobic. You'd never get him out of his village. He's probably from some lost tribe." Wade thought for a moment and then added, "Plus, if you were leaving of your own free will, I expect you'd be going with someone from a more developed country and, well, it would be a bit of a dick move to allow the guy to walk around in his regular threads. He'd stand out like a sore thumb and would be mocked ceaselessly."

"How the hell do you know all that?" asked Elsu sceptically.

"Discovery channel dude!" replied Wade brightly.

"That is excellent work, Wade," said Aarde patting his shoulder, appreciating the effort his colleague had put in to claiming this information. "Tell me," he added earnestly, "did you find anything that might shed a light on who the attackers were?"

"Actually, I did!" said Wade grimly. "I'm afraid it's not as comprehensive as the ID on the victims though."

"Anything is better than nothing mate," chirped Elsu, who had been listening very attentively.

"Well, the biggest clue, and thankfully the police will not be able to make head nor tail of it is this!" began Wade as he rummaged in the evidence box again and produced a sealed plastic tub containing a thick, black oily goo. "Ectoplasmic slime!" he exclaimed tossing the tub to Aarde who held it aloft and rolled it around, making the viscous fluid ooze from one side of the pot to the other.

"What do you reckon, demon?" asked Aarde to Hoowo3oow who had leant in close to Aarde for a better look.

"Could be!" replied Hoowo3oow, squinting at the pot. "We can find out quick enough though, pass it here!"

Aarde handed the tub of slime to Hoowo3oow, who popped open the lid and then, with a quick snatching motion with his free hand, grabbed a spider from a nearby web and dropped it into the pot.

For a few seconds nothing happened, except for the spider lifting its legs in turn and trying to clean them. Suddenly, the spider began to convulse. A little a first, then violently. It began to frantically run around the inside of the tub as though it were panicking, rubbing the ooze onto its body, yet it made no attempt to escape. Hoowo3oow angled the pot to allow the spider to leave without effort and for a moment the spider looked as though it would be fine, but then, most curiously, it began to weave a new web. Everyone watched with bated breath as the spider worked, lovingly creating its intricate pattern. When it had finished, the group gasped with shock. The web was littered with religious symbology. A pentagram, an ohm, a crucifix, the star of David, a nine-pointed star, a Dharmachakra, the name of Allah written in Arabic, eight trigrams, a Shinto, a Hindu swastika, the Chinese character for Tao, the symbols went on and on, looping in a giant swirl to the centre where the web seemed to pulse like a heartbeat. Upon this pulse, the spider sat, immobile save for the rhythmic silent thud of its perch.

Aarde was just about to voice his shock and disbelief at what they had just witnessed when the web began to vibrate. The spider thrashed around in the centre of the web and it looked for a second like it might be thrown from its purchase, but then the vibration stopped, and to the dismay and disgust of those present, the spider cannibalised itself. By the time it had finished, only its head remained, glued to the web that was fluttering in the cool breeze.

"I want to go home!" whimpered Gyasi, his voice thick with fear.

"Yeah! That's messed up, dude!" added Elsu who looked most perturbed.

"Oh, man up!" said Aarde testily.

"Frank should see this!" added Hoowo3oow, overlapping his hands, forming a window and singing the many toned reflect song.

Visible in the space between Hoowo3oow's fingers and thumbs, was Barry. He hadn't noticed Hoowo3oow appear in one of the mirrors back at the control room, and believing he was alone, was attempting to dislodge a bogey from his left nostril.

"Dig any deeper and you will hit grey matter!" sneered Hoowo3oow who looked rather disgusted.

Alarmed, Barry retracted his finger and tried to look nonchalant. He hadn't realised he had pulled out a string of snot, which now sat on his upper lip.

"You, er, have a little something just here," mumbled Hoowo3oow gesturing to his own lip.

Flushing with embarrassment, Barry felt his lip and grimaced as the string of mucus stuck to his finger. He quickly wiped it off with a hankie from his pocket and tried to pretend like it hadn't happened.

"Hoowo3oow, good to see you, how goes the investigation?" asked Barry enthusiastically.

"Good. I am actually contacting you to report some slime… but I see you already have some," replied Hoowo3oow who seemed pleased with himself for making a joke.

Barry rubbed his nose convulsively, then with a weak smile asked. "What kind of slime is it?"

"We think it's demon, but it produces unusual effects when touched by something living," replied Hoowo3oow conversationally.

"All demon slime makes living things go a bit weird, doesn't it?" asked Barry confused.

"Not like this! Where's Frank?" enquired Hoowo3oow.

"He's just pinching one off," replied Barry without thinking.

"Y'know, 'bathroom break' would sound so much more professional!" muttered Frank who had just entered the room behind Barry. "What have you got Hoowo3oow?"

"Slime!" offered Barry.

"I had not realised you had changed your name," growled Hoowo3oow.

"What? Oh, er, sorry!" said Barry, lowering his head as he wheeled his chair out of view.

"So, slime? It's pretty common at supernatural events," said Frank rubbing his hands together. "Is there anything specific that makes it odd or out of place?"

Hoowo3oow gave Frank a 'don't patronise me' look, then said, "Wade confirms that the slime is ectoplasmic, Aarde and I agree that it is demon, what we are struggling with is this…!"

Hoowo3oow inverted his hands so that Frank could see what Hoowo3oow could see and aimed the window straight at the gigantic web.

"What the ffff…?" exclaimed Frank, who felt amazed and alarmed, in equal measure.

Aarde, who had moved into view explained to Frank what Wade had discovered at the crime scene and also what had happened with the spider. Frank's jaw had remained agape throughout the entire explanation and by the end a small trickle of drool had begun to pool on his lower lip.

"Does this mean anything to you?" Aarde asked after a few seconds of silence during which the pool of drool had bungeed from Franks mouth.

"It's got me stumped," replied Frank, still astonished. "I am unaware of any demon that transcends that many religions." He thought for a moment, then shrugging added, "Leave it with me for now. I'll bounce an image of the web around the departments and see if anyone else can shed a light on it. Did you get any other info relating to the attackers… besides slime I mean!"

All heads, and Hoowo3oow's hands, turned to Wade who was pushing a tree that was obviously too big to move. "That's gonna fall down in three years!" he said cheerily.

"Fascinating," said Aarde blankly. "But unless it's going to land on the killers, then I hardly see how it matters."

"Ooh, it won't land on the killers, but it will be caught in a flood during a storm in eight years' time which will cause it to slam into the bakery where you got your sandwich."

"THE KILLERS WADE!" bellowed Aarde who did not have time for whimsy. "Three demons of unknown origin, responsible for a seemingly random murder, do you have anything to add?"

"Three demons and a child, you mean?" replied Wade calmly, ignoring Aarde's flustered admonishment.

"What?" asked Frank, shocked.

"There was a child with them. In fact, I'm pretty sure that the kid, whoever they are, did most of the beating… and the killing… to be honest I don't think the demons did much at all except keep the victims from escaping," explained Wade matter-of-factly.

"How," began Frank, "and feel free to be as specific as you like, do you know this?" There was a very grave and serious edge to Franks voice as he spoke. It was clear that this news troubled him more than anything else he had heard this evening.

"The devil's in the detail mate," said Wade. "For a start, the impact marks on the skeletons were made by fists, feet and elbows, no doubt about that. But the contusions affect a small area, too small for a full-grown man, too small in fact for someone with dwarfism, their hands may be small but there is greater width in the fingers."

Aarde looked sceptical but Frank pressed Wade to continue.

"There is also the fact that many of the blows delivered to the victims were at an upward angle. Consistent with being hit by someone much shorter, not the same height or higher…" Wade thought for a moment, then as though thinking out loud, added. "I suppose they could have been kneeling, or sat down."

"Anything else man, this is important!?" implored Frank.

"There is also the gun shot!" said Wade dreamily.

"Someone was shot?" asked Frank puzzled.

"Not exactly…" began Wade hesitantly. "The shotgun fired and it definitely hit something, but…"

"But what, Wade?" bellowed Frank. "Stop trailing off on your damn sentences and tell me what happened."

"Oh, I am sorry!" snapped Wade, who for the first time that evening had lost his cheery airy manner. "Perhaps one of you would like a moment to present your findings!" Wade cast a scornful look around the group and everybody, including Frank, stared bashfully down at their feet.

"No? Then I'll continue," he said at last, drawing in an almighty breath before speaking with great haste and obvious annoyance. "The professor was the one who fired the shotgun, he has gunshot residue on the remains of his shirt. There is also a streak of rubber I believe has come from a training shoe, leading from the centre of the room over to where the shotgun was found. In addition, I found a professor-shaped crater in the living room wall and a fracture caused by recoil on his left shoulder. The shot from the cartridge is lying in a pile on the floor next to the shotgun as though it was emptied into a hand and dropped. There is no evidence of blood from anyone except the victims and the abductee shows no signs of trauma by wounding with a shotgun. I hypothesise, that the professor had an opportunity to shoot the killers but his attempt was thwarted by someone rushing across the room at great speed and placing an obstruction over the barrel causing the shotgun to blow backwards taking the professor clean off his feet. This obstruction is probably a body part of the killer as there are no objects in the room that could have resisted the blast, let alone be left unscathed. Demons, while they cannot be killed by firearms, are soft enough in body to allow the shot to enter their skin which would have been carried away with them when they left. As the shot was found, it stands to reason it was the child who stopped it."

A ringing silence followed in the wake of Wade's startling revelation. The whole group seemed lost in thought as their brains lumbered along trying to process the vast amount of information they had just heard.

After several minutes had passed, Frank, who had turned quite pale said. "Come home, now!"

He spoke the words calmly, but there was a trace of panic in his voice.

"Don't you want us to do any more digging around?" asked Elsu, who had been expecting to be tasked, not recalled.

"No," said Frank simply. "We need to discuss this at length with the others. Pack up and get back."

At these words the connection with Hoowo3oow severed and Frank disappeared.

"That was a bit abrupt!" exclaimed Gyasi, surprised at Frank's sudden departure.

"Yeah," agreed Elsu. "What's got him all bent out of shape?"

"Indeed," said Aarde looking at Hoowo3oow. "I understand that this is all quite shocking, but he seemed to take it rather personally!"

Hoowo3oow didn't speak, instead he returned a meaningful look to Aarde, who took this to mean he agreed.

"Well, we can worry about all that later," said Wade, getting to his feet. "The man said pack, so…" Wade grabbed a handful of equipment and crammed it into a rucksack, "…pack!"

Everyone set to work, clearing away and sorting their belongings in silence. When the last zip was closed, Aarde, swinging a bag almost as big as himself onto his shoulder, said. "I guess it's the train again then?"

"Man, it's miles into town, this is gonna take ages." complained Elsu, donning his hat and reigniting his pipe.

"Do not worry about that! We will give you a lift!" said a firm voice from behind them. The accent was very French and did not seem as friendly as the words would have suggested.

As the group turned to face this new arrival, a feeling of dread engulfed them. The police. Three officers in full uniform and none of them looked remotely happy to be there.

"Bonjour, officiers. Quelque chose de mal?" enquired Aarde, trying to sound casual.

"Speak English, boy," said the first officer, a tall, thin man with heavy set eyelids and a carefully trimmed and waxed moustache. "Your pronunciation does a dis-service to our language."

"Fine!" snapped Aarde who was wholey offended by this remark. He had always prided himself on his linguistic abilities, and didn't fail to miss the irony of this Frenchman butchering the English language with too many e's and z's. But he thought better of mentioning it. This was already more exposure than preferred, an argument would only make this worse.

"What seems to be the problem?" asked Aarde in as polite a voice as he could muster.

"You are coming with us to the police station for questioning!" said another officer. This officer was short, fat and was going bald, which was plain to see as he took off his hat to mop his sweaty brow.

"Wh-what?" barked Gyasi. "For what?"

"In relation to the murder of Professor Albert Braskin," said the last officer.

This officer was much younger than the others and his voice was softer. He was of average height and build and his appearance bore nothing remarkable, except for his eyes. He had very kind eyes.

"I'm sorry, who is this, er, professor?" asked Elsu sounding confused.

"He owned this house," said the tall officer, pointing at the wreckage. They all gave quizzical looks at the house.

"The house you came here to see," added the fat officer, impatiently.

"We didn't come here just to see a burned down..." began Elsu but the young officer interrupted.

"A friend of the baker, Françoise Gagnier, overheard you speaking when you entered the shop. She knows a little English and understood enough to know where you were going."

"The death of the professor turned into a murder investigation an hour ago," began the tall officer. "This is a small town and an even smaller village. Word travels fast around here and you have been a novel source of gossip for the locals all day."

"So much so," added the young officer, "that when we decided to issue a public request for information on suspicious individuals in the area, our receptionist already knew about you and tipped us off. We made a quick call to Françoise to confirm the information and, well…" he gesticulated in the group's direction, "here you are."

Gyasi and Elsu stepped forward to stand in front of Aarde and Hoowo3oow.

"Officers, these are children!" began Gyasi. "Surely you don't think they had anything to do with something as serious as murder?" he asked imploringly.

"Heavens no," replied the fat officer, giving his forehead another mop with his hankie. "We think you two did," he finished looking right at Gyasi and Elsu.

"And it is all the worse for dragging these young boys along with you!" said the tall officer who had begun to draw out handcuffs.

"Whoa, whoa, wait!" screeched Elsu in a bit of a panic. "We had nothing to do with this. We were just visiting the area."

"You just happened to be visiting a rural part of France?" began the young officer sceptically. "A place with no tourist attractions, a place where I doubt you have any relatives and just by coincidence happen to be near a murder scene that you already knew about?"

"Well, when you put it like that…" replied Elsu, but he was interrupted by the tall officer.

"IS THAT AN EVIDENCE CONTAINER?" he roared. "YOU HAVE STOLEN EVIDENCE TOO!"

Quick as a flash the tall officer slapped handcuffs onto Gyasi's wrists, binding them behind his back.

"OK, this has gone far enough," said Aarde sighing deeply.

The tall officer gave him a severe look.

"I know," said Aarde rolling his eyes. "Impertinent child, mind my manners and so on."

The tall officer's eyebrows screwed so tightly together they became one long furry line.

"You do not appreciate the seriousness of the situation, boy?"

"Actually," replied Aarde with increasing exasperation. "it's you who are missing the bigger picture here. Now release my friend here or I will have to incapacitate you."

The tall officer wanted to laugh, but there was something in the finality of this statement that stopped him.

"Cuff him!" said the tall officer, nodding to Elsu but keeping his eyes on Aarde.

"Hoowo3oow!" yelled Aarde.

The fat officer had moved to grab Elsu and place handcuffs on him too, but Hoowo3oow got in the way, and within seconds, the fat officer found his hands tied to his belt. Shocked, he spun round to look at his comrade.

The tall officer bore down upon Hoowo3oow, another pair of handcuffs in his hand. "You little…" he cried angrily.

"STOP!" yelled the young officer throwing himself between Hoowo3oow and his colleague. "Look, if you are innocent then ruling you out of our… er… how to say… enquiries…? will help us."

Aarde gave a searching look to Gyasi, Elsu and Wade. They all conveyed a look that made Aarde understand that perhaps a less aggressive approach would be wise. Besides they didn't need Gyasi, Elsu, and Wade, ending up on France's most wanted list.

"Fine!" Aarde conceded. "Let's go to the station, where's your car?"

"We have no car," replied the tall officer.

"Well then how did you get here?" asked Elsu.

"We walked," said the young officer simply.

"Yeah, but we are radioing for a car to take us back!" snapped the fat officer who obviously hadn't enjoyed the exercise.

"As we have detainees, we will 'ave to!" sneered the tall officer. "Handcuff that one," he pointed at Elsu, "while I contact the station."

The fat officer freed his own hands from his belt and looked hopefully at Elsu, who acquiesced to holding his hands out in front of him while he was restrained.

The tall officer, having radioed for a lift, rejoined the group. "They should be here in about fifteen minutes," he muttered to the fat officer.

"You might as well sit down," said the young officer, perching on a tree stump himself.

He said it to the children more than anyone else, but it was the fat officer who responded first.

"*Bonne idée!*" he wheezed as he lowered his round frame onto the edge of the fence surrounding Professor Braskin's house.

Both the tall and young officer tutted in unison, which was ignored by the last, but then everyone followed suit and found a place to rest while they awaited their pick up.

A few minutes passed in total silence. Only the rustling of leaves in the wind disturbed the quiet. Unexpectedly, an owl flew into view and came to rest on top of the charred chimney on top of the ruined house. All eyes fixed upon it as the owl ruffled its feathers and surveyed the surrounding grasslands, likely searching for a mouse or similar prey. On occasion it hooted, as owls tend to do, infrequently at first, but then it became more agitated. The hoots got louder and were sung with increasing rapidity, before long they were incessant. Almost everyone found this irritating. Hoowo3oow was so annoyed by the sound he voiced the idea of killing it with a rock. The young officer, on the other hand, looked petrified.

"*Mon Dieu!*" the young officer blurted out, after nearly five minutes of constant hooting. "*Il s'agit d'un mauvais présage. Les hiboux se comporter comme cette mort prédire!*"

"I'm sorry, what was that about death?" enquired Elsu, who under the circumstance was in no mood for ghost stories.

"Superstitious nonsense," Scoffed the tall officer. "He is full of them! His head is full of rubbish."

"Believe what you will," snapped the young officer. "I just know I'll be happier when we leave this place. It is creepy, *non*?"

"I've seen creepier," mumbled Aarde absently, lost in thought over how he was going to explain all this to Frank.

The young man didn't respond to this, instead, to distract himself from the owl which was making him more and more flustered, he asked Wade to open the evidence case to see what they had actually taken.

Together, the officer and Wade rummaged through the contents, occasionally withdrawing a bag and holding it up to see what was inside.

"What did you take this stuff for?" the young officer asked, puzzled. "It all seems pretty useless to our investigations!"

"They are probably collecting trophies!" growled the tall officer. "I hear that's what serial killers do."

Aarde looked incredulous as he fixed his eyes upon the tall officer.

"Well, they do!" the officer added, defensively.

"I think the only important thing you have is the camera," the young officer continued, speaking to Wade and pretending as though his colleague hadn't said anything. "Can you pass it here? I should look at what photos are on the memory."

Wade, who didn't look nervous, but wasn't speaking either, snatched up the camera and made to pass it over. During the manoeuvre, Wade fumbled with his grip and accidentally took a photo. The sudden brightness from the flash, illuminated the ruined building and dazzled all three officers. The young officer noticed that only the three of them seemed to be caught by the flash, and began to panic again.

The fat officer turned to look at him and frowned. "What is wrong with you now?" he snarled.

"*Vérifiez la photo! Vérifiez la photo! Combien d'entre nous sont sur elle?*" the young officer whined.

Aarde jumped to his feet and snatched the camera out of Wade's hands. He cycled through the photos and found the one that had just been taken. Aarde chuckled at the sight. The young officer looked stunned and blinded, the fat officer had his hands raised in front of his face and appeared as though he was about to be hit by a truck and finally the tall officer was picking his nose, oblivious at the time to the sudden burst of light.

"The three of you," said Aarde to the young officer, gesturing to all three policemen.

"*Non, non, non...*" muttered the young man somewhat manically. "When three people are photographed together, the one in the middle will be the first to die," he continued in a whisper.

"Oh!" replied Aarde jovially. "Well then you shouldn't worry. Your rotund colleague here is in the middle, and judging from his size and heavy breathing, I reckon a heart attack is imminent."

The fat officer mumbled something in French at Aarde, who was sure it was something offensive, but as the brief moment of humour had lightened the mood of this very tense and highly strung young officer, he decided not to challenge it and sat down after throwing the camera back to Wade.

"How you became a police officer, when your head is so full of crap, is beyond me," said the tall officer.

Aarde hadn't failed to notice that the officer spoke in English rather than French. He obviously wanted the group to hear his comment and now seemed irritated by the lack of laughter.

The young man had flushed with embarrassment. His rosey cheeks glowed in the moonlight and beads of nervous sweat twinkled as they rolled down his face.

The tall officer sighed disparagingly, then reaching into his trouser pocket, pulled out a packet of cigarettes.

"Here!" he groaned, thrusting the packet towards his young colleague, causing a single smoke to jut out. "Maybe this will calm your nerves."

The young officer took one cigarette after which one was offered to the fat officer and then finally the tall officer took one for himself.

"*Merde*!" spat the tall officer, patting himself down and searching his pockets. "Does anyone have a lighter?"

Hoowo3oow, Aarde, Gyasi and Wade all shook their heads. Elsu, always prepared for a smoke at every given opportunity said. "I have some matches, they're in the inside pocket of my jacket..." he paused for a moment to look at the tall officer who was waiting for him to produce them.

"I'd love to pass them over mate, but I can't... NO, no point arguing, my hands are tied..." he raised his wrist revealing the handcuffs. "Get it? Hands are tied? Oh, never mind, just reach in."

After a nod from the tall officer the young man extracted the matches and tossed them over.

The officer opened the box, there was only one match inside. He struck the match against the side of the box and a soft, dim light illuminated the gaunt features of the tall officer's face.

"Here, quickly!" he barked at the young officer, who leaned forward and fired up his cigarette.

The tall officer leaned over to his fat friend and used the same flame to light his cigarette. The young officer opened his mouth to speak, but the tall officer anticipating his response, interrupted him.

"Let me guess," he scoffed. "It is bad luck to light three cigarettes with the same match!"

"Well, yes!" said the young officer meekly.

"Well then, allow me to educate you before you get all hysterical again." sneered the tall officer, straightening up and looking quite pompous.

"Back in the war, before our time of course…" he began, oblivious to the condescending look on Aarde and Hoowo3oow's faces, "…soldiers in the trenches were warned not to light three cigarettes with the same match. This is because the first light alerted a sniper, the second light allowed him to judge distance and the third man got shot. Now unless you believe there is a marksman hiding in the trees, I think I will be quite safe."

Wade, whose eyes were focused on something the others hadn't noticed muttered. "I don't know, I think it may be unlucky this time."

"Nonsense!" barked the tall officer and sparked his cigarette with the flame just before the match burned to the end.

He drew deeply on the cigarette, as if this somehow emphasised his point, when he removed the cigarette and inhaled, a moth that had fluttered near, attracted by the light of the flame, was sucked into his mouth and became lodged in his throat. The officer immediately began to choke, rising to his feet and flailing his arms around wildly in panic. The fat officer rose too, as did the young officer and together they attempted to assist their companion. They slapped him hard on the back, tried to make him cough but the dry powdery wings of the moth stuck fast to the moist wall of his throat and closed his windpipe completely. Eventually the fat officer grabbed him around the midriff and attempted abdominal thrusts, but in his desperation and panic, the tall officer convulsed and threw him off. The fat officer, overbalanced and unable to stop himself, toppled over, and with a horrific crunch, fell back onto a shard of broken and burned wood, impaling himself through the heart — dying instantly.

The young officer wailed with misery and terror. One colleague dead and another was dying. He looked around wildly at the others who were trashing their equipment in a vain attempt to locate a bottle that still held some water.

The choking officer's face had turned a dark shade of blotchy purple and the blood vessels in his eyes had haemorrhaged under the strain of struggling to breathe. A few seconds later he had collapsed to the floor, his fingernails tearing at the skin on his throat. The young officer had frozen from shock. He felt helpless as the futility of the situation overwhelmed him and his eyes were fixed upon the visage of his colleague which was wrought with fear and pain. The officer convulsed on the floor as his brain began to shut down from lack of oxygen, a soundless scream contorted his face and then all too abruptly, the body became still. He had died.

"*Cela est mauvais. C'est vraiment mauvais. Je ne veux pas mourir*," whimpered the young officer at last.

He was backing away from the body as he spoke, away from the group and towards the house.

"Calm down," said Aarde in a soothing voice. "Your friends have died in a tragic accident, but that's all it is, an accident."

"NO…!" the officer screamed. "I said they were bad omens, I told them, but they wouldn't listen. Now I'm going to die too!"

"No, you're not. Help is coming, remember?" reminded Elsu, trying to be helpful.

The officer did not seem to be listening, however.

He continued to move away from them, closer and closer to the wall of the professor's home, all the while manically searching the darkness for unseen threats and muttering under his breath. "*Merde, merde, merde…*"

"STOP!" bellowed Wade. "Don't go any further, please!"

"Wade, what's going on?" demanded Hoowo3oow.

"Stop him!" Wade cried back. "If he continues, he will die."

"What?" gasped Aarde. "How…"

"STOP HIM! NOW!" Wade yelled, lunging towards the officer himself.

But it was too late, he was too far away. Lost in the depths of paranoia and fear, the officer backed himself up against the wall, directly below the chimney. At that moment his ears retuned to the persistent screeching and hooting of the owl that was still perched above. It was the sound that had started all of this. In the officer's mind it was the catalyst that had caused these deaths and he finally snapped.

Spinning round and turning his head skyward, he yelled as loudly as he could, "*TA GUEULE!*"

The owl, startled by this sudden and violent outburst took flight, dislodging as it went a brick from the top of the chimney stack. The brick fell fast and heavy right into the young police officer's face. His neck broke as his head was wrenched backwards and shards of bone shot into his brain as the brick smashed open the front of his skull. The officer dropped to his knees, his deformed head lolloping loosely from side to side and finally he fell to the ground leaving no doubt in anyone's mind that he too, was dead.

For what seemed like an eternity, everyone stood stock still, gawping at the scene of dead bodies in disbelief, unable to express in words their surprise at what they had witnessed. "What the hell, Wade!" said Aarde at last, breaking the silence.

"What?" snapped Wade defensively.

"You knew this was going to happen?" asked Aarde angrily.

"Of course not... I mean I knew something was going to happen..." Wade surveyed the bodies and sighed mournfully. "...But not this! I didn't know they would die."

"We have got to get out of here!" whispered Gyasi. "The police will be here soon and I don't fancy trying to explain this when we are already murder suspects."

"Gyasi's got a point, guys," added Elsu. "And while we're at it..."

He raised his wrist and jingled the handcuffs. Hoowo3oow approached him and pulled the chain links apart. Aarde did the same for Gyasi.

"Ah, that's better, thanks," said Gyasi, stretching his arms and shoulders. "They are much more uncomfortable than you would think."

"I don't know..." chuckled Elsu looking at the cuffs still around his wrists. "...I quite like them."

Hoowo3oow gave Elsu a sharp slap on the back of his head.

"OW! What was that for?" whined Elsu.

"Three men lay dead seven feet from where you stand. This is not the time for levity, you should show more respect."

Elsu lowered his head in shame as he rubbed the place Hoowo3oow had slapped. "Sorry... I... I didn't think."

"Enough," whispered Aarde, scanning the horizon for flashing lights. "Let's just get out of here!"

As they gathered up their belongings and turned to move deeper into the woodland, Wade stood still, straining to hear a sound the others hadn't noticed.

"Shhh!" he whispered. "Can you here that?"

"What is it now, Wade?" growled Aarde. "We don't have time for…"

Aarde broke off mid-sentence as what Wade had been listening to became louder and much more obvious. The sound was a strange garbled whispering, like many people trying to speak at once in hushed voices.

"What the…" muttered Elsu, unable to finish his own sentence.

Hoowo3oow rubbed the bridge of his nose with his finger and thumb and sighed. "This can't be good!"

The whispering chatter grew louder and at the same time seemed to be drawing closer to their position.

Before anyone could make sense of it, the voices joined together, becoming one croaky, sinister tone that said. "Ooh, look Rangda, children! Your favourite."

Slowly, everyone turned to see where the voice had come from. Spluttering blood from his mouth and convulsing slightly, the fat police officer had come back to life and was watching them, smiling.

A crunching noise, like two broken bones rubbing against each other, distracted the attention of the group. The young officer, whose head hung limply against his back, was also alive and getting to his feet. "Steady Bushyasta. These are not children." This voice was also croaky but a little muffled. The damage to the front of his face by the brick made him sound as though he had a bad cold.

A violent cough followed by the sound of chewing pricked their ears next. The tall officer had also risen to his feet, and apparently, had hacked up the moth he had inhaled and was now eating it. "He's right!" The tall officer said. "They are elemortals!"

Aarde and Hoowo3oow stared at them in shock. "Yes, Onoskelis, I see it now. Well, what a treat this is. Help me up so I can greet them properly."

Onoskelis, strutted over to where the fat officer, now known as Bushyasta, had been impaled. Rangda did the same and together he and Onoskelis heaved the fat frame off the burned spike and back to his feet. Bushyasta, patted himself down, clearing away dust, dirt and a few splashes of blood. He seemed quite unconcerned by the large gaping hole in his chest, that whistled in a low tone as the wind passed through it.

"So nice to meet you," Bushyasta said in a very smarmy manner. "I have heard about you for so, soooo many years but sadly have never had the pleasure."

"Are you guys not policemen any more?" asked Elsu who was clearly struggling to comprehend the situation.

"We are not guys!" replied Onoskelis defensively. Then looking down at herself and at the others added, "OK, superficially we are men, but be assured, you are in the presence of three ladies."

"And you do look good in uniform!" sniggered Bushyasta.

"Yeah. It's just a shame the bodies are so badly buggered. We could have had some fun in these," grumbled Rangda, whose head was still flopping upside down.

"How have you done this?" demanded Hoowo3oow aggressively. "How did you get to this realm. You were not summoned!"

"Pish posh, my dear little Indian boy. There is no need for summoning in a place like this!" mused Bushyasta.

"I would suggest you elaborate, before the little Indian boy loses his temper," snarled Aarde.

"Don't play dumb!" gargled Rangda as blood trickled up her nose. "We know you've noticed!"

"Yesss!" hissed Bushyasta. "There's a hole in your roof that's leaking and it's letting in more than just water."

"You, breached the barriers?" asked Aarde hoping to capitalise on the honesty of their answers.

"Oh, we helped," cooed Onoskelis. "But we certainly cannot take all the credit."

"Oh no," added Bushyasta. "Everyone's been chipping in. Besides it was damaged already, we're just making it worse."

"And that hole is just getting wider and wider," finished Rangda happily.

"That's not possible. The Gods prevent you from..."

"The Gods," screamed Onoskelis with delight. "don't prevent anything any more."

"Foolish boy," sneered Rangda. "Don't you see…" she moved her upside down face closer to Aardes. "…it was their idea."

"LIES!" roared Hoowo3oow and he lunged forward and grabbed Onoskelis by the throat.

"It's true!" Onoskelis choked, even though she was laughing. "You broke your own rules and now you must face the consequences. We are being given a chance to reign on earth."

"A war is coming," hissed Bushyasta. "A war to decide who gets to reign over this world."

"What rule are we supposed to have broken?" demanded Aarde.

"Someone," cackled Bushyasta. "a delicious, wonderful, stupid someone has caused a paradox. It cracked the borders and here we are with more on the way."

"What paradox?" barked Aarde. "Do you even understand what paradox means?"

"Well, no, not really, I don't get sciency terms," crooned Bushyasta. "But that's what Athuramazda called it… and it was Yahweh who told him."

"Oh, who cares about the hows and the whys?" squealed Rangda with delight. "When the last barrier breaks, demons will be free to walk the earth in our own pure forms…" Rangda examined her host and sneered. "…and not these repulsive sacks of meat. They're a bit too fragile for my liking."

"We will stop you!" snarled Hoowo3oow, squeezing Onoskelis' neck so hard the windpipe collapsed.

"And how do you intend to do that?" asked Bushyasta calmly.

"There are four of us and only three of you," replied Aarde with equal coolness in his voice. "I wouldn't like your odds even if one of us were alone."

Rangda cackled so hard her head swung around to the front of her body. After flipping it over again and regaining composure she turned back to Aarde and said "It's not just us, you moron. Kill us if you can, but there are billions, yes BILLIONS, of demons, spirits, forgotten Gods and every weird thing ever imagined by children just dying to come for a visit."

Rangda and Bushyasta wailed with laughter at the despondent look wrought upon Gyasi, Elsu and Wade's faces. Onoskelis, thanks to

Hoowo3oow, had lost the ability to make noise but she looked happy all the same.

"He knows!" Bushyasta said, pointing at Wade. He's doing the maths in his head now. You elemortals are powerful, but you cannot be everywhere at once. You cannot defend every last man, woman and child on the planet. We demons alone, outnumber your headcount by six hundred to one, you cannot stop us all."

"You will be nothing more than cattle," crooned Rangda as she casually strolled closer to Aarde's side. "And there are so many mouths to feed, all hungry for flesh…" Rangda placed the tips of two fingers on Aardes shoulder and began finger walking down to his chest. "…for souls…" she scuttled her digits to his stomach. "…for pain…" Rangda began to move her fingers to Aarde's pelvic region. "…and well, some thirsts that can't be sated with a good meal."

Aarde slapped her hand away in disgust to Onoskelis' and Bushyasta's great amusement.

"So sensitive," pouted Rangda, circling Aarde as she spoke. "Did I touch a nerve?"

Bushyasta snorted a harsh mocking laugh. "Hah, maybe if someone did touch a nerve, you wouldn't be so uptight."

Rangda's head crunched and cracked, lolloping from side to side as she doubled over giggling.

Aarde clenched his fist tightly and gritted his teeth. The gesture did not go unnoticed. Bushyasta began to walk slowly towards Aarde, eyeing him hungrily, when she finally spoke her lips were quivering with excitement.

"The immortal child," she began in a sickeningly sweet, falsely sympathetic voice. "A man, forever trapped in the body of a boy. And you think 'we' are evil!"

Aarde's face remained expressionless, but his clenched fists tightened up so much, the knuckles cracking was clearly audible.

"You know it's true!" sneered Rangda. "I mean, how old are you two now?" she asked pointing at Aarde and Hoowo3oow in turn. "Two, maybe three thousand years old? A long time to live and never know the love of a woman."

"Shut up!" demanded Aarde, although he said it so quietly it was almost inaudible.

"Maybe I'm wrong," chuckled Rangda. "Maybe you've made sport of that little girl in your group!"

"I said, shut up!" repeated Aarde, a little louder this time.

"Oh, bless him," sniggered Bushyasta sardonically. "She doesn't want him either."

"Well don't worry," spluttered Rangda, struggling to contain her amusement. "There are lots of interesting creatures and demons who are just going to love her..." Rangda looked thoughtful for a moment then added. "...although they have very unusual bodies, y'know, spikes and things and they tend to be a little rough, so she might not last very lo..."

Rangda broke off her sentence due to the sudden and unexpected disappearance of Aarde who had vanished right before her eyes. Bushyasta and Onoskelis also stared in astonishment, even Gyasi, Elsu and Wade looked a little surprised. The only one who didn't seem taken aback by this was Hoowo3oow, instead his face bore the faintest shadow of a grin.

Without warning, the ground erupted below Rangda. Pillars of rock and earth rose from the floor, morphing into two large powerful arms and two gargantuan fists. These giant limbs swooped down upon Rangda and grabbed her arms, raising her into the air and suspending her a few feet off the floor in a crucified position. As a blood-curdling scream left Rangda's mouth, her voice thick with pain and fear, Bushyasta and Onoskelis seemed to rally, channelling their anger onto the only person they could still see and consider a threat — Hoowo3oow. Onoskelis broke free of Hoowo3oow's grasp and swung for him. Hoowo3oow made no effort to stop the blow, and as the fist neared his face, his mouth curled into a wicked smile.

Miraculously, the fist simply passed through his head, causing Hoowo3oow's face and skull to sort of blow away in the wind before reforming again, good as new. Bushyasta joined Onoskelis and together they pressed on Hoowo3oow who parried and deflected their attacks with relative ease. Frustrated, Bushyasta scooped up a large chunk of timber and swung it at her enemy's chest. Hoowo3oow raised his hands to his face and bent at the knee as the wood found its target, splintering and shattering against his forearms. Unperturbed, Hoowo3oow pounced through the debris of falling shards, grabbed Bushyasta by the arm and drove his elbow hard into her shoulder. A deep, grinding crunch accompanied the blow, followed by a resounding wail of pain as Bushyasta ripped herself away from Hoowo3oow causing the arm to flop about uncontrollably in every direction.

Onoskelis, using Bushyasta's attack as a means to come around Hoowo3oow, tried to kick him in the back but Hoowo3oow floated out of the way as if he had been blown by the wind. Regrouping, Bushyasta and Onoskelis rushed him together, attacking in a raging blur of punches and claws. Hoowo3oow, continued to drift around like sand in a desert storm. With two swift punches to the attackers' hands, he momentarily ceased their assault allowing him time to drift between them and clamp a firm hand over each of their mouths. With a wry smile, Hoowo3oow closed his eyes and tightened his grip on Bushyasta and Onoskelis' jaws. At that same moment, Bushyasta felt her ribs break as her chest collapsed as though it had just become a vacuum when all the air was sucked out at great speed. In contrast to this, Onoskelis felt her lungs expand rapidly until they burst inside her. Her insides felt as if they had been liquefied from the explosion and a great deal of blood and gloopy flesh fountained from her mouth and nostrils. Both demons collapsed, writhing and moaning in agony.

"You need to do more than that to kill us!" wheezed Bushyasta.

"Oh, I knew that wouldn't kill you," sneered Hoowo3oow. "But I bet it hurt like hell!"

Meanwhile Rangda continued to scream and curse as the giant hands squeezed their grip on her arms ever tighter. Without warning another pillar of rock, also sporting a fist on the end, but smaller than the others, burst forth from the ground and collided with her abdomen, causing the stone fist to crumble apart. Before Rangda could realise what had hit her, let alone recover from the pain, another fist shot forth and struck her in her left kidney.

Rangda wailed in pain and cursed at an unseen Aarde in an old forgotten tongue. Another fist, then another and another. Her body, or rather her host's body, was being beaten unrecognisable as spear after spear of rock kept crashing and smashing into this frail shell until at last Rangda appeared to pass out. She came to only seconds later, remembering her predicament and flushing with all-consuming dread. She began to frantically swing her head around, desperately searching for where Aarde may be. She hadn't noticed the rubble of pebbles and stones, gathering beneath her feet.

As Hoowo3oow continued to fight Bushyasta and Onoskelis, a fierce wind tore through the battleground, kicking up dirt and debris, obscuring the world from Rangda's view. Suspended in the air, helpless and in terrible pain, Rangda began to cry. As she sobbed, her limp head jiggled up and down and into some very awkward positions. After coming to briefly rest upon her shoulder following an outburst of blubbing, Rangda finally saw where Aarde was.

The pile of rubble had grown several feet and had solidified into a hard granite boulder. It was now so tall it was level with Rangda's thighs, and out of sheer panic, Rangda began to kick out. Her feet battered against the cracked, rough-hewn block but it changed nothing, except to add to her agony. Her toes had broken inside her police issue boots and her ankles were so badly fractured they would never support her weight if she ever got down. Still the boulder grew. As it neared her waistline, she noticed the rock taking shape. There was the clearly defined form of human legs and the start of a torso, like someone had started sculpting a statue but had accidentally broken off the top part. Moments later, the statue was complete and a delicately carved likeness of Aarde made entirely of stone stood before her. Rangda deflated, acquiescing to the inevitable pain that was soon to come, made more real when the rock in the statue began to crack and creak as, unbelievably, it began to breathe.

"JUST DO IT!" demanded Rangda, straining to make her voice heard above the roaring wind.

"KILL ME, OR ARE YOU TOO MUCH OF A COWARD!" she taunted. But it was not much of a jibe. She wanted death, to be released from this body, to return to her realm.

"C'MON, DO IT! DO IT!" she repeated angrily into the expressionless stone face of Aarde's unmoving statue.

To Rangda's relief, the head and upper body of the statue began to change colour and take on a new texture. Soon the real form of Aarde, both skin and clothing was revealed, his garbs flapping in the gale.

"To answer your question," began Aarde, tonelessly, "my kin and I are over seven thousand years old. We've been on this planet since you were nothing more than a dirty little thought in your creator's mind. We have seen most of you abominations being born and I am sure we will bear witness to the creation of many others."

Rangda spat in Aarde's face. "Lies!"

Aarde wiped off the spittle and smiled. "Touched a nerve, have I?" he asked maliciously. "Mummy and Daddy issues run real deep with you freaks, huh?"

"Screw you," muttered Rangda weakly.

"But then most parents don't make bad kids on purpose, do they?" continued Aarde rhetorically without any hint he had heard Rangda speak.

"Spare me the psychoanalyst crap and just get it done." Rangda choked through a mouthful of blood. "But mark my words, we will be back. When all the barriers finally fall, we will meet again and we shall have our own bodies next time."

Rangda, her head dangling upside down, stared deep into Aarde's cold colourless eyes. He did not seem bothered by this forecast of events.

"You should know," began Aarde after a pause, "that I understand."

Rangda blinked confusedly at this statement.

"That you are the way you are, is not your fault."

Rangda's face screwed up in anger this time and she spat on Aarde's chest.

"You cannot help it because that is the way you were made," Continued Aarde, ignoring the spit and looking to the sky instead of at Rangda's pained expression.

"They will always fear that which goes bump in the night. They will always look to lay blame for the wrongs of the world. They will perpetuate the existence of your kind till the end of time, of that I have no doubt."

Rangda could hardly believe her ears. He spoke with such derision in his voice that it bordered on contempt.

"But," Aarde began again, only this time he didn't look so passive, he looked positively sinister. "as long as you freaks remain…" Aarde moved his face to within an inch of Rangda's and glared deep into her eyes. "…so will we!"

143

Rangda felt an ominous shiver trickle up her spine, a feeling of something like horror was swelling within her, it was not a sensation she was accustomed to nor pleased to experience.

"What the hell are you talking abo…"

WHAM! Her words were cut short by a heavy, rock-filled right hook from Aarde. The sound of Hoowo3oow demolishing Bushyasta and Onoskelis filled Rangda's ears as another strong gust of wind swept between them. She swung her head around once again, searching for the signs of battle, a sign that one of her sisters had broken free from the fight and was coming to her aid. Her hopes fell away, as Aarde grabbed her face and twisted her head the correct way around so she could see him properly. He glared into her eyes for a time, like a doctor examining a patient, a look of polite interest drawn upon his features.

"Do you know the problem with possession?" he asked plainly.

Rangda didn't reply, she simply stared gormlessly back at him, she was exhausted and broken and no longer cared for conversation.

"No?" said Aarde, feigning surprise. "Considering how much your kind rely upon this ability I find it incredulous that you are all so woefully ignorant of the fundamentals."

Rangda still didn't speak but Aarde had piqued her interest. Pleased to have regained Rangda's attention, Aarde pressed on.

"More often than not, demons like yourself, possess a living body. The benefits of this are obvious, full mobility, complete concealment and a wide range of sensory input that you are normally excluded from experiencing," Aarde explained, counting off each point on his fingers. "The downside of course is that you are sharing a body, your energy forced in alongside the energy of the host. This means that your grip is tenuous and a lapse in concentration can let the host force you out or you can be expelled with incantations during an exorcism. But it also means you can pop yourself out if, like now, your situation becomes, how shall we say… dire!"

Aarde's voice was menacing now and Randga squirmed uneasily in her restraints.

"On the other hand, there is this little freak show right here," said Aarde, disappointedly gesturing at Rangda's body. "Obviously, it has its benefits," continued Aarde reductively. "You have a body of your own, no longer hitching a lift, not having to share with a dirty soul."

Aarde circled her as he spoke. With each step a pillar of earth rose from the ground providing a place for Aarde to stand, always keeping him at eye level with Rangda.

"And you are nigh on indestructible too, eh?" continued Aarde giving a her a nudge in the ribs and wink as he slid back in front of her. "I mean the punishment you guys have endured tonight would have killed a human outright and had you been sharing, well, the force generated by their soul leaving would have blown you clean out of this universe. But no danger of that tonight, as long as that mushy brain stays intact you just keep on going... kinda like a zombie!"

Aarde chuckled at this, Rangda, was clearly not amused at being compared to a creature she considered beneath her and ground her teeth together so hard that two cracked under the pressure.

"There is of course one drawback to this method. A failing of such magnitude that it, in my opinion, would put me off it entirely. Ten points if you can guess the flaw?" asked Aarde keenly.

"I'm stuck in here!" sighed Rangda, spitting out a shard of tooth.

"You're stuck in there," repeated Aarde, amused.

"Then what say you smash open this melon and send me on my way, eh?" glubbed Rangda through a mouthful of blood.

Aarde didn't reply.

"Fine, I understand, you don't have the stones to finish me off yourself," muttered Rangda. "How about I help you out. Free my hand and pass me that rock and I'll do it myself," she added eagerly.

Aarde still didn't speak.

"You do wrong ignoring me, boy!" snarled Rangda feeling anger flood her gut. "You will regret this moment."

Aarde looked at her, his eyebrows raised.

"That's right, you heard me!" wailed Rangda with increasing fervour. "I will be back, and when I do, I will repay you for this insult."

The wind howled louder and Rangda had to scream to make herself heard.

"When I return, I will make it my mission in life, to ensure you and that scrawny bitch you hold so dear, suffer until the end of ti…"

Aarde clamped his hand back over Rangda's mouth silencing her.

He moved his face close to hers so she could feel his breath on her cheek, and in a voice so gentle it could have been to a lover, he whispered. "You can't come back if you never leave!"

Rangda blanched and her eyes spread wide. She struggled against Aarde's grip and made muffled noises behind his hand, but Aarde no longer cared what she had to say.

"Do you know what my favourite element is?" he cooed softly. "Carbon," he said simply.

At his words Rangda felt a cold, numbness in her neck and her arms and legs became limp.

"It's a wonderful element," continued Aarde. "Found in abundance all over the universe and it is so incredibly versatile."

The cold numbness began to spread across Rangda's body and she began to panic again.

"Right now, your body is rife with the stuff," Aarde looked her up and down and added, "even if it is useless."

Rangda's body now had no feeling anywhere. Her head felt separate, detached from the rest, and though it was a relief to be away from the pain her broken body had been relaying to her brain, her anxiety soared. As she tried to make sense of what was happening, her mind suddenly began racing with the conversation they'd had minutes before. "As long as that mushy brain remains intact, you just keep on going."

With icy dread, a horrible realisation overwhelmed her. It must have shown on her face because Aarde, noticing her aspect changing, smiled malevolently.

"I suspect you have some idea about what I'm doing to you," smirked Aarde, revelling in Rangda's dismay. "But I doubt you fully appreciate the artistry of my talent. You see I am moving all of the carbon atoms out of your body and pushing them into your brain. In turn I am also removing the superfluous elements such as copper, iron and magnesium."

As Aarde spoke, Rangda's left leg fell off and disintegrated on the floor.

Unperturbed, Aarde continued to speak as though it were normal. "Then I delicately adjust the alignment of those carbon atoms into neat little rows. The result is beautiful and perfect in equal measure."

As her sight began to fail, a single tear appeared in Rangda's eye. The salt inside it irritated her bloodied eyelid and she blinked reflexively. As the tear rolled down her cheek it seemed to cut into her skin leaving a black dusty track behind it. It would be the last thing Rangda would ever feel, indeed would ever remember.

Aarde had bestowed upon her a fate worse than death, an eternity in an empty void, with no light, no sound and no thought. Rangda's body began to crumble beneath them, and as Aarde tightened his grip on her mouth, his fingers sank beneath her skin, breaking it apart like dirty sand. As the remainder of her flesh and limbs fell away encouraged by the gale surging around them, a diamond the size and shape of a human brain was revealed, sat in the palm of Aarde's hand. He held it in the moonlight and was pleased to see a misty haze of blueish hue floating among the multitude of rainbows reflected within the crystalline structure.

"Good work!" said Hoowo3oow who was approaching him from behind.

He was spattered with blood and carried a disembodied head in each hand.

"Frank's been moaning for months about updating the mainframe, he will be chuffed to bits with that. Sadly, there's not enough matter left to do that to these two," he added holding the heads up high and examining them. "They're gone. I can kill them properly next time!"

Aarde didn't speak, he just nodded his agreement. Hoowo3oow eyed him for a moment with a mixture of suspicion and sympathy, then when Aarde noticed him staring, he placed his hand on Aarde's shoulder and gave it a gentle pat.

"Why don't you tell her?" Hoowo3oow asked softly.

Aarde stopped walking and for a moment he just stood there, poised and stiff, but then his shoulders slumped and he gave a huge disappointed sigh. He raised the diamond brain in his hand to look at it, gave a breathy half laugh and turned to look at Hoowo3oow over his shoulder.

"Because Rangda was right!" he said at last.

Hoowo3oow's eyebrows screwed together and Aarde sensed an argument but he waved him down with a casual swing of the brain.

"How could we ever be together?" he pleaded as a defiant rage built in his chest. "What we are and what we can do is not a gift, it's a purchase!" Aarde snarled. "One that was made for us… and one that has condemned us to an eternity of solitude and slavery!"

Aarde was breathing heavily now, and there were tears in his eyes.

"I'm sorry my friend!" offered Hoowo3oow, his voice thick with shared regret.

"Nothing done bro!" replied Aarde more softly. "We have the same burden, you know how it goes… I don't know… it has just weighed on me a lot more lately, always close but never near!"

"Love will prevail!" said Hoowo3oow kindly.

There was a smile etched upon his face that looked so forced it was almost scary and he used it to glare at Aarde as he strode past him, but then his face turned suddenly stern again. "If you tell anyone I said that I will kill you and wear your tongue as a trophy!"

Aarde burst into hysterics, dropping the brain as he clutched his own belly. Hoowoo3oow without looking back at him continued walking back to their camp but if Aarde could have seen his face he would have seen a genuine grin propping up the corners of his mouth.

With Aarde still fitting a little with laughter and an occasional chortle further down the path, Hoowo3oow looked around for the rest of his group and spotted Gyasi's left buttock sticking out of a bush which was shaking.

"You can come out now!" he called.

Like meerkats on the lookout for danger, three heads belonging to Gyasi, Elsu and Wade, peeked up from the foliage and scanned the area.

"It's all good," said Elsu nervously as he fumbled with his pipe, trying to light it with shaky hands. "We were just looking for some, er, rope, yeah, to y'know, tie up the prisoners, but, I see now you don't need it, AAHHHHH!"

Elsu gave a very girly scream and fell over as a cloud of purple smoke erupted beside him. The smoke dissipated showing the sensuous form of Nephthys, illuminated in the moon's eerie glow.

"I think I just peed a little!" whimpered Elsu, who looked on the verge of tears.

"Damn right you did!" chuckled Nephthys, pleased to have had such an affect.

"What are you doing here?" grumbled Hoowo3oow suspiciously.

"Frank's been monitoring radio chatter and knows you had a run in with the local police. He sent me to see if... you... needed... a... lift!" Nephthys trailed off as she suddenly became aware of the carnage she was stood amongst. "You do know you're not supposed to kill humans, don't you?" she asked sounding quite surprised.

"They died of stupidity," snapped Aarde defensively. "However, some demons decided to take them on joyride."

"Really?" asked Nephthys gleefully. "Anyone I know?"

"Bushyasta, Onoskelis and Rangda!" replied Aarde pointing to them in turn as he said their names and holding up the diamond brain last.

"Aw, I knew Onoskelis, we go way back," said Nephthys fondly. "We had a thing during the Crusades, no big loss, it was a messy break-up, but still, it's a shame, she was an amazing lover!"

"Nice," said Elsu grinning.

"You still have pee on your trousers!" sneered Nephthys.

Elsu turned scarlet and turned his back to the group and began frantically rubbing his crotch with a cloth.

"Look!" said Aarde pointing through the trees at a series of flashing blue lights. "Backup is on the way, we need to get going."

Everyone gathered around Nephthys and held their breath.

"You know the drill, keep your arms and legs inside the ride at all times and please no flash photography."

"Nephthys!" snarled Hoowo3oow impatiently.

"Oh, for ff..." sighed Nephthys as she snapped her fingers, and in a bright flash of purple light, they all vanished in an explosion of violet fire.

Chapter Eight
Problem Child

During the day, the quaint town of Leamington Spa was peaceful and serene. The tall white buildings and antique structures such as the bath house, gave the area a sense of grandeur despite its diminutive size. People wandered lazily through the shopping centres and groups gathered in the parks for picnics. It conveyed a sense of civility rarely seen in the United Kingdom.

You could be forgiven then, if you happened to be in this town during the day, spending some time inside an office or some other place that shielded you from natural light and then, stepping out into the street after the sun had gone down, for believing you had been transported to another world.

You would be greeted with a plethora of colours and sounds that, for better or worse, would engulf you so completely you would be hard pressed not to feel like being in a party mood. That is, of course, unless a few hours before, you had felt your mind torn open and subjected to a violent and harrowing hallucination, a vision of the future that implied you had done something very, very wrong. Stood on the roof of the "Slug and Lettuce", looming over the hordes of revellers and party goers stumbling drunkenly along the high street, was Ignis, who was experiencing that very problem.

He had been running along the rooftops for hours, trying to calm his thoughts and work off his anxiety. What had he really experienced? Was this the future? Or was it some oddity related to Chloe's, as yet unquantifiable abilities? Maybe part of her power to control people was to show them their fears and amplify them. He had heard Amos' voice, no doubt about that and his tone was pained and frightened. He was blaming Ignis for something... was Amos dying? Was that his fault? It certainly fulfilled the category of 'his fears'. In fact, it was the only thing he was scared of. He didn't want to lose Amos and certainly not like that. Seven thousand years is long time to live, and to have had only one true friend in all that time, well, it was almost tragic. In fact, neither Ignis nor Amos had missed the irony of Amos being like a father figure to Ignis, especially considering the staggering number of years Ignis had on Amos and the fact that Ignis had actually helped raise Amos when he was a mere infant. Ignis rubbed his eyes, he felt weary and was developing a headache.

He had just reached the decision to go home and get some sleep, when loud voices followed by a crashing noise from below caught his attention. It seemed that a group of males had been ejected from the bar with some degree of force by the door staff and they were not happy, least of all the loudest male, who was so drunk he could hardly stand and had been thrown into a rubbish bin.

As the man lay on the floor cursing at the top of his lungs at the bouncer who had put him there, Ignis despaired. "This is who we go out of our way to protect?" he thought to himself, disgusted.

"Is he your mate?" barked the doorman at one of the other men.

"Y-yes!" replied a feeble voice. Ignis could not see who had spoke but they sounded petrified.

"Then I suggest you take him home and put him in bed."

The male whom the doorman had been talking to came into view. He was nodding feverishly in agreement and was trying to drag his loutish companion to his feet with the help of his friends.

"Be warned, mind," said the bouncer as he casually strolled over to them with his hands in his coat pockets, "if I see this prick again tonight, I will be deeply upset and I will be holding you," he withdrew one massive hand from his pocket and jammed a sausage-like finger in the man's chest, "entirely responsible!"

"N-n-no problem!" stammered the male dragging his friend away. "Straight to bed!"

"Yeah! Your mum's bed!" laughed the lout who had regained some degree of consciousness and had swung round to blurt this comment back at the doorman.

Ignis could only imagine the look the doorman probably gave them. He hadn't moved, but something about the bouncer made this group of four men panic and leave at great speed, dragging their companion behind them.

Partly because Ignis wasn't convinced these men were headed home to sleep off their problems and would at some point cause more trouble and partly because he didn't really fancy going home to speak with the others yet, he decided to follow them. Keeping to the rooftops, he tracked them as they wandered through the crowded streets. He watched them pause to vomit in an alleyway, observed them make several attempts to smash a bus shelter and finally saw them rip out all the plants in a flower bed from a nearby park and hurl them at passing taxis, all the while laughing morosely and shouting abuse at anyone who challenged their behaviour.

They were certainly an unwelcome part of society and in Ignis' opinion it was only a matter of time before they caused a real problem that would probably endanger someone's life. Ignis began hoping they would get hit by a bus and be ejected so fast from their bodies they would instantly become ghosts, thus giving him a marvellous excuse to give them a royal beating. He decided, not to hold his breath on that happening any time soon.

Ignis had just reached the conclusion that following these idiots, though mildly amusing, was a complete waste of his time and ought to leave, when the group passed a young couple who were walking home with their arms around each other. The male who had been particularly offensive to the bouncer earlier, chose this moment to swing his arm up over the young woman's head, before bringing his hand down upon her right buttock, slapping it quite hard and giving it a very inappropriate squeeze.

The young girl squealed with a confused mixture of shock, pain and utter outrage.

"Oi!" bellowed her boyfriend, moving himself between the woman and the man and squaring up to him.

"Shesh got a nice arsh that one mate, like a lil' peach," replied the lout, slurring each word as he wobbled from side to side.

The young man, quite unconcerned at this moment for the fact that he was terribly outnumbered, shoved the letch hard in the chest. The drunkard didn't even stumble backward, he simply toppled over with his legs in the air.

"You do that again and I will cave your face in you perverted prick!" barked the boyfriend at the man who was, for the second time tonight, laying on the ground.

The lout's friends stepped forward, one tried to help him to his feet while the other two stepped up to the young man. Ignis, without thinking, moved closer to the roof edge and readied himself to pounce.

"Leave it, John," Pleaded his girlfriend. "Really, it's not worth it, I'm fine! C'mon, let's just go."

John stood stock still for a few moments, rage contorting his features as he stared maniacally into the same face the bouncer had threatened.

"You should listen to the woman, it would be terrible if something happened to you and she were left all alone!" the guy spat back, though there was a tremor of fear in his voice which Ignis noticed, even if John didn't. A few more seconds and a couple of extra tugs on his arm later, John acquiesced and backed away from the scene before turning around and walking off with his girlfriend, occasionally looking back over his shoulder to be sure they were not being followed.

Ignis relaxed and sat back as he watched the group of men recover their fallen friend and lie to each other about what they would have done to the guy if he hadn't walked away.

"Cowards!" hissed Ignis.

He knew it was for the best that his involvement wasn't required. Breaking their cardinal rule of interfering with the business of normal people was not something he needed to be caught doing. Deciding he really had better leave before he did something stupid, he got to his feet and headed off towards the largest of the many parks in Leamington, feeling this would be as good a place as any to hitch a ride on the demon express without being seen.

As he walked towards his destination, he considered contacting Frank to give him the heads up and arrange for a pickup, but every time he put his hands together to call him, he suddenly felt sick and changed his mind. He knew Shui would have shared what had happened at the school with Frank and as she only knew half the story, he knew there would be many questions waiting for him back home, questions he didn't feel like answering right now.

Ignis dwelled on this heavily as he walked and so preoccupied was he, with rehearsing what he might say, he failed to notice that he had reached the park entrance, and unfortunately, the edge of the last building. Stepping into thin air, Ignis suddenly plummeted to the ground and landed with a crunch inside a thick hedge. Spitting out a mouthful of leaves and twigs, Ignis poked his head out of the top of the hedge and peered around to check that his fall had gone unnoticed. Luckily the area was pedestrian free, so Ignis tore himself from the net of branches and brushed himself off. At that moment a door opened behind him, and alarmed, Ignis darted around the corner and hid in the shadows.

"Have a good evening, madam, and we hope to see you again soon," said an exceptionally polite voice from within the building.

It dawned on Ignis that he was currently hiding in the bushes outside a restaurant. The aroma of many delicious foods, floated out of the door and into the cool night air. For a moment, Ignis was entranced by the smell and his stomach growled painfully. He shut his eyelids and allowed visions of succulent meats, and syrup drenched sweets to dance before him in the blackness.

Unexpectedly, a scent quite different to that of food but familiar all the same filled his nostrils. He inhaled deeply, titillated by its enticing nature, and to his surprise, the ballet of food dancing before his eyes gave way to form the shape of a woman. He sniffed again at the flavour in the air eager for more and as he did so his sense memory kicked in. The figure in the blackness sharpened and became detailed, like a picture drawing itself. With a final intake of breath, the figure became clear and Ignis reeled as he became acutely aware of who it was. Ignis slowly opened his eyes and saw with a thrill of excitement that made him blush, Alex Sterling, the teacher from Chloe's school.

"Thank you!" called Alex to the maître d', giving a polite wave as she crossed the road heading straight towards the...

"Ah crap!" muttered Ignis gloomily as Alex entered the park.

Thinking he had better hang back to give Alex time to exit the park before he started summoning creatures that would likely give her heart failure, Ignis scaled a nearby tree to get a better vantage point while he waited. He had just gotten comfortable when the group of anti-social louts he had followed earlier appeared across the road. Worryingly they had seen Alex enter the park and spurred on by their drunken leader had decided to follow her in. To make matters worse, Ignis caught part of what they were saying as they entered the dark grounds and knew that their interest in Alex had nothing to do with the contents of her bag.

The leaves on the tree Ignis was hiding in, dried out, shrivelled up and flashed as they caught fire before burning out seconds later.

"Someone's gonna die!" growled Ignis.

He dropped from the tree, sprinted across the road and disappeared into the shadows a few feet behind the men, following the sounds of their hushed cackling and laughter. He could kill them now, but he had to wait, had to be sure this wasn't just more bravado. Twenty metres ahead of the group, periodically illuminated by street lamps, he spotted Alex and felt a tightness in his stomach that had nothing to do with nerves. Ignis didn't get nervous.

Alex had been holding her coat tightly around her as she strode along the gravel paths that wove between the pockets of trees and bushes. The early November wind had been cutting through her clothes and biting her skin, yet strangely she was suddenly beginning to feel quite warm. So warm in fact that she felt the impulse to remove her coat before she started sweating. She had just lowered the long grey trench coat from her shoulders when she heard a man speaking behind her.

"Yeah baby, take it off!" leered the leader of the four men, grinning and dancing a little on the spot. He was still staggering, but his speech was no longer slurred. He was sobering up.

Startled, Alex dropped the coat completely, revealing the rest of her clothes, a white blouse which was unbuttoned showing a generous amount of cleavage and a long black skirt cut to the thigh. Sadly, this only seemed to provoke the group even more.

"Look at that, lads!" jeered the leader. "I'd pay good money for a ride on that!"

The group laughed their agreement and made a lot of depraved sounds and gestures which made Alex recoil with terror and she fumbled to clench the top of her blouse together and hide her legs as she backed away from them.

"Ah, no need to be modest," sighed the leader in a low murmur as he traipsed towards her. "We're all adults here."

Ignis felt his whole body, flex. If he wanted to spare Alex the trauma of this ordeal he would have to attack and soon.

"Go on," he urged in a low whisper, "give me a reason!"

"Phew," panted the man close to Alex. "I think you got me all hot!"

He grabbed his shirt and wafted it to cool himself down.

"What about you sweetheart?" he asked, reaching out and brushing hair out of Alex's face who was beside herself with fright. "Maybe we should loosen some of this clothing."

The man slid his hand down Alex's face, along her neck and down her chest. For a brief moment his fingers caressed the top of Alex's breast before pinching the edge of her blouse. He pulled it slightly, exposing more of her skin, and licking his lips, said with a dry guffaw. "Must be my birthday!"

Alex reeled from his touch and tried to flee but the man was too quick for her. He grabbed a fist full of cotton and tugged, causing her top to burst open. As tears streamed down her cheeks, Alex tried to scream, but it got stuck in her throat and came out shallow and meek. This was Ignis' cue, his time to strike, but oddly he seemed to be frozen, mesmerized by the sudden exposure of Alex's half naked torso.

The man came behind Alex and lifted her off the ground. "Grab her legs!" he barked at the other men. Together they lifted Alex kicking and screaming into the air and threw her to the grass. As she fell her skirt tore away which had been held on to by the stammering lackey.

Still Ignis did not act, he wanted to help, he wanted to destroy and yet curiously, guiltily, he wanted to see more.

The leader threw himself upon Alex, turned her over and forced her face into the ground while his friends held her arms and legs in place. Alex writhed and bucked but she wasn't strong enough to force them off. As the leader of the gang began to tear at her blouse in an attempt to remove it, Alex let out one terrified, muffled cry.

"PLEASE, SOMEONE HELP ME!"

Ignis finally came to his senses, snapped out of his daze by this heart-breaking plea. He lurched from the shadows like a bullet, a kick chambered and aimed at the thug's head. It would have been a killing blow, but moments before impact Ignis thought better of it, adjusted his position and scooping the brute's arm with his own, rolled over his back and threw him with tremendous force against a wrought iron fence. The malleable metal buckled under the man's weight and began to sag around him as the intense heat radiating from Ignis warped the bars. Feeling his skin burn from the touch of hot iron, the lout clambered to escape the clutter of metal. Everyone stared from the thug to Ignis, struggling to comprehend what had just happened. Alex got to her feet, shaking despite the warmth and Ignis ushered her out of the way.

"Stay behind me!"

"Ignis?" asked Alex, utterly stunned.

Ignis didn't respond, he was concentrating on the group of men who, having realised the attack had come from a little boy, were feeling more confident about retaliating.

Their leader, having freed himself from the fence, nursed his shoulder and his leg. Unable to stand and do anything himself he turned to his companions and yelled. "Don't just stand there, get him!"

The closest male, lunged at Ignis, grabbed his arms and lifted him off the ground. Ignis made no attempt to stop him, he didn't need to. Seconds after the man had picked him up, he let out a scream of pain and dropped him again.

"AHHH! My hands!" he wailed staring at his palms which were red and blistered.

"What are you doing? Grab the little shit and hold him!" demanded the leader.

"I can't!" wailed his friend. "His body... it's... it's like hot coal!"

"Stop being a pussy and smash his face in."

The man with burned hands backed away as another lackey stepped up. Ignis observed his shoulder twitch, the tendons in his neck tighten and his hand ball into a fist. This was too easy. As Ignis knew he would, the man wound up a punch and flung himself forward.

Alex gasped but Ignis simply smiled. When the fist was a few inches away from his face, Ignis took a step back and jabbed the man's hand. A series of cracks erupted along the attacker's arm as the bones in his fist, forearm and humerus fractured and splintered. The man stumbled backwards, observed his arm flopping around like it was made of rubber, then passed out.

The remaining friend, took up a fighting stance but upon seeing Ignis ready himself, thought better of it and fled along with his burned comrade.

"Get back here you cowards!" roared the lout who still lay injured on the floor. Ignis walked over to him, cracking his knuckles as he went.

"You've not had the best of nights, have you?" said Ignis. "That was rhetorical," he added as the thug made to reply.

"By my count that's the third time you have been splayed out on the floor today and I am pleased to have been a contributing factor."

"Wha...?" began the man but Ignis slapped him across the face.

"Be quiet!" demanded Ignis, his tone sharp with impatience. "I am disgusted and embarrassed that you and I are considered the same species. You have no use to anyone and are so vile that a pile of dog crap would command more respect. I feel that I would be doing the world a favour if I simply ended your life, a task I assure you would not trouble me in the slightest."

"Ignis, don't!" whimpered Alex who had begun to sob again. "He's not worth it."

Ignis turned to look at Alex and gave a heavy sigh. "So I've heard."

He turned back to the thug and leaned in close, staring into the man's eyes and grinding his teeth. He rummaged in his pockets, found his keys and wallet and pulled out a series of bank cards and a driver's license. After a cursory glance at each, he piled them in the palm of his hand and held them up to the lout's face as they burst into flames.

"What the hell?" the lout exclaimed, watching his possessions melt through Ignis' fingertips.

"Be seeing you real soon, Matthew!" said Ignis coolly as he got to his feet, took a deep relaxing breath, then upon seeing that he was suitably terrified, booted Matthew square in the face knocking him unconscious.

"H... How did you do that?" stuttered Alex, who aside from being very shaken was beginning to feel cold now that Ignis had calmed down.

Ignis found he didn't have an answer. He just stared at her shivering in the night breeze, taking in her form and once again feeling a strange twisting in his gut that was quite unfamiliar. Forsaking an explanation, Alex ran over to him and kneeling, scooped Ignis into a tight embrace.

"Thank you!" she whispered through a dry sob.

Due to Ignis being the height of a child, he found his face being squeezed between Alex's semi-bare breasts. He flushed so red with embarrassment his face matched his hair colour, but he didn't pull away. Instead, he wrapped his arms around her back as far as he could reach and pulled her close, breathing in her scent and relishing the soft touch of her skin. For what could have been five minutes or five hours, no one moved or spoke until unfortunately, it began to rain. It came down gently at first but quickly escalated into a torrential downpour.

Ignis and Alex broke apart feeling very awkward, both were sweating and flushed. "We had better get you home," he said at last in a soft voice.

Alex gathered up her clothes and tried to cover herself but they were ruined. Ignis was about to remove his top and hand it to Alex when a voice boomed out of the shadows cutting through the sound of the falling rain.

"IGNIS! CAN YOU HEAR ME?"

Ignis knew instantly who it was and panicked. Pretending he had a mobile phone he took a few steps away from Alex, gestured for her to give him a second and then found the puddle containing Frank's concerned face.

"Hello," said Ignis trying to sound casual. "Now's not the best time to…"

"Where the hell have you been?" yelled Frank. "I've been trying to reach you for over an hour."

"Y'know, just keeping busy."

"Busy?" repeated Frank furiously. "I'll give you ruddy busy, we've been in a right state."

"Why, what's happened? Is everyone OK?" enquired Ignis, painfully aware that the conversation was not at all discreet and that Alex could probably hear every word.

"Everyone's fine," Frank shot back. "But it's been an eventful day, let me tell you. Demons running around the place, three police officers dead, not to mention what happened at the school."

"Well, we can discuss that when I get back," replied Ignis, uneasily.

"Yes, and while we're at it you can explain to me why you have been causing hot spots all over Leamington," grunted Frank indignantly. "I've been panicking for the last hour thinking you were going to incinerate a whole town."

"Sorry about that," said Ignis apologetically. "I was just a little worked up but I've calmed down now and so should you!"

"Ha!" laughed Frank. "Unless I intend to spend the rest of the night getting baked out of my skull with Elsu, I really don't see that happening. Anyway, we need you back here, we have some interesting information on the murder in France and…" Frank paused for dramatic effect, "some rather sinister news on the barrier breaches… so get back here."

"Yep, will do," replied Ignis airily. "I just need to…"

"Don't worry about getting to the station," Frank interrupted. "Nephthys is here and she has been running pickups of any late arrivals!"

Ignis could hear Nephthys complaining loudly in the background. "Oh, don't mind me! Nephthys do this, Nephthys do that. I'm not a bloody taxi."

"No really," challenged Ignis. "It's fine, I don't need a lift, I'm…"

"Nonsense," interrupted Frank once again. "We need you back and need you back now. No point in waiting on a train at this time of night."

"Just give me five…" began Ignis, but Frank wasn't listening.

He gave Nephthys a nod who promptly snapped her fingers and with a whoosh of purple flame, Ignis found himself sucked out of the park into a transdimensional rift heading straight for headquarters.

A few seconds later, Ignis emerged at his destination in the central lounge at headquarters. As the purple flames dissipated and the brightly lit room came into focus, he became acutely aware that everyone, Shui, Aarde, Hoowo3oow, Gyasi, Elsu, Wun Chuan, Amos, Frank via a monitor screen, Wade and even Nephthys were all present and staring bemusedly in his direction.

This made Ignis feel a little sheepish and he convulsively checked his face for anything odd, until he realised they were not staring at him, but rather at something over his shoulder. With an increasing feeling of dread, he slowly turned his head to look behind him and wished he hadn't almost at once.

Standing in the background, looking entirely bewildered, dripping wet, shivering and dressed only in her bra, knickers and a partly shredded blouse, was Alex. She had obviously been standing too close to Ignis when Nephthys had zapped him back and been dragged along for the ride. The silence that followed Ignis and Alex's arrival was deafening. Inwardly Ignis mused that if someone were to look up the word 'awkward' in a dictionary, they would be presented with a photo of this very moment, complete with slack-jawed stares and unspoken questions.

The only one who didn't seem at all concerned by this unexpected turn of events was Nephthys. After looking at Alex, then Ignis, then the group and finally Ignis again, she straightened up and said at last, "Well, as amusing as your discomfort is, I do have places to be, things to do!"

She sauntered over to Amos who was just as dumbfounded as the rest and gave him a peck on the cheek.

"Don't be a stranger!" she whispered lovingly in his ear, before turning on her heel and resuming her Bathin form in a whoosh of purple haze.

An electric blue steed erupted from the ground beneath his serpentine tail and thrust Bathin upon the saddle as the mount reared. Whipping his thick black mane of hair out of his face, Bathin gave a guttural roar and spurred the steed's side causing it to leap several feet into the air and across the room. It landed right in front of Alex who had gone very pale with fright. The horse clopped its front hoofs against the marble floor which echoed around the room causing Alex to jump skittishly. Bathin lurched his head towards Alex, bringing his face to within an inch of hers. He gazed into her eyes with his own, the ruby red glow from his irises illuminating Alex's face. With a terrible ferocity and thunder in his deep booming voice, he roared at Alex. "YOUR SOUL IS MINE!" before whipping his snake-like tail through air, causing it to crack like a whip.

Alex finally broke! After everything else that she had been through that evening, this was just too much. Screaming so loudly those present were forced to cover their ears, she bolted from the room straight into Shui's bedroom which had been the nearest open door and with panicked looks at the demon threatening to steal her soul, frantically mashed the keypad inside until the door slammed shut and locked.

Bathin wailed with laughter.

"Well, that broke the tension!" he chuckled before rounding his steed and galloping at the group.

Shui launched herself into the air, aiming a kick at Bathin's head as the adults braced themselves to be run over. But her foot found nothing but air as Bathin evaporated in a cloud of purple mist which did little more than ruffle a few hairs.

Shui landed gracefully and sidled up to Ignis who was now the centre of everyone's attention again.

"Is this going to be a short explanation or do I need to get a snack and sit comfortably?" Shui giggled.

"I'd like to hear this too!" agreed Frank sternly. "What on earth did you do to that poor girl?"

Ignis made to speak, though he still had no idea what he was going to say, but Amos cut across him. "Frank! Mind your tone!" he snapped. "I understand that this is a most unusual circumstance. I am sure that whatever has occurred, it is for the best that Ignis interfered."

Frank looked a little affronted at being admonished like this, but his indignation softened as he glanced back at Ignis who appeared exhausted and thoroughly fed up. "Sorry," murmured Frank. "It's been a testing evening. So…" began Frank again, throwing a furtive look at Amos. "…what has actually happened?"

Ignis sat down and explained the events of the evening as the others sat in a circle around him. Ignis was quite good at telling stories and he narrated the night with impeccable detail. The others 'oohed' and 'aahed' as he recounted the fight and the peril Alex had been in. He even made them all laugh as he described trying to convince Frank not to teleport him back with Alex watching. In the end, everyone agreed that Ignis had no choice but to intervene. However, the matter of what to do with Alex, given everything she had witnessed and the fact that she was now sat locked in a room inside their own headquarters, loomed over them like a dark thunder cloud. Best intentions or not, this was a serious breach and it could not be taken lightly.

"Perhaps Shui should try and speak with her," proffered Wun Chuan, looking at the locked door uncomfortably.

"Why me?" retorted Shui acrimoniously.

"Well, because you are a woman and this obviously needs a woman's touch," replied Wun Chuan feeling this settled the matter.

"And what are you then? Hermaphrodite? Dude in disguise?" argued Shui.

162

"I… well I don't have your, um, interpersonal skills," said Wun Chuan feebly.

"At least have a try," said Amos encouragingly. "Wun Chuan's lame excuse notwithstanding, she is right that you are much better with people than she is and, well…" Amos blushed. "…under the circumstances of her predicament, not to mention her attire…"

"Or lack of!" interrupted Elsu.

"Quite," continued Amos. "A woman's presence is perhaps most appropriate." After a short pause he added, "Besides, it is your room!"

Shui, who had been stood with her arms folded and her bottom lip jutted out so far you could have used it as a tea tray, cast Wun Chuan a very scornful look before throwing her arms to her sides in defeat.

"Fine!" she barked. "But next time I get a pass on this kind of crap!"

"Agreed," said Amos.

Shui marched over to the door of her quarters, muttering things like. "Not in my job description!" and, "Bleeding sexist is what it is!"

When she reached the door, she banged her fist hard against the metal front several times yelling, "I'm coming in… Don't get snot on my sheets!"

When no reply came from inside and the door didn't open, Shui cracked open a panel and hacked the lock from the outside. The door hissed open and Shui marched inside. She glanced over her shoulder at the group giving them a look that silently conveyed, 'You all suck!' and punched the keypad inside, causing the door to close abruptly.

"While Shui deals with our guest, why don't you debrief Ignis on the encounter in France?" said Amos to Frank.

Frank swept his hand through his hair ruffling it to the point of untidy and sighed. "Where to begin?" he asked Aarde who took the question as a cue to take over.

Between them Aarde and Frank, with occasional elaboration from Wade, explained the encounter with the police and the subsequent attack from three demons. Wade described the circumstances of Professor Braskin's death and highlighted any points of note to support his theory that the lead aggressor had been a child. Ignis was particularly interested in this bit of information. His face had turned as grim as Frank's. Amos too looked most concerned.

"What is it?" asked Wade noticing their obvious disdain.

For a few moments no one replied, they just exchanged dark furtive looks. Finally, Aarde spoke up. "They are concerned that the child in question might be an elemortal."

Seeing Wade's, Gyasi's, Wun Chuan's and Elsu's jaws drop in unison might have been funny if the reason were not so serious.

"One of, one of you guys?" asked Elsu who sounded very frightened.

"Kind of," replied Aarde.

"Some years ago, myself, Amos and Ignis were sat around hypothesising possible future threats and what sort of contingency plan we would need if they came to fruition," explained Frank.

"It was surprising how many different methods we discovered to destroy the world!" added Amos chuckling slightly.

"One theory," began Ignis, "was that someone outside the Conclave of Magikal Thought may one day discover how to make children like us."

"Pu-lease!" scoffed Elsu. "Not possible, it's just not!"

"Why?" asked Amos politely. "The Conclave discovered how to make these children thousands of years ago. Understood it and put it into practice with very little knowledge of science and the vaguest appreciation for the arcane and supernatural."

"Yeah, but…" began Elsu weakly.

"But nothing," interrupted Frank. "There are hundreds of occult groups, necromancers, sorcerers, summoners, warlocks, witches, wayward religious factions, all scattered across the globe and all operating outside our control, who knows what people have discovered. It only takes one person to learn and understand the principle of the realms as we do and they could create their own elemortal, their own super child, or worse."

Amos nodded his solemn agreement. "That the supernatural world has been abused and manipulated by so many over the years without anyone actually discovering the secret of creation is, quite simply, down to luck. But to presume that no one would ever figure it out as our predecessors did…" Amos plucked his glasses from his nose and cleaned them on a handkerchief. "Well, that's just blunt minded arrogance!"

Amos' words left most of the group feeling like they had been hit with a brick. As members of the Conclave they had been indoctrinated with the secret Amos spoke of and in turn, it seemed, had all been guilty of the blunt minded arrogance Amos had just condemned.

"Has there been any progress in discovering why the professor and his Peruvian friend had been targeted?" asked Hoowo3oow slicing through the ringing silence.

"A little," replied Frank. "Barry gave the charred photo to Richard in Research and Development and miraculously he found an article in the Cambridge university archives."

"Does it say who the second victim is? Was? You know what I mean!" asked Wade.

"Indeed, it does," interjected Barry proudly, sliding into view on screen. "His name was Pacal Chan and as Wade had correctly deduced, was the village elder in a Peruvian tribe."

Wade smiled broadly. He already knew he was correct but validation felt so good.

"Easy there, Columbo!" chuckled Frank, noticing Wade's beaming grin.

"So how did Albert come to know this Pacal Chan fellow?" asked Amos.

"Well from what Richard told me, Albert and his team had been in Peru looking for evidence of the Mayan empire, when he stumbled across the remote village in a rainforest," explained Barry. "Albert abandoned his entire Mayan adventure and settled down in the forest village to study the tribe who'd had zero contact with any other humans for centuries."

"Hmm," mused Gyasi. "That's all well and good, but it doesn't really tell us anything about why they were executed, does it?"

"Well," began Elsu hesitantly, "it might!"

"I don't follow," said Frank quizzically.

"Hoowo3oow will remember this better than me," began Elsu. "Y'know seeing as he was actually there for this…"

Hoowo3oow frowned at Elsu who recoiled a little under his glare.

"Oh, unclench!" said Elsu, quickly turning his back on Hoowo3oow to avoid his eyes. "Back in the early settlement days, when the English colonised America…"

Hoowo3oow slapped the back of Elsu's head.

"Fine!" snapped Elsu. "When the English invaded America, many foreigners were killed to prevent the location of settlements being revealed to the English."

"So you think this Albert was killed to prevent him revealing these lost tribes to the wider world?" asked Gyasi enthusiastically.

"Maybe," replied Elsu. "In fact, during the 'invasion'…" Elsu drew inverted commas with his fingers and looked at Hoowo3oow with a sarcastic smile. "Many Englishmen, appreciating the lifestyle of our people, switched sides, befriended chiefs and even took native women as wives. This led to a whole mess of bloodshed between tribes as this inclusion of a white man was often seen as a betrayal. The chief was often murdered and the wife of the foreigner brutally slaughtered. The death of Pacal Chan may have been a similar kind of retribution."

"You may be onto something!" replied Gyasi trying to sound intelligent.

"Doubtful!" said Wade and Hoowo3oow in unison.

Wade smiled at Hoowo3oow who did not return the gesture, Hoowo3oow motioned for Wade to proceed with his argument.

A little flustered, Wade elaborated at high speed. "Neither native Americans or any Mayan derived cultures include demons in their belief structures. Spirits yes, deities yes, but demons… no."

"My thoughts precisely," growled Hoowo3oow casting Elsu a dark look as if to suggest he ought to have known better.

"What I want to know," said Aarde bringing up a digital print of the burned photo of Alfred and Pacal Chan on a second display, "is who this guy is?"

Aarde was pointing to a pair of legs jutting out of a burned edge at the bottom right of the image.

"My word!" exclaimed Frank. "How the hell did we miss that."

Barry gave a little cough behind Frank. "Actually we, or rather I, didn't!"

"And…" whittled Frank. "Who the devil is he?"

"Professor Bernard Godfrey!" said Barry proudly. "He is quoted and credited in many of the articles published by Alfred and…" Barry tapped on a keyboard off screen. "one of those articles contains the same photo, which is wonderfully intact."

"Bravo," said Frank clapping Barry on the back. "I always knew there was a reason I kept you around."

Barry looked momentarily pleased, but then fell sullen, as he realised what Frank had actually said.

"Our top priority now is to find this Bernard Godfrey fellow," Boomed Frank in a very hearty voice. "If he is still alive, he can be considered both possible victim and suspect."

"Quite," added Amos. "At the very least he may be able to fill in a few blanks."

Ignis stroked his chin thoughtfully, then looking at Wade asked. "Do you think any of this relates to the paradox that demon mentioned?"

Wade stared blankly back. "Haven't the foggiest mate. I've been mulling it over ever since Bushyasta made mention of it. But I cannot narrow down the cause based on the information we have. We simply don't know enough."

Just then the door to Shui's room hissed open and Shui, looking very flustered, stormed into the room muttering incoherently in Chinese.

"Y'know I can speak thirty-four different languages and not one of those includes 'Jibbering Wreck'. I can't get any sense from her at all, the woman is clearly damaged."

"No success in calming her down then?" asked Wun Chuan politely.

"Suck it!" Shui fired back, glaring menacingly at everyone in the room, daring them to make a comment. She then rounded on Ignis. "She wants you!"

"Me?" asked Ignis tremulously.

"Only thing she said that made sense," said Shui, sounding thoroughly irritated.

"Where's Ignis? I want to speak to Ignis!" moaned Shui in a grim sing-song imitation of Alex whimpering as she rummaged in a cupboard, pulled out a glass and filled it with water. "Wants to get her shit together more like!" she added, draining the glass and slamming it on the counter.

"Best foot forward then m'boy!" chortled Amos, casting Shui a weary glance.

Looking very uncomfortable Ignis began plodding towards Shui's quarters.

"Get her out of my room!" barked Shui as she filled her glass with water again.

"What, oh, yeah… er… right!" replied Ignis trailing off, his voice becoming quieter the closer to the door he got, which hissed open at his touch.

He peeked his head beyond the door and spotted Alex sat in a ball on Shui's bed with her duvet pulled up to her chest. She was rocking back and forth and was still white as a sheet. Ignis glanced back at the others who quickly sat down and pretended not to be watching. Taking a deep breath, Ignis stepped inside and closed the door behind him.

He had only been inside Shui's room a handful of times. She was dreadfully protective of her personal space. This was her inner sanctum and was decorated and adorned with a styling that reflected her unique nature.

The room was completely circular and dome-shaped. The singular wall was comprised entirely of glass and was reformed in places to create shelves upon which Shui had placed ornaments or books. The space behind was very deep, filled with water and lit from above, the light from which shimmered and sparkled on the floor. Various marine creatures drifted along the circumference of the room, occasionally pausing to examine an object beyond the glass barrier or perhaps entertaining a curiosity over Alex. The overall effect of the room was almost like living in a fish bowl and was decidedly tranquil.

Shui had only two pictures in her room. One was a photograph of her with the group, her Conclave brethren. They were stood arm in arm, everyone smiling broadly and standing victoriously upon the badly beaten and subdued body of Lamashtu. Ignis smiled affectionately at Shui in the picture, who was still smiling at the camera but also had Pazuzu in a headlock which was causing the demon a great deal of distress.

The other picture was a Chinese-style ink portrait. The parchment it was drawn upon was very old and worn around the edges, but the ink was still perfectly black and the red stamp by the artist gleamed vibrantly, as if fresh. Shui never spoke about who the man in the portrait was, but Ignis and the others suspected the picture was of her father, a suspicion reinforced by the fact the image was framed behind bulletproof glass.

The rest of the room's adornments consisted mainly of mood lighting which illuminated containers filled with liquids of different consistencies, the centrepiece being a large lava lamp, that oozed thick, orange, viscous wax back and forth from floor to domed ceiling.

Ignis had been wandering aimlessly around the room as he examined Shui's choice of decoration and was surprised to find himself so close to Alex that he could ignore her no longer.

"Alex?" asked Ignis tentatively. "Alex, are you OK?" As soon as he asked, he put his palm to his face. "Sorry, stupid question, of course you're not OK!"

"Ignis," muttered Alex so quietly it was almost inaudible. "Is that thing still outside?" As soon as she finished speaking, she buried her face back into Shui's duvet.

"What thing?" asked Ignis, genuinely confused.

"THAT THING THAT WANTS TO TAKE MY SOUL!" screamed Alex hysterically.

Ignis, whose mind had been distracted since the debrief and had completely forgotten about her encounter with Bathin, tried to imagine what that must have felt like for someone unfamiliar to dealing with demons on a daily basis. Ignis sat on the bed beside Alex and placed a reassuring hand on her back.

"That was a mean trick," began Ignis consolingly, "and I will be having words with Nephthys the next time she pops by."

"That was no trick!" cried Alex, defiantly. "I'm not stupid, whatever that was, it was more than just smoke and mirrors."

"Huh? Oh no," began Ignis noticing the mix up. "I mean that scaring you like that, was a mean trick."

"That thing has a name?" enquired Alex, utterly mortified at the prospect.

"Like I said, her name is Nephthys… although when you saw her, she, or rather he, was Bathin. It's a bit confusing, but then high-ranking demons are not exactly straightforward."

"D-d-demon?" replied Alex meekly. "A really real demon?"

Ignis couldn't help but laugh a little at this. "Yes, I'm afraid so. But as demons go... and her prank not withstanding... she is one of the nicer ones."

"Just what the hell is going on here?" asked Alex her voice growing stronger. "What is this place? Who are they... them... those people outside? How did we get... Where the hell are we?"

"That's a lot of good questions," said Ignis sounding hoarse. "And there are... ahem... good and reasonable answers to all of them."

His mouth and throat had suddenly become very dry, and as he looked at Alex's enquiring face, he realised he didn't actually know exactly how much he could tell her.

"The truth, Ignis, please!" said Alex softly.

"The truth is... difficult," replied Ignis lamely.

"Tell me anyway!" demanded Alex. "Tell me or your efforts to have Chloe join your... 'institution?'... end here!"

Ignis drew in a heavy sigh, sagged his shoulders and flopped back onto the bed. "What do you believe in, Alex?"

"Believe in?"

"Yeah, y'know, religion and stuff."

"I don't," replied Alex simply. "I'm an atheist."

Ignis smirked inwardly. "If only everyone shared your opinion, my life would be soooo much easier... although probably shorter," Ignis added as an afterthought.

Alex scuttled down the bed and lay beside him, staring intently into his eyes, perhaps searching for signs of deception.

After another deep sigh, Ignis elaborated. "I hate to be the one who breaks this to you, but every God from every religion and every angel, demon, monster, creature, beast and spirit associated with each, actually exist."

Alex screwed her eyebrows together and raised herself high enough off the bed to look down upon Ignis.

"I told you I'm not stupid," she began crossly. "You honestly expect me to believe that Gods and that sort of thing are real?"

"Very real!" exclaimed Ignis calmly. "Not just religious notions either," he continued, "but magic, sorcery, witchcraft, necromancy, parallel dimensions, elves, goblins, bogeymen, all the crap that goes bump in the night basically… anything in short, that a child could believe in."

Alex searched Ignis' face again for a sign of deceit, when she found none, she collapsed on the mattress with a heavy flump. She looked more panic-stricken than she had when Nephthys had threatened her.

"Oh God, I'm so screwed," said Alex dithering weakly where she lay. "I'm going to hell, aren't I? My stoic atheistic stance has condemned me to an eternity of pain hasn't it, HASN'T IT?" She was becoming a little manic now.

"Calm down, Alex," said Ignis softly. "You are not going to hell… or any other place of purgatory," he added, guessing Alex's next argument.

"Being an atheist is a fine choice, believe me," said Ignis in a stern but reassuring voice.

To her surprise, Alex found she did believe him. Her panic ebbed away and reason began to return. "So how do you know all this?"

"It's my job to know," grumbled Ignis. "Me, Shui and the other guys spend our time cleaning up the mess of occults and religious fanatics and occasionally fighting demons and spirits. We've even taken down a God or two in the old days!"

"Old days?" asked Alex. "You're like, seven years old!"

"Only physically," groaned Ignis. "This youthful form hides a very, very tired old man."

"How old is old?"

"You tell me teach!" challenged Ignis. "I caught the highlights of the Bronze Age, a glorious period during which time I owned a beautiful bronze armour breastplate," he finished reminiscently.

"SEVEN THOUSAND YEARS OLD?" bellowed Alex in abject astonishment.

"Thereabouts, give or take a hundred years or so," said Ignis in an offhand tone.

"Y-you're older than me?" stammered Alex.

"You're an infant compared to me mate!" chuckled Ignis.

For the next hour Alex and Ignis talked at length about the supernatural world, ancient monsters, legends and prophecies, albeit cautiously avoiding all subjects that explained the hows and whys. Once Alex had moved past the shock of these new revelations, she found herself feeling at ease in Ignis' presence and was soon smiling, laughing and thoroughly enjoying listening to his stories. Moreover, Ignis discovered that he too, enjoyed recounting his adventures to her and found her company to be a refreshing change.

"…So I was in their place of worship and everyone was just staring at me, no one wanted to fight," said Ignis ebulliently.

"Why not?" asked Alex. "Where they too afraid?"

"Nope! Turns out I'd got too hot and burned all my clothes off. Seems that not even nutters want to tussle with a guy whose junk is hanging out."

They both collapsed into hysterics, rolling around on the bed and making a general mess.

They both started, when a loud banging erupted from the direction of the door and Shui's bad tempered voice bellowed in from the other side. "What the hell are you doing in my room dude! If the crazy lady is fine, then drag her bony backside out here and let me have my room back!"

Ignis gave Alex a weak, apologetic smile. "Just because we're old, doesn't always mean we are mature."

Alex chuckled and wrapping Shui's duvet around her, got up from the bed and walked over to the door.

Ignis raised his eyebrows in surprise, he hadn't expected Alex to be so amicable about leaving.

"I guess you had better introduce me," said Alex nervously.

Chapter Nine
Into the Fold

Alex and Ignis' reappearance in the main lounge area of headquarters was awkward to say the least. Shui impatiently shooed them out of the way of her door, entered and immediately began berating Ignis' flagrant disregard for her 'personal space' and yelling loudly about the mess.

Everyone else smiled uncomfortably, not really knowing whether they should speak, look at the floor or play with the nearest available object.

"For those who have not already had the pleasure," began Ignis, "may I introduce, Alex Sterling."

"Delighted to see you again, Miss Sterling," said Amos rising from his chair as he spoke.

"All right!" added Elsu, giving a little nod but not meeting Alex's eyes with his own. His gaze was trained upon Alex's bare legs that stuck out from the bottom of the duvet.

"You've obviously met Shui and Wun Chuan," continued Ignis strolling passed Elsu and elbowing him in the shoulder.

Shui could still be heard complaining loudly in muffled yells. Wun Chuan awkwardly shook Alex's hand and then left the table to try and find her some clothes.

"Finally, this is Gyasi, Aarde and Hoowo3oow."

Gyasi and Aarde waved politely, Hoowo3oow, arms still folded and looking decidedly grim, grunted what could have been a greeting before returning his attention to the photo of Bernard Godfrey.

"So you guys are like the *Ghostbusters* then?" said Alex, who winced at how silly that sounded considering the scope of what Ignis had told her.

"A bit of an over-simplification," said Amos happily, "but in essence, yes, I suppose we are."

"Man, I loved that movie!" said Elsu dreamily.

Alex sat at the table, flinching at the coldness of the seat against her almost bare bum, interlocked her fingers and placed her hands on the table. The change in her demeanour was so abrupt it was startling. She became suddenly very business-like and stern in expression.

"Ignis has explained in a general sense what it is you and these, 'children' do."

Alex drew inverted commas in the air with her fingers as she said 'children' and Ignis couldn't help but grin at how uncomfortable it seemed to make Hoowo3oow and Aarde.

"What I still don't fully understand," continued Alex, "and you must be sure to explain it fully if you expect me to support her transfer, is what Chloe would be doing here."

Considering that they would be giving Chloe a tour of her new place of education in approximately two hours, this was actually a question no one had been expecting. Indeed no one it seemed, aside from Alex, had given Chloe's placement a second thought since last meeting her at school.

Spurred on by the lack of response, Alex continued her interrogation. "Please understand me, I think what you do here is remarkable, certainly commendable, but I also understand that it is extremely dangerous. Chloe does not have the strength, super powers or gift of immortality that these individuals do. In fact, Chloe does not have an extra seven thousand years to add to her age, she really is only five years old. I'm sorry but I fail to see what use she would be to you."

"If you'll forgive my saying so," replied Amos as politely as he could, "your failure to see her use is due to your own shortcomings."

Alex looked quite affronted by this comment and pouted angrily at Amos.

"Please, I mean no offence," Amos added calmly. "My meaning was that, while I am impressed by how well and willingly you have accepted what Ignis has told you about the supernatural world, it is still an alien truth. As such your senses are dulled to the subtle signs a person with an extraordinary talent displays."

"No offence," said Alex, "but you don't have to be able to read subtle signs to see that Chloe is a genius." Her words oozed sarcasm and she overemphasised 'subtle signs', rolling her eyes as she spoke. "But that's the problem, she is really clever, she's not a ninja or whatever."

"First," said Amos coolly, "you ought to know that Chloe's intellect is the tip of the proverbial iceberg. We didn't discover Chloe because she is smart, we found her because she is giving off massive energy readings. So massive that every department, every scientific and supernatural branch within our community has been notified of her presence."

Alex looked aghast. "Is... is she...?"

"Dangerous?" supplied Amos. "No, not at the moment."

"What do you mean at the moment?" asked Alex.

"I mean that right now, Chloe is a sweet young child with a marvellous mind and an innocent disposition. Her thoughts are free from malice or contempt. For many reasons this could change..." added Amos warningly, "...her power, which I'm afraid to say is still a mystery, is likely to have been noticed by others beyond our influence. There may as a result be attempts to coerce her into a darker world. One that would no doubt help to discover her abilities and unleash them upon the world for selfish and destructive purposes."

"And what are 'you' going to do with her?" demanded Alex. "Turn her into a nice weapon?"

"A nice weapon, now that's a novel idea," interrupted Frank who had just reappeared on a display screen. "It could shoot hug bullets and kiss grenades."

"Who the hell are you?" snapped Alex defensively.

"Frank, hero of Yorkshire and conqueror of the northern realm," replied Frank, in a supercilious and over British accent. "Barry, send a memo to Rich in R&D. Nice weapons, finally a way to hug with nuclear arms!" He turned back to look at Alex. "Glad to see you have calmed down Miss Sterling. I need to go through a bit of paperwork with you if you don't mind."

"Paperwork?" enquired Alex, her feeling of frustration rising.

"Yes. Since you have arrived and no doubt before you leave, you have been and will be privy to sensitive and highly classified information pertaining to the supernatural world, the Qin Zhu Institution of

Experimental Science, the Conclave of Magikal Thought and some of its members."

"So you want me to sign some kind of official secrets form?"

"Basically, yes!" said Frank happily.

Above the table and emerging from a compartment hidden in the ceiling, appeared a small machine that looked similar to an upside-down microscope. It spun on a turret so its barrel pointed at the desk space in front of Alex and fired a blue laser against the polished surface. Instead of cutting or burning the desk, it began to print a document complete with text, seemingly out of nothing. When the action had finished the laser disappeared back inside the ceiling and Alex, prompted by Frank, picked up the paper and began to read.

"What does it mean by 'all information retained by the signatory will be destroyed by means of FFL?' What's FFL?" enquired Alex.

"Upon signing this document, you will find it quite impossible to commit any information you learn here to paper," said Frank brightly. "This does not, prevent you from speaking about it, though you would find that difficult too. Any conscious attempt to reveal and or discuss this knowledge with any individual who is not part of the Qin Zhu Institute of Experimental Science or the Conclave of Magikal Thought, will trigger an automatic shutdown in neurons and synapses within the prefrontal lobe. The resulting brain damage would be the equivalent of an FFL, or full frontal lobotomy."

"Is that legal?" asked Alex, shocked.

"We operate within our own system of laws and our jurisdiction is global, legal is simply a matter of perspective. Nonetheless your compliance is mandatory," said Frank seriously.

"And if I refuse to sign?"

"Then that laser will reappear and lobotomise you here and now."

Alex laughed, then stopped abruptly when she realised no one else was laughing and that Frank was not joking.

"Does anyone have a pen?" continued Alex meekly.

"Here you are," said Amos handing her a beautiful black and gold fountain pen. "You will feel a slight sting under your thumb when you write," he added in caution. "The document must be signed in your own blood I'm afraid and there is a needle in the barrel which will extract just enough for a signature."

"Why blood, you're not after my soul as well are you?" whimpered Alex.

"No," chuckled Amos. "Scientifically, it assigns your DNA to the contract which provides a target for the contingency. Supernaturally… well it's always been blood. It is more associated with the idea of a life force than the concept of a soul, which by all accounts is a relatively new idea."

"This is magic paper?" asked Alex trying to bring the conversation to a more understandable level.

"Yes," said Frank impatiently. "It's magic paper with magic words which makes your brain magically implode if you ignore the instructions."

With a half nod and a lot of trepidation, Alex put pen to paper and wincing as the needle bit her thumb, wrote her name with a flourish that glistened scarlet against the page.

"Do you want me to keep hold of this till later?" enquired Amos holding up the signed document and brandishing it at Frank.

"No need, mate," replied Frank who was busy inputting Alex's details into their database. "I'll send Edmond to come and collect it."

"Edmond is our er… mail room clerk," Explained Amos noticing Alex's puzzled expression.

"Aarde?" continued Frank ignoring Alex now. "Barry thinks he has tracked down this Bernard Godfrey's home address. We will send some uniforms round to confirm this, if he's in, we'll bring him to the institute for questioning. I'd like you and Wade to lead the interview if you don't mind."

"No probs!" replied Aarde happily, he liked conducting interviews and liked them even more when he had Wade in his corner. "Should be fun," he added holding out a clenched fist to Wade who bumped his own fist against it and grinned broadly.

Aarde and Wade then got to their feet and headed off to make preparations for Bernard's arrival. Everyone else got up and left too, leaving Amos, Ignis, Alex and a digital Frank alone at the table.

"CHLOE!" yelled Alex, impatient and nettled beyond reason. "You still haven't told me squat about what she would be getting into. What you would use her for!"

Frank looked calmly back at Alex for a moment who seethed back.

"Manners cost nothing, m'dear! Amos, bring her up to speed as much as you are able. Miss Sterling, if you will excuse me, I have other matters to attend to."

At these words Franks image vanished and Alex rounded on Amos. "Well?"

"Well he's right," said Amos placidly. "Manners do cost nothing."

Alex blushed embarrassedly, finally realising how blunt and aggressive she was being. "I'm sorry."

"It's quite all right," said Amos kindly. "You've had quite a day."

Alex gave a weak smile and Amos patted her affectionately on the back.

"The Conclave of Magikal Thought, as I am sure you have guessed, is our frontline against the forces of Evil. When the supernatural world steps out of line and threatens the safety of mortals, we move in and contain the threat, with lethal force if necessary. However, the Conclave comprises of a select and elite group. Ignis and his comrades aside, we have within our ranks incredible men and women who are proud to dedicate their lives to such a noble and worthy cause."

Alex rolled her eyes again. "You cannot use children as soldiers. It is unfair and unjust."

"Ignis has told you his age, yes?" asked Amos plainly.

Alex's eyes flitted quickly to Ignis then back to Amos again. "Yes," she replied quietly.

"Then I hope your misconception of 'child soldiers' can be put aside. No one who is a member of the Conclave or its associated auxiliary task force is under the age of eighteen. I might also stress that openings to join Conclave ranks are highly sought and applied for voluntarily. No coercion is used as none is required."

"So Chloe won't be placed on some sort of frontline then?" asked Alex feeling somewhat ashamed of her accusations.

"No." Amos smiled. "Chloe will be inducted into the Qin Zhu Institute of Experimental Science. There she will be offered an education that cannot be rivalled by any other school on earth and guaranteed a career path that will not only be lucrative, but hers for life."

Alex smiled. "Don't suppose you have any vacancies for a slightly maniacal and hysterical physics teacher?"

"Be careful what you wish for m'dear," chuckled Amos, although there was caution in his tone. "If Chloe accepts a place, she would be required to choose a chaperone, what we call a dovetail. It is someone who will assist her while she studies and handle matters on her behalf that may be too adult in nature for a child to cope with. If, as you say, her parents are too distracted to be interested then you may indeed be Chloe's first choice."

"What do you mean matters too adult for a child?" asked Alex pensively.

"The world that Chloe is soon to be introduced to is cruel and often frightening," replied Ignis before Amos could speak. "Chloe will be taught the extremes of science but also the depths of the supernatural world. To look into such an abyss can, at first, be a truly harrowing experience…" For a moment Ignis appeared to be lost in a thousand-yard stare, preoccupied with a distant memory, perhaps of his own induction, until he said at last. "…believe me I know. She will need a familiar and comforting face."

Alex suddenly let out a shrill, high-pitched shriek and Amos and Ignis both jumped so violently they left their seats by an inch or two. A quick glance at Alex explained the cause of her alarm. Edmond, the mail room clerk as Amos had called him, had appeared out of the desk in front of Alex. His head and shoulders were all that were visible, however, the rest of his body was still somewhere beneath the desk. He was obviously a ghost but he was not pearly white and transparent as one would have imagined. He was coloured in skin and clothing, the same as a regular person, except the colours appeared washed out and greyed, as though they had faded over time. He was also dressed like he belonged in the year 1840. Garbed in yellow pressed trousers, an immaculate white cotton shirt, a reddish-brown waistcoat and a long black jacket, it would have been easy to assume this was a man of business, prior to his death of course.

"I'm here to pick up the indenture," the ghost stated, happily. "Is this it?" he asked holding up the paper with Alex's signature still glistening at the foot of the page.

"That's the one," replied Amos. "And how are things my good man?" he added, sounding interested.

"Not bad, Amos," said Edmond. "Sandra keeps me busy. Wants to renovate the loft. Like I don't have enough on." Edmond tucked the contract into an inside pocket of his coat and climbed out of the desk. "Terribly sorry to 'ave startled you madam," he added with a slight bow to Alex. "Ignis, always a pleasure. Amos." Edmond bowed to the men in turn then faced a nearby wall and ran towards it.

Ignis, sped ahead of him and got to the wall first. Before Edmond was able to pass through, Ignis grabbed his shoulder and Edmond found himself slamming into a very solid, very hard surface.

"Ahhh..." wailed Edmond cupping his nose. "...bleedin' 'ell Ignis, was there any need?"

"What do you think?" asked Ignis wryly as he turned Edmond back to face Alex who was chuckling. "You scared the poor girl half to death mate, least you could do was contribute a bit of slapstick for the sake of levity."

"Yeah..." grumbled Edmond who was still nursing his face. "...is my nose bleeding?"

"You're a ghost mate, you don't have any blood!" replied Ignis incredulously.

"Oh... yeah, well it don't stop it hurtin', does it! Glad to have helped ease your stress m'lady, now if you'll excuse me." At these words Edmond eased his way more slowly through the wall and vanished.

"How did you do that?" asked Alex.

"Do what?" replied Ignis.

"You touched a ghost. I thought they would be all... y'know... not really here. I mean he passed through the table and the wall, but not before you grabbed him and made him crash into it. Also, I thought ghosts were supposed to be see-through and stuff."

"Your versatile and expert use of the English language is a true testament to your position of teacher," chuckled Amos.

Alex cast him a disdainful glare, so Amos pressed on.

"Most spirits are, as you so delicately described, not really here. Although some, normally maligned in nature, develop the ability to interact with their environment, it is usually impossible to touch them or to witness such calamitous collisions like that of our dear departed friend Edmond. However, Ignis and his kin have developed the ability to channel their energy allowing physical contact with ectoplasmic forms. In doing so, contact with someone like Ignis briefly causes the spirit or entity to become corporeal, solid in the real world. It is normally used as a battle strategy, and not for our own amusement…" Amos looked scornfully at Ignis for a second, then breaking into a mischievous smile added, "…that was pretty funny though."

Wun Chuan returned to the table holding a pair of blue jeans and a thick black woollen jumper.

"Alex? I think these should fit you. It had to be a jumper though as I don't think my shirts would have coped with your… er… more sizeable bust."

Wun Chuan flushed a very deep scarlet, dropped the clothes on the desk in front of Alex and then rushed off again muttering about her jumper being stretched all to hell.

"Feel free to use a side room to dress yourself, you can find socks and a spare pair of boots that ought to fit in the armoury," said Amos gesturing to a door behind him.

Giving her thanks, Alex stood up from the table and allowed Shui's duvet to slide off her shoulders and onto the chair. She slung the clothes over her shoulder and then sauntered towards the door, in such a casual manner it was hard to believe she was dressed only in her underwear and in the presence of two men she had only met a day ago.

Both Ignis and Amos watched her leave, their eyes transfixed on her swaying hips and supple frame. Then catching each other's eyes, quickly faced forward, only to look back at each other, grin cheekily, then glance at Alex again, just in time to see her turn around and close the door.

"She's quite a woman," said Amos, a sly look on his face. "I can see why you would be taken with her."

"What?" said Ignis a little louder than he intended. "I'm not, I don't…"

Amos gave Ignis a pitying smile. Ignis sighed heavily and slumped forward.

"I can't be having feelings, Amos. I mean look at me. For as old as I am, the body is still a child's. If a woman really looked at me that way, I'd have to consider placing her under arrest."

"No one will ever know the sacrifice you make," said Amos sadly. "Hoowo3oow, Shui and Aarde included. All your powers and strengths and abilities, can never make up for being condemned to an eternity of solitude. That you bear such a burden without complaint is a true testament to your characters."

"Yeah," said Ignis weakly. "Gotta have character."

"It's nearly morning," said Amos, changing the subject. "We should get ready to meet Chloe. We'll take the train again. A car can bring us to the station, I think it best to avoid Alex using any more magical transportation for now, we wouldn't want to break her."

"I'll grab a quick shower," said Ignis. "I got a little muddy from that fight earlier."

"I'll wait for Alex and we shall meet you topside in twenty minutes," said Amos, pleased to be on the move again.

By the time Ignis had made it to the ground floor level of the Qin Zhu Institute of Experimental Science, Alex and Amos were already outside, enjoying the early morning sunshine. As Ignis exited the building to join them, he took in a deep breath and sighed blissfully. He liked their headquarters and loved his room, but it was very stuffy sometimes and the aroma of four children who lived there and four adults who worked there often became overpowering.

"I recognise that building!" Ignis heard Alex say as he moved within earshot. "It's a museum that's home to a magnificent collection of butterflies. My father brought me here as a child and afterwards we went for an ice cream just over there. I can't believe we are in Flksqrkglk!"

For a second or two Alex looked like she was going to vomit. She clapped her hands over her mouth and stared confusedly at Amos, who was smiling serenely.

"Thrkuksknng!" said Alex before gagging again. "What the hell, Amos? I can't say Sknrrgflrup... thrpmnn!" Alex gave up her attempt to speak before she gave herself an aneurism.

"No," replied Amos. "You cannot say the name of this city as currently you are using it in the context of naming the location of the Conclave of Magikal Thought. Something you are contractually forbidden from disclosing."

"Most people puke the first time they try," added Ignis gleefully. "I'm impressed that you made three attempts and still have your breakfast."

"I haven't eaten since last night," said Alex. "Perhaps that is why my stomach isn't protesting."

"Well, we shall have to remedy that on the train," said Amos rubbing his hands together briskly. "They do a marvellous bacon and egg sandwich in the buffet cart which is served in a crusty bap."

"Breakfast of champions!" agreed Ignis, rubbing his own hungry belly.

"Then let us make haste," began Amos jovially. "We do not want to be late in meeting Chloe."

All three climbed into the back of a black Ford people carrier and got comfortable. Alex laughed for nearly ten minutes at Ignis' sulky rant when Amos jokingly asked him if he required a booster seat. After the laughter died down, they travelled almost eight miles in silence until at last Amos broke the silence.

"Are you all right, Miss Sterling? You seem distracted with worry."

"Do her parents know we are coming?" asked Alex, who was growing increasingly concerned over how they would react.

"They do," said Amos. "Mrs Penton, Chloe's current headmistress, who of course you know, phoned ahead to make them aware of the offer our institution wishes to extend. In addition, a representative of the Qin Zhu Institute was dispatched yesterday evening to explain at length the process of transferring to our establishment, the benefits this would bring to Chloe's future and to answer any burgeoning questions they may have had."

"So we won't have to sit and chat with them?" asked Alex tentatively.

"No..." replied Amos, giving her a solicitous look, "...are they really so inhospitable?"

Alex shuffled awkwardly in her seat. "It's not that they are inhospitable, just really tense and not exactly overflowing with patience."

"From what I understand their jobs are quite demanding..." began Amos but Alex cut across him.

"It's their relationship that's demanding!" spat Alex, then realising she sounded more bitter than she had intended, turned her gaze to stare out of the car window.

Amos turned to look at Ignis who replied by shrugging his shoulders and stretching out the corners of his mouth.

"Am I to understand that you and Chloe's parents have come to blows in the past?" enquired Amos cautiously.

"Not blows," said Alex sadly, "just heated words," she sighed deeply then added. "I know they love their daughter and I'm sure they are good people, but they do not pay Chloe enough mind. Her parents argue incessantly with each other and abuse the fact that Chloe is wise beyond her years by assuming she can take care of herself. They seem to have forgotten she is a child and it is nothing short of neglect."

Amos considered these words for a moment, then said at last. "It is rare to see a teacher having such vested interest in a student these days," he mused. "She attends your class but once a week and only for a few hours, yet..." Amos looked appraisingly at Alex for a moment. "...you rally to her defence as though you yourself had birthed her into this world."

Alex did not look at Amos, instead she continued to glare out of the car window, though Amos could see her frown had softened.

"That dedication will serve you well as a dovetail," said Amos softly and he patted Alex gently on the shoulder.

The rest of the journey to the train station was carried out in silence, as though each person were sat in a bubble of thought that was impregnable from outside interference. So much so that words were not spoken again until Amos requested three tickets to Stratford-upon-Avon.

As they boarded the train the smell of freshly cooked sandwiches stirred their moods and all thoughts turned to food and the promise of a hot bacon and egg bap. It was like feeding time at the zoo. A silence had fallen upon them again, but it was not brought on by awkward questions and gloomy thoughts, but a desire to sate a ravenous appetite caused by an absence of sleep and no food at all since the late hours of the day before.

Amos read a paper while he ate, taking bites in between the turning of a page. Occasionally he would make a muffled remark and show Ignis an article or extract from whatever story he was reading. Ignis on the other hand had crammed his entire bap into his mouth and was holding it in his cheeks like a hamster storing food. He reclined in his seat, placed his arms behind his head and smiled serenely. Alex had just begun to wonder what poor table manners Ignis had been subjected to when she noticed small puffs of smoke billowing from the corners of Ignis' mouth. Remembering what talents Ignis had, she reasoned he must be cooking it a little more inside his mouth. "Like a little baby dragon," she thought to herself with a chuckle.

Meanwhile Alex herself was not eating with any element of refinery. She devoured the sandwich as though she hadn't eaten in days and was quite oblivious to the large splotch of egg yolk that had been projected onto her, or rather Wun Chuan's, jumper during a particularly hearty bite. She remained unaware until she had finished eating, dabbed delicately at her lips with a napkin and noticed Ignis almost choking on his food as he struggled to contain both laughter and contents within his mouth.

"Ah, crap!" said Alex grimacing at the thick, yellow yolk dribbling a shiney track down the front of her top.

Amos, peered over the top of his paper, smiled and handed her his own napkin which he had not needed.

"Thanks, Amos," said Alex as she mopped up the mess, screwed the napkin into a ball and with a mischievous grin, threw it at Ignis.

Ignis responded by opening his mouth wide and sticking out his tongue upon which sat the charred remains of his breakfast.

"Ironic, really!" smirked Alex.

"What is?" asked Ignis swallowing hard.

"That Chloe is a child yet behaves like an adult, while you are an adult who behaves like a child. The phrase 'Act your age!' seems to have lost all meaning."

"Yeah, well be sure to let me know if you find someone my age who acts differently. Oh wait, there is no one else my age except Shui, Aarde and Hoowo3oow and they do act the same… except Hoowo3oow but he's just grumpy… and let's be honest, Shui makes me look like the pinnacle of maturity."

An announcement rang through the train. "The next stop is Stratford-upon-Avon where this service terminates. Please ensure you have all your belongings before you leave."

Amos folded up his paper and slid it into a pocket inside his suit. "Let's not keep our new charge waiting," he said merrily, then stood up sharply and marched toward the train door.

Ignis and Alex got up at the same time. "After you," said Alex politely, gesturing for Ignis to step ahead.

"No, no!" said Ignis flatly. "I must insist. My height tends to put me at bum level and for as much as I love Amos, I would be much happier squared up to your backside than his."

Ignis leaned closer to whisper. "He tends to trump as he walks, it's like following a boat with a broken motor."

Alex giggled under her breath and moved ahead to join Amos. As she walked, Ignis had the distinct impression she was putting more emphasis on swaying her hips than normal. Indeed, Ignis was so focused on the hypnotic motion of Alex's rear that when the train stopped abruptly at the platform, he lost balance and found his face buried between her buttocks. He recovered quickly but his face was flushed with so much blood he looked as though he might pass out.

Alex seemed quite unabashed and gave Ignis a cheeky smile over her shoulder which eased his sense of embarrassment.

The morning had flourished into a bright and clear day. It was also remarkably warm considering it was now November and Amos elected to remove his jacket which he folded over his left arm. Alex too was feeling warmer than she would have preferred but as she was dressed in nothing but Wun Chuan's jumper, could only compensate by rolling up her sleeves.

Amos checked the time on a beautifully ornate pocket watch, which he had stowed in his waistcoat.

"It is now a quarter to eight," Amos exclaimed brightly. "If my geography serves correct, we should be able to walk from here and arrive at Chloe's place of residence by ten minutes past eight."

186

"Eight on the dot, if we head this way," proffered Alex, pointing down a side street."

"Excellent!" said Amos. "By your leave then, Miss Sterling! Lead the way and see us follow."

Pleased to be doing something useful, Alex strode off across the road and disappeared down the alley she had indicated with Amos and Ignis in hot pursuit. When they emerged from the passageway, it was into a square that had a grassed seating area, enclosed by low lying walls and was beset on all sides by various shops and businesses.

To Amos and Ignis's great delight, stood in front of a park bench with an amplifier to his left and a guitar case laid before him, was the busker boy they had spoken to the same day they had met Chloe and Miss Sterling.

He was wearing his long black leather coat today, which looked very dramatic as it blew lazily in the wind as the musician deftly flitted his fingers up and down the fret board as the sound of 'Texas Flood' filled the air.

"Ah, now this takes me back!" said Amos, casting a crisp five-pound note into the boy's guitar case before drifting off into blissful reminiscence.

The boy, noticing someone dropping money into his case, turned to show thanks and recognised both Ignis and Amos at once. Beaming, he bowed low in gratitude to Amos, threw in a quick bar of 'Problem Child', to show he remembered Ignis and then paused playing altogether and gestured for Amos to pick a song this time.

"Well now, that is kind," said Amos excitedly. "But what to pick? What song would you like, Miss Sterling…? Er, Miss Sterling?"

As Amos turned around, he noticed Alex was missing. He scanned the square and spotted her talking to a young boy.

"Excuse me one moment." Amos said to the waiting boy, who although appeared perplexed, was not offended and opted to play Pachebel's 'Canon in D', with some very complicated flourishes while he waited.

Amos signalled to Ignis and together they went over to where Alex was stood and from what he could hear, was apparently interrogating a boy in his early teens. Ignis recognised the boy as soon as he saw his face. It was Quentin Farrowfield the Third, the obnoxious boy from Chloe's class, or more precisely, Miss Sterling's class.

"Quentin, answer me, what are you doing here?" demanded Alex. "You should be heading to school. Quentin? Quentin?"

Quentin appeared not to be listening. His expression was vacant and none of his features gave the slightest hint that anything Alex was saying was reaching his brain. Ignis walked over to him, placed his hands on either side of Quentin's head and pulled his face closer to stare straight into the boy's eyes. The only sign of life Ignis could see was his own glassy reflection staring back.

"What's wrong with him?" asked Alex, her voice shrill with concern. "He looks like he's got brain damage."

"No, not brain damage," said Ignis, still peering into his eyes. "I think he's sort of hypnotised."

"Hypnotised?" repeated Amos. "Hypnotised to do what?"

"Not sure, hang on!" said Ignis as he raised a finger in front of Quentin's face.

He moved the digit around saying. "Follow," over and over out loud until at last Quentin's eyes began to track its movement.

As soon as Ignis was certain Quentin was fixated on his finger he moved it through the air and rested the tip on his forehead. Quentin's eyeballs had followed the finger so diligently that they now appeared to staring into the inside of his skull. A look that was creepy, but encouraging.

"Where are you going, Quentin?" asked Ignis, his voice so soft it bordered ethereal.

"Far away," replied Quentin tonelessly. "Can't come back… just go… far away."

These words jolted Ignis' memory of yesterday's encounter with Chloe. He remembered the fight she'd had with Quentin and more importantly remembered her screaming at him, 'Why don't you… don't you… go far away and never come back!' It seems Quentin had done just this and Ignis wondered if Quentin had even returned home yesterday or if he had left school and just continued going. Was this as far as he had got and if they left him would he just keep going until he found the sea. Or would he even die of exhaustion or hunger? Self-preservation certainly did not appear to be a high priority at the moment.

"Amos," whispered Ignis, beckoning him close. "Chloe did this!"

Amos looked taken aback. "Are you sure?"

"Positive!" said Ignis firmly. He thought a moment then added. "We had better take him with us, if we leave him here, he will just continue to wander off. Besides if Chloe can do this, she may also be able to put him right again."

Amos heaved a deep sigh. "It's certainly not conducive to our plans for today, but I see no alternative. Miss Sterling perhaps you could contact this boy's parents and inform them he is safe. If he has indeed been out all night, they will no doubt be worried."

Flustered and completely at a loss as to what she would say to the Farrowfields, Alex withdrew her phone and released her grip on Quentin who immediately began to shuffle off in an arbitrary direction.

Amos pulled Quentin to one side. "Ignis, would you mind?" he asked nodding at the boy.

It was a testament to their relationship that Ignis understood at once what Amos wanted. He moved behind the boy and discretely jabbed two fingers into three different places along his spine. Quentin froze mid-stride in an almost comical manner. Unbalanced by the weight of his leg jutting out, he toppled forward and would likely have fallen to the floor rigid as a plank of wood had Amos not steadied him.

Seeing that Alex was still busy with her phone call, Amos headed off to continue speaking with the musician. Meanwhile Ignis amused himself by posing Quentin into silly positions before eventually arranging him into a seating position on an unoccupied bench.

As Amos approached the musician, he noticed he was now playing, *The Times they are a Changing* by Bob Dylan.

"They most certainly are," chuckled Amos with inference to the song.

The boy turned to look at Amos and smiled broadly, pleased that this near stranger had also understood his songs to be conversation.

"About my song choice," began Amos genially. "I'll give you another five bob, if you can play *Cliffs of Dover* by Eric Johnson."

The boy grinned mischievously and used his foot to crank up a dial on his tiny amp. He then pushed a little white button labelled, 'Overdrive' and raked the strings in the chord of C. He then proceeded to blare out an intricate solo introduction to the piece which caught the attention of the entire square. By the time he had reached the first bridge of the song, almost forty people had gathered round and were cheering their appreciation of the musician's effortless execution of so many notes.

Waving his goodbyes to the boy, Amos turned back to where Ignis was still toying with Quentin, only to find Miss Sterling joining in.

"He's like a giant doll," Alex said brightly, adjusting Quentin's hand to allow his finger to be inserted in his nose.

"Miss Sterling please, he is your student," sighed Amos, rubbing the bridge of his eyes where his glasses normally sat.

"Yeah, but he's an obnoxious little twat," chuckled Alex indifferently.

"This is exactly the kind of thing I expect you to be doing!" Amos said as he rounded on Ignis. "In any case time presses on, let us use our musically minded friend's talent, to leave without anyone noticing that this child," he pointed at Quentin, "is completely paralysed."

"Good idea," replied Ignis.

Together, with Quentin posed to sit comfortably on Miss Sterling's back, they departed the square and continued on to Chloe's home.

"What did you tell the Farrowfields?" asked Amos a few minutes later.

"I said that we had found Quentin and that he was safe," replied Alex sounding a little flustered. "Apparently they reported him missing when he didn't come home yesterday and they've had the police out looking for him all night. I mentioned that he also seemed a little out of it and that we are going to take him to the hospital, but we need to pick up another child first. I said I would call them once he has been admitted."

"Jolly good," said Amos. "That at least gives us a chance to remedy the boy before he is seen by his parents."

"Next left here." panted Alex, who after carrying Quentin for nearly ten minutes now, was starting to feel quite tired.

"Do you want me to carry him for a bit?" asked Ignis helpfully.

"Thanks," replied Alex, "but I think it looks weird for me to be giving a teenager a piggy back, let alone someone who for the sake of appearance is a seven-year-old."

"Not to worry," said Amos examining a door number a little ahead of them. "We are here. Ignis, could you assist Alex in positioning Quentin in a jaunty pose against the fence… Er, try to make him look casual… and see if you can do something with his face, he looks like he's had a stroke."

Amos strode up the path to number 33, Windcrest Way. It was a large semi-detached house in the centre of the street, that was surrounded on all sides by a very tall hedgerow which opened in an archway over a gate.

There was no grass on the front, nor any slabs, just gravel which crunched beneath Amos' shoes. He knocked on the door in a brisk but tuneful manner and waited.

"One minute," yelled a voice from the other side.

A few moments later the door swung open revealing a tall, muscular man with chin length wavy hair and dressed in a grey shirt and brown tie. He was pre-occupied with trying to pull on his suit jacket, so much so, that at first Amos did not think anything of not being greeted. After a while though the scene became uncomfortable so Amos, decided to do it for him.

"You must be Chloe's father, Mr Gibson," said Amos politely.

The man gave Amos a very stern look, then simply nodded his agreement.

"Quite…" said Amos, a little put off by this rather unfriendly welcome. "Well, pleased to meet you, I'm…"

"Late?" supplied Mr Gibson.

Amos began to explain their delay, but Mr. Gibson ignored him. Instead, he just turned around and walked off inside the house. Amos turned around to spot Alex spying on them from behind the hedge. Amos raised his eyebrows and Alex gave him a look that clearly said, 'told you so'.

Considering Mr. Gibson had left the door open, Amos took this to mean 'come inside', so with a deep steadying breath, he entered the house.

It was not what he had expected. Their living room was like a miniature museum. There were statuettes, wood carvings, stone relief sculptures and paintings, all with distinctly different religious leanings and they littered every flat surface that wasn't used for walking on.

Amos counted tributes from at least thirty different cultures, both alive and dead, and for a moment, Amos wondered where they could have come from. Mr Gibson was an architect and although he travelled, he would not have had time or perhaps even the inclination to concern himself with collecting historical knick-knacks. Besides, there was a space in the far corner of the room that housed a drafting table and had its own small collection of miniature structures. Perhaps Mrs Gibson then? She, Amos knew was a translator, who assisted ambassadors both at home and abroad. She also commissioned her talents to various museums and institutes deciphering archaic scriptures. This certainly made her more likely to be responsible for such a collection, but it still didn't quite fit. The artefacts were so nuanced and obscure, that only an expert would see them for what they were. Before Amos could think any more on the subject, Mr Gibson joined him.

"Chloe is upstairs in her room waiting for you," said Mr Gibson curtly. "She is unsure what to bring and would like your help."

"Chloe does not require a thing, we will provide all she requires to begin her studies," replied Amos reassuringly. "But I shall go and greet her nonetheless. I wouldn't want to be rude."

Amos headed towards the stairs, but before he embarked, he turned and asked, "Will I meet Mrs Gibson before we depart?"

"My wife is not well this morning, it is unlikely she will emerge from the bathroom any time soon," replied Mr Gibson with a bitter edge in his voice.

With an understanding nod, Amos left Chloe's father and climbed the stairs to the landing. Amos had imagined Chloe's room easy to spot. A young girl likely had her name on a sign hanging on the door or perhaps stickers. To his disappointment, he was faced with four plain, identical, glossy white doors. As he moved past the door closest to the stairs, he heard the sound of a woman vomiting. "Bathroom!" he murmured under his breath. The second door opened into an airing cupboard which was full of towels and a boiler.

"Ooh, Egyptian, very nice," cooed Amos, ruffling the plush fabric with his hand.

As Amos made to close the door, a small, white plastic object fell from a high shelf and clattered noisily to the floor. Amos hurriedly knelt down to grab it, his joints aching with stiffness and as he did, he noticed it was wet. Whipping out a napkin from his trouser pocket he grabbed a long protruding edge of the object then stood up to see it in the light.

At first glance it was quite unremarkable, that is until he twirled it around and saw a little window with a blue plus mark sat in the middle. Amos' face gave a grimace. He was holding a pregnancy test and shuddering as he thought it, understood precisely why it was wet. This thought also coincided with another heaving splash sound from the bathroom next door and Amos nodded knowingly to himself.

Amos dropped the test back onto the top shelf with a movement that was something like a disgusted spasm and hastily closed the door.

"Maybe that is why Mr Gibson is so testy this morning?" wondered Amos quietly. "Wasn't expecting to be expecting, eh?"

When he came to the next door, Amos decided to knock instead, he'd had enough personal information for one morning. Waiting with his ear close to the door, Amos heard someone slide off a bed and two little feet land on the floor promptly followed by the sound of scurrying footsteps rushing towards him. The next second the door had been flung open and Chloe was standing before him looking elated.

"You came!" she exclaimed brightly.

"But of course," chuckled Amos. "Did you think we wouldn't?"

"Fifty-fifty," said Chloe rocking a flat hand side to side. "Adults have a tendency to be unreliable."

Amos leaned close to Chloe and with a grin whispered, "I tend to agree, they are just so…"

"Overflowing with insouciance?" supplied Chloe.

Amos laughed heartily which emphasised his surprise. "Couldn't have put it better myself."

Chloe blushed a deep rouge but smiled all the same.

"Are there many kids like me at your school?" she asked and when she spoke, it was more reserved and shyer, than before.

Amos considered her a moment, then crouching to look her square in the face said softly, "Perhaps not quite like you, but extraordinary nonetheless."

Amos noticed the look of concern still etched across her brow and added, "My dear, I think you are going to fit in just fine."

Chloe's tension dissipated and she instantly became more energetic, bouncing on the balls of her feet. "What should I bring?"

"Just your fabulous self and any items you think will help you feel comfy and safe…" said Amos. "Oh, and perhaps a coat. My old bones are of the opinion that the weather will turn sour later this afternoon," he added, rubbing his neck poignantly.

"What about clothes?" asked Chloe sounding confused. "I thought this was like a boarding school, that I would be sleeping there throughout the week."

"And you are quite correct," said Amos. "However, a wardrobe of clothes and various uniforms befitting the unique activities you will be involved in will also be provided, we will get you measured during the tour."

Amos held out his hand towards Chloe and with a warm welcoming smile fixed upon his face asked, "Shall we?"

Chloe grabbed a satchel that had been sat on the bed beside her, took Amos' hand and together they left the room.

As they passed the bathroom Chloe's mother emerged looking queasy and rather bedraggled. "Oh Chloe, are you leaving?" she asked.

Chloe gave a nod and realigned her satchel strap on her shoulder.

"I'll miss you sweetheart, be good and do your best OK," said Mrs Gibson, leaning down to hug Chloe and kiss her cheek.

"Do not worry, Chloe is in good hands and we have an open-door policy to family members of our students," said Amos consolingly. "If you are able, feel free to come by and pay Chloe a visit. I have left a contact card on your hallway table, the number will provide you with a car to take you directly to our institute… it can be awkward to find if you don't know the way."

"Thank you," said Mrs Gibson attempting to make her hair neater. "I'm Cassandra, I assume you have already met Daniel, my husband."

"I have," said Amos a little coldly.

Cassandra sighed deeply. "You'll have to excuse him, we have been under a lot of stress lately."

"I understand," said Amos, winking and patting his own belly knowingly.

Cassandra looked suddenly mortified and dragged Amos by the arm into the bathroom, leaving Chloe alone on the landing.

"How the hell do you know I'm pregnant?" snarled Cassandra under her breath.

Amos thought of the pregnancy test and as he did, it occurred to him that perhaps the test had been hidden and nobody else knew.

"My dear, you are radiant, positively glowing, in fact," he invented wildly. "Besides, old codgers like me have a knack for spotting this kind of thing."

"Please, please, don't mention this to anyone else, certainly not Chloe... not yet!" Cassandra pleaded.

"Of course," said Amos. "You have my word."

Cassandra seemed to relax for a moment, then heaving she spun around and vomited loudly into the toilet again.

"It was, er, nice to meet you Mrs Gibson," said Amos loudly, trying to be heard over the sound of sick splashing into the bowl. He gave a feeble unseen wave and without further hesitation, he left.

Wasting no more time, Amos headed to the front door with Chloe hot on his heels. As he reached the door, Amos turned to look at Chloe, who was standing right up against him eager for the door to open. "Aren't you going to say goodbye to your father?" Amos asked

"Nah," replied Chloe glumly. "Daddy's not been happy to be around us lately." She stared down at her feet looking positively miserable and Amos found himself lacking for something to say.

As the pair stepped outside into the bright morning light, Chloe's aspect changed completely when she spotted Alex at the end of the path.

"Miss Sterling," she exclaimed with delight. "Are you coming too?"

"I am, chick!" said Alex happily. "You can't get rid of me that easily."

Chloe ran forwards and gave Alex a very enthusiastic hug, something that surprised Amos as he had seen her neglect to offer such affection to her parents. Chloe spotted Ignis from around the side of Alex's waist and quickly stepped around her legs to greet him.

"Hi, Ignis," she said giving a tiny flick of her hand that Ignis assumed to be a wave. "Is Shui with you?"

"Not today, she's er, having a day off," said Ignis. "But you will meet her again later."

"That's goo…" Chloe stopped mid-sentence, her eyes had just found Quentin and for a moment she looked apoplectic with rage.

"WH, WHY IS HE HERE?" bawled Chloe verging on tears. She spun around to face Amos and there was pain and pleading anguish wrought upon her tiny features. "He's not coming too, is he? Please, he'll ruin it! I don't want to go if he is!"

"Chloe, please, calm yourself," said Amos in a soft but firm voice. "This boy is not attending the institute, I promise."

"Really?" replied Chloe trying hard not to sound mistrustful. "Then why is he here?"

"He is here because of you," said Amos simply.

"Me?" said Chloe.

"Yup," said Ignis grinning. "His brain is a bit addled at the moment and I have a sneaky suspicion that you are the reason why."

"Me?" repeated Chloe defensively.

"Ignis, don't…" began Alex, but Amos waved her down.

"Oh yeah!" continued Ignis still smiling as he cast her a surreptitious glance. "I think your mad skills ran away with you a little bit and you boiled his bonce."

Chloe stared wildly at Ignis and her jaw gaped open, words had completely failed her.

"Done it myself loads of times," said Ignis, acting as though he hadn't noticed Chloe's shock. "Remember that time I burned all your hair off?" he added turning to look at Amos who gave a subtle wink in return.

"Oh yes," said Amos. "I also remember the toupee."

Ignis rounded on Chloe again. "Show me."

"Show you what?" murmured Chloe meekly.

"How you did it. I want to see," replied Ignis, no longer smiling.

"I don't… I can't… I…"

"What?" sneered Ignis. "Can't what?"

Chloe didn't answer, instead she stared at the floor and shook her head from side to side. Ignis raised an upturned palm towards Chloe and formed a swirling, blazing hot fireball that floated an inch above his hand. It was about the size of a tennis ball, but all present could feel its radiating heat and it looked terrifying.

Chloe retreated back into the hedgerow and as Ignis advanced on her, Alex lurched forward, but again Amos pulled her back.

"Stop it please," whimpered Chloe.

"Stop what?" demanded Ignis.

"Why are you doing this? You're scaring me," blubbed Chloe as Ignis brandished the fireball close to her face. "Please get it away from me, it's burning."

"Make me!" breathed Ignis menacingly, his face eerily illuminated by the glow of the flame.

Without warning, as tears streaked down Chloe's cheeks, a torrent of rain burst forth from the apparently clear sky and doused Ignis and his fireball which sizzled and vanished in a puff of smoke.

What's more the rain, apparent to everyone except Ignis who was thoroughly drenched, was pouring on nobody else.

Ignis laughed and looked at Chloe. He was smiling broadly and his eyes conveyed affection where there had been malice before.

"I knew it," Ignis yelled jubilantly. "I bloody knew it." Ignis slicked his wet hair back out of his face and looked at Chloe. "Just before it rained, what were you thinking of? Just for me to leave you alone or was it something specific?"

Chloe, still looking stunned but no longer scared, gave a slight, almost imperceptible nod. "I thought of you being washed away by a waterfall."

Ignis choked as he inhaled a few droplets of water. "Good job your talents are under developed," he spluttered. "Look, I'm sorry for scaring you but I had to prove a point." Ignis looked down at his sodden clothes and added, "Of course I'm not entirely sure what that point was now. I wasn't expecting physical manifestations, I just figured I'd probably feel the effects of mind control like you did with Quentin over there."

Chloe glanced over to where Quentin was still leaning against the fence in the same frozen position.

"He isn't moving," said Chloe. "What's wrong with him?"

"He's a flight risk," interjected Amos.

"Yeah, he kept wanting to wander off!" chuckled Ignis. "Like he needed to go away and never come back!" he added raising an eyebrow at Chloe, whose face suddenly illuminated with comprehension.

"Where was he going?" asked Chloe, aghast at this revelation.

"No idea," said Amos. "But he had been walking to his supposed destination all night. His parents were quite concerned, as you would imagine."

"The question that remains is…" asked Ignis. "…can you put him right again?"

"Did I really do this?" asked Chloe.

"Right after your scuffle in the corridor at school," replied Ignis. "Don't feel bad for not knowing, I was there and still missed it and this kind of thing is part of my job."

"Let's go somewhere more secluded," suggested Alex, ever aware of her proximity to Chloe's parents.

"That's wise," agreed Amos. "I'm surprised we have not drawn more attention to ourselves already, we aren't exactly being quiet."

"Then let's cut to the chase," said Ignis holding his hands aloft before he quietly whistled and sang in multiple tones.

The back of Frank's head came into view and over his shoulder he saw Elsu sat facing him. They were both slumped lazily in plush, leather chairs and smoking Elsu's pipe which they passed back and forth with what seemed like a tremendous amount of effort.

"Really, Frank?" snapped Ignis, the scorn in his voice impossible to miss. "It's twenty to nine in the bloody morning."

Alarmed at the same time as drawing from the pipe, Frank fell into a coughing fit. He had lost none of his composure, however. "It may be pushing nine in the morning to you m'laddo but when you are approaching the end of a thirty-six-hour shift, it is just a time before I sleep. Besides, it's eight in the evening in Australia."

"If you are not too baked, could you arrange travel back to HQ," asked Ignis, testily.

"I thought you were using public transport today on account of picking up that new girl?" enquired Frank through a mouthful of smoke.

"We were," interjected Amos, "but there have been complications."

"There always friggin' is!" sighed Frank

"Perhaps we should explain Nephthys to Chloe…" said Amos giving Alex a furtive glance, "…to avoid what happened with Miss Sterling."

"Don't bother," groaned Frank. "Nephthys won't be coming!"

"Why the hell not?" demanded Ignis.

"She is attending some sort of party for the dearly departed," said Frank.

"Dearly departed?" scoffed Ignis. "She doesn't consider anyone dear."

"No," replied Frank. "I dare say she doesn't but those three demons that Aarde and Hoowo3oow demolished, were apparently close friends."

"Do we have any summoning packets prepared for anyone else?" enquired Amos sensibly.

"Yeah, a few…" said Frank looking around his office without actually moving, "…hang on a sec!"

Ignis watched Frank get to his feet, take a huge hit of Elsu's pipe then wander out of view. They could hear drawers and cabinets being opened and slammed shut again and the tinkling of glass mixed with the various rustling of fabrics. Occasionally a drawstring bag would fly passed Ignis' view and land on Frank's chair. When Frank reappeared, he was pulling one bag open and peering inside.

"This should do!" said Frank.

"Who is it?" asked Ignis.

"Vapula," replied Frank.

"VAPULA! C'mon Frank, Vapula's a dick," snapped Ignis.

"Language," sung Amos, indicating Chloe with a shift of his eyes.

"Like Nephthys is any better," retorted Frank.

"Yeah, but with Nephthys it's zip zap! Vapula can only fly and it takes ages," whined Ignis.

"Then take the bloody train if it's such an inconvenience," barked Frank feeling very harassed.

"Vapula will suffice," said Amos with forced civility. "Will he be summoned here or do we need to await his arrival?"

"Nah, I'll order him to appear in front of Miss Gibson's abode," said Frank more calmly.

"Thank you," said Amos. "And might I suggest you have Barry man the mirrors if you are at the end of your shift. Much the better way to enjoy your free time in peace."

"Good idea!" grumbled Frank who cast Ignis a lingering dirty look before the connection broke.

"Douche!" muttered Ignis into the empty space between his fingers.

Amos gave Ignis a disapproving look then turned to Chloe. "It would perhaps be best to explain who Vapula is before his arrival," said Amos nervously. "It's important not to be scared, he cannot hurt you, but… well… er…"

"I'm not scared," interjected Chloe. "I know he's a demon. I've never seen one before though, I'm really quite excited."

"Y', you know about demons, do you?" enquired Ignis, as equally surprised as Amos.

"Yep. It's one of those, 'I just know' kinda things," said Chloe brightly. "For example, I know that Vapula is a duke of Hell and he commands thirty-six legions. I also know he's pretty good with science and mechanics."

"Do you also happen to know what he looks like?" asked Amos.

"A winged lion. Front claws and wings of a griffon," replied Chloe matter of factly. "Kind of like that!" added Chloe pointing over Alex's shoulder.

Ignis and Amos followed her finger and raised their eyebrows in unison. Alex hadn't turned round. At the same time Chloe had gestured, Alex had felt a strong blast of hot and heavy breath on her neck, a breath she instinctively knew couldn't have been made by a human.

"Vapula," hailed Amos, "so good of you to join us."

"It has been a while!" said a deep raspy voice from behind Alex.

"Not long enough!" mumbled Ignis so quietly he knew only Vapula with his feline ears would hear.

"Ignis, still as impertinent as ever I see!" said the bassy voice. "Why are you wet?"

"I've just seen your mother, she says 'hi', by the way!"

"You know, I don't mean to be rude, but would you mind turning around to face me or at least moving to one side," rumbled Vapula.

For a moment, Alex thought the voice had still been speaking to Ignis but then a feeling of dread trickled along her spine as it dawned on her that the voice was actually addressing her. Slowly, Alex turned on the spot, her eyes clenched tight. Finally facing the other way, she cracked open her eyes and saw a giant lion's maw inches from her own face. Steeling herself she opened her eyes wide to take in the full sight of this immense demon. Sat on his hind legs, yet still towering above her at a massive eight feet high, was a gigantic lion. As though determined to impress, Vapula spread his wings above him. The feathers at the wing tip caressed the guttering along the roof and the bulk of these limbs was flecked silver and gold which caught so much sunlight it blinded Alex momentarily who stumbled to the floor in a dazzled and awed stupor.

"You're really pretty," said Chloe who wore the expression of a star-struck fan.

"Thank you, tiny human," said Vapula sounding amused. "And I'm sure you are quite delicious," he added with a sloppy lick of his lips.

For a moment no one seemed sure whether Vapula was joking, no one except Chloe who had moved next to Vapula and was eagerly stroking his mane saying. "Who's a pretty kitty."

"Perhaps we should think about getting this show on the road!" said Amos.

"Yeah, kitty!" said Ignis a little obnoxiously. "Mush!"

Vapula directed a gutteral growl at Ignis. "Quiet, the grown-ups are talking! Amos, where can I take you?"

"We need to head back to our headquarters rather sharply," said Amos his voice thick with concern.

"The boy got you into trouble again, has he?" said Vapula.

"Not this time, no," said Amos.

"What do you mean, not this time! Since whe…" began Ignis but Amos forestalled him.

"It's the young man beyond the gate," Amos explained pointing at Quentin. "He's a bit damaged at the moment."

"Understood," said Vapula. "I can get you there in about ten minutes. If the woman and girl sit forward of my wings, you and the statue over there can ride upon my back." Vapula turned to look at Ignis. "You can ride upon my arse and fair warning, about an hour ago I ate a harpy that I'm pretty sure was ill."

Ignis made a series of rude hand gestures at Vapula who ignored them with a smile.

"Not to be awkward," began Alex who had finally got to her feet, "but how are we supposed to ride a humongous winged lion through town without being seen. I mean, seriously, I can't say the name of a city without gagging on my own tongue, but this is fine?"

"For a start we wouldn't be going through town so much as over it," said Amos reasonably.

"Quite true," agreed Vapula. "Plus we will also be phasing out of this timeline for the duration of the flight so no one should see us anyway…" He paused for a moment then shrugging added. "Well, no one that matters."

"I'm sorry, but what?" asked a flustered Alex.

"It means he will be taking us beyond the fourth dimension and out of sync and visual range of anyone experiencing our time. Like all fifth dimensional beings he is not limited to experiencing time in a linear fashion like us," said Chloe to everyone's utter astonishment.

"So we will be going to a different point in time?" asked Alex.

"No," continued Chloe, "rather we will be everywhere and nowhere all at once. We will see all time within the current confines of our own branch of the fifth dimension, as far back as the big bang but no further than our next choice."

"Forget I asked," muttered Alex rubbing her temples.

"A surprisingly concise summation," said Amos, bewildered.

"You just became my new favourite human." Vapula grinned and beckoning with his head, gestured for Chloe to climb on his haunches.

Before long everyone was seated upon the back of Vapula including Ignis who was perched upon the lion's buttocks and Quentin who was jammed between Amos and two enormous wings.

"Hold on!" called Vapula over his shoulder as he reared on his hind legs, roared majestically and then with a tremendous sweep of his wings, sped skyward with his cargo.

Chapter Ten
Angels and Demons

Within a matter of minutes, Vapula had pierced the scant covering of clouds and had levelled off to glide high above Stratford. Chloe gripping tightly to Vapula's mane chanced a look down to the distant buildings below. She had never even flown in a plane before so the experience of soaring through the sky upon the back of a demon was somewhat of a shock. Nonetheless, as the wind swept her face causing her eyes to stream, she could not resist opening her arms wide and embracing the adventure. The strong air current buffeted Chloe backwards into Alex who was sat behind her, cowering low to Vapula's back and hanging on for dear life.

"Are you OK, Chloe?" bellowed Amos, straining to make himself heard above the whooshing wind.

Unable to raise her voice loud enough, Chloe jutted out a fist with a tiny thumb raised above it signalling she was fine which made Amos chuckle.

"And what about you my dear?" enquired Amos as he patted Alex gently on the shoulder. She was shaking, and from what little he could see of her face, looked decidedly pale.

"F... fine!" Alex stammered back. "Just let me know when we land."

"Everybody, brace yourselves!" roared Vapula over his shoulder. "We are about to slip out of time which can be somewhat nauseating for the inexperienced."

"Roger that!" replied Amos.

"Whatever!" sighed Ignis who was sat leaning back-to-back against Amos and looking out into the distance behind the group.

Alex buried her head inside her jumper and tightened the hold she had with her feet under the crook of Vapula's wings. Chloe seemed incensed by the prospect and leaned deep into Vapula's mane like a cub hunting in long grass.

A sound almost like whale song filled the air as the sky before them began to shimmer and ripple as though viewed through a heat haze. As Chloe watched on, the ripples increased in size and the tranquil sound of whale song changed to something like metal being violently twisted. Ghostly shapes of who knew what faded in and out of sight as the distortion built, sending waves of bent light crashing over the group. The entire world, sky and earth alike seemed to be building up in front of Vapula like water at the bow of a submarine before splashing past them. It was like carving through a sea of mercury which reflected the world around it, scattering blobs of reality in every direction which reformed into windows of history. A high pitch squeal joined the metallic wails which grew to an agonising volume causing everyone except Vapula and Ignis to cover their ears and wince in pain. The giant waves of reality swelled to immense proportions making it impossible to determine which direction was sky and which was ground. It made Chloe feel dizzy and she slumped against Vapula's neck to stop herself falling. Alex was beyond dizzy at this point. She swung her head over the side and vomited loudly. Vapula, noticing just in time, dipped his wing to prevent it being sprayed with sick, but this caused Alex to topple from her position. Amos lurched forward to catch her and hold her steady, but he moved so suddenly that the force dislodged Quentin as well. Ignis, brought to attention by the abrupt movement of Amos and the trail of sick lining the sky turned just in time to see Quentin fall. With a grin that became a grimace, Ignis leaned forward over Vapula's rear and allowed himself to fall. Twisting in the air as he dropped, Ignis grabbed the lion's tail and swung beneath him. His feet connected hard with the frozen form of Quentin and he slammed the boy deep into Vapula's chest.

"Make yourself useful and hold that!" yelled Ignis still yanking the tail hard to brace Quentin against Vapula's body.

Wheezing and winded, the demon wrapped his front paws around Quentin, securing his safety and allowing Ignis to release his feet.

Dangling below the giant lion and blowing in the wind, Ignis mused how much fun this all was. This thought was cut short, however, as a final giant tsunami of twisted world bore down upon them. Everything began to vibrate and the squeal increased in pitch, harmonising violently with the deep groan of bending time and space. Amos, Alex and Chloe clutched at their bodies as they passed into the wave, their bones and muscles feeling like they would shake themselves to atoms and for Amos and Alex, it was all too much as they both fell unconscious.

Far below, a young musician was busy shredding on an electric guitar, making light work of the solo in 'Bark at the Moon' by Ozzy Osbourne. A man dressed in a black tailored suit and carrying a briefcase had just passed the boy and stopped to listen to him play. Rather than toss him some change and pick a song, the man had elected to give the musician a dirty, condescending look before walking off. Both drew to a complete stop, as far above them, there came an almighty reverberating bang that trembled the air. Confusion quickly gave way to mirth, as the massive thunderous boom was quickly followed by a stream of vomit which drenched the man in the suit as he attempted to walk off.

"Should've picked a song mate," chuckled an old man, who was also stood near the musician, before he flicked a pound into the boy's guitar case and climbed inside a nearby newspaper stand.

Back in the sky, all had become somewhat calmer than before. The giant waves of distorted space time had abated in favour of a gentler yet choppy environment.

Looking to the ground, the effect of moving through fourth dimensional space was much more apparent. Tides of time crested and broke over each other revealing things that were not there before. As one wave rolled beneath them, Chloe saw a gathering of shanty huts surrounded by people wearing rags and dancing. As the next wave crashed over the same spot, the scene changed to reveal a bloody war involving what appeared to be Saxon warriors. The wave after that held nothing but barren land charred by lava flow.

The sky was equally surreal. Dense noxious cloud formations, storms, rain and blazing heat washed over them plunging them into darkness in one moment and dazzling them with midday sun the next. Flocks of birds materialised out of nowhere and streaked past them as though pushed forward by the waves under current. Vapula had to swerve dramatically at one instant when a pteranodon burst into being in front of them, its long beak gaped wide and its immense form bearing down upon them.

This terrifying visage was swept away seconds later, by a spitfire plane caught up in a dog fight with a German Messerschmitt.

Ignis who was still dangling from Vapula's tail had a spectacular view of this as a stream of bullet fire ripped passed him.

"Oh shit! Amos did you see that?" laughed Ignis.

"Do not be afraid," yelled Vapula. "Although we are able to witness these events in time, as long as you are within my reach, we are not part of the space and cannot interact."

"Sorry, but I can't hear you over the sound of me not caring!" yelled Ignis in sardonic reply. He reached up and shook Amos' leg. "Yo, grandad, you still with me...? Amos?"

Concerned, Ignis swung back around and mounted Vapula to sit behind Amos again and checked him over. "Oh, for f... he's passed out!" grumbled Ignis indignantly.

"So has Miss Sterling!" chuckled Chloe who was repeatedly poking her in the forehead with her finger in a futile effort, to prop it upright.

"It's the result of breaching dimensional walls. At the highest threshold the experience is like pulling over fifty Gs." explained Vapula in a proud manner that made him sound like a tour guide.

"Still don't care!" muttered Ignis.

Reaching inside Amos' jacket Ignis rummaged around for a moment before withdrawing a small glass bottle that appeared to be full of cotton wool. Ignis pulled off the lid and jammed the bottle into Amos' right nostril. For a second or two it appeared to do nothing at all, but then Amos suddenly lurched upright and began slapping at Ignis' hand, his face contorted with revulsion.

"Wh... stop, what's it? What? Oh, it's you... and we're here!" spluttered Amos as his voice changed from highly confused and irate to pleasantly surprised and giddy.

"Here use this on Alex," said Ignis as he handed Chloe the bottle.

"How long was I out for?" enquired Amos in a tone so casual he could've been asking about the weather.

"Little over a minute," said Ignis.

Amos looked around and took in his bizarre surroundings. "My word, this takes the eyes some getting used to, eh?"

Another giant winged reptile soared past and Amos whooped with delight. "Now this is how history should be taught! Remind me to discuss fourth dimensional lectures with Rich when we get back."

"If its ideas of science you're after then I'm your guy!" said Vapula importantly. "After all the scientific method is part of my demon class."

"Oh, here we go," groaned Ignis.

Amos cast Ignis a 'play nice' sort of look and then addressed Vapula. "What ideas can you grace me with today then?" asked Amos indulgently.

"How about… oh, you know how the roads in your godforsaken country get all clogged up with snow and ice which for some unknown reason brings your entire society to a standstill…" began Vapula. "Well why not use a similar technique to that applied to rear windows inside automobiles?"

"It's the twenty-first century, Vaps," interrupted Ignis. "Just call them cars, that way you're less likely to sound like a twat."

"THE STRIPS OF COPPER…" continued Vapula, loudly and under the pretence he hadn't heard Ignis, "could be applied to the roads. If the temperature falls a thermostat could activate the wires, thus heating the roads whilst preventing ice and damage to the roads through extreme contraction and expansion."

"That's a bit beyond our remit I'm afraid," said Amos consolingly. "I'd recommend donning your human guise and contacting a member of parliament."

"Wow, that was so boring I think I just had a stro…" began Ignis, but broke off as his attention was drawn elsewhere, drawn to the sound of a shrill whistle from somewhere out in the distance.

Suddenly and moving purely on instinct, Ignis weaved his head backwards just in time to dodge an arrow, gilded with silver and gold, which whizzed by leaving a streak of light in its wake. Ignis hardly had time to recover before he heard the sound again. This time he lunged his hand forward and caught the second arrow in place, just centimetres from Amos' cheek.

"Vapula, we've got company!" called Ignis.

"Who is it?" replied Vapula.

Ignis scanned the skies, searching for any sign of his attackers against the fluctuating ocean of time. Out of the corner of his eye, Ignis saw the faintest hint of a pearl-coloured wing, backlit by golden sunlight.

All at once he spun around to face the rear and clasped his left hand over a bow already drawn and held the arrow that was knocked and ready to be loosed in place. His right hand still held the arrow it had snatched from the air which Ignis proceeded to jam against his aggressor's throat.

"You mean who are they?" growled Ignis through clenched teeth.

"Angels!" said Chloe in surprise.

"You want to explain yourself while you still have the ability?" demanded Ignis pressing the arrow tip hard against the angel's neck.

"Harut! Lialah! Show yourselves."

As commanded, two more angels appeared either side of Ignis, clothed in silky robes that hung loosely off their bodies. One was a female, the other two including Ignis' hostage, were males and both of the new arrivals were armed with swords. Everyone, including Vapula who had come to a stop, were all looking over their shoulder awed and amazed at this unbelievable meeting. Chloe couldn't help but notice how beautiful the angels were, how smooth their skin was, their finely etched muscles and the soft downy feathers in their wings, which no matter where they were viewed from, or what was happening behind them, were always lit from behind by warm golden sunshine. She also couldn't help but notice the lack of a belly button and the strange absence of nipples, which looked most bizarre on the angel whose form resembled a woman as her left breast was exposed and yet was completely smooth and featureless.

"You have no business being in this place!" snapped the second male angel, Harut.

"We were warned of your presence here and we came to remove the contamination!" sneered the female angel, Lailah.

"Contamination?" scoffed Ignis angrily.

"Your continued stay in this dimension risks the timeline, this is not acceptable," said the angel at Ignis' mercy.

"And you are?" asked Amos politely.

"I am Puriel."

"My word, you're quite the celebrity aren't you! Well, Puriel, you have no right at all to prevent our travels through this space and while we have no quarrel with you, force will be used if required," explained Amos keeping his tone friendly.

"We have every right!" roared Puriel. "In the name our lord G…"

"YOUR lord…" interrupted Amos loudly emphasising the first word. "Not ours. You know who we are!"

"We all know who you are," sneered Lailah. "Infidels and abominations who ally themselves with demons, the unclean spawn and you do so under the pretence of making the world a better place!"

Lailah took a moment to scoff and share the joke with her companions. "Safer by destroying spirits and wreaking havoc among the dead and supernatural."

"You forgot to say how good we are at doing it too!" supplied Ignis smiling. "If not for us your poxy kingdom would be rammed so full of souls it would be easier to find seat on a train in Dehli."

"You defend murder?" asked Harut.

"I defend this entire bloody planet!" barked Ignis who was beginning to feel his temper rise.

"You have no right to interfere, it is his plan, his will!"

"His bullshit!" boomed Ignis. "Your kind never cease to amaze me. The arrogance and breathtaking stupidity your blindness grants you. You have superiority complexes that border megalomania and yet display ignorance equal to the humans you look down upon."

Lailah brandished her sword, her face was contorted with rage and blood lust filled her eyes. Any trace of the apparent beauty Chloe had seen on their arrival had vanished, and as she raised the blade high above her head, it shone bright and golden as though imbued by the touch of God.

"YOU SHALL NOT SPEAK ILL OF THE ALMIGHTY!"

A deep thud of flesh against bone washed over the crowd as, before Lailah was able to finish her attack, Ignis buried his fist hard into her sternum. The blow struck with such force that Lailah appeared to vanish as she was sent careening backwards through the sky at incredible speed. A shock wave that resonated from the impact spread out in all directions knocking Harut and Puriel away and sending a giant gust of wind beneath Vapula's wings.

"You really know how to make friends, don't you!" laughed Vapula as they sped through the air.

"Can you outrun them?" asked Amos.

"Outrun an angel?" mused Vapula. "Not a chance, but I might be able to outmanoeuvre them."

"I guess we'll find out," said Ignis watching their flanks.

The shrill whistle of arrows in flight returned and with no time to think, Ignis commanded Vapula to dive. Vapula gave a great heaving sweep of his wings, folded them tight to his body and tilted to plummet. He acted too slowly, and Ignis was forced to parry and deflect a barrage of arrows which, without his intervention, would have have turned Amos' back into a pin cushion.

The group bombed through the air, swerving and darting between Boeing 747s, prehistoric birds, flaming meteors and World War Two anti-aircraft shells. As Puriel attempted to give chase, Ignis shot his own barrage of firey energy balls across the sky holding him at bay.

Harut was the first to catch up with them. He came at them from their blind spot, striking Vapula's underside with a formidable shoulder barge which narrowly missed Quentin. Vapula and his riders were sent careening across the heavens causing them to spiral out of control. Despite the injury, Vapula recovered fast but Lailah was upon them a second later and was poised to drive her sword through Vapula's skull.

Ignis scrambled around Amos and Alex and yanked Chloe out of the way just in time to kick the blade off course. A furious fight ensued inches above Vapula's head as Ignis traded blows with Lailah and defended against more arrows shot from Puriel's bow. It would have been a difficult fight at the best of times, but attempting to battle two angels on the relatively small space provided by Vapula's neck whilst simultaneously defending his companions as Vapula rolled and banked in an effort to shake them off was proving overwhelming.

Unfortunately, the situation only worsened as Harut joined Lailah in combat, quickly followed by Puriel who had stashed his bow and was now armed with two daggers.

It was an epic contest that, regardless of fear of falling and dying, the others couldn't help watching even though the combatants moved so fast their actions were almost impossible to see. The fight seemed evenly matched with all three angels unable to score a hit on Ignis, while Ignis with his hands full was unable to land a decent blow on any of them. That was until Lailah lunged with her sword which Ignis seized with his hands only to have Harut swipe at his neck with his own blade. Ignis bent over backwards to avoid the blow but saw Amos in the line of attack. He released one hand from Lailah's sword and grabbed the edge of Harut's scimitar which saved Amos from having his head severed from his neck, but came at the cost of a deep gash against his palm. Lailah capitalised on this moment of weakness and pushed with all her might against the hilt of her weapon which sliced deep into Ignis' other hand and pierced his gut.

Puriel, believing Ignis bested, launched a flurry of strikes with his daggers that shone brightly against the light of his wings. But Ignis fought him off with Harut's blade, having wrenched it from his grasp, and with a mighty roar released a giant arc of fire from his chest, a solar flare which blasted the angels back, liquefying their weapons in the process which then fell apart in the wind and scattered like metal droplets of rain.

The angels fell behind, blinded by the flame and encumbered by singed wings. Ignis knew he only had a minute at the most before they regrouped and continued their assault. He squeezed out the molten metal from his stomach wound which cauterised itself and turned to face Amos over the heads of Chloe and Alex who looked pale and mortified.

"Amos, I need you to man up mate," said Ignis trying to sound cheery despite the pain. "If I fight them again like this, some, if not all of us will die."

"What's the problem?" asked Vapula nervously.

"Too many targets to defend and not enough space to do it on," Ignis replied simply.

"I hope you're not thinking what I think you're thinking!" snapped Amos outraged.

"Considering that you normally know what I'm thinking a good half an hour before I've thought it, I reckon that's exactly what I'm thinking," sniggered Ignis, touched by Amos' disapproval.

"But you could be lost forever," said Amos, his voice thick with concern. "How would you even get back?"

"What on earth are you two talking about?" demanded Vapula who did not like being made to feel ignorant.

"Ignis is going to separate from us in an effort to draw the angels' attention allowing us to escape and get back to our intended time and space," said Amos emotionlessly, as though saying the words out loud had drained him of fight.

"You fool!" growled Vapula. "You leave my influence and you could wind up sharing your home with dinosaurs."

"I always wanted a T-Rex," chuckled Ignis weakly, but noticing the arguments beginning to form on three concerned faces, he steeled his determination. "There isn't any choice, none of you can fight them and I can't battle freely if I'm worrying about you lot. What I need is a way back and I need it now."

Vapula and Amos worked their brains hard, they were after all the most knowledgeable and most likely to come up with an answer. Panic, however, had made rational thought impossible and neither could offer suggestion.

Like someone who had ran out of patience while waiting for a child to add two and two together, Chloe let out a massive audible sigh and blurted out, "Take a piece of Vapula."

She spoke as though it had been the most obvious thing in the world and yet, no one really seemed any the wiser.

"A piece of me?" asked Vapula who did not like the sound of this one bit. "What would that achieve?"

"Your influence is not a manifestation of will, it's physical!" explained Chloe with exasperation. "If a part of your body is held by Ignis he can stay in temporal flux for as long as he needs to."

"That is inspired," said Amos in astonishment. "I don't know why I didn't think of it myself."

"And exactly what do you intend to take?" barked Vapula angrily. "You think I'm just going to let you start hacking off limbs to give... AAHHH!"

Vapula's argument was cut short by Ignis who had back flipped over the lion's head, grabbed hold of his mane and sunk his knee into Vapula's jaw dislodging a tooth which Ignis caught and pocketed.

"Damn it!" wailed Vapula in pain. "A warning would be nice, asking for my permission even better!"

"What, and listen to you whine for ten minutes? Don't have enough time to be polite I'm afraid," replied Ignis seriously, though it couldn't have been more obvious he was trying not to smile. "Chloe, how do I use the tooth to get back?"

"Get back to the ground, move to where you want to be and wait… preferably near something that can give you an idea of the date and time," said Chloe knowledgeably. "When the wave containing the time frame you want to be in passes over you, throw the tooth at least five metres away from you. This will clear you of Vapula's influence and drop you out of forth dimensional space and into our own."

"You…" began Ignis kissing Chloe on the forehead. "…are epic!"

Chloe blushed and swelled with pride while Amos sulked jokily. "How come you never kiss me?"

"It's that tash, dude!" chuckled Ignis. "Gives me a rash."

The brief moment of hilarity was brought to an abrupt end when another of Puriel's arrows streaked past.

"Here we go again. Wish me luck," said Ignis winking at Amos. "Vapula, you in the mood to throw me at a bunch of angry angels?"

"Always!" snarled Vapula in response as he came an abrupt stop which toppled Ignis off his neck.

As Ignis free fell, Vapula dived through air after him, eventually overtaking. Ignis grabbed hold of Vapula's back legs and felt his speed increase dramatically as Vapula levelled off and came about to face the angels head on.

With a dramatic burst of speed, both Vapula and the angels rushed at each other, Vapula with his teeth bared and Ignis in tow, the angels with their blades poised. For a moment it looked as though they would collide, but Vapula pulled to the side sharply and heaved his back legs around. Ignis felt his speed double and he released his grip leaving the group behind and slammed into three very surprised angels. A cloud of fists, metal, blood and feathers erupted from the epicentre of the collision and as he looked on Amos smiled proudly. When unencumbered and free to fight without restraint, Ignis was truly unbeatable which the angels were now discovering at their cost. Lailah and Harut retreated to recover from their sudden and severe injuries leaving Puriel unprotected and to fight Ignis alone. Ignis took out a good deal of his frustration upon the angel's once handsome features, he was angry and full of indignation. He was annoyed by their arrogance, irritated by their cowardice, livid at being run through by Lailah's sword and every meaty punch filled him with satisfaction.

Before long, Puriel was hanging limp and lifeless in the air, suspended only by the wind caught in his wings. Ignis stood with his feet in Puriel's gut and braced by a fistful of the angel's robes, he looked around for the others. They were some thirty feet above him and were horror struck at the damage this small boy had inflicted upon their leader. As he gazed up at them, Ignis spotted Vapula disappear into the distance, they were safe now, they had time to return home. Slowly the angels sank through the sky to Ignis' level and cautiously floated closer. They looked at Puriel's mis-shapened face in wonder, it was obvious that they had not seen such carnage wrought upon an angel since their war with Lucifer and it filled them with fear and dread.

"Go home!" said Ignis. "Save yourself and spread the word."

"And what word would you have us give voice to?" asked Lailah nervously.

"You will explain the consequences of interfering with the Conclave of Magikal Thought."

"Which is?" demanded Harut impatiently.

Ignis suddenly leapt into the air above Puriel as a brilliant and unexpected white flash filled the world as a giant bolt of lightning cut the air with a tremendous bang. It channelled its way from Ignis, through Harut and arched towards the earth. Unlike a regular lightning bolt, it continued to stream filling Harut with more energy than he could take. The angel screamed loudly as his body burst into flames before a final surge of plasma sent by Ignis caused his charred frame to explode.

"Death!" said Ignis simply but menacingly as he landed back on Puriel and swept burnt bits of flesh and feathers off his hair and clothes.

"Y... y... you said we could leave!" stammered Lailah, panic stricken.

"Nooo, I said 'you' could leave. I wasn't talking to the other guy!" replied Ignis scathingly. "I'd jog on now, if I were you, before you say something stupid and I change my mind."

With a last look at the scattering chunks of smouldering body parts falling to the ground, Lailah expanded her wings and with a forceful flap and a flash of golden sunlight, she was gone.

"Just you and me now mate and I reckon it's time to wake up," said Ignis, looking at Puriel's unconscious face. He clambered up onto the angel's shoulders and grabbed hold of the root of his wings. Puriel stirred and Ignis leaned close to whisper in his ear.

"Do you remember when angels didn't have wings?" asked Ignis almost conversationally.

"Wh...ahhh... what are you talking about?" mumbled Puriel through the pain of talking with a broken jaw.

"Your wings. You didn't use to have them!" continued Ignis brightly.

"You're a blithering idiot who knows nothing. We have always had wings, it is how he made us," replied Puriel with as much spite as he could muster.

"You are a dense bunch, aren't you?" said Ignis rhetorically. "You were made this way, but not by your God mate. In fact, if I remember correctly you didn't turn into birds until about four hundred years after Jesus died."

Ignis pulled the angel's head back to look into his eyes, they were tired and vacant. "You really don't remember what it was like...?" asked Ignis with a false pout. "Well let me remind you!"

Puriel's expression turned from exhausted and broken to wildly panicked and frightened and he frantically looked over his shoulders trying to see what the boy was up to.

Puriel wailed in agony as Ignis, still with a firm grip on the roots of the angel's wings, put his feet against Puriel's back and pulled hard. The flesh between his back and the humerus of his wings began to split as the skin overstretched. Puriel's cry was momentarily silenced by the loud crunch of bones being separated and for a moment he seemed too shocked to process the new sensation. With one final heave accompanied by an ear-splitting tortured scream, Ignis tore the wings off Puriel's back completely and cast them aside to let them drift uselessly away through the air.

Both bodies began to fall to earth, slowly at first but it wasn't long before they reached terminal velocity. Not content with the damage he had already inflicted on Puriel, Ignis guided his body to the tumbling unconscious wreck that was the angel and grabbed a scruff of his hair. Angling the limp body so it was falling chest first, Ignis moved to the angel's back and turned to face the sky. Holding his arms out wide, Ignis roared as he burst into flames, every inch of him covered with a raging inferno. With a satisfied smile, Ignis whispered, "Here comes the boom!", as he lurched his arms forward. The raging fire seemed to be sucked from his body and into his arms and exploded out of his hands in a long stream of blazing heat. The force of the jet accelerated Ignis hard into Puriel's back, who in turn, was carried along for the ride.

They hurtled toward the earth at blistering speeds leaving a giant trail of fire behind them, and unfortunately for Puriel, he regained consciousness just in time to see the ground, distorted by waves of time, rushing closer. Somewhere in Scotland a little over a billion years ago, there appeared a flash of light in the sky. In that instant a colossal pillar of smoke and flame appeared connecting heaven and earth and with it an explosion that tore through the lands destroying everything in its wake. The explosion could be seen for miles around, yet this momentous impact was witnessed by minds no more complex than a handful of eukaryotes.

As Puriel had met the earth, he had also met his demise and as such had been thrown out of temporal flux landing 1.2 billion years in the past. The energy of Ignis' attack had been transferred into that time frame and had exploded with the force of twenty kilo tonnes of TNT. Puriel was vaporised in the blast, and as Ignis lay in the epicentre, exhausted and bruised with time washing over him while people, animals and buildings came and went above him, he mused how easily he could have been destroyed along with the angel had time not continued to move leaving the damage behind. But then Ignis was, like his brothers and sister, remarkably intelligent and had already known that he would not be caught in his own attack. As he withdrew Vapula's tooth from his pocket he laughed and marvelled at his own brilliance before getting unsteadily to his feet, patting off the dust and setting his mind to purpose.

Ignis surveyed his surroundings and felt overwhelmed at the sight of forever changing time around him, at ground level the sheer scope of his predicament seemed to swallow him.

"Anyone know where I can find the twenty-first century?" he asked lamely.

Chapter Eleven
Know Thy Enemy

Without their pursuers, Vapula and the others made it to the location of the Qin Zhu Institute in good time. As an expert in fourth dimensional travel, Vapula had no difficulty in selecting the correct period from the swirling mass, and with a wobble and a pop the group emerged safely back in their own space and time unscathed.

"Thank you, Vapula," said Amos with a tremulous voice as he dismounted the giant lion and recovered Quentin from the demon's front paws.

"Yeah, thanks," agreed Chloe who was much more cheerful in disposition as she slid off Vapula's neck and gave him a massive hug.

Amos saw an awkwardness fall upon the lion's face and felt sure Vapula was blushing beneath his fur.

"Miss, miss, we're OK now, you can come down!" said Chloe releasing Vapula and proceeding to prod Alex repeatedly in the leg.

Alex looked very care worn as she slid off Vapula's shoulders and landed in a heap on the floor, hugging the ground as though it were a long-lost friend.

"No offence, Mr Vapula…" began Alex rolling onto her back and glaring up at the sky. "…but I never want to do that again."

"Miss Sterling makes a good point," interjected Amos. "I have had smoother journeys."

Vapula looked at Amos with concern. "My friend, I feel I must point something out to you that has troubled me since our encounter."

Amos moved closer to allow Vapula to speak in hushed tones.

"I have travelled between the realms, dimensions and time for longer than I can remember and I have never been accosted or ambushed in such a manner as today… it just doesn't happen."

"Well, it stands to reason that eventually even with the size of…"

"This was not a coincidence!" interrupted Vapula brusquely. "Didn't you hear them? They said they had been warned of our presence and had come to remove us. They were ordered to hunt us... or more likely hunt you and yours."

"Well, that's preposterous," blustered Amos. "Angels cannot be ordered by anyone except..." Amos trailed off to a stunned silence, unable to voice the rest of his sentence.

"Precisely," said Vapula. "You, the boy or anyone of these..." the demon gestured to Chloe, Alex and Quentin, "...have been marked for execution, that's my guess anyway. If that's true you have a powerful enemy after you."

"Well I can hardly say I'm surprised, we do step on an awful lot of toes in our business. It seems there may be weight to Bushyasta's words after all."

"Bushyasta!" growled Vapula in disgusted tones. "You have broke words with that abomination?"

"No, not I," said Amos reassuringly. "Aarde spoke with her and her companions at length before he and Hoowo3oow parted their heads from their bodies. Before their timely demise, however, reference to an approaching war was made."

"A war?" repeated Vapula who, to Amos' surprise, appeared just as confused as he did.

"You've not heard anything then, no? Well apparently, the demon world is gearing up for an invasion. We assumed on the back of our intel that the Gods were just standing idle, allowing it to happen and seeing who comes out on top. But if they are taking an active role... well, that's much more serious!"

"I will trawl the underworld and see what I can find out about this war," said Vapula defiantly. "I'll get back to you if I learn anything."

"That is appreciated," said Amos weakly. "I fear a difficult time lies ahead of us and we will need all the friends we can get."

A solemn nod of understanding passed between Amos and Vapula before the giant demon took to the skies again and vanished.

"Right!" said Amos clapping his hands together and rubbing them briskly. "It is bang on nine o'clock, Chloe I know I need to induct you but

I think our first point of business is trying to fix Quentin here, do you agree?"

Chloe thought about it for a second, her reluctance was obvious, but she nodded her agreement all the same.

"Marvellous. Miss Sterling if you are not too ill could you help me hoist him inside and we can get him over to R&D. If Chloe can't fix him maybe Rich can offer an alternative solution."

Together, Amos and Alex grabbed a limb and carried Quentin inside the grand building. It shocked Alex to note, that despite the fact they were carrying a young teenage boy, who superficially looked quite dead, no one seemed surprised or bothered by it, as if this was normal. As soon as they had entered the lobby, Gyasi came bungling over calling Amos' name.

"Good, you're back!" panted Gyasi. "You need to come quickly!"

"What's happened? Is someone hurt? Is it Ignis?" replied Amos hurriedly, eager for answers to the cause of alarm.

"No, we are all fine but there is something you need to see! Please come quickly!" implored Gyasi.

"Have Rich from R&D come and escort my guests to a spare lab," called Amos across the room to an old lady sat at the reception counter. Amos then turned to Chloe. "Go with Miss Sterling and get comfortable, I will join you shortly once I have been brought up to speed."

Chloe and Alex smiled and nodded their assent leaving Amos free to follow after Gyasi back to the Conclave headquarters.

All the way down in the elevator Gyasi was unusually quiet and anxious. He barely looked at Amos, fidgeted incessantly and when the doors opened to the living room, he bolted out so quickly you would have thought him a man desperate for air.

Everyone except Ignis was present in the room, a sight which jarred Amos a little as he thought back to where they had left his friend. As Amos stepped forward all eyes turned to look at him and their expressions were very grave.

"Anyone care to fill me in?" enquired Amos, a little agitated now by the lack of information.

The holographic head of a very disgruntled, tired-looking Frank was the one who volunteered an answer.

"There has been another significant attack."

"Murder you mean!" corrected Hoowo3oow with a growl.

"Don't start!" snapped Frank. "I'm tired, stressed and really stoned. I'm in no mood for semantic bullshit."

Hoowo3oow said nothing but nodded his apology. Amos thought that for Hoowo3oow to apologise the situation must be serious indeed.

"Twenty minutes ago, the self-proclaimed high-priest of the 'Church of Cosmic Rebirth', was murdered in what appears to be a pseudo sacrificial manner," said Frank.

"Church of Cosmic Rebirth?" asked Amos, puzzled.

"A New Age cult, based in middle America," explained Aarde. "It has quite a large following too, especially considering its radical ideology."

"I'm probably going to regret asking but…?" said Amos, trailing off at the end and simply shrugging.

"They all worship this dumb ass who got himself murdered," interjected Shui who did not seem at all sorry for the man. "He used the principles of Panpsychism to convince his flock that his mind had created the universe."

"My word, that's a bold claim," chortled Amos. "And the rest of us are what, figments of his imagination?"

"His creations actually," scoffed Frank. "All the flora and fauna in the world, the world itself and the universe in which it sits were apparently given life during a dream."

"Yeah, and get this!" said Shui, mockingly. "He had his followers believe that upon his death he would become as one with the universe proper and in doing so the energy released from his corpse would unlock a gateway into another dimension where all who believe in him would be granted bodies of light and live forever in the true universe."

"Please, tell me you're joking!" said Amos incredulously.

"Not a joke and like I said there was a huge following, all true believers," added Aarde. "So you can guess what happened next!"

Amos removed his glasses and cleaned them on his hankie, pausing a second to rub the bridge of his nose with his fingers before replacing them. "A doorway opened and took the faithful to another dimension?"

"It's like you were there," grumbled Frank sarcastically.

"So what? The killer wanted to speed up his ascent and off'd the high-priest, case closed. Well at least the exposure risk is reduced. Anyone with him would have probably been devout and…" Amos snapped his fingers together, "…gone."

"It's actually a tad more complicated than that," groaned Frank convulsively rubbing his temples again.

"How so?" asked Amos.

"The high-priest was trying his hand at televangelism at the time of the murder. The whole thing was broadcast live on the *Religion for You* channel," sighed Frank. "It's been a media frenzy, every major broadcast network in the western hemisphere have been reporting on it, the damn thing's even on YouTube, 45,000 hits and rising."

Amos said nothing for a moment, he just clapped his hands to his cheeks and dragged them off again pulling his face into a gaunt expression. "Well…" began Amos, smoothing back his hair and cracking his neck, "…unless this brings credibility to the, er, the… what was it called again?"

"Church of Cosmic Rebirth!" chuckled Elsu through a lung full of smoke.

"Yes, them!" said Amos excitedly. "Anyone devout has vanished and is most unlikely to return, let's make sure this woefully self-indulgent twaddle disappears with them. Have we been able to get any units in position to tweak the facts?"

"Of course," said Frank defensively. "Do I look like a newb? We have successfully attributed the bright lights of inter dimensional travel to an explosion, a terror attack by an anti-Church of Cosmic Rebirth movement. The line is that everyone was obliterated by the force of the blast, we have of course made the place look proportionally damaged enough for the story to seem believable."

"I say again then, case closed," repeated Amos.

"And I say again, more, bloody, complicated!" retorted Frank perhaps more sharply than he had intended. He sighed apologetically. "Sorry, I didn't mean to snap. Please just sit and watch the video, it will be easier to see the problem afterwards."

Amos sat himself at the large circular table in front of a monitor that had been lowered from the ceiling. Frank made a few sweeping movements with his hands and a second later a standard definition video popped up on screen.

On the video could be seen a congregation of some two hundred plus people sat in a large theatre-style room. From the decor, and the view from the windows, Amos deduced this was a country house, probably purchased for use by the movement as a place to worship.

The camera view panned to see the whole stage. Upon it were five individuals, four men and one woman. All but one, were seated in comfortable leather chairs and were silently gazing up at the man who had remained standing. He was dressed in what could only be described as a Victorian nightgown which was festooned with beads, flower chains and a thick black stole which had been embroidered quite badly with nonsensical symbols and patterns. He stood at a lectern which held a loose gathering of papers, and was in the throws of preaching with fire and vigour, occasionally gesticulating violently at the camera.

"…and my sons and daughters I say this unto you. Join us, believe in me and find happiness on the dawn of rebirth. Stop fighting against what I have created, return to me, become one with me again and rejoice as my death gives life to all who believe in me, a harmonious rebirth in the sixth dimension. Just as I am your father, I will become your mother, this world is my womb and I will push you forth into the true universe and nourish you with my energy like milk from maternal breasts. And as we return to our home, we will shed our flesh and live forever with bodies made from my holy light, our sins and desires swept away as we allow truth and knowledge to spread throughout… through… what in tarnation…?"

The high-priest had broken away from his sermon, distracted by what appeared to be a simultaneous epileptic fit experienced by those seated on stage. The high-priest moved quickly to support the female as all four of them slid from their soft seats to the stage floor, convulsing wildly. The man supported the woman's head with one hand and with the other waved down the sounds of concern from the assembled masses.

"Don't be concerned my children, these are my most devoted followers and they are obviously affected by the power my presence brings. They are more in tune with the vibrations of the sixth dimension and have been preparing to leave their mortal frames."

223

Surprisingly, the congregation not only seemed to readily accept this explanation without question, but they seemed happy for the four on stage as they started their journey, but whom, in Amos' mind, really ought to be receiving medical attention.

Eventually the fitting stopped and the people on stage fell limp and without pause to check that all were still breathing let alone thought for placing them in a recovery position, the high-priest returned to his lectern, and fixing his gaze back onto the camera, continued preaching. "Come sons and daughters, come and feel my power…"

Amos tuned out the rest of what the man was saying, he was repulsed by the arrogance of it all, but it wasn't this that made him stop listening. The four individuals on stage had begun to stir and Amos had noticed a faint trickle of black liquid oozing from their mouths and ears. There was a mild, almost jealous applause from the crowd as the devotees got to their feet, seemingly unharmed if not a little unsteady. But the false smiles and half-hearted clapping quickly turned to gasps of horror and punctuated intakes of breath as all four lurched forward and seized the high-priest.

"Hey, go steady now," said the high-priest initially mistaking the movement as a need for stability rather than a desire to restrain. He soon grew wise to the truth of the matter, as their grips tightened upon his arms and neck and his head was wrenched back by a scruff of his ever-thinning hair.

"Unhand me!" demanded the high-priest. "How dare you… Waahh!"

The man broke off and cowered in fear whilst frantically searching the ceiling for who knew what. His devotees pulled him upright again and held him ever tighter. "Listen." crooned the woman in his ear.

The high-priest flinched wildly and clasped his hands to his ears.

"WHO ARE YOU?" he screamed manically as tears rolled down his cheeks. "SH… SHOW YOURSELF!"

A minute or maybe two passed by in almost complete silence and the high-priest seemed to be listening intently to a voice no one else could hear. "I'm sorry, please, I didn't mean to cause any harm, please just let me go!" he pleaded.

The crowd had now got to their feet and were uncertain as to whether they should leave or not.

"STAY WHERE YOU ARE!" demanded one of the men on stage, spitting black gloop as he spoke which hissed as it hit the wooden floor, burning into the boards.

"Please don't... I don't want to die... I never meant..." continued the high-priest between thick, heaving sobs before flinching again as the voice no one else could hear seemed to shout him down.

More silence followed, accentuated by the high-priest's weeping which echoed around the room. He occasionally shook his head, perhaps in mute argument to whatever he was hearing, but for the most part he just stood there, trembling and whimpering.

As though acting on instruction, the high-priest's companions moved in unison to pull their prisoner's arms open wide and tore off his gown revealing an aged, rotund body that was scattered with patches of curly grey hair.

The high-priest yelled in protest and fought vigorously to free himself from their grip, but it was all to no avail.

"NOOOOO!" screamed the high-priest one last time before his voice was lost in a torrent of blood that gushed up from his throat. His body had lurched forward a little as if he had been struck in the back, but it was his chest and stomach that bore signs of damage. A fine scarlet spray ejected from neat cuts in his torso spattering the audience and for nearly a whole minute it rained blood. As the old preacher gagged and slowly drowned on his own vital fluid, the men and the woman who had been restraining him, held him aloft supported by his arms and he hung there as though crucified.

Amos waited with bated breath, for although the death had been uncomfortable to watch, he knew what was coming next and he would not miss seeing such a rare spectacle.

It was almost instantaneous. The neat little gashes on the high-priest's chest glowed and light erupted from every open orifice giving him the brief appearance of one who had swallowed a flare. Half a second later all was bright white as what seemed to be an explosion dominated the scene. Disappointingly, Amos was not able to see what happened next as a shard of wood from the destroyed lectern, careened across the room and embedded itself in the camera lens, ending the transmission.

Amos, speechless and a little deflated, looked up from the screen and stared intently at Frank.

"Like I said," said Frank, "complicated."

"The preacher's colleagues!" began Amos thoughtfully. "Demon possession maybe?"

"Probably," replied Frank. "The drop seizure is certainly symptomatic of a head invasion."

"Any idea what actually killed him?" asked Amos, stroking his moustache thoughtfully.

"Not exactly," replied Frank. "But I do have a good idea about who killed him."

Amos' eyes widened and he motioned for Frank to continue.

"Do you remember how I said it had even made it to YouTube?" asked Frank, swiping the air again. "Well, some clever little bugger has done the work for us, look."

The screen that Amos had used to watch the recording of the high-priest's demise switched to a web page which already had YouTube loaded and a video pre-buffered. The video played a loop of the time when the priest received the killing blow. On occasion, text bubbles and marks appeared on the video overlay showing the editor's thoughts and conspiratorial views. Apparently 'Plumbthumb6759' didn't think an anti-panpsychic sect was responsible for this murder any more than Amos did. Overall, the video and associated commentary was all very vague and speculation heavy and Amos was failing to see the relevance, that was until Plumbthumb6759 drew his viewer's attention to a single frame frozen at 1.34 on the timeline. Amos dived forward and grabbed the edges of the screen trying to drag it closer. He could not believe what he was seeing. Frozen at the moment the high-priest received a blow to the back and captured in surprising detail was a truth no one could deny or ignore. Without the blood covering his chest, the neat little cuts on the preacher's torso could be seen in exquisite detail, and to Amos' utter dismay, revealed themselves to be the same collection of religious iconography, they had seen weaved into the spider's web back in France. Furthermore, the same frozen frame had caught a glimpse of the killer, a distinct and separate individual who had not been seen anywhere else in the video. Whoever it was, they were the size of a child, dressed in a black hooded cloak and were moving extremely fast. Yet, despite the blurriness of the figure, Plumbthumb6759 had spotted exactly what Amos had seen and this above all filled him with dread like nothing else had. An eye clearly visible in the shadow of the hood, a pure white eye, with neither pupil nor iris, proof that the worst had finally happened.

"Ooh, I think I preferred blunt minded arrogance," mumbled Amos queasily.

Shui thought Amos was going to be sick and moved quickly to get a bucket.

"Thank you, Shui, but I'm fine. I enjoyed my breakfast too much to part with it now," said Amos forcing a smile onto his obviously worried features. "You can do something else for me though, if you don't mind?"

"Sure thing, what do you need?" asked Shui.

"Can you go over to R&D? I left Alex and Chloe there along with a rather broken young man who Chloe needs to try and fix. If you could help her get started, perhaps give her some tips on focusing her mind… oh and you will need to unfreeze the meridian points that Ignis had applied."

Shui gave a nod and left the room via the lift, while Amos turned his attention back to Frank. Both men seemed suddenly older and more care worn, as though the last ten minutes had aged them ten years.

"You know Frank, it's been a long time since I felt out of my depth," sighed Amos weakly.

"I know what you mean old friend," replied Frank with equal trepidation.

"Did the auxiliaries at least manage to pick up Mr Godfrey?" asked Amos.

"I'm afraid not," groaned Frank. "A unit has been camped at his place of residence all night but he hasn't been back."

Amos took a moment to pause for thought, once again cleaning his glasses and replacing them before speaking.

"I don't… I don't suppose you have been in contact with Ignis?" asked Amos who already knew the answer before he had finished the question.

"No, in fact I was going to ask you about that. Why isn't he with you?" replied Frank.

Amos explained the morning's events and how Ignis had separated from them to allow their escape. He even told Frank about Vapula's concerns and how he would scour the underworld for more information.

"Angels? Hells bells Amos you could have said something earlier," said Frank. Amos simply returned him a look of incredulity.

"Fighting with angels," said Hoowo3oow unexpectedly. "Ignis really does get to have all the fun doesn't he."

"Too right," chuckled Aarde. "Well, I'm telling you now, we are calling dibs on this assassin!"

"Yes, it will be an epic contest," agreed Hoowo3oow smiling. "I must take a trophy when we win."

"What like his hood?" asked Gyasi.

"I was thinking his eyes!" replied Hoowo3oow with such sincerity it bordered on being sinister.

"Wade, do you want to weigh in on this?" asked Frank.

Wade looked mortified as all eyes turned to him expectantly. "Wh… what? You can't be serious…" began Wade looking wildly from face to face. "…I am a thinker not a fighter, that kid would tear me limb from bloody limb."

Frank chuckled and slapped his hand to his forehead. "No, you prat! I mean what are your thoughts on all of this. Is it safe to assume that this assassin we see here," Frank gestured to the YouTube video again. "Is the same culprit that murdered the departed Professor Braskin?"

Wade collapsed into his chair with obvious relief. "Oh, that, of course. Well yes, I have already run all the measurements taken at this scene and compared them to those I extrapolated for the attackers at the wreckage in France. My conclusion is that either it is the same killer or…" Wade hesitated a moment, whatever his next words were, they seemed to have left a bad taste in his mouth.

"Don't leave us hanging Wade!" demanded Frank. "C'mon, out with it. Or what?"

"Or there is yet another one of these assassins running around!" Wade finished quickly.

"Peachy!" said Elsu with sarcasm that didn't disguise his unease.

"That's enough!" said Frank sharply as the group began to erupt into fierce muttering at Wade's pronouncement. "We have work to do and bugger all time in which to get it done."

The attention given was absolute, everyone was in a mood to do something, whether it be research or simply beating something bad to death.

"OK men… and woman," began Frank adding the last part hastily as he caught Wun Chuan's disgruntled glare. "I will keep this brief. Wun Chuan, Gyasi, Elsu, I need you out and about hitting the underground, whoever this kid is he belongs to someone. Take Hoowo3oow with you, use whatever force necessary to get people talking and don't come back till you have something for me. Aarde, you and Shui need to support the auxiliary in the field, the barriers between realms do not seem to be healing and the bleed into reality is becoming more severe, more than our units can handle. No captures, it's search and destroy until events decrease. Wade, I need you man, I need you to focus, I need to know why our victims are being targeted, anything that connects them together. You are to do nothing but solve that question. If I see you so much as take a shit without giving me an answer first, I will have your grandmother sacrificed to Quetzalcoatl."

"Quetzalcoatl, demanded a sacrifice of butterflies, not people," mumbled Wade disconcertedly.

"Wade, I will eat your face!" yelled Frank. "You all know what to do, so go do it!"

Frank turned to Amos. "For now, continue with Chloe and Miss Sterling. I am still unnerved by that child and won't be happy until I know that her abilities are under her control."

Amos gave a weak smile and made to stand but Frank held his hand aloft, signalling for Amos to pause a moment. "Ignis… is perhaps the most able man I have ever met, he will be back, of this I have no doubt. The fact we haven't seen him yet probably means he dropped out of time a little ahead of where we are now."

"I'm sure you are right," sighed Amos. "I just don't know what I would do without him. I know it sounds silly considering his age, but he's like a son and he is my best friend."

"And you will worry no matter what I say," chuckled Frank.

Amos simply smiled and nodded. Suddenly both men started as a loud siren blared out from above.

"What is it?" asked Amos anxiously.

"Someone has activated the spiritual containment system, the building has gone into lockdown."

"Frank, what's the deal dude?" yelled Elsu who was stood by the elevator with the rest of the group who were all covering their ears.

Frank ignored him. He was deep in concentration, desperately trying to discover the source of the alarm. "Got it," said Frank. "The alarm was activated in R&D and… Oh shit, it's Shui!"

"Chloe!" gasped Amos getting to his feet. "Clear the lift," he demanded as he sprinted across the room to the elevator door with Aarde and Hoowo3oow hot on his heels.

Chapter Twelve
The Sleeping Giant

Amos and his companions arrived at the R&D department two minutes later, the siren still ringing loudly overhead and as the elevator doors slid open, they were greeted with abject chaos. The scene that lay before them was similar to the set of a horror movie, except the panic and the gore was very real. People were scuttling back and forth across the room, some trying to clear space and be helpful while others stood stationary whittling to themselves, else trying to flee to the toilets before they vomited all over the place.

The walls were sprayed with blood and what appeared to be bits of brain and pieces of skull and the same was true for many of the staff.

"What the f…" breathed Aarde trying to make sense of what they were seeing.

"About damn time!" yelled a familiar voice from amidst the crowd. "Get over here now!"

Amos, Aarde and Hoowo3oow jostled their way through the swell of people and found Shui. She was deep in concentration and controlling a stream of red liquid that seemed to be trickling in an arc through the air.

"Shui, what's going on?" began Amos at once. "Is that blood? Who…?"

Amos' last question stuck in his throat as his eyes, following the stream of floating blood, found the source of the commotion.

The body of a young man lay on the floor before him. It was drenched with blood and was quite distinctly missing its head. Shui was catching the blood as it ejected from the carotid and cerebral arteries in the neck and was then forcing it back inside the jugular as though attempting to prevent the body dying from blood loss. Kneeling beside the male, panting with exhaustion and looking decidedly ill, was Rich who was busy performing chest compressions to keep the heart pumping.

"Where is Chloe?" demanded Amos.

"Oh, I'm fine by the way," replied Shui sharply. With an impatient sigh Shui nodded in Chloe's direction. "She's over there."

Amos looked over and spotted her just a few metres away. She was perched on a stool and covered from head to toe in blood, brain matter and what appeared to be a bit of face. She was taking short rapid breaths and was wide eyed with fright, evidently suffering with shock.

Amos made to go over to her to check if she was all right, but Shui impeded the motion. "She will live!" barked Shui angrily. "This one won't, if we don't get him sorted soon."

Although Amos wasn't happy to deny Chloe care, he knew Shui was correct, this was obviously much more important. "Let me take over for a moment Rich, you look like you are going to collapse yourself."

Grateful to be relieved, Rich moved out of the way, slumped against a desk and rolled up a cigarette. He had just placed the tip in his mouth and withdrew his lighter when a shimmering silver whisp screamed past him, closely followed by thirteen giggling teenage girls who were in hot pursuit. They clambered over Rich, barely giving thought to the fact he was there at all. By the time they had all moved on, Rich was looking very bedraggled and his cigarette hung limply from his lip, broken in two.

"I don't get paid enough," he sighed.

"What are they chasing?" enquired a breathless Amos, who had turned his head to observe the calamity behind him as he continued to pump the boy's chest.

"It's the boy's soul!" informed Shui as she continued to control the flow of blood with motions akin to someone leisurely engaging in Tai Qi.

"With the building on lockdown the soul is trapped here," offered Rich. "But damn, that shit's harder to catch than a baseball pitched at light speed."

"Hoowo3oow, can you help keep the body oxygenated? We need to minimise the overall damage."

"Minimise the damage!" scoffed Aarde as Hoowo3oow began pushing air down the throat with movements similar to Shui. "He's got no head left!"

"Then why don't you build him a new one!" retorted Shui. "C'mon, oh master of molecules, put him back together."

"With what, most of what was once his noggin is scattered around the room!" replied Aarde incredulously.

"Is there nothing you can do?" pleaded Amos.

"Sorry Amos, but there isn't enough matter left for me to work with," sighed Aarde grimly.

Amos' mind began racing. This was unacceptable. How could he tell the Farrowfields that their son, who Alex had assured them was in good health, was now dead because his head had exploded. No, this would not do at all, there must be a solution. He cajoled his brain into action in an effort to think if any of the vast resources the Conclave had at their disposal could make a difference, but nothing he could think of could replace a head. He had just naysaid demon intervention when it hit him, the perfect solution and it was even in the building just a few floors away.

"Of course," said Amos excitedly. "I'm so stupid, I should have thought of it sooner."

Amos turned to Aarde. "Pick him up and follow me, Shui. Hoowo3oow, stay close and keep, er, doing what... well, whatever it is your doing."

With a grimace Aarde heaved the blood-soaked corpse onto his shoulder and together the four of them headed back to the lift.

"Get that soul under control," Amos yelled behind him. "Oh, and Rich, can you take Chloe to Mother Westa for a shower and some hot chocolate?"

As the doors began to close, a pair of small hands forced them back open.

"I don't want hot chocolate," said Chloe quietly as she stepped inside and let the door close behind her.

There was a momentary flash on Shui's face of an expression which Amos didn't quite recognise straight away. It was gone in an instant but Amos was sure she was impressed by Chloe's attendance, an emotion she so rarely felt.

"This thing is starting to stink," said Aarde.

"Agreed!" groaned Hoowo3oow. "Amos, which floor do you need?"

"Sub-level seven. Archives," replied Amos with a knowing smile.

There was a sharp intake of breath from everyone in the lift. The surprise of their destination could not be more apparent and as the lift descended, they were accompanied by silence, interrupted only by the sloshing arc of blood and bubbling rushes of air being circulated through Quentin's limp and lifeless body.

A few moments later the lift came to a halt and a little chime rang out signifying they had reached their desired floor. The doors opened and Aarde hurried out to escape the smell that his cargo had created. The floor crunched beneath Aarde's feet and he looked down to see a loose powder all over a white rocky floor.

As the others poured out of the lift the same gravelly crunch marked their footsteps, and together, they surveyed the room.

It wasn't the largest room in the Qin Zhu Institute by any means, but neither was it small. It was heptagonal in shape and the walls comprised of the same white rocky substance that covered the floor. Little crystals of it glistened across every surface reflecting the orange glow from the seven candelabras that stood in each corner of the room. Upon each wall face was a door, each uniquely different from the other whether by design or the material it was constructed from and each was adorned with glyphs and iconography. The ceiling tapered inwards at brief intervals like sloping steps which led to a giant hole within which, what appeared to be a view of the night sky, could be seen.

Sat directly below the starry blackness in a neat triangle were three people. They were wearing dark purple robes with hoods pulled far over their heads obscuring their faces and were each sat on a plush black satin cushion which was held off the ground by a wide wooden stool the edges of which held a few odd looking artefacts, personal possessions of some description, the use of which known only to the owner.

The three individuals were silent and staring at a glass dome sitting in the middle of their triangle which reflected the starry sky.

"I often wondered if I would in my lifetime be afforded the opportunity to greet the famous elemortals," came a soft female voice from somewhere beneath one of the hoods. "Pray tell, what fortune favours that causes you to grace us with your hallowed presence?"

"We broke our toy and now we need a new one," said Shui.

"Show some respect!" whispered Hoowo3oow angrily.

"Whatever dude!" groaned Shui. "Hallowed presence? Puuurlease, I got your hallowed presence right h…"

"Apologies for my companion," interrupted Aarde clamping his free hand over Shui's mouth.

"It's quite all right," chuckled the female voice. "People rarely ever come. After being down here for so long with only these two for company, it is a refreshing change."

Amos stepped forward a few paces, the crunch, crunch of his footsteps suddenly magnified by the increased awkwardness of the situation. "Madam, if you please, we are in quite a hurry. We must commune with the conduit before it's too late."

"This must be a very precious toy," mused the voice.

"Who are they?" whispered Chloe to Amos, but in the silence her voice carried and was loud enough to be heard by all.

"We are the Wisemen. Keepers of secrets and jailers to the wayward and lost. As our forebears did before us, we each gave a part of ourselves in payment for sight into the Akashic Hall of Records and in turn we each wear the name of the original three. I am Mizaru. My friend to the left of me is Kikazaru and to my right, Iwazaru."

Chloe let out a low 'Wow!'.

"You know of us child?" asked Mizaru softly.

Chloe nodded. "You have no eyes," she supplied without pretence.

Everyone was taken aback by this, including Iwazaru who shifted his head slightly at her pronouncement.

Mizaru dropped her hood and faced Chloe. She was a young woman, no older than twenty-five and would have been startlingly pretty, were it not for the garish damage inflicted upon her eyes. They appeared as though someone had forced an odd shaped key into her eye sockets and twisted the flesh out of shape. In that position the skin had frozen leaving only a warped keyhole behind to mark the place where an eye had been.

"You are not an elemortal, yet your voice betrays your youth. How can you possibly…"

"Errr… I hate to interrupt," began Amos, unsettled by her visage, "but we really cannot wait. Our cargo is spoiling by the second."

Mizaru smelled the air. "You brought death to our sanctum?"

"He's not actually dead yet!" ventured Shui. "His spirit is roaming the floors of R&D."

"Then you must be quick," said Mizaru as though the group had been wasting time by chatting.

Shui elbowed Aarde in his ribs as she barged passed him and gave him a look of outrage for daring to silence her. Aarde returned a sheepish look and then quickly avoided her gaze.

"The door you require is directly behind me," continued Mizaru oblivious to the incredulity of the others. "There is another door behind it. You must close the first door before the other will open."

"Is that really necessary?" asked Hoowo3oow who did not relish the thought of once again being crammed into a confined space with his friends and a smelly corpse.

"As it prevents our universe from collapsing into the one beyond the second door, I would say it is entirely necessary."

With this precarious thought in mind, the group crunched their way around the wise men to the door Mizaru had pointed out. It was a giant, heavy polished steel door that was circular in shape much like the entrance to a bank vault. There was no obvious lock or means by which to open it.

"How do we get in?" enquired Amos who was beginning to sound quite desperate.

"Just pull that lever," replied Mizaru pointing at a long bar that jutted out from the edge of the door frame.

"It's not locked?" spluttered Amos with disbelief.

"Of course not. There's nothing evil behind that door," replied Mizaru smiling. The smile quickly faded though as she pointed to the entrances to her left. "Those doors however…" Mizaru gave a shudder.

Hoowo3oow, still waving air into Quentin, grabbed the lever, wrenched the door open and stepped inside. It was at this point Iwazaru raised his hand, signalling for him to stop.

"Oh for… now what?" snapped Amos.

Iwazaru scooped up a handful of white crystals from the floor and scattered them over his arm.

This action was met with rather blank and confused looks from the group.

"He wants you to scatter salt on your bodies before you enter," explained Mizaru.

Without hesitation they all reached down and grabbed a handful of salt and scattered it over themselves. Everyone that is except Shui. "I don't like salt, it makes me taste like seawater!"

"You aren't being seasoned for consumption, Shui," grumbled Hoowo3oow. "Just do it!"

Shui punched the wall withdrawing a fist full of salt which she lazily threw into the air. The little crystals seemed to melt on contact with her skin and hair and Shui gave a little shudder. "That's disgusting."

"Can we go now?" barked Amos, eyeing Quentin's headless body with increasing agitation.

They bustled into the narrow gap between the doors and Aarde heaved the steel aperture closed behind them. For a second or two they stood in pitch blackness fumbling around in the dark for a way to open the second hatch. To their surprise and delight, the door made an unlocking sound and seemed to open of its own accord.

A dazzling light pierced the blackness, blinding everyone for a moment. It was almost so bright as to be painful but a shadow fell across their faces which provided temporary respite.

Blinking to clear the green blobs from their vision, the group began to make out the cause of the shadow. It was a head that was peering around the side of the door and while the face was obscured by heavy shadow, they all had the feeling they were being carefully examined.

A hand belonging to the figure that had greeted them appeared and beckoned them in as the door was swung fully open. Interestingly, the bright light that had dazzled them so thoroughly did not increase but instead vanished almost instantly and the group stepped out of the dark to a most awe-inspiring sight. A seemingly infinite space lay before them. A wide expanse scattered with clouds that hung at waist height that appeared to spread through the air like milk dropped in water. They walked on what felt like a hard white marble ground and the echoes from their footsteps hung in the ear for longer than what would be considered natural. Somewhere in the distance a large shape like a mountain sat alone, bathed in fog and ethereal light and from it, long strands of what resembled hair flowed from the highest peaks like torrents from a waterfall and stretched out into the emptiness like soft streams. The ground around the mountainous structure was rich with grass, flowers and trees which bore succulent looking fruit and they swayed in a wind that nobody could feel.

"It has been so long since we were last here," said Aarde breathing in his surroundings and exhaling a blissful sigh. "I forgot how beautiful it was."

Hoowo3oow placed a hand on Aarde's shoulder. He had no words to convey his own pleasure at being here again but the gesture was unmistakable. Aarde placed his own hand on top of Hoowo3oow's and patted it gently.

Shui turned to Chloe who was quite obviously having her mind blown as she stared up into the never-ending sky. "Do you know where we are?" asked Shui.

Chloe nodded.

"This is where you were born isn't it?"

Shui laughed. "In a manner of speaking, yes."

She observed Chloe for a moment, a deep quizzical stare mixed with bewildered amazement.

"In all my years… and there have been many…" began Shui, "…I have never met one as curious to behold as you."

"Is that a good thing?" asked Chloe tentatively. "Most people think I'm weird and they are uncomfortable around me… especially adults. I think it's because I know too much."

Shui continued to look amused but her smile softened and she took hold of Chloe's hand.

"It's not so much what you know but the bluntness with which you say it."

Chloe shied away and she looked like a child being told off. Shui understood her reaction and lifted up Chloe's chin to look at her again.

"People don't like the way I speak sometimes. I speak my mind and do so without concern for the feelings of those who hear it."

"I know," mumbled Chloe.

"Of course you do," chuckled Shui. "My point is that I have no time for the emotional baggage and insecurities most people carry with them, I have too much on my mind and so do you. I like the upfront and forthright way in which you present yourself and I will happily kill anyone who tries to change you. Whatever the reason for you being the way you are is not important, I like it and so does Amos."

"But everyone else…" began Chloe but Shui cut her off.

"Everyone else can kiss my ass."

Chloe said nothing but gave a muted giggle. Shui had said a naughty word and right now, in this moment of uncertainty and self-doubt, it was a glorious word, the best word in the world. For although it offered neither wisdom nor comfort, it transported Chloe's innocent mind to a place in the playground, where secrets are whispered out of the teacher's earshot and nobody cares that Chloe is the smartest child on the planet.

The figure who had allowed them access to this strange place floated passed Chloe and Shui, pausing for a second to get a good look at them both before darting off towards the others.

It was now that Chloe and Shui were able to get a good look at who they were. It was a young-looking woman, slender and tall with an impish face that seemed to be in a constant state of surprised amusement. She had small pointy ears and oddly enough, was not only completely naked, but was also completely devoid of hair. Not even eyebrows. More perplexingly still was the way she moved. It had appeared at first glance as though she were flying gracefully through air, but as she moved away it became quite apparent that she was swimming. Her body and legs undulated like a fish and she cut through the emptiness like it had heft and lift.

The strange female swam over to where Aarde, Hoowo3oow and Amos were stood and darted between them, an ecstatic look of fascination permanently drawn upon her face.

The woman paid special attention to the headless body of Quentin who was no longer being preserved by Hoowo3oow and Shui. She looked inside the gaping hole atop his neck, unabashedly prying the wound further open with her fingers to get a better view. After her examination was completed, she looked up at Hoowo3oow and Shui in turn and tutted whilst giving an admonitory wave of her finger. Both Shui and Hoowo3oow looked mortified. Being inside this place had proved so distracting they had completely forgotten to continue keeping Quentin's body alive. Together they lunged forward to resume their task but the female, her impish face alive with intrigue, raised her hand to order them to stop. She then tapped Aarde on the shoulder with the tip of her finger and beckoned him to follow her as she swam away toward the mountain.

The group followed the female at speed for nearly five minutes as she playfully dived and weaved through the air ahead of them. She was fast and Chloe struggled to keep up so Shui resorted to carrying the child on her back. This soon led to a race, as Amos, who was sprightly despite his age, overtook her.

Soon it became a free for all contest as, not wanting to be outdone by either their sister or an old man, Aarde and Hoowo3oow joined in the game.

The race came to an abrupt end, when the female who had been leading the way became aware of what they were doing and in her enthusiasm to take part, shot off like a bullet leaving a contrail behind her along with everyone else. When they eventually caught up with her at the base of the mountain she was bouncing around victoriously, her hands clapped together in triumph above her head.

"I… call… shenanigans!" wheezed Amos a second or two later as he sat down, huffing and puffing.

"Either way I got here before you, so you still would have been beaten by a woman, OOOSH!" stated Shui proudly, throwing her shoulders forward and tensing her arms to emphasize the last word.

"Such velocity would have shamed Ignis," chuckled Hoowo3oow who seemed to relish the idea of Ignis being outstripped for once in a contest of speed.

"Please do not tell me we have to climb that thing!" groaned Amos pointing at the towering alp. "Why do deities always have to live at the top of some big bloody mountain?"

The woman laughed almost fit to burst and Aarde, Hoowo3oow and Shui laughed with her. They obviously knew something Amos didn't.

"Am I missing something?" enquired Amos genially, who didn't get the joke but still saw a funny side. The group continued laughing.

"Chloe, I don't suppose you know do you?"

Chloe opened her mouth to speak as if about to give an answer but then her eyebrows screwed together and she closed it again. She shook her head and shrugged.

This surprising gap in Chloe's knowledge brought the others to their senses. "Finally," said Aarde smiling, "an actual secret that's still secret!"

"How come you don't know?" Chloe asked Amos with polite curiosity.

"Because… well I… Hmmm…" said Amos trailing off with no hint of an actual explanation.

"Well," interjected Aarde speaking directly to Chloe, "Amos knows where we are and what is in here, but he has never actually been here before, so he doesn't quite grasp the scale of it all."

"I already know what's in here too," explained Chloe with the same forthrightness that Shui found so charming. "A God lives here, a bespoke built deity created by the Conclave a long time ago. You call him the conduit and that…" Chloe pointed to the woman swimming above them, "…is his wife whom you call the 'Groomer'."

Aarde looked quite flabbergasted for a moment as he gormed at Chloe with his jaw gaped open.

"I just don't understand why expecting to find him at the top of the mountain is funny!" finished Chloe entirely bewildered.

"Because he is the mountain!" supplied Hoowo3oow.

"Good heavens!" exclaimed Amos, stumbling backwards as he gazed up the side of the enormous mesa. "This… *this* is the conduit?"

"Yep," Chortled Shui. "Big bugger, isn't he?"

Chloe was filled with equal awe. Her eyes traced the peaks and valleys up the near face until her view was lost in low hanging cloud at which point, she muttered a barely audible, "Wow!"

Now that it had been mentioned it was possible to see that the cliff edges were actually the fall of the conduit's clothes from his knees and Chloe could even make out a massive rocky bare foot.

"You know when people say, 'He can't get any deader'?" said Shui. "Well Quentin here can, so what do ya say we attend to business. You two can be all impressed later!"

Amos and Chloe were not entirely sure what 'people' Shui was quoting, but they snapped from their reverie and nodded their assent, however, Amos' expression quickly turned to puzzlement.

"How exactly are we going to do this?" he asked with mild embarrassment.

"If you wouldn't mind," said Hoowo3oow turning to the groomer as she lazily floated around the group. The groomer gave an excited grin, clapped her hands together and with a wiggle of her dainty feet, she was off at speed toward the low hanging clouds.

The group soon lost sight of her and they sat and reclined to wait for her return. Several minutes passed and Amos began to feel anxious. "Surely this is taking too long, I mean how big is he?" ranted Amos suddenly. "Oh, what am I going to tell the boy's parents? They'll be mortified. We'll have to lobotomise them… yes, yes… no other way!"

"AMOS!" boomed a voice from behind.

A little alarmed Amos spun round to see who had called him. He found himself looking at Aarde, who had a very placating expression on his face.

"Relax!" continued Aarde in a soft soothing tone. "This here…" Aarde shook Quentin's pale and very rigoured body, "…this 'aint no thing!"

Shui gave a grunt of a giggle. "Stop… please… for the love of all that's good in the world… 'this ain't no thing!'" imitated Shui drawing quotation marks with her fingers. "…brother I'm saying this 'coz I love you… you can't talk street… you just can't!"

Aarde flushed with embarrassment which was made all the more obvious by the grey skin of Quentin slumped on his shoulder.

He recovered quickly though and with as much bravado in his voice as he could muster yelled. "Baby please, you wish you were as cool as this!"

"Cool people, don't say cool… or baby!" mumbled Shui disinterestedly, her attention had been pulled elsewhere and was no longer bothered about teasing Aarde.

She was staring straight up into the sky, her hand held above her eyes and her lips pursed in deep concentration. "What the hell is th… OH SHIT!"

Her last remark had come as a giant plateau of rock appeared out of the clouds. It had raced towards them and for a moment looked as though it would smash right on top of the group. So convinced of this was Shui that she had decided to revert to a liquid state.

Braced for impact but still on his feet, Aarde turned to look at the puddle of water that was Shui and laughed.

"Shit yourself much?"

Shui burbled what Aarde assumed was a string of abuse through the water as her maddened face reformed and rose up out of the tiny pool of liquid.

Having fully reformed and feeling a bit more like herself, Shui glanced up at the giant table of rock that had come to a stop directly above her. It was shaped like the back of a giant hand, with gnarled and cracked knuckles and an occasional scattering of grass where hair might have been. The groomer, still wearing an elated and somewhat manic expression of delight, peeked her head out over the edge of the massive thumb and held out a hand to help Shui onboard. Shui ignored the gesture and leaped high into the air before landing gracefully on the tip of the hand's index finger and turning her back defiantly on the groomer. The young impish woman, unperturbed, shrugged off Shui's affront and proceeded to help the others climb up instead.

When everyone was safely upon the giant hand the groomer gave the palm a couple of pats with her own and they began to swiftly rise into the clouds and up the mountainous side of the conduit.

Looking up as they breached the clouds the group could see a vast expanse of starry sky above them which was periodically sliced by a wave of energy, much like the aurora borealis except these streaks varied wildly in colour and at their most vibrant appeared to form scenes containing people that nobody recognised.

Amos' eyes found the peak of the mountain-cum-deity and in doing so realised that the fall of water streaming from the top that he had previously noticed, wasn't water at all. It was in fact long flowing strands of silver hair that fell from the conduit's head and cascaded to the ground to form what he had assumed were small rivers.

Amos did not have time to stand and marvel, as the giant hand was soon brought level with the conduit's face whose eyes were staring fixedly at Quentin's carcass. Considering the conduit's face was constructed of granite which was cracked causing a fault line to run over his left eye, he was surprisingly handsome. He had a strong muscular looking face with a broad jaw and a heavy-set brow, yet was endowed with delicate cheekbones and a very straight, narrow nose. He had a long, thick beard which like the hair on his head, was silver and flowed like water, an ethereal quality that was even shared by his eyebrows. Silence devoured them for a moment as they stood in the shadow of this colossal face, sharing confused and uneasy glances with each other, daring somebody to speak.

Eventually the groomer who found the situation highly amusing, tapped Amos on the shoulder and gestured for him to speak to the Conduit.

"Me?" asked Amos who had rather lost his nerve.

The groomer gave a soft smile and nodded before unexpectedly shoving Amos forward into a prominent position beneath the Conduit's gaze.

"Eh, good day," began Amos rather lamely.

"HOW CAN I SERVE THEE?" boomed the conduit scaring everyone out of their wits.

"You can start by not talking so loudly," muttered Shui clutching her chest to feel her heart beating manically beneath.

The conduit raised an eyebrow at Shui, but it was impossible to determine if he was vexed by her comment.

"Sorry…" hastened Amos. "…ignore her, she does not speak for all of us."

Shui looked ready to retort but Hoowo3oow clamped his hand across her mouth. "Hold your tongue or I swear I will throw you from this ledge where you can wait at the bottom for us to return."

Shui knocked Hoowo3oow's hand away and crossed her arms sulkily. "All right… you don't have to be a dick about it."

"Please," continued Amos ignoring what the others were doing, "this boy cannot be allowed to die." Amos pulled Aarde forward as he spoke and slapped the cold, clammy skin of Quentin. "Can you restore his life and his head so that I may finally return him to his parents?"

"I WILL NOT. HIS LIFE IS OF NO CONSEQUENCE!" said the conduit firmly, although he spoke as softly as he could the sound still reverberated through everyone's chest. "HE HAS NO INFLUENCE ON

THE PARANORMAL WORLD, AS SUCH HIS DEATH WILL HAVE NO IMPACT ON OUR EXISTENCE."

"This is not true!" argued Amos. "His death jeopardises the secrecy of our work, it risks exposure of the Conclave and more importantly may have a profound negative effect on the future learning of a new but extremely gifted student."

The conduit did not appear to need to ask who this new student was as his head turned with an almighty grinding noise to face Chloe directly. He leaned his massive face closer to hers and surveyed her for a moment. Chloe, already a small child, seemed to diminish in size even further but she did not shrink from his stare.

"DO YOU WISH THE BOY'S LIFE RETURNED TO HIM?" asked the conduit sternly.

"Y… yes!" replied Chloe nervously.

"EVEN THOUGH YOU DESIRED AND STILL DESIRE HIS DEATH?" pressed the conduit.

"I didn't… I don't…"

"YOU CAN LIE TO YOURSELF IF YOU WISH BUT DO NOT TO LIE TO ME," growled the conduit. "YOUR EFFORTS TO REMOVE THE INFLUENCE YOU HAD OVER THE BOY FAILED BECAUSE YOUR THOUGHTS WERE CLUTTERED WITH ILL INTENT!"

"I… I…" whimpered Chloe.

"LEAVE HIM DEAD!" boomed the conduit once more. "HE HAS CAUSED YOU NOTHING BUT MISERY AND PAIN, HE DESERVES THIS END."

Chloe shook her head violently as tears streamed down her face.

"YOU HAVE WANTED HIM DEAD FOR YEARS, HAVEN'T YOU?"

"No, please, I… AHHHH!" Chloe collapsed to her knees clutching her face like a person gone mad.

"YES, IT'S RIGHT HERE INSIDE YOUR MIND, ANGER THAT OVERFLOWS, A DESIRE FOR REVENGE, FOR RETRIBUTION."

Chloe rolled around on the conduit's hand in agony and Amos lurched forward to come to her aid but at a look from the conduit, the groomer pushed him back before darting off into the midst of hair streaming around them.

"IT HURTS, IT HURTS, AAHHHHH, PLEASE STOP!" begged Chloe.

"ACCEPT THE DARKNESS INSIDE AND THE PAIN WILL GO AWAY," snarled the conduit.

"STOP! I DON'T WANT TO! GET OUT OF MY HEAD! GET OOOOOUUUT!"

"MAKE ME!" demanded the Conduit with such volume that everyone clasped their ears in pain.

Chloe let loose a scream that shook the fabric of space around them. She roared with such intensity that Amos' glasses shattered and new cracks split the already scarred face of the conduit. Her scream increased in pitch and volume and as she writhed on the floor a strange blood-coloured smoke began to rise from her eyes, ears, mouth and nose. The group began to feel themselves growing faint and their vision blackened as Chloe's wail and force of will gained more momentum. Just when it seemed as though consciousness was about to leave them, an explosion which bore no flame, erupted between Chloe and the conduit. It had so much force that Hoowo3oow and Shui were blown clean off the conduit's hand while Amos and Aarde were saved by a thumb and a finger. The force of the blast caused the conduit's head to recoil backwards and a large chuck of his cheek sheared off and crumbled to the ground below.

All was, at last, quiet, and when Amos, Aarde and the Conduit recovered they were greeted with the visage of Chloe vomiting reddish goo, the peculiar smoke now dissipated.

"CHILD? CAN YOU HEAR ME?" asked the conduit who was no longer aggressive in tone, but kind and gentle. "CHLOE?"

Chloe groaned and shuddered and wobbled on all fours, but with a great effort forced herself upright and raised her head to see the conduit smiling back.

"AH, GOOD! FOR A MOMENT I THOUGHT I HAD PUSHED TOO FAR!" said the conduit with a heavy sigh of relief.

Amos, who was nursing his head and assisting a dazed and confused Aarde to his feet, did not feel quite so relaxed. "What the bloody hell is going on?" he roared unexpectedly.

"CALM YOURSELF OR I WILL EJECT YOU FROM YOUR PERCH AND YOU CAN WAIT AT THE BOTTOM WITH THE OTHERS... ASSUMING YOU SURVIVE THE FALL!" said the conduit forcefully.

Chloe got to her feet and massaged her belly. It may have been sore or it may have felt empty, either way she seemed quite content and not at all perturbed by the rather grim looking puddle of mush laying at her feet that had up until a few moments ago been inside her.

"What is it?" asked Chloe looking to the conduit expectantly.

"UNFINISHED BUSINESS!" replied the conduit simply.

"I don't understand," said Chloe. "My unfinished business? Or yours?"

"I CANNOT BE CERTAIN BUT I SUSPECT IT IS HIS!" replied the conduit implicating Amos with a glance.

"Mine?" spluttered Amos outraged. "What are you blithering about, how can I be the cause of that?" he added pointing at the disturbing looking puddle of vomit and looking very offended.

"A GOOD QUESTION, BUT ONE I AM UNABLE TO ANSWER," said the conduit in a tone that made him sound quite unconcerned.

"Then how on earth do you justify your outlandish accusation that implies I am somehow responsible for her illness," continued Amos

"IT WOULD PERHAPS BE EASIER TO SHOW YOU," replied the conduit. "HOLD TIGHT NOW!"

Chapter Thirteen
By a Hair

The conduit raised his massive hand up beyond his face, moving Amos, Chloe and Aarde to the top of his head. He dropped them off in his hair near the crown where the shimmering swirl of silver strands looked like a whirlpool. Out of the deep gathering of strands emerged the groomer who was smiling jubilantly at Chloe as she wrestled with something beneath the thicket of flowing hair.

"CAN YOU SEE IT!" asked the conduit calling up to them.

"See what?" enquired Amos sharply.

The groomer raised a hand for Amos to be patient a moment as she continued to tug and pull at something as yet unseen.

"CAREFUL!" boomed the conduit with a wince. "YOU DO NOT WANT TO PULL THIS ONE FROM ITS ROOT!"

After a bit more pulling and rummaging, the groomer finally raised her arms above the sea of silver, but to the surprise and disappointment of those watching produced just another hair.

"That it?" scoffed Aarde bemused. "All that effort to show us another frickin' hair!"

The groomer gave Aarde a look of dismay and slapped a free hand to her perfectly smooth scalp. She then grabbed Aarde by the hand, dragged him closer and pointed aggressively toward the root. Aarde, failing to see the big deal peered closer, shifting his gaze deep between the shimmering shafts and after a moment or two gave a soft 'ooh' of amazement as his eyes widened with intrigue.

"What?" asked Amos, his curiosity getting the better of him. "What do you see?"

Aarde beckoned Amos and Chloe over and together they followed the groomer's still outstretched finger to observe for themselves what held such fascination. At the base of the long single strand of hair held by the groomer was another. It was shorter than the first and was so tightly wrapped around the longer strand that at first glance it almost seemed as though the two were part of the same shaft.

"I don't get it!" said Chloe blankly.

"Neither do I!" agreed Amos. "You have a tangle, nothing a good brushing couldn't cure."

Aarde chuckled loudly at a joke shared only by the groomer who giggled mutley. "Hell's bells, Amos. I can't believe how little you know about this place, especially as it was your idea to come here."

Amos puffed himself up indignantly. He took pride in his work and had enjoyed many years of being the 'Go to guy', the 'Man in the know'. This gap in his knowledge frustrated him, a sensation that was as uncomfortable as it was unfamiliar.

"Just get to the point, Aarde!" he snapped, brusquely.

"These hairs," began Aarde cautiously, "are a tangible representation of every human life on the planet."

"Really?" asked Amos.

"Yes, really!" replied Aarde with a smirk. "The older someone is, the longer the hair."

"Really?" asked Chloe.

"Really!" replied Aarde somewhat impatiently. "What's odd about these two is the tangle… this rarely happens and when it does it implies a deep and intrinsic connection between souls."

"Really?" asked Amos again in wonderment.

"Oh my God, yes frickin' really!" barked Aarde.

"So why is this one important?" asked Chloe.

Aarde opened his mouth to speak but then realised he didn't have an answer. "That's a good question," he said turning to the groomer. "Who are they and why should we care?"

The groomer appeared to have been waiting for this question and smiled sagaciously. She held the long hair aloft and gave it a wiggle then without further preamble pointed at Amos.

"You want me to hold it for you?" asked a confused Amos.

The groomer's face turned a blotchy red shade of annoyed and she took a deep calming breath before directing Amos' gaze skyward at the waves of colour that danced lazily above. The groomer concentrated hard, gripped the hair tightly, and unexpectedly, began to sing. It was a song without words, a simple tune, yet it was eerily melancholic and each ear that heard it felt the weight of a thousand emotions press heavily on their hearts.

As she sang the waves of light in the sky transformed into people, acting out their lives unaware of an audience. It continued to change from one moment in time to another and always featured a man who seemed familiar but unrecognisable.

It wasn't until a scene in which a young man dressed in tweed embraced a small fiery-haired boy that Amos yelled out in startled comprehension, "It... it's me!"

The groomer, satisfied that her point had been made, dropped the hair and the scene broke. When Amos returned his eyes to meet hers, she repeated the motion of pointing at the hair, then at Amos.

"That hair is my life?" he asked tremulously.

The groomer nodded and Amos tottered unsteadily on his feet. Even Aarde was blown away by this revelation and stood with his mouth agape unable to find words.

"S... so who does that belong to?" enquired Amos nervously pointing at the shorter strand.

The groomer gave Chloe a meaningful pat on the head, intimating that she was the owner and Amos' legs finally buckled.

"DO YOU SEE IT NOW?" bellowed the conduit, reaching up and scooping Aarde, Amos and Chloe back into his hand.

As the conduit brought them back down to his eye level Amos felt overwhelmed with questions unanswered.

"I still don't understand." Amos whimpered. "What does it mean?"

Chloe stood next to Amos and held his hand to show her support and while he was grateful for the gesture, he felt sickened with guilt.

"I CANNOT OFFER MORE THAN I KNOW," began the conduit consolingly. "WHAT I CAN SAY IS THAT SOMEHOW YOUR DESTINIES HAVE BECOME INEXTRICABLY LINKED AND A RAGE OF VENGEANCE THAT WAS ONCE YOURS BECAME INADVERTANTLY GIFTED TO THIS CHILD."

"But that's impossible, I have no rage!" blustered Amos defensively. "And I have no outstanding vengeance for that matter!"

"What about unfinished business?" asked Aarde in an attempt to be helpful.

"My word Aarde use your head. Unfinished business is for the dead and I am quite certain I continue to live."

"TRUE ENOUGH. BUT THIS CHILD'S SOUL IS OLD AND HAS BEEN CONTAMINATED BY BETRAYAL SINCE THE DAY SHE WAS BORN."

"That still doesn't explain how it's got anything to do with me. I still have my soul!" pleaded Amos.

"WHAT YOU HAVE SEEN IS NO MERE TANGLE. HER HAIR GROWS FROM YOUR ROOT AND AS SUCH YOUR SOUL HAS HAD AND WILL CONTINUE TO HAVE A PROFOUND EFFECT ON HERS."

"Can you separate them…?" asked Amos optimistically but the conduit interrupted with thunderous volume.

"NO. THE POWER THAT BOUND YOU TOGETHER FAR EXCEEDS MY OWN. TO ATTEMPT IT COULD SEVERELY DAMAGE YOU BOTH AND MAKE YOU LESS COMPLETE… LESS HUMAN."

"Oh, I see," said Amos disappointedly. "Well can we at least get rid of this vengeful temperament you said inhabits her?"

"IT IS ALREADY DONE. CURED BY HER OWN HAND!"

"I must have missed twenty minutes!" said Aarde scratching his head. "When did that happen?"

"WHEN SHE COMMANDED ME TO GET OUT OF HER HEAD," said the conduit simply. "HER FORCE OF WILL, AIMED AT ME AND WITH THE INTENT TO CLEAR A FOREIGN ENTITY FROM HER MIND WAS REFLECTED INWARD WHEN MY WIFE ACTIVATED HER STRAND. IT PURGED THE DARKNESS FROM HER SOUL, A DARKNESS THAT WAS NOT HERS AND AS SUCH EASY FOR HER ABILITIES TO ISOLATE."

"How are you, Chloe?" asked Amos bemused.

Chloe thought for a moment, perhaps searching her head for signs of ill behaviour. Happy with what she felt, she looked up at Amos and smiled. "I feel fine."

"Well, that is at least something," replied Amos, returning a warm smile.

"Mr Conduit?" shouted Chloe to the monstrous head.

"YES, CHILD?"

"I really would like Quentin to be put back together," continued Chloe in a slightly saddened tone. "He's an obnoxious bully, but he doesn't deserve that!"

"WELL THEN…" boomed the conduit, leaning his head from side to side causing his neck to make several thunderous cracks. "…LET US TEST THE POWER OF A GOD, EH?"

The conduit gave a wry smile and a wink at Chloe and she in turn hugged his massive thumb.

"YOU MIGHT WANT TO START THINKING OF A REASON AS TO WHY THIS BOY WILL SUDDENLY NEED TO START SHAVING!" said the Conduit to Amos.

Amos raised his eyebrows quizzically. "Why, what's going to happen?"

"TO BREATHE LIFE BACK INTO THIS CARCASS A PORTION OF THE LIFE HE WOULD HAVE HAD MUST BE SACRIFICED."

"Whoa, sacrificed?" blustered Amos. "Nobody mentioned this before!"

"Don't panic, Amos." Soothed Aarde. "It's not as bad as it sounds. He means that the energy used to restore the boy will consume a few years of his overall life span, essentially ageing him. It's very safe, in fact it's pretty much how we were made."

"Oh," said Amos more intrigued than concerned now. "So how old will he be after this?"

"Hmm, let's see. He's about fifteen now…" Aarde rocked his head side to side as he attempted a rough calculation. "…around seventeen years old."

For a moment Amos stared glassy eyed at Quentin, his thoughts flitting from imagining what the boy would look like when restored and marvelling at the new information he had just received. He would soon have a tremendous insight into how Ignis came to be. No sooner had this last thought popped into his head, when a new terrible worry overpowered it.

"Oh, oh, wait…" stammered Amos.

"What's wrong?" enquired Aarde.

"He won't become super strong like you guys will he?" whittled Amos. "He can't be trusted with such power!"

"Nah, we were healthy and alive when seven years were burned off our lives," explained Aarde simply. "The energy had nothing to repair so it remained inside us and enhanced our bodies instead. I've no doubt he will feel invigorated for a while, but his muscles will be no better off in the long run."

"HERE WE GO!" boomed the conduit.

Surprised but excited, Aarde, Amos and Chloe turned to look up at what the conduit and the groomer were up to. The groomer was braced against the back of the conduit's ear. Her feet were pressed hard against the granite head and a medium length hair was wrapped around her right arm which she clenched tightly in both hands. She looked as though she might be about to go abseiling.

"HEAVE!" bellowed the conduit.

Upon command the groomer pulled on the hair as hard as she could, her cheeks flushing with the effort. Her back arched as she attempted to gain better leverage and for a while Amos imagined the hair might suddenly pop free and the impish woman would be sent flying backwards. But it didn't budge, whatever they were attempting appeared to be futile. Shortly after, and to Amos and Chloe's intense curiosity, the groomer began to make progress. The strand seemed to come away from the conduit's head, only an inch at first but then a foot and then a metre. Amos had expected the hair to come out at the root, but instead it was growing. The longer it became the brighter its silvery body shone, and turning to Quentin, they all marvelled at the sight of new veins, flesh and bone growing and knitting together out of the now healing neck. Before long Quentin had a brand-new head, a five o'clock shadow, and a very shaggy hairstyle.

"THAT'S ENOUGH," said the conduit as he clamped a finger over the hair's root preventing the groomer who was getting rather carried away from extending it too much.

"ANY MORE AND THEY'LL NEED TO CONSCRIPT HIM INTO THE CONCLAVE."

The groomer sheepishly allowed the hair to slide from her grip and with a slightly embarrassed grin, slinked down to stand beside Chloe.

"What happens now?" whispered Chloe as she stared at Quentin who looked healthy but still wasn't breathing.

"We wait!" said Aarde simply.

"Wait for what?" asked Chloe.

"For someone to…" began Aarde but he was interrupted by Shui who had just somersaulted onto the conduit's hand.

"Bring his soul in a safe and secure container!" said Shui, finishing Aarde's sentence and smiling broadly whilst holding up a see-through cube with a shimmering silver blue cloud floating inside.

"Safe and secure container!" scoffed Aarde. "It's in a Tupperware box!"

"And?" retorted Shui defensively. "It's not going anywhere, look!"

Shui turned the container over and on the plastic lid, written in blood, was scripture designed to imprison souls.

"Keeps sandwiches and souls fresh for weeks!" continued Shui cheerfully. "Someone from R&D brought it down once they'd caught it. He was just waiting at the bottom of this guy," she gave a nod in the conduit's direction. "I nearly landed on him, poor guy literally fainted!" finished Shui, cackling with laughter as if nothing could possibly be funnier.

"Bring it over!" said Aarde, crouching down and adjusting Quentin's position so his head was raised.

Shui came to where Quentin lay on the floor supported by Aarde and took a low fighting stance. In the next second, she had raised the Tupperware up as if about to throw it but Aarde held up a hand in protest. "Wait, wait!"

Shui lowered her hand and slumped her shoulders forward in exasperation. "What, dude?" she muttered impatiently.

"Not too hard, OK?" pleaded Aarde tentatively.

"Dude!" said Shui in a mocking tone. "It's not like he's gonna feel it and I have wanted to do this since I met the little prick!"

Without further preamble and before Aarde could protest any further, she swung back her arm and then slammed the plastic box hard against Quentin's face with such force that both the boy and Aarde were nearly knocked over the side of the conduit's hand. Shards of plastic scattered across the granite palm and down to the ground below, shimmering like stars as they fell through the air, illuminated by the soul released in the collision which was excited to be so near an empty vessel, a familiar vessel. The pull of such a well-fitting environment was too tempting for the soul to resist and within seconds it had found its way inside Quentins skull via his nasal canal.

There was a general murmur of satisfaction amongst the group and Amos seemed especially pleased as he smiled broadly and sighed, finally feeling the burden and guilt of Quentin's predicament leave him. This contented and sanguine mood did not last, as Quentin's eyes flew open. He sat bolt upright, took one good look at his surroundings and caught sight of a naked, bald woman flying through the air above him. His gaze followed this entrancing sight until his eyes fell upon the giant, animated face of the conduit looming over him.

Outside in the Archive lobby, Mizaru and Iwazaru looked up as the sound of a man's muffled scream came from behind the heavy vault-like door.

"Oh good, he's alive," chuckled Mizaru. The sound cut short, and after a moment's reflection Mizaru added, "Iwazaru, two gold bits say Shui punched him!"

Ten minutes later the circular door to the conduit's domain swung open and in stepped the group waving and shouting their thanks and goodbyes to the groomer and the conduit, even though the portal had already shut behind them. As predicted Shui was carrying an unconscious Quentin who sported a black eye and Shui had a telltale spot of blood on the knuckles of her right hand.

"Pay up!" demanded Mizaru looking at Iwazaru.

"What's that for?" asked Shui.

"I bet Iwazaru that it was you who struck the boy…" Mizaru took a better look at Quentin. "…or should I say 'Man', to silence him!"

"Then you need to give him the coins back, the groomer decked him, not me!" said Shui with grim satisfaction at the look on Mizaru's face.

"But your hand has blood on it!" whined Mizaru.

"That blood is mine!" said Shui. "I asked the conduit if I could feel what it was like to punch a God made of granite and he let me."

"You punched... the Conduit?" asked Mizaru, aghast.

"Yeah!" chuckled Shui. "Check it out..."

Shui held up what appeared to be a stone carving of a canine tooth. "He let me keep it after I knocked it out. That dude's awesome!"

Shui looked like a kid on Christmas morning, while everyone else buried their faces in their hands with mild embarrassment.

"Moan all you like, but how many people can say they've got one of these?" she said twirling the fang with a little toss.

"Well, we must be going but thank you for all your help," said Amos politely.

"What are you thanking them for?" asked Shui bitterly. "Sitting? Stating the obvious? Asking nosey questions?"

"SHUI!" barked Hoowo3oow. "That's enough!"

"No, no..." interrupted Mizaru. "Shui is correct, we do not deserve thanks... not today anyway!" This pronouncement was met with some puzzlement and intrepidation by the group.

"Just don't forget to show gratitude when we do deserve it, OK?" Mizaru added, a slight air of attitude in her voice.

"Sure thing, Miz! Now let's bounce before I eat someone!" replied Shui offhandedly.

As they all crammed back into the lift the mood shifted decidedly to one much more light-hearted. Hoowo3oow was doing his best to avoid having Quentin's buttocks too close to his own face and Shui kept intentionally lowering Quentin's head near Amos' rear, knowing his penchants for dropping bubbly farts whenever he was relaxed. Chloe found the whole thing entirely hysterical and she cackled with mirth every time Quentin's hair flapped in the breeze, but she seemed distracted and on occasion looked disappointed.

"What's wrong?" asked a concerned Amos.

"Nothing's wrong," said Chloe dismally. "It's just... I kinda wanted to see their hairs!" she finished pointing at Shui, Aarde and Hoowo3oow.

Amos turned to look at Aarde. "That's a good point!" he blustered. "Are your hairs not kept with the groomer!"

"Nah, they used to be but they were moved to CERN three years ago," replied Aarde as if this were common knowledge.

"The Conclave has a research lab at CERN who use their time with the LHC to run experiments with our hair's atomic structure," explained Hoowo3oow flatly.

"Why wasn't I informed?" enquired Amos who sounded somewhat hurt and offended at being kept out of the loop.

"You were!" sighed Aarde. "But if I remember correctly, it was around the time Ignis had been cursed by that coven in Somalia."

"That's right!" cackled Shui, bursting into hysterics. "Didn't he have mystical syphilis?"

"Oh, that's right!" agreed Amos as he thought back. "He ended up running a fever and his temperature became so high my living quarters were incinerated."

Aarde, Shui and even Hoowo3oow laughed heartily as they reminisced but Chloe slumped against the wall looking forlorn and dumped her hands in her pockets before heaving a great sigh of disappointment.

"Don't sweat it kid," reassured Shui. "With your brains I have no doubt you'll see the inside of that place before the end of your first year."

Chloe grinned widely at the praise given to her by Shui and for the rest of the climb in the lift her thoughts dwelled on what it would be like to see the LHC, something she had read about after seeing it on the news and had been fantasising about ever since. She never realised that she had already seen the inside of CERN and that it was a memory she was keen to forget.

The group emerged out of the lift and into R&D two minutes later and were greeted by a very dishevelled Richard.

"That's better!" he said looking at Quentin's head bobbing against Shui's back. "Much less... gloopy!"

"Quite!" said Amos genially. "Now to get him home before his parents..."

"His parents are here!" interrupted Rich.

"Wh-what…? Where? What have you told them? How did they get here? Why are they here?" whittled Amos, his voice becoming louder and more panicked with each question.

He still hadn't thought of a good reason for the substantial physical change that had been the consequence of restoring Quentin's life and his mind was coming up blank.

"Calm down, Amos!" said Rich soothingly. "Alex is up in the hospital unit with the parents who are currently sitting beside a marvellous fabrication of the boy which is housed inside a bio-isolation tent."

Amos gawped at Rich in disbelief. "And they believe this facsimile is their son?" he enquired tentatively.

"Yup, we said he had contracted a new strain of virus that caused hyper-senescence in the host cells," explained Richard proudly, it couldn't have been more obvious that this explanation had been his idea.

"You just made up a virus?" chortled Amos who sounded most impressed.

"Yes, I did," laughed Rich. "The Farrowfields were of course mortified when they found out, but once we told them that due to being here at the finest medical research institute in the world it was treatable and that we were going to name the virus after him, 'the Quentescence Virus or QSV-14', they were really quite happy about it."

"Good work that was some quick thinking!" praised Amos.

"Quick thinking?" scoffed Rich. "Hardly! They were kept in the dark for the first few days whilst we 'ran tests!'" explained Rich drawing inverted commas with his fingers. "Of course we were just placating them whilst we…"

"First few days?" interrupted Amos, puzzled.

"Mate, you have been in that room almost a week. Today is the 11th November, Remembrance Day."

"Bugger, I completely forgot about the time dilation," mused Amos wistfully. His aspect soon changed, as his thoughts returned to more pressing concerns. "Ignis. Is he back back yet?" he asked hopefully.

Rich dropped his gaze and shook his head. "Sorry bud, I knew you would ask but as yet there is no sign of him."

"No matter," said Amos, straightening up and stiffening his resolve. "He will be back before long, I'm sure."

"As am I," reassured Rich. "Oh, before I forget. Frank wants to see you when you have a sec!"

"Right 'o!" said Amos with a heavy sigh. "In that case can I leave Quentin and his subsequent care in your capable hands?"

"Sure thing. What do you want to do about Miss Sterling?"

"Send her down when she's free, I still need to induct Chloe and she needs to be present," replied Amos, removing his glasses and massaging the bridge of his nose.

"Roger dodger!" replied Rich with a comical overly rigid salute before heaving Quentin onto his shoulder and heading toward the lift.

Amos, tired and deflated by the lack of news about Ignis, dragged his heels somewhat in reaching the Conclave headquarters. He really did not need any more bad news, but if Frank wanted to see him it could be nothing else. As he approached the solid oak door that led to the common room he pined for a big ploughman's cheese sandwich, a cup of tea and a lie down, even five minutes' silence would do.

"Amos, it's about bloody time!" growled Frank as Amos stepped through the door into the circular room and was instantly greeted with Frank's digital disembodied head floating above the large central table.

It reminded him of the *Wizard of Oz* and he found himself replying with. "There's no place like home."

"What?" barked Frank.

"Never mind, what's been happening?" asked Amos, disinterestedly.

"Another death at the hands of that bleeding imitation!" spat Frank, as if he took the existence of this fraudster as a personal insult.

"Who was it this time?" enquired Amos who was beginning to feel more intrigued than lethargic now and had been keen to hear more news on the little faker's whereabouts.

"A..." began Frank, pausing to read something on a scrap of paper. "DQZS Robinson. He's a recently published author whom according to Wikipedia, wrote a trilogy with religious themes that ruffled a few feathers. The police are treating his death as suspicious and have so far pointed the blame at extremists or fanatics who may have been offended by some of the book's content."

"What was the book called?" asked Amos with polite interest.

"Get this…" sniggered Frank. "…it's called *Magikal Thinking* of all things."

Amos chortled loudly. "Oh, ho! Isn't that the title of the Conclave's *Standard Operating Procedure* manual?"

"I know, go figure!" mused Frank.

"Why are they so convinced he was killed by fanatics?" asked Amos suddenly sounding more business-like.

"Because of this!" said Frank who tapped a button on a keyboard which instantly switched out Frank's face on the display with a photo of the crime scene.

Amos took one look at the image and gagged as a modicum of sick lurched into his mouth. He spat into a nearby bin and hovered over it as his mouth began salivating wildly, the promise of vomiting inching closer each time he sneaked another peek at the picture.

"Yep, pretty grim, isn't it?" said Frank over the comm.

The image on the display showed a slim, middle-aged man on his knees with his hands tied together and supported by the man's very long beard which held them up in a prayer-like pose. Within his hands, the poor man held his own brain which had been removed, judging by the damage done to his cheeks, via his mouth. In addition to this the killer, for reasons best known to themselves, had cut three vertical lines over his eyes and closed them with another long line at each end to look like the Roman numeral for three. As if that were not enough the man's body was propped up by several wooden spikes which had been driven through his chest in an arrangement akin to that required to build a teepee. It was on the whole a most disturbing scene and Amos had the terrible feeling that the poor man had still been alive when he was turned into a tent. As if all of this hadn't been enough, the killer had then gone on to scratch into the grey matter the same spiral collection of iconography, seen on previous occasions.

"What the hell is wrong with that kid?" burped Amos as he forced back another globule of sick. "Have you had a chance to read this book?"

"Afraid not, the publisher only printed a handful of copies, mostly it was sold online. Since the murder the publishers have withdrawn it completely. The police are now the only ones with access to the digital property."

"Have any units been dispatched to the victim's home?" asked Amos.

"Of course, I put Wade on it," replied Frank earnestly. "Didn't do any good though, we still have more questions than answers! Wade spoke to his wife but she was understandably a mess. She didn't know anything and neither do the police," he added disappointedly. "Barry's trying to dig up some better information on how he ties in with the previous victims but they are so disparate I think it's going to turn out to be a futile effort."

"Speaking of victims, have you managed to find Mr Godfrey yet?" asked Amos, hopefully.

"Also a no, and to be honest I was going to ask you that. All that time you spent in the conduit's dimension, please tell me you at least tried to find his strand?" pleaded Frank.

"You know about the strands too!" moaned Amos almost imperceptibly. "I did ask just after we revived the boy. We found the hair and they were more than willing to use it..." said Amos skirting the actual point of the question.

"And... what happened?" asked Frank impatiently.

"We saw nothing but fuzzy clouds and heard a noise like feedback from a speaker," said Amos simply. "Although the cause of the interference may not be mystical..." Amos added hurriedly, sensing Frank's imminent meltdown. "...Shui had just punched the conduit with enough force to dislodge a tooth, so he may have been too dazed to function properly."

"SHE DID WHAT?" bellowed Frank.

Amos was saved the need of having to conjure a defence as they were joined in the room by Chloe, Miss Sterling, Hoowo3oow, Aarde and of course Shui. Everyone had just made themselves at home, grabbing snacks, drinks and arguing over the TV remote when Frank barked Shui's name from across the room, which was promptly answered by Aarde singing, "Someone's in trouble!"

Shui dropped the giant granite tooth into Aarde's lap, causing him to double over and cradle his groin before making her way over to a very irate holographic image of Frank who began yelling at her immediately.

"How are you Miss Sterling?" asked Amos in an attempt to divert attention away from the argument that was now raging in the background.

"Oh, pretty good, thanks!" replied Alex. "While you were busy fixing Quentin, I had a good look around the institute and Richard has introduced me to practically everyone in the building. I've even met his wife, Sarah, we had dinner together on Saturday." Alex giggled. "It blows my mind to think she really believes he is just an IT technician."

Amos smiled softly. "A small lie that in the long run spares her from a panic attack and the subsequent lobotomy that would likely follow."

Alex's expression of amusement vanished as she remembered signing her contract and she gulped hard.

"Fear not Miss Sterling, you display remarkable coping skills. It is doubtful that your end will come from the business end of a high-powered laser." Alex relaxed and felt her spirit lift, that was, until Amos added without any trace of sarcasm in his tone, "It is statistically much more likely that a demon will possess, or eat you." And with that he turned and faced Chloe. "We appear to have some rare free time on our hands so how about I show you around like I promised."

Chloe clapped excitedly and jumped to her feet. "Is Miss Sterling coming too?"

Amos turned to look at Alex who had turned pale and looked queasy. "I think we can leave Miss Sterling to have a nice warm drink, she can catch up to us in the classrooms."

Alex gave a slight nod of comprehension and together Amos and Chloe headed to the lift.

"Aarde, if Frank ever gets tired of yelling at Shui let him know I've gone to induct Chloe."

"So never then!" sniggered Aarde glancing at the wildly gesticulating hologram that was Frank and thinking that Shui was probably wishing someone had installed a mute button when they built this place.

Chapter Fourteen
Study Group

"And if we go through here, quietly mind, we will probably have a chance to see the NoMinds learning what I expect to be fresh theology or arcane scripture tailored to aid our cause."

"Quite," replied Amos who sounded amused albeit somewhat defeated, "but I am supposed to be giving the tour my dear, not you!"

Chloe raised a finger and made to speak as though she had a fascinating point to make, but then stopped, blushed deeply and lowered her head with embarrassment. Amos chuckled warmly and gave her a consoling pat on the shoulder.

"It's quite all right, I see now that giving you of all people a tour was a bit of an empty gesture," said Amos ushering Chloe away from the wall and down the corridor to a spiral staircase. "It occurs to me that you probably know as much as I do about, well everything, because of our... er... entanglement," explained Amos as they walked. "I noticed that when there was a gap in my knowledge, you had one too."

"You think I can read your mind?" asked Chloe cautiously.

"Heavens no, nothing quite so hackneyed as that. I mean you do not know what I am thinking right now, do you?" added Amos suddenly sounding unsure.

Chloe shook her head and shrugged.

"Precisely... and er probably for the best too. No, I think it much more likely that you are referencing my knowledge when you are triggered by a visual clue or sound."

"Like a library?" asked Chloe.

Amos swelled with pride. No one had ever referred to his collective knowledge as a library and he rather liked the idea. "I suppose so," he chortled. "Ah, here we are!"

They had arrived at the top of the spiral staircase and were confronted by a large mahogany double door that had the words 'Common Room' carved into the surface which was gilded with gold leaf.

"I suppose you know where we are?" smiled Amos cheekily.

"Yes, this is a central hub for students like me. It is an open work area where we have access to archive records, databases and technical information on technology researched and developed by the institute."

"Very goo…" began Amos, but Chloe wasn't finished.

"It also leads to our personal quarters and provides direct access to the dovetail quarters which has an exact symmetrical layout to this one."

"Oustandi…"

"There is also a sky lab and a dungeon directly above and below the connecting bridge between the two areas which are used for researching and practising supernatural arts and methodologies."

"Bravo, I'm going to stop you there though or we could be out here all day," said Amos in one quick breath, fearing Chloe may interrupt him again. "Let's go in and see if we can find any of your new classmates."

Amos heaved open the door and light filled the staircase. When their eyes adjusted, Chloe was pleased to see a clean and well-lit room with comfy looking sofas and beanbags scattered here and there among a plethora of expensive looking workstations and computer terminals with instruments that Chloe, and therefore Amos, didn't recognise.

There was a single student in the common room and it was one that Amos instantly recognised.

"Wade," said Amos genially. "How are you?"

Wade looked up from the terminal he was working at and greeted both Amos and Chloe with a warm smile. "Better for seeing a friendly face," he replied.

"May I introduce you to a new addition to the Qin Zhu institute, this is Miss Chloe Gibson," said Amos highlighting Chloe with a sweeping gesture of his arm.

Wade took Chloe by the hand and gave it a little shake. "Getting younger every year," he sighed, a hint of pity in his tone.

"Where are the others?" asked Amos.

"I think Sarah and Fiona are in the library with Gyasi for a cryptozoology lesson and I believe Demi and Stewart are with Professor Gathercole down in the dungeon learning the fine art of anthropodermic bibliopegy."

"Anthropodermic bibliopegy?" began Chloe, her face already screwing up in disgust. "Isn't that where you make books out of... of..."

"Human skin, yes," replied Wade giving a shudder as he spoke. "Bloody creepy but there is a rich history associated with the craft and you would be surprised at how much magic can be created with a book bound in such a fashion."

"I would have thought modern media may have culled its use," said Amos.

"On the contrary," replied Wade. "It has been used in so many horror movies and stories that people believe human leather-bound books are a dead cert' for black magic, necromancy... or opening the gates of hell."

"What classes are taking place this afternoon?" enquired Amos with a worried look at Chloe, the last thing he needed right now was to follow up decapitation with an experience in how to flay a human.

"Combat training in honour of Remembrance Day, followed by this year's inter-departmental tournament. Are you entering this year?"

"Hmmm! We shall see!" said Amos looking Chloe up and down. "What about you?" enquired Amos with unease. "How do you feel about fighting?"

"Sounds good," she replied in a voice that betrayed a total lack of confidence.

"You should have your dovetail bring you some training attire, you will of course be required to choose a weapon but it's perhaps best to swing a few around before you decide which you prefer," explained Wade at his usual speed.

"What do I need a weapon for?" asked Chloe.

"All students and staff are trained in combat. Weapons are mostly used by students as a guide or for ceremonial occasions. Of course sometimes..." began Amos but just then the door opened and in walked a young black-haired girl and a slightly older red-headed boy carrying parcels wrapped in bloody gauze bandages that were being held at arms' length.

265

"Eewwww!" squealed the girl as her thumb pressed hard against a wet spot on her package. "That is…" the girl gagged. "…so very wrong."

"Very wrong!" agreed the red-headed boy as he dropped his parcel into a nearby drawer and closed it with his foot.

"Demi, Stewart," yelled Wade beckoning them over. "This is Chloe, she has just started and will be joining us this afternoon with Elsu and… I expect Shui will be on her own?" he added to Amos looking uncertain.

"I'm afraid so, Ignis is still on a mission so Shui will run the lesson alone unless perhaps Aarde is available," replied Amos solemnly.

Ignis' absence still weighed heavily on his mind, even more so since he discovered the extra time they had spent in the conduit's dimension.

"Well, it is nice to meet you," said Demi happily. "It's about time we had a girl closer to my age. So what's your special skill?"

"My special skill?" asked Chloe confused.

"Yeah, we all have a thing. It's why we get invited to learn and eventually work here, because of a unique talent that is of use to the Conclave."

"Well, I er…" mumbled Chloe, she was after all unsure what her talent was and stating that she had somehow hijacked Amos' brain didn't really seem like an appropriate response.

"Chloe's talent is one that we are still trying to understand," interjected Amos who had noticed Chloe's discomfort. "But it's one that bridges both pure intellect and the supernatural, a mix that can have… ummm…" Amos thought about Chloe making it rain and the accidental manslaughter of Quentin. "…a profound effect on the world around us. I suspect vocifery with a dash of pathifery, but I cannot as yet be sure."

"Wow," cooed Demi, obviously impressed. "Me I'm just real smart. I have an eidetic memory and have read almost every book in the London library, only takes me about ten minutes to read one, assuming it's no more than four hundred pages long that is!"

"Assuming of course you can actually be bothered to pick up a book in the first place," scowled Stewart.

"And what do you call this?" asked Demi sarcastically as she threw her blood-stained package at Stewart who recoiled in disgust allowing the book to drop to the floor and out of it coverings.

"Arts and craft don't count and what the hell Demi, that's... that's..." reeled Stewart frantically trying to brush blood spots off his shirt.

"Grim?" supplied Chloe.

"Yes, grim, thank you," sighed Stewart, electing to remove the shirt and replace it with one from a nearby trunk. Feeling smart again and a whole lot fresher he turned back to Chloe and assumed a commanding posture. "I would add that Demi is not doing herself justice. She has total recall which is to say she remembers everything, which I dare say is more than a little annoying at times."

There was a short pause of silence during which Stewart gave a little cough. When no one seemed to be paying attention he drew back his shoulders and loomed over Chloe. "Would you care to learn my talent?" he asked rather brusquely.

Amused, Chloe gave a friendly nod but interrupted Stewart as he was about to speak.

"Let me try and guess instead," said Chloe giving Amos a sly and unexpected wink.

Amos was surprised but delighted to see this new confidence she had gained since her encounter with the conduit beginning to bloom. She was more at ease and was clearly having a bit of fun for a change so Amos remained silent and waited to see where this was going.

Chloe closed her eyes and placed a couple of fingers against her temples. Her eyebrows furrowed together as she massaged the sides of her head slowly and she said 'Hmm!' a lot as she slowly moved closer to Stewart.

Everyone drew close, expectant but patient and as a silence fell over them all Stewart began to look concerned.

"Well for a start your name isn't Stewart!" said Chloe so suddenly it made everyone jump. "It's... James, no wait... Derek, no... Percival...? or is it... Antonio...? No, it really is Stewart!" prattled Chloe with an air of mystery and uncertainty.

"Th, that's remarkable!" exclaimed Stewart with a slight stutter.

"Not as remarkable as your career history!" replied Chloe with a respectful smile. "Invented nitro-glycerin? Wow! And here I was, thinking it was invented in 1846!"

"Well, you see…" began Stewart, trying to explain.

"Yes," interrupted Chloe excitedly. "I do. You have genetic memory! A full and complete memory of every blood relation through to the beginning of the human race."

"Duuude, she has so got you nailed!" laughed Demi in awe and amazement. "Do him some more!"

Chloe grinned at Demi and then proceeded to mentally examine Stewart again. "Unfortunately, it's more complicated than just memories though isn't it?" asked Chloe as she took hold of Stewart's hand.

Stewart gave a solemn, dumbstruck nod.

"A side effect of this collective memory is dual personality, or in your case ad nauseam personality as there are so many. Sometimes the driver takes a rest and the passengers take you for a spin?" Chloe asked rhetorically.

"Boosh!" bellowed Demi adopting a macho double arm flex pose as she spoke. "That's gotta be embarrassing!" screamed Demi hysterically. "Getting schooled by a newb on her first day."

Stewart frowned at Demi, but as he turned back to look at Chloe his expression softened, he was after all not angry at her — he was impressed.

"That is astounding! How did you know all that?" asked Stewart quietly. "Are you psychic?"

Chloe beckoned for Stewart to lean closer and when his head was close enough, she cupped her hands around his ear and whispered, "I'm not psychic, I just happen to know everything!"

Stewart looked confused and made to move away but Chloe held onto him, she wasn't about to leave things unbalanced. When she spoke again it was in a whisper that was so quiet even Stewart struggled to hear it. "I know all about you the same way I know that Demi has an irrational fear of Sellotape. Something to bear in mind the next time you hide your diary."

A look of surprise gave way to a wide and malevolent grin that spread across Stewart's face as he glanced at Demi out of the corners of his eyes. Demi no longer looked amused, in fact as she hurried off to sit at a desk at the far end of the room, she appeared positively worried.

"I can see you are going to be a valuable addition to our little unit!" said Wade with a wry smile. "I have sent a message to your dovetail, she should be here soon with your change of clothes. I would suggest heading down to the war room a little earlier than the others so you aren't busy choosing a weapon in front of everyone... it can be an... intimate experience!"

"Good point!" agreed Amos. "I remember choosing mine like it was only yesterday. I had the loudest argument I have ever had in my life, I'd never... and never since... been so angry!"

"Why?" asked Chloe through a timid gulp.

"I think it's better to discover that for yourself, that way you have no preconceptions clouding your judgement," replied Wade.

"Does everyone have a weapon?" asked Chloe, curious as to how many lethal objects were currently in the same room as her.

As if the question had been a command to bare arms, Amos, Wade, Demi and Stewart all withdrew a weapon that had been concealed about their person. The sound of several blades being unsheathed all at the same time was unsettling but Chloe was too impressed by the wares on display to feel anything but awe. She had never given much thought to weapons and had always regarded them as boys' toys, but as they gleamed in the morning sunlight, Chloe found herself almost salivating at the idea of having one of her own.

"What's that one called?" enquired Chloe pointing at Stewart's odd, crescent-shaped blade.

"This is Ethaneal," replied Stewart simply.

Chloe gave a slightly churlish giggle. "I meant what kind of weapon is it, but you gave it a name?"

"Oh, I see," said Stewart shyly. "Well, I didn't... I mean it was already called... it's a sickle," he finished somewhat deflated.

"Way to explain, bro!" cackled Demi from the far end of the room. "Don't worry about it, kiddo, all will become clear when you get to the armoury."

"I've just come from there!" wheezed Alex as she entered the room panting, holding a bundle under one arm and dragging a gigantic battle-axe behind her with the other.

"What on earth...?" chuckled Amos at the sight of the huge weapon that, if stood on end would have been taller than Alex.

"I know, right?" replied Miss Sterling heaving the axe forward and propping it against Wade's computer terminal. "I thought it was a joke at first, but he made a very convincing argument," she added grinning as she gave the blade a gentle stroke.

"You have a weapon too?" asked Chloe sounding disappointed.

Alex wiped her brow with the sleeve of Wun Chuan's sweater and turned to face Chloe.

"Sorry sweetheart, but I have had a lot of time to kill and apparently it's a requirement. It's pretty cool though," replied Alex gleefully as her eyes flitted to the blade again and widened with excitement.

"I have some clothes for you, Chloe. Do you want to try them on now so I can check I brought the correct size?"

Noticing that Chloe still looked a little forlorn she added. "There are some for me too, we can try them on together."

Chloe beamed, skipped over to where Alex stood holding the pile of black fabric items, and taking her by the hand, dragged Alex off in the direction of their personal quarters. Amos watched them leave, arm in arm and giggling like sisters and was once again reminded of Ignis. He thought back to when he first joined the Conclave and how Ignis had raised him, how he had found a brother, how the first face he remembered seeing is Ignis' and how much he missed him right now. A tear welled up in Amos' eye, he was beginning to lose hope that Ignis would return, that he would be lost in the tides of time and the thought terrified him.

"Amos?" whispered Wade. "Are you OK?"

"I'm fine, dear boy," Amos replied, dabbing his eyes with his handkerchief, and with a soft smile that didn't reach his eyes added, "Thank you."

"I think Sarah and Fiona are back," exclaimed Wade, cutting through the awkward tension and allowing Amos to straighten himself.

"Why do you say that?" enquired Amos sounding more like his usual genial self.

"Because I have just solved this equation that I have been working on for the last four hours and I have no idea how," chuckled Wade.

Swinging round on his chair, Wade turned to face the door just in time, to see two little girls step inside. The girls were aged eight and were physically identical in every way except their hair. Sarah had long, curly, almost white blonde hair which was plaited on each side and tied at the back with a blue scrunchie. Fiona, on the other hand, had short, jet-black hair which was very straight and, with the exception of a few strands that hung either side of her face, was brushed back and stuck out behind her head like she was stood in a strong wind.

They both wore the same black keikogi adorned with a white sash and thick velvet cloak and each had the same blue eyes and matching grins which were currently fixed upon their faces as they doted on a contented looking round faced baby with leaves over its eyes. The baby was lying on a metre-square patch of earth covered in gravel and a few stones, which had the appearance of a piece of road. Sarah and Fiona carried this odd load between them and rather than watch where they were going, 'coochi cooed' and blew soft sounding raspberries to the baby's apparent delight.

"Ooh, a baby!" squealed Demi with glee as she looked up and caught sight of the creature. "Where did he come from?" she added rising from her chair and rushing to the twins to get a better look.

"He, is a konaki jiji!" replied both Sarah and Fiona in unison.

"That's a weird name for such a lovely baby," said Demi in an overly cutesy manner whilst tickling the baby's belly.

Sarah and Fiona chuckled together, then looking at Demi said. "That's not his name, it's his species." They laughed some more.

"Oh!" said Demi a little perplexed. She shook off her puzzlement quickly though and returned to gazing affectionately at the baby burbling away as it fidgeted on the piece of road and added. "Can I hold it?"

"I wouldn't if I were you!" said Chloe as she headed back into the room with Alex in tow. They too were now clothed in black keikogi but theirs were adorned with violet fixtures in contrast to the white of the twins.

"Looking sharp, ladies!" said Amos with a doff of an imaginary hat. "Very dapper, in a lethal sort of way!" he added with a chortle.

"Why can't I hold it?" asked Demi who sounded very deflated.

"A konaki jiji is a creature that looks like a baby which usually lies in a road and cries. When some sympathetic soul wanders by, and wanting to help, picks the baby up off the road, the konaki jiji increases its weight until the victim is crushed beneath it!" reeled off Chloe without hesitation. Amos looked at her and simply smiled.

"Then how are these two holding it?" enquired Demi, annoyed that the twins were carrying the baby without much effort.

"Because," interjected Amos, deflecting Demi's aggression away from Chloe and toward himself instead, "the twins are not carrying the konaki jiji, they are carrying the road it lays on and as it cannot see, it doesn't know someone is around to trick."

"What about the noise?" asked Demi sounding incredulous. "I have been talking to it and tickling it."

"It doesn't understand English, Demi." Amos smiled. "And it is probably so calm due to the twins' influence. Oh, and speaking of…" Amos held out his arm to indicate the twins. "…Chloe, this is Sarah and Fiona."

Amos thought for a moment then with a chuckle at how well she performed with Stewart added. "Care to have a crack at them too?"

Chloe, her eyes flashing with excitement and thrilled at Amos' interest, shuffled forward toward the twins rubbing her hands together. Understandably the twins were a little taken aback by this strange girl heading straight at them and looking like she was trying to generate static electricity.

"What is she doing?" they asked in one concerned voice.

"Shhhh!" hushed Demi forcefully. "You'll break her concentration."

The twins looked at each other and then turned their heads to face Chloe, who to their surprise was already upon them, standing a foot away with her arms outstretched, her index and middle fingers tapping rapidly against her thumbs. The twins reeled and almost dropped the piece of road.

"Whoa! Careful!" whittled Wade who made to brace the road from falling out of their grip.

"Jeez dude, be quiet!" snapped Demi. "Go on Chloe, what do you see?" she continued with deep interest.

Chloe appeared to be deep in concentration and she was humming again. Behind her, knowing it was all an act, Amos did his best to suppress a giggle.

A few seconds later, Chloe snapped open her eyes and recoiled in terror away from the girls, her face looked mortified.

"What is it, what's wrong?" asked Demi fervently as everyone in the room gathered closer.

Chloe looked solemn and cold as she glared at the girls with awe. "That's… incredible!" whispered Chloe at last. "You… you are…" she continued stammering as actual realisation of the twins' power washed over her.

"What? What is it?" said Demi eagerly.

When Chloe spoke at last it was in a toneless, vacant voice.

"These girls are the most dangerous people in the world!" she said as she stood there staring blankly at them.

Demi burst into hysterics and almost fell to her knees laughing. "You're kidding right?!" she wheezed between giggle fits. "I've told jokes more lethal than these two!"

"You are wrong to mock my dear!" said Amos shooting a cautious glance at Demi.

Demi's laughter broke off almost immediately, petering into small chuckles before another look into Amos' eyes halted them completely. Demi looked confused and a little scared as she eyed the twins suspiciously.

"But I've seen these two, fight…" said Demi "…and no offence…" she added waving her hands at the twins in an apologetic manner. "…they suck!"

"The danger is their ability… or curse in some regards!" interrupted Chloe who still looked stunned.

Demi was suddenly interested again. As far as she and the others knew, the twins' ability was one that promoted good feelings and stimulated the brain functions of living creatures which caused anyone within the field of their 'aura' to be more productive in their task. What was dangerous about that?

"You can never be separated can you?" Chloe asked the twins in a surprisingly sad voice.

Amos suddenly looked concerned but recovering quickly he laughed and said, "That will perhaps do for now." He made to usher Chloe away.

The twins looked very shocked and indignant at Chloe's pronouncement and together they bellowed at her. "What did you do?"

Chloe jumped backwards in fright at the sudden outburst and angry reaction the twins were displaying.

"What did you see?" the twins demanded in unison. "Tell us now!" they roared as they advanced on Chloe with konaki jiji held aloft.

Everyone in the room began imploring the twins to calm down and not drop the baby, but they did not seem to care.

"How dare you rummage in our minds without permission!" they raged as together they bore down upon Chloe.

Amos darted forward and stood between the twins and Chloe and opened his arms wide. "That's enough!" he barked.

The authority in Amos' voice was unmistakable, the twins stopped in their tracks at once and lowered the konaki jiji. Looking shy and bashful they both stared at the floor and swung the baby back and forth. Eventually they mumbled, "She started it!"

It was so quiet it was almost imperceptible but Amos was close enough to hear.

"She did nothing of the sort!" argued Amos. "I assure you," he added quickly noticing the twins were about to speak, "no one has been inside your minds, that's not what her ability does."

Amos gave them a reassuring smile. "I promise and if I'm lying you can have my last KitKat."

Placated by the idea of chocolate they'd never see, the twins returned their attention to the konaki jiji and so did Stewart.

"So why do you have that… konapi jelly, anyway?"

The twins squealed a high mocking laugh. "It's konaki jiji and he is for the tournament later," said Sarah.

"It is a test of strength that Frank thought would be entertaining…" continued Fiona.

"…and we are looking after him until then," finished Sarah.

Unperturbed by the creepy way in which the twins spoke, Amos had brightened considerably at what they had said. He loved the inter-departmental tournament, he thought it really brought out the best in the competitors and almost everyone who worked at the institute entered each year.

"Oh-ho!" chuckled Amos merrily. "It ought to be a good event this year, eh?" he asked Wade in an effort to redirect the conversation. "I look forward to seeing how long the elemortals can keep it raised. Why don't you go and put the konaki jiji safe for now so there are no mishaps before the tournament," continued Amos to the twins.

"OK!" replied the twins excitedly, it was obvious that they too were keen to see Shui and the others brace against a weight that would increase for eternity and knew how fiercely competitive the four of them could be.

"What about you Wade?" enquired Amos giving him a firm pat on the back. "Are you going to have a crack this year?"

Wade smiled nervously but nodded enthusiastically while casting sideways glances at the twins who were carrying the konaki jiji to their quarters. Stewart, capitalising on the sudden calm of the room, leaned in close to Amos and Wade and in a hushed tone whispered. "I wouldn't bother Wade, I reckon this year might be *my* year!"

"You sound very confident, you know something we don't?" replied Wade with a sly look at Amos.

Stewart grinned broadly and gestured for Amos and Wade to move closer.

"I have figured out how to choose who gets to man the wheel when I catch some shut-eye," explained Stewart proudly. "Half an hour before the tournament begins, I will neck a couple of sleeping pills and Alcibiades will take over, he has been itching to throw down for a long time!"

"Alcibiades?" asked Wade confused.

"Bloody hell!" exclaimed Amos in awe. "Wasn't he an Athenian general?"

"Yup!" chuckled Stewart. "He was quite the badass too, he might not be much of a challenge for the elemortals, but as they have their own contest anyway, I may be in with a good chance."

"Isn't that cheating?" asked Wade who suddenly wasn't feeling so keen to enter the tournament himself any more.

"No, it's perfectly legitimate," answered Amos who sounded amused. "and I might add quite clever!" he added winking at Stewart. "I'm quite looking forward to pitting my own skills against such an esteemed warrior."

"You are entering?" asked Stewart sounding mortified at the idea. "Amos, sir, no disrespect but I really don't think th…"

"Underestimating your opponent is a sure-fire way to lose before you begin!" interrupted Amos with a wry smile. "Old I may be, but I am no stranger to combat and you will find me a very formidable opponent."

"Yeah!" agreed Chloe who had come to stand by Amos' side, drawn in by the conversation that was no longer being carried out in low voices. "Amos is hard as nails, he's a legend," Chloe gave a knowing wink at Amos. "He knocked out Kokou in a bar fight and he is a warrior god."

Chloe sighed and crossed her arms resolutely. "Unless you have a demon in your bloodline buddy, I think you're still gonna lose!"

Stewart slumped into his chair, this unexpected news had stunned him into silence and he was feeling much less confident about his chances.

"If it makes you feel any better," began Amos consolingly, "I was a young man when I beat Donn!"

Stewart looked up with a hopeful expression on his face. "And how old are you now?"

"Old enough to know better than to answer that question dear boy!" replied Amos cheerfully.

Stewart moaned loudly, got to his feet and left the room muttering under his breath, slapping the leaves of a few desk plants in a tiny tantrum on the way.

"I think someone needs a cuddle," chuckled Wade.

"Agreed," said Amos who was grinning. "And on that note and with little time to get you prepared, I think we should head off to the armoury and see about choosing you a weapon," he added turning to Chloe whose face lit up with excitement.

"You smile now!" said Wade darkly and giving Chloe a warning glance gave a sharp harsh laugh. He too was smiling but there was a look of anguish in his eyes as he spoke and for a while, he looked lost in thought, then unexpectedly he blurted out. "I'm not a lickspittle!"

Wade, realising that he had spoken this out loud went red, gave a sheepish cough and swung round in his chair to face his workstation.

"Quite right, Wade!" said Amos patting him on the shoulder. "No lickspittle here!"

Chloe bit her lip, she was half amused, half concerned and wasn't sure whether to laugh or be afraid. As Amos escorted Chloe and Alex from the room, Chloe felt an unexpected and overwhelming sense of trepidation that she had not as yet experienced since being at the institute in spite of all that had happened recently. Still following Amos and Alex toward a set of double doors that led to the lift she suddenly realised something which hadn't occurred to her before.

"Amos?" she began tentatively.

Amos looked down at her as he swung the door open and held it aside for them all to pass through. He had the same kind smile he usually wore when interacting with Chloe and had raised his eyebrows, gesturing for her to continue.

"If I know what you know and you have already been through this weapon choosing ordeal, why don't I know what it's like?"

Amos chuckled. "Because what you are about to experience has nothing to do with knowledge, it is about feelings and emotion."

Chloe looked puzzled so Amos pressed on. "It isn't a learned fact or a piece of information per se and as you don't seem to have access to my personal thoughts and feelings then it stands to reason that it will remain obscured until you have experienced it yourself."

Chloe looked a little disheartened to hear this, as though this discrepancy in their shared mind had somehow diminished the whole by this one flaw.

Amos noticed her face grow sullen, and guessing the reason, pressed the button to call the lift before kneeling down to look Chloe in the eye at her own height.

"My dear child," he began softly. "In the short time we have known each other I have come to cherish the connection we share, both its unique nature and the bond it has obviously begun to form between us."

Chloe still seemed saddened so Amos reached forward and raised her chin with his finger so she was looking into his warm kind eyes.

"Remember that it is important that you have your own life too Chloe. While what you have gained from me will serve you well, utter reliance upon it will only hinder your progress, both in your education and your life."

Unable to stop himself, he leaned close, gave Chloe a peck on the forehead and swooped her in for a hug which she returned.

"We should all strive to be better than the sum of our parts and I would be proud to know you have surpassed me in every way!" Amos whispered in Chloe's ear.

A soft chime rang out in the corridor and the doors to the lift slid open. Amos glanced at the lift and gave Chloe a little squeeze. "The path to such an achievement begins here, with the unknown," he added softly.

Chloe released Amos from the hug and looking into his eyes smiled. "It's a shame you never had children," said Chloe sincerely. "You would have been a great dad!"

Chapter Fifteen
All Out for the Parade

Deep in the heart of London, amongst the throng of people and din of traffic, calm and orderly preparations were being made for an event later that day. Busy streets were blocked off and traffic was redirected as a route was carefully carved through the increasingly empty roads leading to the Cenotaph in Whitehall. Londoners along with other people from different parts of England and indeed Europe had begun to gather along the barriers the MET Police had erected along the pavements and each person wore an imitation poppy on their left breast.

Inside the Houses of Parliament all was abuzz with activity. The prime minister dashed about checking his itinerary, making sure his staff were doing what he had asked and praying that his wreath was about to magically appear like it should have done half an hour ago. In almost every room, speeches were being rehearsed, uniforms and suits were checked and plans were recited.

Buckingham Palace was no different in this regard. Those under the employ of Her Majesty were hot stepping, performing their duties double time. The queen, Her Royal Highness Queen Elizabeth II, was reviewing the events of the coming day. Already dressed in a smart black blouse and skirt, she had already chosen which coat she would be wearing, a knee length, black fur overcoat along with a black fur hat.

The queen placed down the paper she had been re-reading and looked at a clock on the mantle and then over at the bedroom door.

"Philip!" she beckoned.

There was no reply.

"PHILIP!" she repeated, much louder than before but still gently.

There was a sound of footsteps moving towards her then the bedroom door swung open. He marched through the threshold and was donned in his naval tunic, his rank of admiral emblazoned along his left breast, his aiguillette arranged neatly on the opposite side and his ceremonial sword twinkling in the low early morning sun.

"Yes dear?" enquired the prince kindly.

"Oh Philip. You do look handsome!" replied the queen with an affectionate smile. "I was just checking to see if you were ready and, here you are," she added, taking his hand and giving it a little shake.

"Feels a bit heavier this year," said Prince Philip, tugging his lapels straight and looking a little downcast.

"That's the weight of too many years!" chuckled the queen as she got to her feet and gave her husband a gentle hug.

"Just one more thing we have in common!" said the prince with a grin as he gave his wife a little wink.

Queen Elizabeth faced her husband, brushed off his epaulettes with her hand and nudged his tie a little straighter. "Have you read the notes I gave you regarding the gentleman you shall be greeting? A Mr Bogdan Bogomolov I believe."

The prince gave a little chuckle. "Yes, I did!" He smiled again but then gave his head a little shake. "It's quite the mouthful. Did you say there would be a translator with him?" he enquired hopefully.

"I have appointed someone we have on retainer," replied the queen simply.

"Oh? Which one might that be?" asked the prince with ill-disguised disappointment in his tone. "Please don't tell me it's Jonathan!" the prince continued as he reminisced on the last occasion. "He's a lovely fellow but he ruins my jokes with his monotonous droney voice. My dontopedalogy gag is priceless, but he has no delivery. One would have better success using Siri!"

"Then you'll be pleased to learn it's not Jonathan, it's Cassandra," replied the queen with an exasperated smile.

"Miss Gibson? That's splendid, she at least has a funny bone… and she doesn't always smell of boiled cabbage… I mean really, what does Jonathan do, sleep inside a golabki?" the prince continued in a mutter.

"It's not that bad, he's a nice boy, he just… well… has an aroma!" replied the queen in a placating tone.

"No, he bloody stinks and it drives me mad because he is always with me!" growled the prince.

The queen chuckled as she turned back to her paperwork. "You grumpy sod!" she added, just loud enough so the prince would hear. "So what does Cassandra smell like?" the queen continued as she rifled through the stack of pages.

"She smells like lavender most of the time, on occasion she has the faintest hint of lemon but I quite like it… smells clean!" said the prince matter-of-factly. "I've noticed she hasn't been feeling well lately," he added almost as an afterthought.

"Really?" mumbled the queen who was concentrating on what she was reading. "Perhaps, Jonathan should fill in for her after all!" she added jokily.

"That's not even remotely amusing!" replied the prince with a glance at the time. "In fact, she should be here by now, I think I'll go to the library and make sure she came."

"Good idea!" agreed the queen. "You're distracting me anyway and I really do need to make sure there are no mistakes in this."

The prince chuckled affectionately, kissed the queen on her head and left the room, closing the door behind him.

Her Highness sat in the silence for a moment and allowed herself time to feel the weight of the day's itinerary wash over her.

"The old bugger's right!" she thought to herself as she spotted a jewel encrusted poppy broach on the desk and scooped it up in her hand. "It does feel heavier!"

Watching the gems on the broach glimmer in the sunlight the queen seemed momentarily lost in thought. Memories of her father, King George VI, surfaced in her mind. She remembered watching him preside over the Armistice Parade when she was a child and she swelled with affection and pride. As thoughts of past and present collided and became muddled, she became acutely aware of a low and unusual sound that snapped her from her reverie.

It was a rhythmic humming sound that seemed to pulsate. There was something very familiar about it and the queen strained her ears to hone in on the sound, but almost as soon as it had appeared it was gone. The queen who was no longer a young woman, indeed not even a middle-aged woman, was used to the occasional tricks her ears played on her and for a moment she mused over the idea of tinnitus, but the sound which had seemed somewhat tuneful, had almost been recognisable, like a song that she couldn't quite place. Suddenly becoming acutely aware of the time and turning her attention back to her duties, the queen chalked it up to old age and shook thoughts of it from her mind.

Meanwhile, Prince Philip had just made it to the gallery. He meandered along the extravagant room lazily casting his eyes between the various masterpieces that had earned a place in the Queen's Royal Gallery. The prince did enjoy the collection and had a keen knowledge of each work, yet he seldom had chance to appreciate them alone. More often than not his presence in the gallery was accompanied by a plethora of guests and dignitaries who assembled here prior to being escorted to the ballroom for some formal occasion or another.

The prince's eyes scanned over the closest painting, a canvas in oil which stood over a metre in height entitled *The Assumption of the Virgin Mary*. Created by Rubens, its vibrant colours and heavenly depiction made it a firm favourite with many visitors. As the prince continued walking his eyes flitted to other works which he no more than glanced at, *The Mystic Marriage of St. Catherine*, *A Lady at the Virginials with a Gentleman: The Music Lesson*, *The Passage Boat* and *Summer: Peasants Going to Market*. He stopped in his tracks, for an extended look at *Cleopatra with the Asp*. He gave a little smile at the sight of the asp held against Cleopatra's milky white breast and chuckled inwardly. "Lucky little bugger!" the prince thought to himself.

He was near the door to the library when the prince spotted an object that was completely out of its place. A didgeridoo made of eucalyptus. The prince recognised it as the same instrument that had been presented to the queen by the Coolabah community group back in the year 2000. It had been left propped up against the door frame as if someone had used it, got bored and just put it to one side. Feeling somewhat aggrieved by this disregard for the queen's possessions, the prince made a mental note to scold the entire staff and maybe, if he got to the bottom of it properly, sack the person who had left it there. He reached out to grab the instrument with the intention of leaving it safely in the library until the end of the day, when the didgeridoo appeared to play entirely of its own accord.

The sound was quiet at first and the prince, refusing to believe any instrument would simply play without a musician behind it, stuck a finger in his ear and gave it a good wiggle. To his discontent, upon removing his finger he discovered that the didgeridoo was still playing. Not only that but it was louder than before and had begun to include the imitation vocals of the dingo and kookaburra. The prince recoiled from the didgeridoo in horror, he didn't believe in the supernatural but he couldn't ignore his senses either. The tune grew in volume again and each chirp that shot through the hollow tube caused him immense physical pain inside his head. Collapsing to his knees in agony, the prince wailed with anguish as his skull felt as though it were ready to explode. He clawed at his scalp as if trying to tear open his head to allow the sound to escape. Skin gathered beneath his nails and blood trickled down from his crown and over his face. He hunched over into a ball on the floor, pressed his forehead against the thick rug that ran the length of the gallery and began smashing his head against the ground. Over and over again he hammered his skull into the floor, creating a dark red puddle beneath him. The prince screamed one last time, expecting it to be his last as his skull began to vibrate with the rhythmic hum of the didgeridoo.

It was not how he expected the day to go, it was not how he had expected to meet his end, neither did he expect to feel a soft and warm hand gently grab his own and hear a kind voice, thick with concern ask. "Excuse me, Your Royal Highness... but are you OK?"

The prince, suddenly free from pain and entirely unable to hear anything but the voice of a woman echoing around the gallery, looked up from his pose. He was shocked and more than a little mortified to see Cassandra Gibson staring down at him, a look of genuine worry written clearly on her face.

Trying his best to recover himself despite his obvious confusion, the prince got to his feet and straightened his tunic. His face was flushed with embarrassment but that was the only red on him, he was quite uninjured, no claw marks, no blood.

"Miss Gibson," the prince said heartily, overcompensating for the awkwardness of the moment. "I didn't see you come in."

"I heard you yell from the library," replied Miss Gibson. "I thought, well, I was worried when I saw you on the floor!"

"Oh that!" replied the prince off-handedly, "I, er, had lost a contact lens!" he continued trying his best to appear nonchalant. "I found it of course, the blasted thing was still in my eye, just not where it should have been!" finished the prince with an unconvincing laugh.

"If you are sure!" said Cassandra, instinctively reaching forward to hold the princes arm to comfort him, but then remembering, he is the prince and one does not simply grab the prince.

"Quite sure," replied the prince who had noticed the gesture and reached forward with his own hand, placed it on her shoulder and gave it an affectionate pat. "But thank you!"

Cassandra placed her own hand on top of the prince's and smiled. "If you are feeling up to it, shall we discuss this meeting with the war veteran you are having today?"

"Lead the way, m'dear, lead the way." instructed the prince feeling steadier now.

They had just entered the library when the prince remembered the didgeridoo still propped against the door frame in the gallery and regardless of the 'senior moment' he felt he had just experienced, he was still resolved to bring it in with him and give someone a sound tongue lashing later. Unfortunately, when he peered back through the door into the gallery to retrieve it, the didgeridoo had gone without any trace that it had been there in the first place.

The prince instead resolved to lecture his doctor about the side effects of his new medication and rejoined Miss Gibson for a stiff drink, an in-depth overview of Russian customs and notes on a few choice phrases for greetings and farewells. At the far end of the gallery, a door stood ajar. In the gap, unnoticed by both the prince and Miss Gibson, two white pupilless eyes blinked, creased narrow from an unseen smile, then vanished as the door clicked shut.

Chapter Sixteen
Kindred Spirits

Amos, Alex and Chloe arrived at their destination one minute and fifteen seconds later, but as the lift slowed to a stop on their floor the doors didn't slide open as Chloe had expected. Instead the computerised voice of the global ordinance and divination system, or 'GOD', sounded through an internal speaker.

"Attention! Only one person is permitted to enter this section of the armoury at any one time. Please identify yourself by placing your hand on the pad to your right."

At her words a small rectangular pad appeared out of a panel on the lift wall and a quiet chime played impatiently like that of a cash machine waiting for a customer to collect their money. Chloe spun round to look at Amos, her eyes were wide and her mouth downturned, she was obviously panicking and waiting for Amos to come to the rescue.

"Sorry Chloe," began Amos in a soft but firm tone. "I know you are hoping I can pull rank or jiggle the system, but on this occasion I can't, it really is a solitary affair."

Chloe turned to Alex instead. "You'll come though, right?" she asked hopefully. "You are my dovetail after all and should assist me with this kind of thing, yes?"

Alex looked down at her and tried to appear upbeat, but her face betrayed her sadness at having to refuse her as well.

"No, Chloe!" she whispered. "Amos is right, this is something you must do alone."

Chloe looked as though she had been informed that she was about to be sold into slavery, her eyes were pooled with tears and her bottom lip quivered dramatically, for Alex it was a heart-wrenching sight. Amos saw Alex faltering and expected her to try and placate Chloe, but to his surprise and satisfaction Alex reverted to what he assumed was a classroom persona.

She stood up straight, crossed her arms and loomed over Chloe with a commanding glint in her eyes. When she spoke, it was with unquestionable resolution, brisk and to the point and Amos knew there would be no further argument thereafter.

"Chloe, as you have seen from the big bloody axe I have been hauling around, I have been through this too and as such I can promise you two things," said Alex holding out a hand to count the points on her fingers. "The first is that while you may feel afraid there is absolutely no danger, there is nothing at all that can actually harm you in that room… OK, yes I know weapons can hurt you but nothing will be 'trying' to harm you!" she added the last part quickly at an 'are you kidding me' glare from Chloe.

Regaining her composition after an encouraging nod from Amos who was stood behind Chloe, Alex pressed on. "Finally, and this is important to bear in mind sweetheart, you will be gaining a brand new and lifelong friend, a companion who will always be by your side and no one should ever choose your friends for you!"

Chloe looked at Alex as though she were mad. She was talking about choosing what basically boiled down to a finely crafted lump of metal, not a puppy. But Chloe understood that she would not be able to persuade either adult to come in with her, so with slumped shoulders, she turned about, lifted a slightly shaky right hand and slapped it against the pad in a very defeated manner. As she did so she didn't notice Amos and Alex quickly shuffling to the back of the lift and against the wall.

"Identifying. Gibson. Chloe. Student GC01," spoke GOD almost immediately.

The lift doors opened in front of Chloe but as they did another set erupted from the lift walls and closed behind her, sealing her off from the adults and leaving her alone to look down a deep, dark corridor.

Chloe spun around and banged on the door behind which Amos and Alex now stood, but the echo of each clang sounded off behind her in the depths of the corridor and this made her feel nervous so she quickly jutted her arms back down by her side.

For a few seconds she stood there with her eyes closed, her fists clenched and her breath held. When the sound had faded away, she let out a slow breath and opened her eyes. Slowly but with stiff resolve she turned around and peered into the gloom. As her eyes adjusted to the dim light within, she could start to make out what looked like a sign that stood alone against a black wall. It had a brass frame and a slender pole for a stand, all supporting some black text upon a white background. Chloe rather thought it looked like the sort you would find in a museum. What was written on the sign Chloe couldn't be sure so she began inching forward into the corridor to have better look.

Shhh!
Quiet In The
Armoury Please!

Having read the words eight metres ago, Chloe now stood only inches from the sign. The information that had been scribed was so anti-climactic, that Chloe had gone from feeling silly at how terrified she had been over all of this, all the way to annoyance that she was now stood in a corridor with poor lighting, no other exit and a sign that, now she came to think of it, came across as a little bit rude.

"Maybe someone has already taken the weapons!" she thought to herself disappointedly.

Bizarrely, the sign suddenly spun around to reveal a second notice. To her surprise the sign read:

Shhh!
If you must think, then do it quietly!

Feeling more than a little sheepish Chloe, in as much of a whisper as her imagination would allow, thought. "So, where do I go from here?"

The sign span around again only this time instead of revealing the original message that was on this side before, the notice read:

Please wait one moment
while we adjust the lighting.
Thank you for your patience.

The lift doors at the other end of the corridor quietly hissed closed, eliminating the only source of light. Chloe stood in the darkness for a moment, nervous, but unafraid. She heard the sign turn again. As she looked toward it, she saw bright green words floating against the black.

Please remain still while
the chamber walls are in motion.
Flash photography is not permitted :)

As the sound of the walls moving rumbled around her, Chloe couldn't help but crack a smile and wondered if Miss Sterling had thought the emoticon was funny as well. The sound of the sign creaking around again pierced the darkness as the green letters vanished to be replaced with:

Miss Sterling laughed at
all my jokes m'dear. We had a nice chat
she's quite the conversationalist.

"Oh!" thought Chloe with embarrassment. "I'm terribly sorry, I... I thought you were just a clever sign, I didn't think..."

That's quite all right,
I am clever and a sign :D
Mind your eyes, this might seem really bright!

A thin shaft of intense light pierced the darkness as the corridor Chloe was stood in seemed to crack in two. As the walls separated further, both disappearing into the floor and raising into the sky, the light they had been keeping at bay overwhelmed Chloe's face, forcing her to shield her eyes. A cacophony of noise met her ears. Thousands of voices all trying to converse and desperate to be heard above the others created an insurmountable din that was painful to experience. While it was impossible to hear any dialogue distinctly enough to understand anything of what was being said, Chloe could hear one word clearly, a word everyone seemed to be using over and over again. It was her name.

The sound of the sign spinning could be heard again. Louder than before, it was able to cut through the noise, its metallic squeak purposefully amplified so much, that all chatter ceased instantly leaving the screech to echo in the seemingly endless light.

Chloe dared a peek from beneath her arms to see what was written and, as her pupils shrank to size of pin pricks in the glare, she could just make out the thin black letters that made up the message that had brought an abrupt end to the commotion:

SHUT UP!

An affectionate smile spread across Chloe's face. She was liking the sign more and more. "See Mum," she mused thinking back to her mother's pile of paper work all written in upper case and the debate that had ensued, "writing in capital letters *is* shouting!"

Once again, the squeak of aged metal sang out in the silence intimating that the sign had something else to say, so Chloe, still struggling to see clearly in the all-encompassing light, moved closer to get a better look.

Sorry about that!
People come down here so rarely
that when the walls part, excitement
tends to get the best of those who live here.

"It's OK," whispered Chloe as the light began to fade and was gently replaced by a soothing darkness once more. "I'm kind of excited myself!"

As you should be.
This armoury is home to the most
valuable weapons in existence!

"And I get to have one?" asked Chloe enthusiastically, clapping her hands together and bouncing up and down on the spot.

Not exactly!
Please try to bear in mind as you browse
that these weapons are not so much possessions
as they are possessed!

Chloe looked wholly perplexed by this statement. She was about to voice her confusion when the sign, anticipating her question, spun again.

Consider me if you will!
What am I?

This was a difficult question to answer and Chloe did not know how to reply. She had plenty of responses to give, an antique sign, probably enchanted, at a push possibly created by some clever engineering and computer programming… but considering the conversation they'd been having Chloe wanted to give the sign more credit… it had been engaging, had made jokes, it had even lost its temper. If this was a piece of AI Chloe was certain it would pass the Turing test used to assess such programs. Not wishing to offend and feeling it would perhaps be best to leave the question as a rhetorical one, Chloe shrugged and waited for a response.

Very diplomatic! ;) and no! I'm not a gadget!
My name is Gowin Knight and
my spirit inhabits this sign!

That this hadn't occurred to Chloe earlier made her feel woefully dumb, it was sort of obvious now he had said it. Chloe silently nodded her understanding and peered up into the darkness which was now complete. She scanned the emptiness for a sign of anything that might look like a weapon but couldn't see anything in the void. Suddenly in the periphery of her vision a singular dim, soft blue light appeared in the black. It was impossible to tell how far or close the light was but it didn't matter as soon many other soft blue lights were lighting up all around her, which hung in the dark like ice crystals.

As the seconds passed the light grew brighter, and in their progress, slowly illuminated small patches of land on the ground beneath them. The land under each light Chloe noticed, was exactly that, land. Under some lights was thick, lush grass that blew in an unfelt wind, below others soil or rocks and the occasional cobbled road. Each was clearly a representation of a separate location, like large dioramas illuminated from above with a singular spotlight.

In the centre of each scene Chloe could at last see the resemblance of what she thought were bladed implements, embedded in the ground or some other fixed object. The metal sign which housed Gowin spun with a creak. It no longer bore glow in the dark letters as it too was now lit from above by a soft blue light. Gowin had obviously registered the confusion on Chloe's face and had prepared a suitable explanation.

In case it isn't apparent, the armoury is also a sort of multi-dimensional nexus. It connects different places and different periods of time together, allowing the weapons that reside within to
be gathered here for safe keeping!

Chloe gave another look around the expanse as she pondered Gowin's words.

"It's so beautiful!" whispered Chloe, unable to restrain herself. Her eyes bulged and sparkled in the twinkling lights, she looked almost tearful.

Finally, someone has an appropriate response
to seeing something of this magnitude and sheer splendour.
My compliments, you are clearly wise beyond your years and humble
beyond your need.

Still entranced by the breathtaking vista of pocket worlds that spread out into the vast space before her, it took a moment or two for Chloe to register what Gowin had said. It wasn't until the sign made an impatient squeak that Chloe turned to look at it and, reading in a rush, blushed wildly at both the compliment and the fact she had been accidentally ignoring it.

Pondering the dark shadowy void that webbed between each lit scene, Chloe leaned in close to the sign, cleared her throat and then with a quick furtive glance over the sign at the darkness again whispered. "So, um... what do I do now?"

Gowin responded in kind, not only with another helpful phrase which read:

Now we walk and see if anything calls out to you,
so to speak!

but now the sign had begun hopping off into the shadows, pausing briefly to face Chloe and tell her with a tiny screech:

Come on then, this way!

before bouncing off again into the dark making a clunking noise as it went. Chloe followed cautiously, placing her foot tentatively into the black space to be sure there was a floor to stand on. Satisfied that the ground was there and indeed solid, she hurried off to catch up to Gowin who was now several metres ahead.

Gowin stopped next to the first pocket world and displayed some helpful information on his fascia which explained where it was, when it was and a little bit about the weapon, a short dagger which was embedded half the blade length into a grassy field.

Chloe came and stood next to Gowin so she could read the information he had provided:

This is the magnificent pugio that was wielded
by Sempronius Densus in 69AD. He died here in Rome outside the
palace defending the
Emperor Galba against a thousand strong horde in one of the most
epic one-man stand-off's in history.

Chloe raised her eyes to look at the dagger that, aside from being coated in blood, appeared quite a lot less than magnificent. Questions began to surface in Chloe's mind but before she could voice them Gowin gave another squeak.

Calm down Sempronius, I am getting to that just be patient, this all needs explaining!

Chloe stared for a moment at Gowin's sign, puzzled. She hadn't heard anyone speak and nothing like words had appeared on or near the dagger.

When nothing else happened, she tapped the top of Gowin's sign and feeling a bit frustrated exclaimed. "I can't hear anything!"

Always ready with an answer Gowin spun again. Perhaps it was just her imagination, but the way the sign turned seemed a little impatient and Chloe wondered if she had perhaps interrupted a conversation and she knew how much adults hated to be interrupted.

Of course you can't hear anything, you are alive
and unable to simply tune your ears to hear
the random mutterings of a single spirit!

The way it was written seemed to confirm Chloe's suspicion that Gowin was indeed annoyed and grew concerned that she had done something wrong. As she thought it, tears welled up in her eyes, Chloe disliked being disliked!

"Sorry!" she mumbled quietly.

Squeak!

Oh, Chloe, I'm sorry. I wasn't upset with you, it's Sempronius, he's being rather demanding!

Chloe nodded her understanding, but was startled by another very abrupt squeak!

Yes, you are and you bloody well know it!

"Am I able to speak with Sempronius?" asked Chloe, in a tone she hoped sounded helpful.

Yes, and it's perhaps for the best that we crack on.

replied Gowin with a brisk spin. Another creak of metal.

Step into the light, walk across the grass and take hold of the dagger's handle, DO NOT pull it out!

With a look of mild intrigue at Gowin, Chloe shrugged, gave a quick look about the scene, and holding her breath, stepped onto the grass. She heard it gently crush beneath her feet and instantly felt a rush of warm summer wind wash over her. She inhaled deeply and caught the faint aroma of salted fish. The sun was bright and she closed her eyes for a moment and appreciated being out of the oppressive darkness of the armoury.

She looked down at her feet and surveyed the dagger. Lying next to it and previously unseen due to grass growing over it, was a wooden cudgel that had almost as much dried blood on it as the dagger. Grimacing uncontrollably, Chloe knelt down and closed her hand over the handle. She felt the leather binding flex under her grip and gave a little shudder at a touch against the patches of dried dirt and blood on her skin.

"CAN YOU HEAR ME?" boomed a voice out of nowhere.

The sound made Chloe jump so much she released her grip on the handle and toppled over backwards. She sat on the soft grass a moment waiting for her heart to stop racing. She understood what had happened and was managing quite well to suppress a giggle fit at how daft she must have looked. She glanced at Gowin and tittered thinking how alarmed she had been.

"He's a bit loud, isn't he!"

Well, he is old!

Chloe got up and knelt beside the dagger. Feeling resolute and prepared for the volume of Sempronius' voice, she reached forward and wrapped her fingers around the leather-bound handle once more.

"Jumpy little thing, aren't you?" said Sempronius, keeping the volume of his voice more reasonable this time.

Chloe gave a weak smile and shrugged. "Sorry," she said quietly.

Sempronius barked with laughter.

"Sorry?" he repeated incredulously. "I made you fall over with fright and yet you're apologising to me?" he added laughing harder still. "We need to find you a backbone, little girl!"

Chloe didn't reply. She lowered her eyes to look at the dagger clenched in her hand and gave it an appraising look. She tried to imagine squaring up to a single armour-clad soldier who would have had a sword and a shield while she would have been holding what basically amounted to nothing more than a posh kitchen knife. It was ridiculous.

"Penny for your thoughts?" said Sempronius who had not failed to notice the lull in conversation.

Chloe twisted the dagger in the ground and churned up some of the soil. "You fought 1000 men, with this?" asked Chloe amazed.

"That and my trusty cudgel, young lady!" replied Sempronius in a gruff but hearty voice. "Yes, we lost and the emperor was slain but they rued the day they stepped up against me, slaughtered hundreds of the fuc…"

YES! Thank you, Sempronius!

interrupted Gowin with a forceful ear-splitting squeak. Quite apart from disliking obscenities, he was very much mindful of Chloe's age and shuddered to think of her returning upstairs with several new additions to her vocabulary that would likely get him fired.

Something that had been puzzling Chloe swam to the front of her mind and, feeling now would be a good time to change the subject turned to Gowin and asked. "Why could I hear everyone speaking my name when I first entered the armoury, but I can only hear Sempronius when I hold his weapon?"

That is a good question and the answer is quite simple. It's down to collective will. A single spirit tethered to an earthbound object cannot communicate without physical contact because the quantum vibration of a single thought is not strong enough to traverse the limitations of our dimension.

Chloe read Gowin's words enthusiastically and nodded her understanding as Gowin spun again,

When many think as one, the accumulation of that many thoughts resonating at the same frequency is enough to stimulate the molecules in the surrounding matter which in turn create sound waves that we can hear.

"Load of mumbo jumbo!" exclaimed Sempronius haughtily. "Like 'quantum' is a word!"

Gowin made half a squeak as though he were about to spin and respond but Sempronius ploughed on. "The nature of spirits and the afterlife is, I'm afraid, too complicated for someone as young as you to understand!" continued Sempronius loftily. "All you need to know is that Mercury imbues the weapons with his power and that allows us to chat when in direct contact with each other, but he is much too busy to be bothered with relaying messages back and forth, his time is too important! I dare say Jupiter keeps him occupied with actual important matters!"

Chloe looked dumbfounded. Indeed, Chloe found that Sempronius' alternative explanation made her brain ache. "How does a planet help anything?" asked Chloe looking at Gowin.

"What the ruddy hell is a planet?" scoffed Sempronius. "Is your mind addled child? Are you speaking in tongues?"

"What...? No...! What?" stammered Chloe.

"As I said, too complicated for a child." sneered Sempronius. "Stick to playing with dolls and leave adult topics and adult objects to... well... adults!" he finished with a loud guffaw.

"But you said..." began Chloe but Gowin interjected with a loud squeak.

He doesn't mean the planets, Sempronius is referring to the Roman Gods named Jupiter and Mercury.

"Don't waste your breath, Gowin…! or oil… or whatever it is you have!" growled Sempronius impatiently. "This one is too dull witted to stand at my side! I won't pair with her, I just won't! The cheek of it, bringing a child to me like I'm some sort of bloody nurse maid. That's right, move along, maybe there is a barbarian down the way willing to lend his hammer to knock some sense into her! Yes, in fact I'm sure an intellectual equal, sits in the south corridor, it's a lump of wood possessed by Larry the Lazy who accidentally killed himself when his club rolled off a shelf and hit him the face while he slept!"

Outraged at the ludicrous ranting of an antique, an antique moreover that had the nerve to question her intelligence when the simple concept of a planet was a foreign notion, Chloe released her grip on the weapon, stood bolt upright, shook with impotent rage and gave the dagger a half-committed kick before storming resolutely off the grass and into the shadows where she couldn't be seen.

Perhaps not this one, eh?

offered Gowin with a slow awkward whine. Chloe said nothing. She just stood there with her arms folded and glared at Gowin who gave a sheepish squeak,

Moving on then!

The subsequent offerings that followed were, in Chloe's opinion, scarcely better than Sempronius. There was a long bow that belonged to Arthur White who was famed for performing impressive trick shots in market squares across England. He sadly met his demise when an arrow ricocheted off a cooking pot and hit him in the forehead. Undeterred he kept trying to convince Chloe to take pot shots at Gowin to see if she could make his sign spin. Then there was an ornately carved axe that housed the spirit

297

of Ebba Eriksson, a viking shield maiden who once raided an entire village without any assistance leaving everyone dead before heaving over a tonne of treasure a distance of twenty-two miles back to her home. Unfortunately, she complained incessantly about Chloe's scrawny build and her natural aversion to torture and murder. Chloe even viewed a pair of cestus that belonged to Flamma, a Roman gladiator who was so successful in the arena that he won his freedom four times. An honour he refused because to Flamma, killing was life, and while he was agreeable to pairing with Chloe his constant "WHOOs" and screams of "GET SOME!" or, "WE GONNA BATHE IN BLOOD!" very quickly became annoying and Chloe, as politely as she could, had to refuse making the excuse that the cestus was simply too heavy for her to wear.

More than two hours later Chloe, feeling defeated, plodded out of a scene in China after being resolutely informed that, "Chinese secrets, were for Chinese people!" by Liu Fei Hua, a Shaolin monk who lived inside a gigantic dao and was xenophobic to the extreme. As Gowin and Chloe made their way further along the pockets of time, Chloe found herself dragging her feet, she was exhausted and had been berated so often her will and enthusiasm for the task had all but waned.

Come on, Chloe. Persevere. Your match is in
here somewhere, I promise!

"Bullsh.." began Chloe, but Gowin cut her short.

Language! If you go upstairs repeating words you have heard in here,
I'll be sent to the scrapper's yard!

"Sorry!" sighed Chloe thickly through a wide yawn. "I'm just feeling a bit fed up, this is obviously pointless, I am just not compatible with brave and fierce people." Chloe gave a little kick at nothing and slumped forward.

Yes, you are! It is an arduous task for everyone, but they all succeed in
the end and so will you!

Chloe was about to argue but Gowin squeaked. Upon reading the sign, it was obvious he was responding to a nearby weapon and not offering further words of comfort as she expected.

I'm afraid you are mistaken, her name is Chloe!

Chloe had read with only the vaguest amount of interest and was about to wander off and leave Gowin to converse alone until the next reply from Gowin which read:

Of course I am sure! I know Amos, he works here at the institute, and as a matter of fact, is currently in the lift waiting for Chloe to return!'

Squeak!

You can't, that's not how it works and you know it!

Her curiosity piqued, Chloe jumped inside the scene which consisted of an old Japanese courtyard that led to a two-storey building that was nestled against the broad cliff face of a humongous mountain. Ignoring the squeaks made by Gowin as he tried to communicate, Chloe darted forwards toward the delicately bound handle of a katana sword which, unlike the other weapons she had seen, was not embedded into anything, but instead rested gracefully upon a wooden stand beneath a winding tree which was raining cherry blossom like soft pink snow. She seized the handle and demanded to know why the warrior within thought she was Amos.

The voice of an old man, thick with a Japanese accent, responded.

"I could feel his ki!" he said simply. Chloe thought she could hear a note of urgency in his voice as he spoke.

"His ki?" said Chloe.

"We all have an energy that runs through us, each unique to the individual!" said the old man politely, although there was still a hint of impatience in his tone. "We Japanese call it ki!"

"And you think mine is the same as Amos'?" asked Chloe with such eagerness she almost pulled the sword off its stand.

"Had I not been corrected by Gowin, I would have thought you one and the same!" the sword replied.

Chloe's eyes widened. Considering what she had discovered about the connection between Amos and herself during the visit with the conduit, it made a surprising amount of sense.

"Who are you?" asked Chloe eagerly. "How do you know Amos?"

"My name is Yoshiro Tokugawa and I know Amos because he saved my life!"

Chloe considered his response a moment, if Amos had saved his life, he didn't do a very good job considering Yoshiro's current situation. Deciding this would be an inappropriate response, she enquired as to the whens and hows of this incredible revelation.

"It was during the First World War!" replied Yoshirou. "Amos was based in Singapore at the time and his unit came under attack by a mutiny force comprising of Indian troops. I was part of an infantry unit sent in to provide ground support to our naval fleet who were helping to suppress the assault against the British!"

Chloe's mouth gaped open. Although she knew for a fact that this was true, that Amos had left the Conclave to serve in both wars and could even recite his service number, it was still unreal to imagine the venerable old man laying down fire in the thick of battle.

As no one had spoken, Yoshiro took it as a cue to continue. "As my unit rushed the Indian forces, we were devastated by friendly fire from one of our battleships. A single artillery shell reduced the company from eighty to nine in the blink of an eye. Capitalising on the sudden reduction in our numbers the mutinous dogs advanced on us, one hundred and fifty sepoys that had broken formation surrounded us and opened fire."

Yoshiro fell silent a moment lost in the memory, then with a dreamy quality to his voice said. "I felt certain my demise was imminent and I wanted a warrior's death. I drew my blade and yelled at the top of my voice, 'Cowards! Fight me like men!' Then I stood up from my cover and took up a stance with my blade raised to eye level. The gun fire ceased and some of the sepoys laughed. They pulled their sabres from leather scabbards and with a cocky arrogance that boiled my blood, strolled toward me with an air of someone undertaking a chore. I knew I could not beat them all but I did not care. Though I was prepared to die, I intended to kill and maim as many of them as I could before I fell."

Chloe gulped, Gowin remained silent, both sublimely lost in Yoshiro's narrative.

"The first to reach me was a massive man, tall as he was broad and clearly thought me weak as, when I was alive, I was small and slender — his mistake!"

To Yoshiro's delight, Chloe gasped. "Did… did you kill him?" asked Chloe.

"I did and it was all too easy!" said Yoshiro who sounded almost disappointed. "Before he had fully swung his sword, I had sliced off his head which landed next to my feet. I kicked it towards the nearest sepoys and raised my blade again."

A darkness suddenly swept over Chloe. Unbidden and most unexpectedly, a scene which showed from afar a head falling from uniformed shoulders and landing next to a short Japanese man unfolded in her mind. With a jolt Chloe realised the man was Yoshiro and what she was imagining was in fact a memory. That she borrowed knowledge from Amos was accepted if not understood, but borrowing memories? This was new! Before she could contemplate the matter further, Yoshirou continued his tale.

"The men who fought me next were more cautious and attacked in groups!" said Yoshiro fervently. "I injured many, but received several deep cuts in return. An attack from behind opened up the back of my leg and I dropped to my knees. Before I knew it, I was surrounded. Together the sepoys raised their sabres and brought them down upon me. I knew this was the end. I lowered my sword and opened my arms to embrace my death with honour… but it never came."

With the invading memory still playing in her head, Chloe instantly knew why. "Amos!" she said in a soft but pleased tone.

"Amos!" agreed Yoshiro. "He had sprung forth from his own regiment and barged into the group knocking them to the ground, their weapons clattering away from them. I am not sure what else he did, but none of the men rose to fight again."

Chloe who had been visualising the fight with perfect clarity excitedly spoke up to fill in the blanks.

"He opened their throats with his combat knife during the collision! Two circular swipes as he spun through the air, they were dead before he crashed into them. Y'know, this is why ninjas shouldn't do ballet!" chuckled Chloe with a dreamy, hero-worshipping expression melting over her features.

There was an awkward silence following this pronouncement, but then a five-year-old girl talking about such a violent act like it was the most awesome thing in the world should be awkward.

"I see," said Yoshiro. "Well as you are already aware, Amos continued to battle while I struggled to get to my feet again. I fought off the odd man who had managed to get past Amos or had flanked our position to come at us from the rear, but none were successful in their attacks. I could not say how long we fought for, but by the end I was back-to-back with Amos, he supporting most of my weight and bodies of the slain littering the clearing!"

Chloe closed her eyes and nodded her agreement of the description. "Amos is as unclear on the matter as you, most of the memory is a blur, clouded by red mist!"

Blood drunk!

"Precisely!" said Yoshiro. There was another long silent pause.

"Mr Tokugawa?" Chloe said at last.

"Please, call me Yoshiro."

"Chloe smiled. "OK, Mr Yoshiro…" Yoshiro laughed but didn't correct her. "If you don't mind me asking…" Chloe hesitated a moment, "…if you didn't die in this battle then how did… how did…?"

"How did I meet my end?" supplied Yoshiro helpfully. Chloe simply nodded. "My death was a matter of honour!" said Yoshiro flatly. He was not angry at the question but it was said with great finality. "I will perhaps tell you the details one day, but for now we must act quickly, you say Amos is nearby? I must speak with him, it's important!"

I've told you, it's not possible!

The floor is sealed with a spacial rift and will not open again until a pairing has been made!

"You never told me THAT!" bellowed Chloe. "You're telling me I'm locked in here until I pick one of these?" she added gesticulating with broad exaggerated sweeps at the weapons surrounding her.

I'm afraid so… sorry!

"Sorry?" snapped Chloe. "How long have I been down here? Have Amos and Miss Sterling been stuck in the lift this whole time?"

Not exactly.
You have been inside the armoury
2 hours and 26 minutes.
Amos and Alex have been waiting in the lift
2.0569327 seconds.

"Time rift!" added Yoshiro, displaying a level of understanding that Chloe had not thought him capable of.

Chloe said nothing but snorted instead. She was obviously frustrated, but then so was Yoshiro.

"I appreciate that you are in a rush to get out but my need is greater. Please I must tell Amos about what is happening, people are in danger!"

Well that simply cannot happen!
Amos can't re-enter the armoury whilst his current
companion is still in service and you
can't leave unless you pair with a member!

"If I pair with someone else, then Amos won't be able to communicate with me! Please…" implored Yoshiro. "…lives will be lost if we do not act soon, there must be a way!"

An idea steeled over Chloe. She sat thoughtful a moment while Yoshiro continued to beg Gowin for help beside her and found she liked the idea more and more. She did after all quite like Yoshiro, he was interesting and, perhaps because of the memories, was relatable in a way the others weren't. Plus, if their ki was the same or similar...

"Yoshiro?" said Chloe. Yoshiro stopped pleading to Gowin. "Why don't you pair with me?"

"I mean no disrespect because I do find you clever and intriguing, you remind me in many ways of my own daughter, but it must be Amos, only he will understand!"

"I thought you'd say that, but I don't think it matters," said Chloe gleefully. "Amos and I, well we're sort of the same!"

"What do you mean?" asked Yoshiro uncertainly.

Chloe explained to Yoshiro everything that had happened since she'd met Amos. She explained about how she was somehow able to access his brain like a library and told him all that had been said when they had met the conduit. Yoshiro had been particularly interested in the part about the entangled hair.

"...plus, you said yourself our ki is the same!" said Chloe, trying her hardest to sound convincing. "Maybe that connection will allow you to communicate with Amos once we get outside!"

Yoshiro pondered this a moment. A pragmatist at heart he thought worst case! If she was wrong, he could still relay the basic message to Amos through Chloe. It wouldn't be the same, of course it wouldn't but he would at least be out and that meant a chance, he could still stop it if they were quick.

"I agree!" said Yoshiro with resounding conviction. "Gowin, how does this work?"

Chloe, you need to take Yoshirou from his resting place, draw the blade, and placing the cutting edge against your hand, make a small cut. This will bind Yoshirou to you.

"Whoa, whoa, whoa!" said Chloe raising her hands up in alarm. "Miss Sterling promised me... PROMISED... that I would not be harmed in here!

I guess she lied!

Best do it quick and get it over with!

Making a mental note to scold Miss Sterling for this disgusting breach of trust once she was out of here, Chloe grabbed the scabbard with her free left hand then, keeping it horizontal, lifted it gently from the stand. With her right hand still on the handle she pulled her arms apart and the blade was revealed with a pleasant soft 'snikt!'. The steel glinted brightly in the glow of afternoon sunlight and for a moment, Chloe let the reflected light dance over her eyes. It was, in a strange way, hypnotic and Chloe felt a calming warmth grow in her chest.

Lost in the moment Chloe brought her left hand over the blade and slowly lowered it to the upturned edge. Her skin had barely brushed the metal, when a trickle of blood ran across the width of the sword and dripped onto the ground. For a second Chloe wondered where the blood had come from. She hadn't felt any pain. That was at least, until she examined her hand and saw a surgically thin cut running from one side of her palm to the other. Her face immediately screwed up, her lip jutted out and curled, tears welled up in her eyes and as her downturned mouth widened to let out an almost imperceptible whine, she convulsed and began to sob uncontrollably. Chloe screamed and cried for, what seemed to Gowin, to be an eternity. All she wanted was for someone to scoop her up and give her hug. For someone to kiss her and tell her it would be OK. Gowin had tried to soothe Chloe, spinning frantically from message to message, but her eyes were screwed up and so full of tears she hadn't read a single thing.

As Chloe continued to bawl, she rocked back and forth with her knees to her chest, her injured hand cupped to her clavicle and shielded by the other. She rocked so hard, she ended up toppling over, and in an effort to stop herself falling, she nudged Yoshirou.

"Finally," chuckled Yoshiro. "Keep hold of me, I can heal your hand!"

Distracted, Chloe's crying reduced to an occasional blubber and wet sniff. Gingerly, she inched her fingers over the handle and grabbed hold. An itchy tingle appeared in her the palm of her injured hand. She wanted to scratch at it and rub it. Perhaps sensing this urge, Yoshiro said softly, "Leave it!" and then to everyone's surprise, began singing a lullaby in Japanese.

Chloe closed her eyes and swayed side to side in time with the song. Before long, her hand felt normal again and her sadness had ebbed away completely.

That's incredible!
I had no idea you had this ability!

"My education in the ways of the warrior included more than just how to swing a sword," said Yoshiro. "I learned many secrets, including Ninjutsu, the skill of the Shinobi. In life these techniques were useful but limited. I have been locked inside this blade for a long time, and I have had nothing to do but meditate. I have mastered my ki and broken those limits!"

You made her stop crying with your ki?

Yoshiro laughed heartily. "Heavens no! When my own daughter was born, I had to become an expert at soothing boo-boos on little girls. It's what fathers do!"

Chloe scooped the sword into her arms and hugged Yoshiro. Gowin mused if metal could blush, Yoshiro would have turned a brilliant shade of rose gold.

"Well then!" said Yoshiro bracingly once Chloe had released him from her embrace. "Time is against us! We had better get to the lift, there is much to discuss, we'll need a plan and if I have not stressed this enough already…"

"We need Amos!" said Chloe pointedly.